1

Beth took a deep breath as she crept past her aunt's front parlour that sunny but cold morning in March 1912, but the harsh voice stopped her before she could reach the back door. She sighed and went to the parlour door, where Aunt Helen was busy at her sewing machine, her left foot working the black metal treadle in a steady rhythm.

'Let me look at your shoes before you go,' her aunt commanded without looking up. Beth smothered her anger, her blue-green eyes smouldering with suppressed passion. She was a woman, not a careless child, and would hardly leave for such an important appointment with dirty shoes. They were smart shoes that fastened with two buttons at the side and made of black leather, which shone so she could see her reflection in them

'I spent ages on them last night,' Beth said. She stood where her aunt could see her in her neat grey ankle length skirt, white blouse and darker grey jacket that nipped in at her slim waist. Her thick pale tresses were swept up neatly at the back of her head and she wore a black velvet hat that shaded her face and hid her hair. She carried black gloves to match her highly polished shoes. The colour did nothing for her pale complexion, but Beth had not yet ceased mourning her mother, who had died less than four months earlier. Besides, she would be expected to wear grey or black for work, or perhaps a uniform.

'You look washed out, girl,' Aunt Helen frowned, 'but I suppose you can't help that. You will merely be a salesgirl, so I dare say it does not matter.' She removed her sewing from the machine and snipped the thread with a small pair of fancy silver-plated scissors. 'Come straight back when your interview is over.' She looked at Beth over the glasses she wore for her sewing.

'Yes, Aunt,' Beth replied meekly, though inside resentment stirred once more.

She was almost two and twenty and this was the first time she'd had to apply for a commercial situation. Beth's mother, Jessie Grey, had been an invalid for most of the past ten years, since her husband died of a terrible fever. Mr Grey had been a brilliant doctor and their lifestyle had been comfortable, though after his death the money had been tight. When Jessie Grey's inherited income died with her, Beth was left with very little. The news that her mother's few possessions would be sold to pay their debts meant Beth was forced to accept an offer to live with her aunt, whom she knew through her infrequent visits over the years, though she sensed her aunt's resentment and wondered at it. She could only think that Aunt Helen resented the fact that for a while Jessie had been loved and happy, while she had never married.

'But why did she never tell me we lived beyond our means?' Beth had asked her aunt when the solicitor had told them the awful news. The inheritance in her mother's name was finished and nothing was left for Beth. 'I could have perhaps worked...'

'Jess was ever a little fool,' Aunt Helen had said sharply. 'She might have married anyone with her looks and background, but she chose a doctor who devoted his life to the poor and consequently left her nothing but a few pounds. Your mother lived off what our father left her and never thought of the future. You may live with me, but you must find work for I cannot feed and clothe you.'

'I am perfectly happy to work, Aunt,' Beth had said proudly, but unfortunately thus far she had not been able to find a suitable job. She was properly brought up and from a decent family, which meant she could not work in an inn or a factory. Aunt Helen thought she ought to look for work as a lady's companion but, although Beth had applied for two such positions, she had not been lucky enough to be chosen from amongst the many applicants.

'Well, I do not know why you were not chosen,' her aunt had grumbled when she was told Beth had not been selected. 'You've looked after an invalid mother for years and are capable of running after an old woman, I imagine.'

'Lady Vera said she wanted someone with experience and Mrs Thompson said I was too attractive, because she has sons...'

'Tush!' Aunt Helen had looked disgusted, for it was obviously unfair. 'Well, you must work, Beth – we shall look through the newspaper this Friday and see what is advertised...'

The large advert wanting staff for the new department store in what Aunt Helen said was the wrong end of Oxford Street took up half a page of the local paper. There were all kinds of positions on offer, including cleaners, office staff, as well as a floor walker, salesgirls and supervisors. The advert made it clear that Harpers was to be a prestigious store, set over four floors, with lifts, a café on the top floor and, it said, merchandise to rival anything in London.

'It says here that training will be given,' Beth had read aloud. 'We are invited to write an application for an interview...'

'Shop girl...' Her aunt's mouth had twisted in disapproval. 'I must say that I never expected my niece would work as a common shop girl...'

'I don't think it is a common shop,' Beth replied. 'Harpers is to be a prestigious store.'

'Your grandmother would've died of the shame,' declared

her aunt dramatically. 'She was the daughter of a gentleman. Your great-grandfather was Sir James Mynott and you should remember that, even if grandmamma did let the side down by marrying into trade...' She had sighed deeply. 'If your mother had put a little by for you, you might have been saved the indignity of having to work – but she never had an ounce of sense.'

'Mama was ill.' Beth had defended her mother loyally. 'She suffered from terrible headaches and I dare say it was all too much for her after Papa died.'

That discussion had taken place more than a week previously. Beth had written in answer to the advertisement and received an appointment to attend promptly.

The interviews were being held that morning at a small hotel just off Berwick Street, which veered off Oxford Street itself. The Malmsey Hotel was normally frequented by travelling salesmen and businessmen who stayed in London for a few nights before moving on. However, it boasted a large conference room. When Beth arrived, she was told to take one of the hard wooden seats in the conference room, which had been divided by various screens to give a little privacy.

Perching on the edge of her seat, Beth glanced round nervously, because nearly all the chairs were occupied. So many girls, men and older women had turned up that her heart sank. It was hardly likely that a girl of no experience would be given a job when there were so many applicants.

'Am I late?' a cheerful voice asked Beth and a very pretty girl with reddish-brown hair, a red felt hat and a red-flecked tweed coat sat down next to her. Beth noticed that she wore a faint trace of lip colour and her hair was naturally waved down to her nape with a fringe that curled over her forehead. 'I'm Sally Ross,' she said and offered Beth her hand. 'I've worked in Selfridges and in Woolworth's, an' all – what about you, love?'

'I'm Beth Grey and this is the first time I've applied for a job in a shop,' Beth replied. Somehow, Sally's smile was making her feel less nervous. 'After Papa died, Mama was ill and I looked after her until she died a few months ago... since then I've done nothing but help my aunt in the house.'

'Rotten luck,' Sally said and reached across to squeeze her hand. 'I never knew either me dad or me ma. I was brought up in an orphanage until I was sixteen and they kicked me out. I've been livin' in an 'ostel for the last two and a 'alf years. I 'ad to fend fer meself...'

'That's even worse,' Beth said, horrified. 'I had to live with my aunt when Mama died. She lives in Holborn, so it won't be a long bus ride for me if I get a job...' She paused, sighing as she thought she'd been happier in her father's little house in Clerkenwell than her aunt's, even with her mother an invalid for years, and her sudden heart attack had devastated her. Sally grinned as her name was called. 'Oh, that's you...'

'Yeah, only just made it,' Sally chirped and got up to follow the thin, rather sour-faced woman, dressed in severe black, towards the screens. As they disappeared behind them, Beth saw a girl of perhaps sixteen looking at her from two seats down.

'I've been here ages,' the girl said and looked nervously towards the screens. 'They haven't called me yet...'

'Is it your first job, too?'

'Yes... I'm Margaret Gibbs, but everyone calls me Maggie,' the young woman said. 'My father wanted me to stay on at school and become a teacher, but...' She took a sobbing breath. 'He had an accident at work last month and is confined to bed. The doctor says he may never walk again and Muma can't manage without his wage.'

'Oh, I'm so sorry. I know how it feels to see someone in pain...'

'It's awful...' Maggie's eyes flicked nervously towards the screens again. 'I hope they give me something. I don't mind what I do...'

'Yes, I feel the same. It's all so exciting. The papers say the new owner is American, very rich and handsome. I've been up to see the store, have you?'

Maggie nodded. Her dark brown hair was swept up at the back in a neat roll and drawn back from her face, but the wisps that escaped curled in her nape and about her pretty face.

'It has blinds on all the windows so you can't see inside, but I think it will be lovely – almost as good as Selfridges or Harrods, though not as big as Harrods...'

The new store was set at the other end of Oxford Street to Selfridges and just up from Soho Square, a fact that had made Aunt Helen look down her nose and warn Beth never to stray into what she described as a disreputable area, because ladies of an unsavoury nature walked there. She had decided to overlook it in the end because Beth need never venture there. She would come home straight after work on the bus and eat her packed lunch in the staffroom.

'Oh, that is exciting,' Maggie said but looked even more nervous as she realised the importance of the store. 'There are so many people here. I'm sure there are far more than is needed, so I'll be lucky to get anything, though I'd love to work with clothes or hats...'

'Oh, I think they want junior staff as well,' Beth reassured her. 'You've got a nice voice and manner and I'm sure that's half the battle with a store like Harpers. I think it's a matter of always being polite and respectful to the customers. I hate it when assistants hover over you and try to influence your choice.'

'Oh, yes, so do I...'

'Miss Margaret Gibbs please...' A man with slicked-back dark hair, slightly greying at the sides, called Maggie's name and, with a nervous look at Beth, she stood up, straightened her narrow ankle length skirt and followed him behind one of the screens

Beth twisted her gloves nervously. Maggie wanted to work with clothes or hats, but she just wanted a job. Her mouth was dry and she had butterflies in her stomach. Aunt Helen would be annoyed if she failed again.

She saw Sally Ross emerge from behind one of the screens.

A big smile was on her face and she gave Beth a 'thumbs up' as she passed her and whispered, 'I'm in – good luck...'

Beth nodded, but her mouth was too dry to speak She watched several men go behind the screen at the far end and two older women and then the severe-looking woman came back and called her name.

Beth rose to her feet and followed her behind the middle screen. Her stomach was tying itself in knots as she wondered what to say and do. The woman sat down behind a desk, but there was no chair and Beth was not invited to sit.

'You are Miss Beth Grey?' The woman's eyes went over her critically as if seeking a fault.

'Yes, ma'am,' Beth's voice croaked with nerves.

'I am Miss Glynis Hart,' the woman said. 'I shall be the floor walker for the women's department and the ground floor at Harpers. It is a position of responsibility and that is why I've been asked to help select the staff. We are looking for young women to work in one of several departments.' She looked at the letter in her hand. 'You have no experience of shop work, I see. What made you think you would like to work for us, Miss Grey?'

'I need to find a position and I thought it would be a good place to work...'

'No doubt a hundred others thought the same.' Miss Hart's voice was sharp and stinging. 'You do realise that this is a prestigious store? We expect our girls to be bright, hard-working and a credit to Harpers! To work here is a privilege and every young woman taken on must be aware of it. Why should we take you on rather than a dozen others?'

'I suppose there is no reason,' Beth said honestly. 'I can only say that I should be grateful and work hard for my employer. I believe I learn quickly and I can add up swiftly and accurately – and I have patience...'

'Yes, I see.' Miss Hart's eyes narrowed. 'That in itself is very necessary when serving customers, some of whom may be difficult. One thing you must remember, the customer is always right as far as you are concerned. If their complaint is beyond your level it will be taken to your supervisor, then the floor walker, which is me, and then the manager, should it be serious enough.' She eyed Beth up and down and nodded again. 'Well, you are nicely spoken, neat, clean and honest. Training will be given and experience is not always necessary. I shall put you on my list of possible candidates and Mr Stockbridge, the manager, will make the final decision.'

'Oh... thank you,' Beth said, dispirited. She turned to leave.

'You will have your letter in two days, Miss Grey – and, if accepted, you must report to the store for training the following day. All those fortunate enough to receive a place at Harpers will receive three days training and then the next day will be spent preparing the stock for the opening...'

'Yes, I see, thank you,' Beth said, then, drawing more courage, 'What would I be doing if accepted, Miss Hart – and what is the wage?'

'That is not my decision,' she replied primly. 'I am here to pass on details of suitable applicants. The details of employment offered will be in your letter. Good day now...'

'Good morning, Miss Hart,' Beth said and turned to leave. As she did so, she almost collided with Maggie, who had come from behind a screen further down. She was smiling and looking pleased with herself.

'Hello again,' she said and sounded excited. 'I've been given the job of junior salesgirl. I'm going to sell hats... or at least help Mrs Craven. I will keep things tidy and assist – and they will pay me six shillings a week to start...'

'Oh, lucky you,' Beth said and wondered why she had not been immediately selected. It was worrying that both Maggie and Sally had been taken on straight away but perhaps they'd seen a senior member of staff, above Miss Hart's level. 'I have to wait to see if I am selected, I am on a list...'

'Good luck,' Maggie said and smiled warmly. 'I hope you get it...'

Beth nodded, her eyes drawn to a woman in a smart black costume as she came from behind one of the screens. The good-looking man with slicked back hair was smiling at her and talking animatedly and she looked pleased. The things that made her stand out from so many others were the red felt hat with lots of veiling she wore on her dark honey-blonde hair and shiny black patent court shoes, with big buckles. She looked as if she came from a better-class family and the man's eyes followed her as she walked from the interview room. Clearly, he was taken with her, and Beth momentarily wondered who she was as she emerged in to the cool of a damp spring morning, caught her bus to the corner of High Holborn and began to walk home, feeling apprehensive.

Beth sighed because it had started to drizzle with rain as she began to walk past the local shops. Mr Rushden, the local butcher, had a queue outside his door. His assistant, Andy, was taking something from the window and waved at her, bringing a blush to her cheeks. He always talked to her and smiled a lot when she went into buy their weekly purchases, mostly braising or stewing meat, bacon, ham and either a small chicken or some chops at the weekend. If his boss wasn't looking, he always gave her good value for money, which was why Aunt Helen frequently sent her shopping.

Beth smiled but did not wave, because, as her aunt would say, it was not ladylike. Grandmother had come from gentry, so Beth had been told many times. She'd married a haberdasher, who was successful for many years until he became ill and his business dwindled away. He'd left both daughters a small inheritance that was secured to them by means of a trust for their lifetimes but unfortunately died with them. Aunt Helen had never married, supplementing her slender income with the genteel art of sewing for ladies of breeding. Beth did not know why her aunt had never married, though she believed her grandfather might have had something to do with it, expecting his elder daughter to stay at home and look after him. It would explain why she so resented her sister's marriage. She was strict, sometimes cold, but at least she'd made sure that Jessie was decently buried and she'd given her niece a home. Beth had hoped they might be friends, but her aunt was a difficult woman to get close to; however, she was grateful and wanted to be able to pay her way.

Aunt Helen was a skilled seamstress and went out to measure and fit her ladies at their homes. She seemed to know lots of people, but Beth suspected that she was lonely, even though she gave no sign of it. Had Beth shown a talent for needlework, her aunt might have taken her on as her helper, but Beth's stitches were not neat enough and she had tangled her thread twice when she used the machine so had been forbidden to touch it!

As Beth passed, a youth was selling newspapers outside his employer's shop which smelled of tobacco and, for some reason, strong peppermints. He was calling out to people as they went by, trying to make them buy.

'Survey says two per cent of the nation die of cold weekly,' the boy hollered. 'Read all about it, come on, lady, buy me paper, do! Only a penny, 'appeny. Read about them ladies what smashed up Piccadilly...'

He was referring to the Suffragettes who had rioted and smashed the windows of shops in the West End of London earlier that month.

Beth fumbled in her purse for two pennies and waited for her change. She did not often indulge in the daily paper, but if her interview did not result in a situation she might have to apply for others.

The fishmonger's shop had the door open and smelled strongly as Beth continued on her way. In his window was a large selection of fresh fish, including plaice, cod, hake and bloaters, resting on beds of crushed ice. There were two large red lobsters on an enamel tray and Beth thought they must be very expensive. She'd never tasted lobster, though her father had taken her and her mother for a crab tea at Southampton on a day trip when she was small and he was strong, healthy and loving.

A wave of grief went over her at the memory, because she'd loved both her father and her mother, despite her mother's increasing selfishness as her illness gained on her and she demanded all Beth's time and energy. Aunt Helen would have condemned her sister to the infirmary, but Beth kept her mother at home and never minded what she did. She wished with all her heart that she could have her parents back but knew that the past was gone and she must move forward.

Beth arrived at her aunt's small terraced house in Broughton Street, a few minutes' walk from her bus stop at High Holborn. It looked in need of some paint on the doors and windows, but the white stone step had been scoured by Minnie, who came in for two hours three times a week to do the rough work, and the lace curtains were spotlessly clean. She thought that it was a cheerless, respectable place but could never be a home, though as Aunt Helen often reminded her, had she not taken her in, Beth might be living in one room somewhere that smelled of boiled cabbage and damp. It was smaller than the house in the East End where her father had set up his surgery, but the district was nicer.

Taking a deep breath, Beth entered the hall, which was redolent of lavender polish, her pulse quickening as she heard that infernal treadle machine. Would Aunt Helen's house ever feel like home to her or would she always tip toe round like a stranger?

2

Maggie let herself in through the back door of her home, a small end-of-terrace house in Jameson Street, not far from Cheapside. It was a narrow road with houses on either side, their paintwork peeling, a shop on the corner and children playing hopscotch on the pavements. Yet despite the dilapidated state of many of the houses, the net curtains at every window were spotless and the white doorsteps scrubbed every morning.

She could hear no sound from the kitchen and suspected that her mother had either gone to the market or popped to the corner shop. Her heart lifted, because Muma was inclined to complain in a loud voice, mostly about how much she had to do and how hard it was to manage now that Poppa was an invalid. Maggie was always afraid that Poppa would hear and be hurt; she was his only child and knew that she meant everything to him, as he did to her and every time she saw that stricken look in his eyes, it was like a knife thrust in her heart.

His accident, while working as a foreman at Dorkings, an importer of grain and other foodstuffs on the East India Docks, had turned him from a happy, cheerful man into an invalid overnight. A crane lifting a crate had snapped a wire and the falling object had caught Poppa a glancing blow on the back of his neck despite a warning that had saved his life. However, the injury to his spine was such that he was unlikely to work again. He'd been earning good money as a foreman and being a thrifty man had hoped to secure a good future for his girl, but the accident had robbed him of the use of his legs and her of all he'd promised her. All Maggie cared about, though, was that he should live and his pain should ease.

Running upstairs, she went quietly into her father's bedroom, not wanting to disturb him if he was sleeping. His head turned towards her on the pillow and he smiled.

'You're back then, love. I think your mother went shopping...'

'Yes, I expect so. I told her I would go when I got back, but she says she gets the best bargains.'

'She probably does,' Poppa agreed and his hand reached for hers as she sat on the edge of his bed. He couldn't use his legs properly, though his hands and arms were still able to move and his fingers closed lovingly over hers. 'We have to be careful with money until my compensation comes through...'

'Have they told you how much it will be?' Maggie asked. Because it was a fault with the machinery at the docks that had caused the terrible accident, the owner had agreed to pay compensation, but her mother said it would be no more than a fraction of what he'd earned.

Her father smiled at her lovingly. 'Not yet, love. I may get a lump sum or it may be a few bob a week – we'll have to see.'

'I got a job at Harpers,' Maggie said, the excitement bubbling out of her. 'I start next week, but we have training before that; I shall get six shillings a week to start, but when I've finished training in three months, I'll get twice that...'

'I wanted you to stay on at school and go to college,' her father said, frowning. 'You could have been a teacher – or even a doctor, Maggie. The wages would be better and it is a more fulfilling life for an intelligent girl.'

'I'm not clever enough to be a doctor,' she said and squeezed his hand gently. 'I might have been a teacher if I'd gone to college as we'd both hoped.'

She saw the twist of pain in his face. 'I'm so sorry, love; I've let you down. I know how much it meant to you.'

'It doesn't matter, Poppa,' Maggie denied, even though it had been hard to let go of her dream. She bent her head to kiss his hand and hold it to her cheek. She knew that he loved her very much and returned his love wholeheartedly. 'My wage will help a little, though I know it isn't much – but there were so many applicants that I feared I wouldn't get anything.'

'They know a good thing when they see it!' He smiled lovingly at her. 'Could you get me a glass of fresh water, love? It gets warm after a while...'

'Yes, of course,' Maggie said. She picked up his glass and the jug of water and took them downstairs to the kitchen. It took a couple of minutes to run the tap enough for the water to be cool and she washed both the glass and jug, placing them on the tray to take back to her father. She was about to leave when the door opened and her mother came in, a rush basket over her arm.

Joan Gibbs was a small, thin woman with bright eyes, dark hair pulled back in a bun and a neat figure. Still attractive, she might have been pretty had she smiled more. She'd had two children, first Maggie and latterly a son who had died a few days later; the doctors had forbidden Joan to have more children and she habitually wore the face of a martyr. Until her husband's accident, she'd had a part-time job in a local dress shop and resented having had to give up something she'd enjoyed to care for her invalid husband. Never a very caring woman, her husband's accident seemed to have brought out the worst in her.

'How did you get on?' she demanded. 'I hope you didn't waste your time and my efforts to iron your best white blouse?'

'I got a job,' Maggie told her and took the tray. 'I'll tell you after I take this up for Poppa. It pays six shillings a week...'

'I got more than that for my part-time job...' her mother frowned and shook her head. 'I shall be making a pot of tea in a moment – but take the water first if you want. I've been up there enough times this morning...'

Maggie went out quickly. She knew that Poppa's accident had made life harder and did her share of the running up and down stairs. She didn't mind what she did, but Muma thought it unseemly for a daughter to wash her father and so she was only allowed to do hands and face and fetch and carry, though she plumped pillows, read their favourite books and anything else she thought would help to ease him.

Maggie frowned as she realised that her mother would have to do even more when she was working. Maggie would see Poppa had all he needed before she left for work in the mornings and at night, but during the day it would all fall on her mother. The six shillings she'd been promised suddenly seemed very little for the change in their circumstances. Now, she knew that Muma would sneer and say it was hardly worth Maggie's time, but it was she who had pushed Maggie into leaving school and applying for the job; it was unlikely that she could earn more until she had some experience. In fact, she'd been surprised to be told immediately that the job was hers, when others were being told they would hear in a few days. Mr Stockbridge had been very kind to her in her interview, seeming almost paternal in his attitude and he'd told her she was just what they were looking for at Harpers.

'Girls with good education and speaking voices are just what we need,' he'd said, smiling.

She watched her father sip his cold drink.

'That's better, love,' her father said 'My mouth gets so dry, but I don't like the taste of warm water.'

'Would you like me to fetch you a bottle of pale ale?'

She saw the hesitation in his face, for he'd always enjoyed a drink when he got home from work in the evenings. 'It's a waste, love,' he told her. 'I know your mum is struggling to cope, and she liked having her own small wage to buy what she wanted. We'll wait and see what the firm pay me before we buy luxuries...'

Maggie nodded, understanding his reluctance. 'Muma is making a pot of tea – would you like one?'

'Yes, please.' He nodded to her and she saw his wince of pain. 'Will you give me a spoon of my medicine please, love?'

'Is the pain very bad?'

He grimaced and she fetched the small brown bottle from the dresser, pouring a tiny amount into a teaspoon and mixing it in a medicine glass with water. Her father took it and drank it down eagerly, then relaxed back against the pillows.

'Go and talk to your mother, tell her your news,' he said and closed his eyes.

Tears were hovering as Maggie walked down the stairs. She knew he suffered terrible pain and the medicine gave him relief for a time. He would sleep now, so there was no point in taking up a cup of tea until he woke later. She would share the tea with her mother and tell her what had happened at the interview...

* * *

Beth's letter came two days later by the second post. She was baking when she heard the letter box and ran into the hall to scoop the envelope up, tearing the seal and reading eagerly. For a moment, elation filled her as she saw that she had been offered the post of second sales assistant in the women's millinery, gloves and scarves department. She would be working under Mrs Rachel Craven, who was to be her supervisor. Her wage was fifteen shillings a week for a start and would rise to one guinea when she had been working at the firm for six months. She reread the letter with mixed feelings, because she'd hoped the wage might be more, but perhaps she was lucky to get in at all.

Reading the second page, Beth saw that she would need to go in to begin her training the next morning. She would be required to wear black court shoes, silk stockings and either a black or grey dress. One black dress would be supplied when the shop was opened and after that she would have to buy them herself. At least she would have one free uniform, she thought. She would otherwise have worn the black dress Aunt Helen had made when her mother died. If it was suitable, she might be able to wear it as her reserve dress, though it was possible that all the assistants would be required to wear the same style. It would be expensive to buy a second uniform out of her wage. Her aunt was sure to ask for something towards her board and lodging.

Aunt Helen accepted the letter when Beth offered it and nodded. 'As I thought,' she said. 'Had you been taken on by Lady Vera, you would have had fifty-two pounds a year and your keep. Perhaps now you see why I thought the post of a companion would be much better for you?'

'In six months' time, I shall earn more.'

'Yes, that is true,' her aunt agreed. 'I shall take seven shillings and sixpence now and ten once you're earning more.'

'Yes, Aunt,' Beth said, feeling her excitement evaporate. It would leave her just enough to pay for the bus to work and buy her lunch, which she'd estimated at sixpence a day. Her letter had said there was a staff discount, so she might just be able to afford a cup of tea, and have her shoes repaired now and then, especially if she walked to work on fine days. It left little for extras like new clothes, even with what looked like a generous staff discount.

'You have a decent black dress,' her aunt said. 'If that is acceptable, you will not need to buy another, but if it must be a certain style, I can probably copy it for half the price.'

'Yes, I know – thank you,' Beth said, hesitated, then, 'I'm not ungrateful for all you've done for me, Aunt.'

'Jessie was a fool, but I know my duty,' Aunt Helen said, her tone a little softer. 'My sister had hopes that you would marry well, but it did not happen.'

'I could not leave her...' Beth turned her head. She was too proud to tell her aunt that she'd once had hopes of being loved. She had lost what she thought of as the love of her life and did not expect to get another chance. Her pain had been sharp but was muted by time now, though occasionally it came back to haunt her. 'I loved her.'

'You were certainly a devoted daughter.' Aunt Helen's mouth twisted wryly. 'Well, you have taken a step on the ladder, Beth. Work hard and who knows what may happen. Should you be made a supervisor or a floor walker, you would earn quite a bit more then, perhaps as much as thirty-five shillings or more.'

'I intend to work hard and make something of my life,' Beth smothered a sigh. Rebellion flared in her heart, but she fought it down. She did try to be thankful and helped her aunt by doing housework and baking, at which she was quite good. Aunt Helen thought her scones were excellent and her chocolate cake, although kept for special times, was mouth-watering. For now, she must accept what she had been given and be grateful. 'I shall do my very best, aunt.'

'Yes, I know you will.' Aunt Helen offered a rare smile. 'I have nearly finished my work and shall start on a new order this afternoon. Please make a pot of tea and we'll have one of your excellent cheese scones with some soup for our lunch.'

Beth nodded and left her aunt to finish her work. Had she had a choice, Beth would have found somewhere she could live on her own, but it might be years before she could afford it.

Beth told herself she was luckier than many young women in her position. Had her aunt not taken her in, she might have been in a precarious position and perhaps a part of her understood her aunt's loneliness and resentment, because she too had given up a life of her own to care for an ailing parent. She just wished her aunt would be a little more satisfied with her efforts to please.

Sighing, Beth returned to the kitchen and finished her baking. Once she started work, she would either have to bake in the evenings or very early in the morning. Her life would be harder than it had been, but at least she would meet people at work and perhaps make friends...

3

Beth was early for her appointment the next morning. She found a queue of young women outside the shop, which still had blinds at all the windows. Across the road, a small crowd of bystanders had gathered to watch, clearly keen to see what was going on. Beth spotted some cameras, which could only belong to newspaper reporters in the crowd forming. It wasn't Harpers opening day, which was the following Tuesday, so what were they hoping for? Some gossip they could splash over the head-lines or had they been asked to come?

Only a few of the male employees had turned up yet, but as Beth saw two faces she recognised, she smiled and beckoned them to join her.

'Are we queue jumping?' Maggie asked, looking nervously at the woman standing behind Beth. 'I thought we didn't start until next week, but the letter said to come today, Friday...?'

'It's for training – and Beth saved our places, didn't yer, love?' Sally's cheerful cockney accent raised a few eyebrows, but she ignored them and stood resolutely beside Maggie, her arm pinioning Maggie to her side. 'I hope we all get to work in the same department...' Beth noticed that her voice alternated between her natural cockney and the posh voice she would use for customers.

'I've been told millinery,' Beth offered and smiled.

'Yes, me too.' Maggie looked happy at the idea.

'I think that's where they will put me.' Sally made a wry expression. 'I wanted clothes. It's what I know best, but it sounds as if we'll be working together – at least that's something...'

The front door was opening and Beth, Maggie and Sally were among the first admitted. The woman who had interviewed Beth was holding a clipboard and directing people to their various departments. Beth hardly had time to take in the look of luxury on all sides – tiled floors of grey marble, glossy pale wood and sparkling chandeliers overhead were all a blur as the floor walker spoke to them. Her excitement and nerves were churning inside her, making her mouth dry and the palms of her hands damp.

'Ah yes, Miss Ross, Miss Grey – and...' She frowned at Maggie over her gold-rimmed glasses.

'Maggie Gibbs,' she supplied timidly.

'Ah, the junior... Yes – you are all to report to the first floor. You may use the lift, if you know how to, if not take the stairs.'

'I can work the lift,' Sally said confidently and led the way into the small cage, sliding the outer and then the inner doors closed and pressing the buttons on the wall next to it. 'We had these at Selfridges... I expect there will be an operator when we open...'

'Did you work at Selfridges?' Maggie looked at her in awe. 'Why did you leave?'

'Because the floor supervisor couldn't keep his hands to himself,' Sally said with a grin. 'He was always touching me as I passed him and I'd had enough. At least we shall have a female supervisor here.'

'Yes – Miss Hart is a bit of a dragon, isn't she?' Maggie said ruefully.

'I've known worse,' Sally told her grimly. 'You stick with me, Maggie love, and I'll put you right.'

The lift had reached the first floor. Sally opened the wire cage and sliding doors and they trooped out into a large department with glass counters covered with paper wrappings one of which had been torn open, things that looked like hat stands still wrapped in layers of brown paper, and many large cardboard boxes.

As the girls hesitated uncertainly, a woman who looked to be in her early thirties walked in from what they later learned was the stockroom. She looked directly at them and smiled, coming forward with her hand outstretched.

'You must be my assistants,' she said. 'I am Rachel Craven. I've had experience of running a haberdasher for a while. During working hours you will address me as Mrs Craven, but I hope we shall get on well and perhaps become friends.' Her bright eyes moved over them. 'Miss Sally Ross, you are my senior assistant, because you have the most experience...' She looked at the right person. 'I've been told why you left Selfridges – and if you have that kind of trouble in future, come to me first and I will sort it.'

'Thanks,' Sally nodded.

'Now, before we go any further, I should tell you what I know about the store. We're on the first floor and next to us are the dress and lingerie departments; above us is the men's department, which is subdivided for suits, coats, hats, gloves, underwear and shoes, and next to that is the shoe department. The women's shoes are also on that floor, a mistake I feel, and also children's clothing. On the third floor is a restaurant which serves snacks like a cup of tea and a scone for both customers and staff, also the staff rest room, where you may go if you feel unwell. On the fourth floor is Mr Stockbridge's office, Mr Marco's room and the accounts office, which is where we send our invoices and cash for change. Then, of course, there is the basement...'

'What happens there?' Maggie asked.

'It is the domain of our caretaker, who brings up our stock and keeps us all going...'

'Only one?' Sally Ross said. 'We had several at Selfridges...'

'I dare say we'll manage for the moment.' Mrs Craven turned her gaze to Beth. 'I think you must be Miss Beth Grey, you are the second assistant, but you will have the gloves and scarves counter, and Miss Margaret Gibbs, you will be my assistant for the time being. That means you tidy up after I've served a customer and fetch whatever I need. It will also be your job to dust and remove covers in the mornings. Miss Ross has leather handbags and costume jewellery – two counters – and I am in charge of the millinery. If one or the other of you is very busy, I may send Miss Gibbs to assist you. I shall, therefore, instruct all of you in the way merchandise is to be handled, how to address customers and how to take money and send it by way of our ingenious machine up to the office for change. For a start, if I am free, I shall supervise the money taken, but there may be times when I simply do not have the time and you will have to do it alone.'

'Yes, Mrs Craven,' they all said and she smiled.

'I am sure I don't have to warn any of you about personal hygiene. We insist on clean short nails, no make-up or perfume for work and your hair must be tidy and clean.' Her eyes swept over them. 'Nothing to complain of here... Good – now I think that we shall have Miss Ross in the role of customer for a start. You will serve her with gloves, Miss Grey – and you will watch, Miss Gibbs...' She turned her brown eyes on Sally and Beth noticed the glint of mischief. 'I want you to be as difficult as possible, Miss Ross – so that our ladies understand just how much patience it takes to be a sales assistant in this kind of department.'

'Where do I stand?' Beth asked and was told to take her place behind a counter which had several graduated wooden drawers inside. Most of the wrapping had been taken from this counter and Mrs Craven snipped away the rest with a small pair of silver-coloured scissors that hung from a chatelaine at her waist.

'Now, Miss Ross, address the assistant – and tell her you need the gloves to match some shoes for a wedding.'

Beth took her place and Sally approached. She looked at the counter, appearing to study it, and then touched her hair. 'Miss, I need some pale grey gloves,' she said in a voice that shocked Beth, because it sounded high class and completely unlike the voice Sally used when speaking normally. 'Size five and a half please...'

'Yes, madam,' Beth answered in her normal tone. 'We have silk and leather... would you like to see both?'

'I'm not sure,' Sally turned up her nose. 'I don't want cheap leather – and silk is difficult to keep nice. Don't you have anything else?'

'The knitted gloves are more for winter,' Beth improvised. 'I can assure you that these leather gloves are beautifully soft and well made...' She pulled out a drawer at the back and pretended to take some gloves out, placing them on the counter.

Sally pretended to pick up one pair, looked at them, shook her head and then picked up the next. She smoothed her fingers and admired them for a moment and then sighed.

'The leather is good – but they're too dark. I need something lighter... What about those – I'd like to try those, please...' She pointed to another drawer in the counter.

Beth went and pulled out another drawer, pretending to take out more gloves. Sally went through the motions of picking each pair up again and comparing them, and then shook her head.

'These are too plain. Do you not have something with a bow or a little fancy fastener? It is for a special occasion...'

'I'm not sure, madam,' Beth said and turned to Maggie. 'Miss Gibbs, would you ask Mrs Craven if she could please come for a moment – and if she is busy, ask her if we have any more grey gloves not out on show...?'

'Excellent,' Mrs Craven said. 'That is always a good ploy if the customer is too difficult. However, you have made the most common mistake all shop girls make when they start...' She turned her bright gaze on Sally. 'Can Miss Ross tell you what that is please?'

'Do not get too many items out at once,' Sally said promptly. 'If a customer says she doesn't like something and asks to see other examples, then put away the ones she rejected in your personal drawer at the top. You can sort them when you've finished serving. Otherwise, if she is dishonest, and even the posh ones sometimes are, you may lose things like gloves, scarves, costume jewellery...'

'That is why I've put you in charge of that section as well as the handbags, Miss Ross,' Mrs Craven nodded approval. 'The leather handbags are the most expensive items we stock and some of the jewellery is too good to be classed as costume jewellery. They are handmade, individual silver pieces from America, and must be put away in my office safe at night...'

'Oh, I didn't realise.' Sally's expression brightened. 'I like handling good things. When will the stock arrive?'

'Not until next week,' Mrs Craven said. 'Today is to be given to learning how to serve our customers, where the different departments are – and also learning the rules, which are quite strict. We do not allow assistants to eat or drink anywhere in the store but the restaurant, or the staff restroom, which is on the third floor.' She paused, then, 'I think it is quite expensive to eat in the restaurant, and my advice would be to bring sandwiches and take them to the restroom in your lunch break. I would advise you to find somewhere cheap to have a cup of soup midday if you prefer; your tea break will be in the staff room and is no more than fifteen minutes in the morning and afternoon. You take it in turns and being late back is liable to a fine of one penny a minute, as is arriving late in the mornings. We work until five thirty, finishing when the last customer has left the department, even if that is several minutes past our time...'

'Do we all wear the same style dress?' Beth asked. 'Are we allowed to make our own or do we have to buy it from the store?'

'You will be given one dress and any other you buy or make must be the same style. Mine is a slightly different style, but you three all have the same. It has a white lace collar, which you can change rather than washing the dress every time. If you choose good material, sponging should be sufficient.'

Beth nodded, feeling relieved. She would be able to buy material from the market and ask her aunt to make the dress.

'What are the other rules?' Sally inquired.

'You are expected to be here by a quarter to eight in the mornings. First of all, we shall be addressed by the manager and told of any important events and then we say prayers. It will be frowned on if you do not attend the briefing. After that we tidy and prepare the department for customers.' She placed a sheet of paper on the counter. 'Study the list and you won't forget...'

Sally nodded. 'I can see there is a pulley system to send the money up to the office. Do I have to check every payment with you, Mrs Craven?'

'Unless I am very busy, I would advise you to do so for your own benefit, Miss Ross. However, you could ask either Miss Grey or Miss Gibbs to check if that is easier.' The supervisor looked at Beth and Maggie. 'The reason I advise you to have someone check what the customer gives you is because occasionally you might be told you were given more than you were – and it is awkward. We would then have to confirm it with the office and they might be busy, which could cause a problem... I find it is best to write on the invoice the denomination of the note given and repeat it to the customer before you put it into the capsule and send it upstairs.'

Beth and Maggie nodded. It had never occurred to either of them that their customer might say they had given more money than they had. There was such a lot to learn.

'There are so many rules,' Maggie whispered to Sally

anxiously. 'I shall be frightened of breaking them without knowing.'

'You don't smoke, so you don't have to worry about that one,' Sally consulted the list Mrs Craven had placed on the counter.

'I'm glad we can't, I don't like it,' Maggie replied softly.

'What other rules are there?' Sally asked.

'No jewellery is allowed to be worn other than a wedding ring – engagement rings must be left at home. Taking them off and leaving them in a handbag is unwise – as is leaving more money than you need for the day. Clean handkerchiefs are expected and shoes must always be polished. No ladders or holes in stockings, in case they are seen if you bend down – Miss Ross, I think you are wearing perfume today. Please do not do so for work.'

Sally nodded. 'Sorry, Mrs Craven. I think it's on my dress.'

'I think it unnecessarily harsh, but it is one of the rules,' Mrs Craven smiled at them. 'I think I've covered most things – and if you think the rules are severe, remember that until recently many large stores insisted that their girls live in a hostel of the firm's providing. Had that been the case, you would have had strict rules there, as well as a curfew of nine o'clock at night...'

'Don't tell me, I know,' Sally groaned. 'The hostel I live in is murder. The rules here are easy compared to some there. I hate it and as soon as I can afford it, I'll get a place of my own to rent.'

'You would live on your own?' Maggie stared at her in surprise and Sally grinned.

'Just give me the chance – but if I could, I'd live with other women. Friends I could trust would make it more fun...'

Beth smiled but her aunt would say the idea was reprehensible. Aunt Helen would not think that a young woman should live in lodgings without an older woman to supervise her, unless she was a widow and forced to it.

'Well, we'll remove some of this paper,' Mrs Craven said, looking about her with a frown. 'The cleaning staff should have done it, but they haven't got round to us yet. I want it off so that we can see what space we have available and then we can do some more training...'

Beth accepted a pair of scissors and she and Maggie began to snip away the brown paper and pile it in a corner so that they could see the counters more clearly. For the millinery, there were two tall glass counters with glass shelves, where the most expensive hats would be on show, and another counter where the hats would be placed on stands, both on top and inside the glass. Several hat stands came out of more brown paper, most were adjustable and could be placed either on counter tops or dotted about the department.

'I shall do the displays,' Mrs Craven told them, 'but you will keep them free of dust, Miss Gibbs. I'll show you what to do as we go along...'

Beth studied the counter she'd been given. There were about twenty graduated wooden drawers, which would show off the gloves and scarves on display.

'If I were you, I would use one side for gloves and the other for scarves,' Mrs Craven said, coming to stand by her. 'It is a good idea to put colours into separate drawers, and keep glove sizes together if you can. Perhaps the black and grey at the bottom and come up with the brighter colours and finish with white lace and cotton at the top – and the closed drawer at the top is for you to place your order book, your receipt book, your pen and scissors, and it is a good idea to put things in there if you need to refold or tidy up. The bags printed with Harpers logo will go on a shelf underneath the counter. And if you have to leave the counter, put your items away, as I warned earlier, otherwise you may return to find something missing. It is very difficult if you have to ask what happened to a scarf, for the customer will be outraged and march off...'

Beth felt that she had learned a great deal that morning. The time flew by as they worked and asked questions, and it wasn't long before the girls were told they could take half an hour for something to eat or drink.

'We shall work for two hours this afternoon, but then you may go,' Mrs Craven said. 'However, I shall come with you now and show you where the other departments are...'

'Thank you,' Maggie said, looking relieved. 'I don't want to get lost and be fined for being late back to work...'

'I think we can be lenient today,' Mrs Craven smiled at her. 'But, Miss Gibbs, the rules are meant to be kept – and I shall be strict once the shop is open...' She hesitated then, 'Just one more thing – and this is personal – I am widowed and have no children. I tell you this so that you know and will not be embarrassed by asking questions about my family...'

None of the girls answered, because it would not be appropriate to offer sympathy to their superior. Mrs Craven nodded her head and smiled.

'Very well, I think that is all for the moment...'

4

Sally took Beth and Maggie to a small café a short distance away. It was clean and busy but the food was cheap. For sixpence they could buy a double sandwich and a pot of tea.

'I thought we could share,' Sally said. 'If three of us came, they would give us extra cups and it would only cost us tuppence each...'

'That is much cheaper,' Beth agreed, 'but you wouldn't get a lot to eat...'

'We could buy three buns for a penny 'appenny' Sally said. 'We could easily cut the sandwiches into three, have a cup of tea each and a bun to fill us up... it's just an idea. Of course, on warm days we could sit out in the square on one of the benches and eat a packed lunch...'

'I wouldn't mind sharing sometimes,' Maggie answered first. 'I can bring a sandwich most days, but it would make a nice change to visit the café...'

'I'll be cooking at night and I'll bring a few bits in,' Beth said. 'Do you think they will notice if we eat our own stuff?' She looked at the woman behind the counter, who smiled and nodded to her but looked as if she could be formidable if she chose.

'That's Bessie, and her husband, Mike, owns the café,' Sally said and nodded to the woman. 'I helped her when she fell down in the street and took her to the hospital in a cab. She lets me do what I like – as long as we buy a pot of tea and a sandwich, she'll turn a blind eye to the rest...'

'You have some useful friends,' Maggie said admiringly.

'We mustn't take too much advantage,' Beth said, 'but in the summer we can sit out and eat our food, though not in Soho. My aunt would have a fit...'

Sally's eyebrows went up, so Beth took the opportunity to explain her aunt's strictness.

'We could go to Bedford Square if we walk fast, but it takes so much time to get there and back, that's why I come here. I only just made it here some days when I worked in Woolworth's and had to run all the way back...'

'I asked if they needed anyone at Woolworth's,' Maggie said, 'but they told me they have a list of girls who want to work there...'

'I know – a lot of girls like working for them,' Sally said. 'I wanted to work with clothes, but it's far harder to find a job in the smart shops because they have loads of girls waiting for a position.'

'I've just remembered,' Beth said. 'Didn't Mrs Craven say we took it in turns to have our tea breaks – do you think it will be the same for lunch?'

'Never thought of that,' Sally admitted. 'Still, we could come after work and share something – less expensive than eating supper alone. I hate going back to the hostel too early...'

'My mother will expect me home straight after work,' Maggie said and looked disappointed. 'It's because of helping with my father...' She'd already told them of his accident and they gave her sympathetic looks.

'My aunt has warned me of the perils of being out after dark.' Beth grimaced. 'She wanted me to be a lady's companion, but I couldn't get a position.'

'You're too attractive, Beth – or you could be,' Sally said, looking at her frankly. 'If I were you, I'd have my hair cut to collar length and if you wore a little lip rouge…'

'Mrs Craven said we were not allowed to wear make-up or perfume for work,' Maggie said and Sally made a wry face.

'Aunt Helen would throw me out,' Beth said and laughed, touching her hair self-consciously. 'I'd like to be friends with you, Sally, and you, Maggie – perhaps we'll get to come together for lunch sometimes, but it's not easy for me to get away.'

Sally nodded, clearly disappointed. 'As soon as I can afford it, I shall find a place to live – a room or an apartment…'

'An apartment would be so expensive,' Beth said. 'Aunt Helen makes dresses and costumes for a wealthy widow she knows and she pays more than a hundred and fifty pounds a year for her apartment. I took a parcel there for her once and it was beautiful, with a lift and a porter…' She sighed. 'Like you, Sally, I'd love an apartment of my own, but I could never afford anything like that.'

Sally looked at her hard. 'But we could – if we put together, all three of us, don't you see? Oh, it wouldn't be posh like the one you visited, Beth – but it would be ours. If we shared the rent and the expenses, it wouldn't cost much more than we have to pay now…'

'I couldn't,' Maggie said, looking upset. 'I have to be at home for my father… Muma couldn't cope.'

'That's a shame,' Sally said. 'You could though, Beth. If we found a third to share the expenses…'

'I don't think my aunt would approve.'

'Would that matter?' Sally asked.

Beth was silent. What Sally said was true, but it was in Beth's opinion a very bold thing to do. Three young women living alone without an older woman would be seen as very fast and she did not wish to be thought cheap or amoral.

'I'm not very happy at my aunt's,' she admitted thoughtfully.

'Yet, I think we should need someone older to balance us out. Otherwise, we might get a reputation.'

'Oh, who cares?' Sally said, but Beth saw her flush. 'We could ask around, there may be an older woman that works at the store and lives alone who would like to share...'

'Yes...' Beth glanced at the clock. 'We must get back. We do not want to make Mrs Craven angry on our first day.'

The girls stood up and went out. Sally stopped to talk to Bessie and then caught up with the others. 'Bessie says that if either of you go in alone, she will serve you with one sandwich and a cup of tea for a threepenny bit because you are my friends.'

'Oh good,' Maggie said, glanced back and smiled as she saw the woman watching them.

'That is very kind of her,' Beth said. 'I could afford that some days, others I'll just bring my own lunch – but I do like a hot cup of tea.'

They ran the last few steps back to Harpers, but as they entered the building, they saw Miss Hart. She glowered at them over the gold-framed spectacles she wore perched on the end of her pinched nose.

'Decorum, ladies,' she said tartly. 'This is your only warning. Any member of staff seen running, either in the store or on the street, will be fined a penny from their wages. We cannot have our staff bringing the store into disrepute. Straighten your hat, Miss Gibbs!'

'Mean old biddy,' Sally hissed as she pressed the lift button to take them up to the first floor. 'What harm were we doing?'

'It's just the rules,' Maggie said. 'Though I think she just made that one up – Mrs Craven didn't mention it.'

'I imagine Miss Hart will introduce whatever rules she thinks fit,' Beth told the others.

They nodded in unison and went into the department to discover that all the brown paper and string had been cleared away and the carpet swept with the sweeper that resided in the stockroom. A man dressed in a dark suit was there. He turned to look at them, his face serious.

'Good afternoon, ladies. I am the store manager and I wanted to see you were all getting on all right. I understand Mrs Craven is making you all aware of the rules...' Nodding to them, he smiled in Maggie's direction. 'Are there any questions while I'm here?'

'No, thank you, sir,' Sally said, because everyone was silent. 'Mrs Craven is looking after us.'

'Good, good,' he said and then left.

'Oh, I should have done that,' Maggie said, a flush in her cheeks as she saw their supervisor putting the cleaner away. 'I'm sorry...'

'It will be your job in future,' Mrs Craven assured her. 'I wanted to get tidy because I intend to do more training – and some of the stock is here early...' She looked pleased.

'What has arrived?' Sally asked, her interest sparked.

'A box of millinery and some gloves,' their supervisor said. 'I have opened the boxes and now I'll show you how to record the stock as it comes in. Miss Grey, this is your stock, so please take your stock book from the drawer...'

Beth took out the long book covered in a green fabric with a red binding and a pencil.

Mrs Craven shook her head. 'We need a pen, Miss Grey. You will require a fountain pen and you will find one on the desk in my office...'

Beth went into the office and saw the impressive brass pen tray. She selected a black fountain pen and made sure it was filled with ink and then picked up a piece of blotting paper and took it into the showroom.

'That's right,' Mrs Craven nodded approvingly. 'Now, look here at what we have unpacked for you. Six pairs of grey gloves and six pairs of black, all in fine leather, also six pairs of white lace evening gloves, in sizes from five to six and a half, I think.'

Beth looked at the gloves on the counter. She picked up each pair and examined them before putting them into the counter, the grey and black in the bottom drawers and the white lace at the top.

Mrs Craven had written the date in the left-hand margin of the book and then indicated that Beth should add the stock. 'Write six pairs of gloves in black leather, six pairs of grey gloves in leather, and six pairs of lace gloves, and in the right-hand column we shall put the price.'

'Should we not write in each pair individually?' Beth asked. 'They were different sizes, Mrs Craven, and it would be easier to check what is sold if we make a mark in the left-hand margin next to the pair that has been sold...'

'Yes, quite right,' her supervisor nodded and smiled. 'I am happy you worked that out for yourself, Miss Grey. It does not apply to scarves, of course; they are described by colour and material and price.'

Beth wrote carefully the size of the gloves in the space left between the margins and then showed the ledger to the other girls. Sally nodded but looked as if she knew it all, but Maggie smiled.

'You have a very neat hand, Beth.'

'Yes, I suppose I do,' she replied. 'My mother had a neat hand, but my father's scrawl was hard to read...' She smiled at the memory. 'He was a doctor and there is something about doctors, hardly any of them write with a neat hand. I sometimes took prescriptions for his colleagues to the pharmacy and then delivered them to patients.' Sadness swept over her and, though she did not know it, was reflected in her eyes. 'I loved going with Father to his surgery and everyone said what a wonderful man he was...' Unconsciously, she sighed. 'Well, I've done the gloves, shall I write up the scarves now?'

'I can help you,' Maggie offered, because there was a big box of silk scarves to unpack.

'Beth needs to know her stock, but you can certainly help her,' Mrs Craven said. 'Sally, will you come into the office. As the senior saleslady, there are things I want you to take responsibility for...'

Sally followed Mrs Craven into the office and Maggie began to unpack the scarves, handling them with reverence. 'This is pure silk,' she said to Beth, 'and I think the colour is magenta...'

Beth looked at it and nodded. 'Yes, that is how I would describe it. It is lovely, isn't it – and priced at two guineas. That is such a lot of money for a scarf, but it is very beautiful...'

'I wonder who priced all this stuff,' Maggie said. 'I thought Mrs Craven might do that, but the tickets are already printed and attached by a fine thread.' She considered. 'Do you think that was done by the owner or the buyer?'

'The buyer, I should think,' Beth said thoughtfully. 'It would be easy to pull that off if I wasn't looking – I'll have to be sure I know what the prices are...'

'There's so much to learn,' Maggie said. 'I thought it would be so easy working in a shop, didn't you?'

'It hadn't occurred to me that some customers might try to steal something,' Beth said. 'My family would think that beneath them – and I don't like to think it of anyone...'

'No...' Maggie glanced towards the office. 'Sally is lovely, isn't she? I'd love to go out with her after work, but I have to look after my father...'

'Of course you do,' Beth agreed. 'My aunt wouldn't like it if I wasn't straight home, but I might stay out for special occasions...'

'Oh yes,' Maggie agreed. 'Mrs Craven is a bit strict...'

'I think she is very fair,' Beth replied. 'The ones we need to watch out for are Miss Hart – and Mr Stockbridge.'

'Oh, him...' Maggie blushed and looked hard at the scarf she was selecting. 'He interviewed me and he was very kind...' She looked embarrassed and Beth was surprised but didn't say anything. Had the manager flirted with her at the interview?

She picked up a scarf that was a mixture of blue and green with a pattern all over. 'What would you describe that as?'

'Oh, I think that is swirls in green and blue,' Maggie said and Beth smiled.

She wrote: *One swirls silk scarf/green & blue, priced at thirty-five shillings.*

'It's less money than the magenta,' Maggie said. 'My mother would like it, but I could never afford to give her that for her birthday.'

'Don't forget the staff discount. We're allowed to buy one thing a month at a twenty per cent discount...'

'So I would get seven shillings off...' Maggie nodded. 'If it doesn't sell in a year, I might save enough for Muma's birthday next year...'

'It's awful, knowing all these lovely things exist and not being able to buy them, isn't it?' Beth smiled and picked up another pale blue scarf. 'This one is only thirty shillings. Perhaps some of them will be less... or there might be a sale one day...'

Maggie nodded, smiling. 'Before my father had his accident, Muma always went to the sales in Oxford Street to buy clothes for us. We used to come early in the morning and queue up – and the queue sometimes stretched round the corner.'

'Yes, it's fun doing things like that,' Beth said. 'When I was little, my father took me to see a Christmas display at one of the big toy stores. It was wonderful and I never forgot, though I was too little to remember which shop we went to. I never thought I would work in a shop like this...' She picked up a dark crimson scarf and looked at the price tag. 'Oh, look, Maggie – this is only seven shillings... I wonder why...'

Beth looked carefully at the label. 'It is artificial silk and rayon,' she said and nodded. 'That is the difference, of course – the one you liked was pure silk.'

'This is nice,' Maggie said, 'but my mother would think the colour fast...'

'Yes, my aunt would too – like you, she would prefer the swirls...'

They had finished unpacking all the scarves now and the open drawers were half filled. Beth felt a little tingle of excitement. She couldn't wait for all the stock to be in and the store to be open.

Mrs Craven returned, followed by Sally, who looked pleased with herself. They both looked at the counter and the supervisor read Beth's entries in the staff book.

'Very nice and colourful,' she said. 'Now, which scarf have you described as swirls? No, don't tell me...' She looked at the counter and then pointed. 'I would guess that one?'

'Yes, just right, we both loved that one – and the magenta,' Beth said. 'But there are a few that are not as good as the others...'

'Oh, really, why?' She looked concerned.

Beth explained that about four were only artificial silk and Mrs Craven frowned.

'I'm surprised they've been included. You must make certain you tell a customer the difference when you show them, Miss Grey.'

'Yes, I shall,' Beth assured her.

'Good. I think we've all learned a lot today – and since there is nothing left to do for the moment, you may all go. I look forward to seeing you all next week – and remember what I told you about being on time. Persistent lateness might result in dismissal; it is considered one of the worst sins, together with rudeness and theft...'

The warning sobered all three girls and they thanked Mrs Craven and left to get their coats. As they walked down the stairs, they saw Mr Stockbridge talking to a rather attractive man. His dark hair was a little long and he was wearing a bright blue scarf around his neck, his jacket was a darker blue and his trousers pale grey. Mr Stockbridge signalled to them.

'Ah, girls,' he said. 'This is Mr Marco, our window dresser. You will get to know him when he comes to your departments.

We're privileged to have such a talented artist – so make sure you keep your counters looking as attractive as his windows.'

'We'll do our best, sir,' Sally said and grinned at the window dresser, who winked back at her.

Giggling together, the girls ran down the stairs and stood for a moment on the pavement saying their goodbyes. Then Maggie saw her bus approaching the stop and sprinted to catch it.

'Good thing Miss Sourpuss isn't about,' Sally said and grimaced. 'Maggie would have lost half her money before she starts...'

'There are a lot of rules,' Beth agreed. 'I should get home I suppose – I look forward to working with you, Sally.'

'Come and have a cup of tea first,' Sally said. 'My treat. Your aunt will not be expecting you yet, will she?'

'No, not for another hour or more,' Beth acknowledged. She sensed that her new friend was lonely and smiled, 'I'd love to, Sally. You know Oxford Street better than I do – tell me where I can find all the best bargains...'

Sally's face lit up and she tucked her arm through Beth's. 'As soon as I was thrown out of the orphanage, I headed up West; I found a cheap hostel and I was lucky to get into a gift shop as a junior for a few months and then I went to Woollies' and then Selfridges... but I think I'll be more content here.'

The two girls linked arms, smiling happily as they went off together.

5

It was five o'clock when Beth and Sally finally left the café after laughing and talking their way through a pot of tea and a shared bun. Beth was feeling happier than she'd been in ages when she parted from her new friend at the bus stop. Sally was walking home, because she had nothing in particular waiting for her at the hostel, and Beth was waiting for the next bus when a man's voice made her jump. She turned to look at someone she hadn't expected to see again.

'Mark... Mr Stewart,' she said, blushing. 'I didn't see you approach.'

'You were lost in thought,' he chided her with the smile that had always set her heart racing. He was a doctor, newly qualified when her father had died, and he'd been there to lend a shoulder when she'd wept out her grief. Serious, attractive, with dark hair and eyes, Mark had been an infrequent but consistent visitor to her home for years – until nearly two years previously, on Beth's twentieth birthday, when he'd asked her to marry him. She hadn't seen him since she'd refused his proposal.

'I've been sharing a pot of tea with a new friend,' Beth told him, feeling shy as his eyes moved over her searchingly. 'I'm starting a new job at Harpers next week and I went in for training...'

'Really? I've heard the owner is an American.' His eyes darkened. 'I heard about your mother – I should have visited or written, Beth. I am sorry...'

'I didn't expect it,' she said, feeling close to tears. 'You were angry when we parted.'

'Yes, but I understood after a while. I've been abroad for two years, Beth. I took a position in Africa. At the time, I couldn't bear to stay in the same country and know I couldn't be with you...'

'Oh, Mark...' She wished that the ground would open and swallow her, feeling sick and hot all over. 'I'm so sorry. I never meant to hurt you – but I couldn't leave my mother...'

'I told you, she could've lived with us...'

'Yes, but...' Beth shook her head. How could she tell him that her mother had acted as though she was betraying her when she'd said they could all live together? Beth's heart had been torn in two as her mother wept and begged her not to desert her, cajoling and threatening until she gave in.

For a moment, she closed her eyes as she remembered.

'I'll be dead soon enough,' her mother had cried out after some hours of pointless discussion. 'Surely you can wait for a few years?'

The memory was still vivid, still hurtful.

'But you would still be with us,' Beth had replied, silently begging her to smile and say she was happy for her, but she hadn't, instead she had fallen back on the pillows. 'I love him, please let me marry him and live with us...'

'You must do what you want with your own life, Beth, if your conscience is clear,' her mother had said then and closed her eyes as if in pain. 'I'll just stay here in this bed until they take me into the infirmary...'

Beth had tried to win her mother round, but she'd insisted that Beth must not think of her and refused to be a burden to her, claiming that Mark would grow tired of having her in his home and she did not wish to be the cause of quarrels. Despite the regret and pain it gave her, in the end, Beth had told him she could not marry him.

Mark had taken her refusal badly. He'd thought she did not love him, because all she would say was that she could not leave her mother. He'd pleaded, but when she told him it was no use, he'd stormed off, angry and bitter. It had broken Beth's heart and she'd hoped that he would come back and be her friend again, but he hadn't visited or written even when her mother died.

'Mother couldn't face leaving her home – or the thought that she might be a burden to us. If I'd left her, she would have died in the infirmary...'

'Oh, Beth,' he said and looked stricken. 'Is that what you feared?'

'She – she would not live with us and...' Beth shook her head as the tears stung her eyes. 'I shouldn't – it is so disloyal of me...'

'Disloyal – you?' Mark sounded. 'You were the most loyal of daughters and she used you – yes, she did, Beth. You broke my heart and perhaps your own for a selfish woman...'

It was true. She knew that he was speaking the truth as it seemed to him, but he hadn't been there and seen her mother's fear, and he didn't have the ties and the memories that had bound Beth to the invalid's side. Mark might think her spineless and weak for giving in, but in fact it had taken strength to do what she knew was right despite her own longings and her heartbreak.

She could not bear any more of this!

'I must go.' Beth tried to move away, but he caught her arm. 'Please, I know you're angry but...'

For a moment, the passion flamed in his dark eyes and his handsome face looked almost cruel; she thought that if they were alone he might have kissed her or hit her and did not know which she expected. She did not know what she wanted, whether the love she'd had for him once was still there. Then, all of a sudden, the heat was gone and he smiled wryly.

'It nearly killed me to leave you,' he said, 'but it hardly matters now – I'm married to a wonderful young woman and Lily adores me...'

There was something about the way Mark spoke, half gleeful, half angry, that made Beth look at him and the expression in his eyes gave her a jolt. It felt as if he'd plunged a knife into her heart.

'Why are you looking at me like that?' she asked and her voice shook. 'It's as if you hate me...'

'I both hate and love you,' he said in a quiet vicious tone. 'Seeing you opens old wounds, makes me remember...'

His words, combined with what seemed like cold anger now, made Beth nervous. Fortunately, her bus drew up at that moment and she jumped on, looking back at him as he stood staring after her. His arm came out, almost as if in supplication, and she felt her heart twist with pain, but the bus was turning the corner and the conductor told her to move along.

'Sit down, ducks, or you might fall and harm yourself...' he said and gave her a cheery grin.

Beth nodded and moved numbly towards the nearest seat. She discovered that she was shaking and feeling a little sick. For a moment, she'd thought Mark might hurt her, but when he'd held his arm out to her at the last, it had been pain she'd seen in his eyes.

'Tuppence please, ducks,' the young conductor said as Beth asked for High Holborn. 'You came up early this mornin' – had a good day?'

'Yes, thank you.' Beth swallowed hard, trying to rid herself of the hard knot of misery in her chest. When she saw Mark, she'd thought that he might still love her, that now there was a chance to find the happiness that had been denied her, but then he'd spoken the words that had broken any dream she might have held. He was married – to Lily, who loved him, and he despised Beth, thought her faithless for choosing her mother over him.

The tears burned behind her eyes, but she couldn't give into grief in a public place. Years of strict discipline made her raise her head and hold back the tears. They would come later, when she was alone in bed. It was only now that Beth realised she'd been hoping that Mark would return one day and ask her to be his wife again. Now she knew the dream had finally gone.

'It's going to be a lovely day again tomorrow,' the cheerful conductor said and winked at her. 'They say the weather is settled for a while now, but more than likely it will rain all summer.'

'I do hope not...' Beth replied but couldn't force herself to smile. She looked unseeingly out of the window. She would soon be home and could hide her tears in her room.

* * *

Aunt Helen was in the kitchen and the smell of vegetable soup cooking met Beth as she entered. Her aunt turned to look at her expectantly.

'How did you get on then?'

'I like it there,' Beth said. 'I'll change quickly, Aunt, and then finish the supper...'

'Just change and come down. I finished the costume I was making – and Mrs Wayman has ordered two summer dresses for her daughter, but I do not need to start them until tomorrow.'

Beth nodded, forcing a smile before escaping to her bedroom to change her dress for a comfortable old tweed skirt and a jumper. Aunt Helen knew nothing about Mark and she would not tell her. It was a private hurt that she must learn to put aside. Her future was at Harpers and she would probably grow old there and become a floor walker like Miss Hart...

6

Sally lingered in the shops. She knew all of them on her route back to the hostel well and spent as much time as she could every evening wandering towards New Oxford Street and Bloomsbury, looking in the windows or browsing the counters in those that opened late: anything to delay her return. It was hateful at the hostel and she longed to find a place she could call home, but that was something she'd never truly had. All her young life had been spent in orphanages run by nuns and she'd been passed from one to another, because the nuns said she was rebellious and flouted the rules. Sally supposed it was true, but she'd hated the nuns' sombre attire and their stern faces and longed for someone to laugh and play with her, as a mother would – and yet she knew now that mothers did not always love their daughters. That dream had been shattered when she was sixteen and Mother Superior had called her into her office and told her that she must leave.

'We took you from your mother, because the life she led was not suitable for bringing up a child...'

'My mother...' Sally had recoiled as though she'd been slapped. 'My mother is dead...'

'Of that I have no certainty,' the nun had said sourly. 'By her lifestyle, I would imagine she must be dead long since, but she abandoned you to the care of our order and we have brought you up as we do all motherless children...'

Sally's eyes had blazed with anger, because she'd been passed from one home to another like a parcel. She'd pleaded then for more details of a mother who might yet live. The nun denied knowing more than she had already told her.

'You were the child of a woman of the night and one of her clients. She was ill and begged us to take you, that is all I've been told.' Mother Superior had hesitated and then removed something from the drawer of her desk. She had placed a tiny silver locket on the desk. 'Your mother asked the sister who took you in to give this to you one day. Since I do not expect to see you again, Sally, it is yours, and now it remains only for me to wish you a good life.'

Feeling angry, torn with regret and bitter at being sent out alone to fend for herself, Sally had snatched up the locket and left the nun's office. Tears had blinded her eyes, but she had forced them back. Her mother had given her to the nuns, condemning her to years of a cold, sterile existence, because she did not want her. So much for her dreams of a loving mother!

Sally shook her head, refusing to weep. It did not matter. She would never think of her again or long for something she could not have. Sally had ceased to grieve. She was strong and had learned how to manage alone.

Sally reached Selfridges and stood outside the window, studying the way the window was dressed. It was so stylish and the clothes were lovely. Sally's dream was to work in the dress department, and perhaps to help dress the windows. She admired the way the clothes had been draped on the dummies but also the fact that the theme of the window was women dressed to go motoring and cycling and an old-fashioned penny farthing cycle had been brought in to make you smile and stop to look. Everyone marvelled at the window dressing at Selfridges and people would often crowd around a new display. Sally would have liked to continue working at the busy store. Unfortunately, that had become impossible for her and she'd been forced to hand in her notice, something that had annoyed her immediate supervisor.

'I thought you were reliable,' she'd told Sally crossly. 'If you continue to leave your work every few months, no one will employ you...'

Sally hadn't told her that it was Mr Jago's fault, because Miss Robinson would not have believed her. Some of the firms she'd tried after leaving her last post had been reluctant to give her a chance – but she'd been lucky. Harpers needed experienced shop girls and fortunately her story had been believed.

She moved along to the next window and studied it. This was given over to a display of sporting clothes for men with cricket bats and various other items such as shooting gear and a sports rifle. She frowned slightly, feeling that something was missing; it didn't quite have the interest of the first window in her opinion.

'Have you noticed it too?' a voice asked and Sally looked at the man who had spoken. She knew the owner of Selfridges by sight, and this gentleman wasn't her former employer. Tall, dark haired with an open, fresh-faced appeal, he had the look of a sportsman. He was a gentleman, though, by his clothes, which were well cut and expensive, and she thought there might be a faint American accent. 'Something's missing – but I'm not sure what...' he said more to himself than her.

'There's no life to it,' Sally spoke for the first time. 'Yes, there are two dummies, but both are men – it needs something to represent the way sport is enjoyed... a woman in a summer dress with a parasol. She's there to watch and applaud the cricket, of course – or even some models of a fox or game birds.' She cocked her head on one side and grinned because she could see it all in her mind's eye. 'It needs more to give it movement...'

'Yes, I agree,' he replied and she laughed inside as she saw him making notes in a little black book. 'That is just the answer

Marco would give. You are an intelligent young woman – are you employed here?'

'No, not now,' Sally said, wondering if he meant the Mr Marco she'd met earlier at Harpers. Was this man employed there too? 'I did work here for a while but... I'm going to work for Harpers now.'

'Why did you leave – were the wages better?'

'No...' Sally's cheeks burned. 'It was something personal...' She turned to move away, feeling that she'd said too much.

'Forgive me, miss... I did not mean to embarrass you, especially after you were so helpful.'

'It's all right,' Sally said. 'I should go now.'

'Yes, of course – good luck in your new job.'

'Thank you,' Sally said and moved away, a little flustered. For a moment, she'd thought he was going to proposition her and wondered if her open manner had given him the wrong idea. She'd liked the look of him and even a few minutes spent talking with a stranger was better than returning to the cold cheerless place where she lived. Yet Sally didn't want to be thought fast and needed to protect her good name. Men often tried to take advantage of a pretty young woman with no family and Sally was determined not to end up like the street walkers she often saw in Soho Square.

Refusing the temptation to glance back, Sally walked steadily on. Even the shops with later opening hours were closing now and she would either have to spend a few pence buying a cup of tea or return to the hostel and make a cup of cocoa before going to bed. There was nothing else to do when she got there because the canteen would be filled with girls she had nothing in common with, so she kept to her own room most of the time.

Sally had been lucky enough to have a friend when she first arrived, but Jane had fallen pregnant and her boyfriend had married her. She'd invited Sally to pop round whenever she liked, but Sally was uncomfortable with Roger, Jane's husband.

For some reason, he didn't like her, though she'd done nothing to upset him.

She'd never managed to make friends at the orphanage. Sally wasn't sure why, but she thought it might be because she was a rebel and often punished and the other girls thought they might get punished too if they were her friends. At Selfridges, she'd tried to make friends and one or two had been nice to her, but then she'd had to leave and she hadn't seen them since.

Feeling lonely and still reluctant to return, she walked on towards Clerkenwell and finally turned the corner into the dingy lane that housed the hostel for young working girls. In itself it was respectable enough and the rules were strict. Another twenty minutes and the door would have been locked for the night.

Across the street there was a rowdy pub that was noisy on Friday and Saturday nights when the working men got paid; it doubled as a working man's club and on Saturday nights there would be music, singing and laughter. The King Billy was always busy and she'd been told the food at the bar was good but had never dared to venture inside. The men took their wives there on special nights and Sally had seen them coming and going from her window that overlooked the lane. Occasionally, there was a fight in the lane and early one morning she'd woken to the sound of pounding feet and police whistles, but that didn't happen often.

As Sally paused at the hostel door, waiting for it to be answered, a man came out of the pub and grinned at her. Mick was Irish and ran the bar for the owner. He always looked at her as if he wanted to say something, but she wasn't in the mood for flirting, and it seemed that was what most men did when they met Sally. Mick had tried to be friendly, but she did her best to avoid speaking to him, though now and then he would deliberately come across the lane to speak to her.

She escaped inside as the door was opened by Mrs Hobbs,

who was in charge of locking up for the night and for making breakfast for the twenty young women who lived in the hostel.

'Oh, it's you,' she said, sniffing in disapproval, and glanced at the American wall clock. 'Leaving it nearly to the last minute as usual, I see. You won't get any supper now. I've cleared the counter.'

'That's all right, Mrs Hobbs,' Sally said cheerfully. 'I had something to eat out.'

'Lucky you can afford it!'

The custodian gave her a suspicious look, sniffing again as she went back to her private room and Sally made for the stairs. She could hear voices from the landing above. Three girls were arguing, two shouting at each other and the third trying to keep the peace.

'That bitch Jean was in my things, I tell you – and my garnet beads are missing.'

'She's a liar. Tell her that she's a lying cat, Bessie. I never touched her beads. I wouldn't be seen dead in them...'

'What are yer starin' at?'

Jean's sharp voice directed at Sally made her start.

'I'm just going to my room...'

Sally turned away from the unpleasant scene. Jean and Violet were always arguing and Bessie tried to keep the peace between the roommates. It was at times like these that Sally was glad she paid three shillings a week and had a room to herself rather than sharing. She'd had a run-in with Jean herself occasionally and it was best to stay clear.

Her room, which she always left locked, was so small that it was filled by a bed, a chest of drawers with a swing mirror on top and the single bed. There was no wardrobe, so Sally hung her clothes on hooks behind the door. It wasn't ideal and looked untidy, but if she'd folded her spare dresses in the chest they would have needed to be ironed every time she wore them.

Even though tiny, it was better than living at the orphanage, where the nuns were so strict it bordered on cruelty and the young girls were turned out as soon as they were old enough to fend for themselves. Nuns were supposed to be the brides of Christ, but how could they justify their unkindness to God? Sally wasn't sure she believed in God at all, and if she did, it wasn't the one those awful women worshipped, she was sure of that...

Sally took off her jacket and dress and hung them up on the hooks, put on her bathrobe and then brushed her hair in front of the mirror, in the lamplight it glowed with red highlights. She picked up her towel and soap bag and went down the hall to the bathroom. Luckily, it was empty and she took the chance to wash her face and clean her teeth. Sometimes, she had to queue for the privilege, but most of the residents didn't bother to wash at night. In the morning, there was always a rush and some girls shared to save time.

Returning down the hall, she saw one of the other girls, Sylvia, come upstairs. She nodded to Sally. 'I just made it,' she said. 'Mrs Hobbs is on the warpath again.'

'Yes, she hates latecomers, as she calls those who stay out to the last moment...'

'It's ridiculous,' Sylvia said. 'If I want to stay out, I shall.'

'Don't blame you...'

'Goodnight then...'

'Goodnight, Sylvia...'

Sylvia was one of the few girls at the hostel that talked to Sally. She wondered what the young woman found to do every night, because Sylvia was never back until a minute or so before nine. Sally found it hard to find anything to do alone past a certain time, but Sylvia always seemed to be in a rush.

Sally looked around the cheerless room as she locked her door behind her. She'd learned to do it all the time, because otherwise some of the girls would just barge in unasked. There were some cheap pictures on the walls that she'd picked up on the Portobello Market, but they didn't make the place look any better.

She sat down on the edge of the bed and then lay down on her side, bringing her knees up to her chest. Her private life was so empty and lonely, Sally longed for friends she could share things with, a place where they could be together and laugh and talk as they made supper or did each other's hair.

One day, she vowed to herself as she lay curled up on the bed, one day she would get out of this dump and find a place to call home and someone she could trust and rely on as a friend...

7

Beth woke in the night with tears on her cheeks again. She'd been dreaming about the terrible time when she'd begged her mother to let her marry Mark and Mrs Grey had refused to listen. Throwing back the covers, Beth padded down the hall to the bathroom and locked the door before washing her face. She didn't want Aunt Helen asking why she'd been crying.

It was ridiculous to cry, of course. Life was looking better for Beth than it had done in a while because she was looking forward to starting work the following week. She'd found it exciting to discover all the new things she would have to learn, and handling the merchandise was lovely. As yet, her counter was only half filled, but the soft leather gloves and the fine silk scarves were quality and she would find it satisfying to show them to customers.

Beth made herself think about her new friends at Harpers. Sally was lonely, she could tell. She seemed full of confidence, but Beth had seen beneath to the vulnerable girl she was and wished she could help her. Beth thought her aunt's home must be far more comfortable than the hostel that Sally had to endure.

Her mind moved on from Sally to the younger girl. Maggie

seemed a gentle, pleasant girl but perhaps a little timid, Beth thought. She liked both her and Sally and knew she would enjoy meeting the two girls at work every day. Beth felt thankful she'd been given the chance to work at Harpers and Aunt Helen had seemed more relaxed that evening and they'd got on reasonably well. Perhaps her life would begin to improve now. It would be better for both of them if Beth was out at work and earning a little money.

The only dark cloud was bumping in to Mark and the way he'd reacted, as if she had let him down deliberately. Beth shook her head. She wouldn't let the chance encounter with Mark ruin her pleasure in her new job.

As she went softly back to bed, because it was still only four o'clock in the morning, Beth wondered about her supervisor. She knew hardly anything about Mrs Craven, except that she'd told them she was widowed. However, she seemed nice enough – strict but fair – and that was what was needed in a supervisor, of course.

Beth climbed back in bed. She hadn't heard Aunt Helen stir, which was a good thing. Her aunt worked really hard and needed her rest. The glass of sherry they'd had to celebrate Beth's job must have helped her to sleep. She smiled as she remembered her aunt's flushed face after the unaccustomed drink; it was a treat for them both.

Turning over in bed, thoughts of Mark kept her wakeful, but she made an effort to settle down and forget the chance encounter that evening. Beth was being silly, worrying over something which couldn't possibly matter. She'd known it was all over long ago, when Mark had stormed off... hadn't she?

Determined to get some sleep, Beth put the meeting from her mind. She had several things she needed to get done this weekend, because once she started work properly there just wouldn't be the time...

* * *

Rachel Craven lit the gas ring in in her room, boiled her kettle and made a pot of tea. She'd been lying awake for the past half an hour and it must be nearly six o'clock anyway. She would need to get up by six in future if she was to arrive at work early and set the girls a good example. Besides, she didn't need much sleep these days. She'd got out of the habit of a full night's rest when Paul was dying.

For a moment, the pain of her husband's death struck her hard. Was it only two years since they'd told her his illness was incurable and she'd watched the slow descent into terrible pain and a wretched death from a wasting sickness that made her weep tears of blood inside? Rachel knew that she would never forget those last weeks and days when she'd known she had lost him. He'd gone from her before death took him, his pain making him angry and bitter – angry at the woman who had loved and tended to him so faithfully to the end, bitter because he was dying and she would live on. At the very last, he'd told her he'd always loved her and begged her to forgive him; she had done so, but the hurt had gone deep.

Afterwards, she'd felt drained and empty, too tired and worn down to grieve properly. It had taken her six months to return from that hell and then it had been necessity that had brought her back. She'd been shocked when she realised that Paul's savings were almost gone. The doctor's fees and their expenses over the months of his illness had used up much of what had been saved. Paul had worked in an office as a manager, but his wage had never been high and he'd been a generous man, always giving to charity and friends in need, never imagining that the day would come when he could not work. There was enough to live on if she was very careful, but she'd had to give up her pretty little house and take a room in a boarding house. She'd been lucky to find Mrs Malone, an Irish widow who ran a small boarding house for respectable ladies. Three other women lived under the same roof as Rachel, one a widow of slender

means and two spinster sisters who eked out a precarious living
by taking in sewing.

Paul had always refused to let her take a job. She was his wife
and he was the provider; he wanted her at home, caring for his
needs and enjoying her life as she pleased. Rachel might have
continued as an assistant to her father in his office as a lawyer
had he not died just after her marriage, but Paul hadn't wanted
her to go anywhere else to work and she hadn't minded. They
had both longed for children, but during his illness he'd told her
that he was glad they had none, for any child of his might have
inherited his illness.

His words had broken Rachel's heart. She had lost both her
parents to typhoid when she was twenty. Her only blood relative
was a sister who lived in Hastings-on-Sea and ran a boarding
house with her husband. They had three children, but Hazel
only sent cards at Christmas and was too tied up with her own
family to write even when Paul died; she'd sent just a card with a
black edge that Rachel couldn't bear to look at and threw away.

Rachel had decided to seek work outside the home after
Paul's death because she did not want to risk the kind of genteel
poverty that the spinster sisters endured and for six months she
had run a small haberdashers for a Jewish couple. Mr Samuels
had been ill when he took her on, but now he was well again
and, though he wouldn't say, Rachel had known he wanted her
to leave the business to him. He'd given her a glowing reference
for Harpers and she'd gone round to thank him after she was
given her new position.

He'd been pleased for her, but she'd sensed there was relief
too. Rachel sipped her tea and thought about the job she'd taken
on at Harpers. It was a good job and paid more than twice what
Mr Samuels had thought fair. She might earn enough to find a
home of her own again one day, though she would need to save
a decent nest egg first, because she didn't want to have to worry
over how she would pay the bills. For the moment, she was
comfortable here. Mrs Malone was honest, cheerful and

friendly, though a little nosey. Rachel suspected that she went through her tenants' things when they were out. Nothing was ever taken, but little things were disturbed. Perhaps she just wanted to be sure that her lodgers were what they claimed, Rachel thought with a wry smile.

Mrs Malone provided her with breakfast of toast with marmalade and grapefruit out of a tin, and would, if asked, cook an evening meal. Tinned food had been thought of a century earlier and was a boon to people like her landlady, who used it at every opportunity rather than cook fresh. Rachel usually ate soup for lunch at work and then bought ham and made herself a salad or a sandwich in her room at night; she was not fond of the heavy stews and pies the spinster sisters devoured hungrily each night. Her appetite seemed to have disappeared with the peaceful sleep she'd once enjoyed.

Life without Paul had seemed bleak, despite the pain and grief of his illness. Hopefully, at Harpers she would find a new purpose and even some new friends.

Smiling wryly at her foolish thoughts, Rachel finished her tea, washed her cup in the small sink and then went along the hall to the bathroom. She would be washed, dressed and ready to leave long before the sisters stirred. They were very polite ladies and always asked Rachel if she needed the bathroom first, because, as they were fond of saying, 'You have to work, dear.' The exquisite embroidery they did, which brought in barely enough to cover their lodgings, was not work – because work would not have been acceptable for Papa's daughters. Rachel had heard all about their stern father who had kept the sisters at home to wait on him, refusing to let them marry and then leaving them in poverty when he died. His property had been sold to pay his debts and they would have starved on their tiny income if Mrs Malone hadn't found them a few customers from amongst her friends.

Rachel was thoughtful as she dressed in her neat grey dress with its collar of white lace fastened at the throat with a cameo brooch set in gold, and then, remembering the rule of no jewellery at work, removed it again. Minnie and Mildred did beautiful work. She thought they might have charged more for their embroidery if they'd known where to sell it, but they were ashamed to take anything for it and would only reluctantly accept the small fees Mrs Malone's friends were prepared to pay.

At Harpers, there was room for a range of stylish evening gowns with beautiful embroidery. Rachel had looked through the rails and thought what little stock had arrived so far was not as exclusive as it might be – but perhaps Harpers was the wrong end of Oxford street to be offering exclusive gowns with the handmade touches the sisters might provide. It was more a ready-made market rather than bespoke. Besides, it wasn't her department and the sisters would probably be too frightened to offer their work even if she suggested it...

Rachel's mind moved on. She had assessed the three girls working under her in Harpers store. Sally was the senior assistant and seemed to know her business, though she was inclined to be a little rash and sometimes outspoken. Rachel would have to keep an eye on her for a while. Maggie was a sweet girl, a little shy but very willing – and Beth... A smile of approval touched Rachel's lips. Beth was hard-working and intelligent, very much like she'd been at her age. Rachel liked her and thought she would like to know her better; though she could not relax her position as their supervisor, she hoped to enjoy good relationships with all the girls.

Rachel had the weekend to herself. She decided that she would take a bus trip and visit Paul's mother, who lived in a leafy suburb on the outskirts of the city. Rachel's mother-in-law had married for a second time late in life and, though now yet again a widow, had sufficient funds to live comfortably. To give Edna her due, she'd offered to take Rachel in when she learned that Paul's savings had almost gone. Rachel had thanked her but refused. She and her fussy mother-in-law had never truly got on. Paul had been her only child and she tended to be possessive, though she was decent enough in her way. Rachel continued to visit occasionally, because her mother-in-law had few friends and Paul would have wanted her to keep in touch.

She would stop by the little local bakery run by a French chef and take some fancy cakes. Edna was very partial to a Bakewell tart or a cream horn...

8

Beth left half an hour earlier than necessary on her first real day at work. She'd wanted to make a good impression and so arrived at exactly the same moment as her supervisor. Mrs Craven glanced at the little silver watch she wore pinned to her tailored jacket; it had big black Roman numerals but was otherwise plain. As it was necessary to keep a check on things, it was not quite jewellery. She was wearing a dark grey dress that flirted just above her neat ankles, a white collar and a matching grey jacket and her hair was caught back in a soft knot at the nape. Beth noted how attractive her supervisor was and thought it sad that she'd been widowed so young, though she was glad she had told them so that they knew the truth; otherwise there would be gossip and rumours.

Beth was wearing the new black dress she'd had for her period of mourning for her mother. It had been sponged and pressed the previous evening and she had attached one of the lace collars that were part of the uniform she'd been given. The white collar relieved the stark lines of the dress and Beth had no idea how lovely she was, never seeing beyond her pale skin and wide, clear eyes when she looked into a mirror.

'I know we're just setting out stock today,' she told her supervisor as they went up in the lift together. 'I wasn't sure if this dress would be approved. If it isn't, my aunt can make one exactly like those we were issued so I have a spare.'

Her supervisor nodded and took off the jaunty red hat that enlivened her sober attire, taking it into her office. 'It looks neat and tidy to me – but we shall consult Miss Hart,' she said. 'I would wear your regulation dress for opening day – as I shall.'

'Yes, Mrs Craven,' Beth replied. 'I wanted to keep it smart as I thought we might have dusty boxes to unpack today...'

'Yes, I dare say...' The words were made superfluous as they entered the department and saw boxes piled everywhere. 'Well, it looks as if we shall be busy.'

Beth took off her jacket and hung it in the space provided at the back of the stockroom. There was a small alcove for the girls' jackets, bags and pegs for hats, but everywhere else was given over to racks and cabinets.

She and Mrs Craven had just begun to unpack the first of the large boxes, which contained beautiful hats, when Maggie came in, hurrying but being careful not to run, though she was breathing heavily.

'I'm not late – am I?' she asked.

Mrs Craven looked at her watch and smiled. 'You are three minutes before time, Miss Gibbs,' she replied. 'Did you have difficulty in getting away?'

'My father was in a lot of pain,' Maggie said. 'I had to call at the doctor's surgery and missed my bus. I managed to get another but I got off and... walked quickly from the other end of Oxford Street, because there was an overturned lorry and the bus couldn't get through...'

'You must have walked very quickly,' Mrs Craven said and glanced up as Sally entered the department. 'Just in time...' she said and Sally smiled and nodded. 'Take your coats off, girls, and you can start opening some of the other boxes.' She paused and then went on, 'These have been delivered to the porter's office and were shipped over from America. I believe everything has been priced again, but I do have lists to go with them and if anything isn't priced, we shall check it…'

Sally and Maggie went off to hang up their coats. When they returned, Sally started on the boxes nearest to her counters and the cries of delight and excitement from the girls made both Beth and Mrs Craven look round.

'Shall we see what they've found?' Mrs Craven asked Beth.

'May we?' She deposited the beautiful creation of silk tulle and straw on to the counter and followed the supervisor to the counter where Maggie and Sally had been unpacking and immediately saw what the other two were so excited over. There were about twenty beautiful leather and skin bags on the counter. Beth had never seen such lovely things before, except in the window of a large department store, never this close, for she had not dared to touch or ask to see something she could never afford. 'Oh, those bags are lovely…'

'Very expensive,' Sally remarked and picked up what Beth thought was a handbag made of crocodile skin. 'This is ten guineas… and that one is twelve…'

'Good gracious, that is a lot of money,' Mrs Craven said. 'Are you sure, Miss Ross?'

'The tickets are already inside – look…' Sally opened one of the bags and showed it to her supervisor. 'Do you think anyone has enough money to want to pay that for a bag?'

'Oh, yes, a great many ladies do,' Mrs Craven said. 'The bags are obviously authentic. I knew some of the stock was valuable, but I thought we would stock good leather or mock crocodile, not the real thing. I'm not at all sure they are suitable…'

'I've seen the copies and they're nothing like these,' Sally said, her eyes bright. 'Shall we start on the costume jewellery next?'

'Not until you have all these listed and safely displayed inside the cabinets, Miss Ross. Check your inventory very carefully please and make certain nothing is left to chance. With such expensive merchandise, we must take extra care.'

Beth looked at the beautiful bags. She wondered what kind of people could afford to spend so much on just one item. Crocodile skin was popular with rich women, but Beth wasn't sure she would want one herself. It seemed an extravagance and rather cruel to her. Many families had less money to keep them in food and clothing for a month and it made her wonder just a little about the balance of things. However, she thrust the thought to the back of her mind. This was a prestigious store and it was not for her to judge such things.

She and Mrs Craven unpacked all the hats. Beth listed them all neatly in the relevant stock book and Mrs Craven told her to unpack the smaller boxes containing the scarves and gloves and took over arranging the hats herself. After a few moments, she called Maggie to her and they began to discuss the care that must be given to such gorgeous creations.

Sally had finished listing and her precious bags were safely inside cabinets that locked. She had begun to open the smallest cardboard boxes, which Beth could see contained costume jewellery. However, she was busy listing and arranging first her gloves and then the silk scarves. There were so many that she could not find a space for every pretty scarf and so she listed some as stockroom and took them through in their boxes.

'What are you doing with those?' Mrs Craven asked and Beth turned.

'I've listed them as stockroom. I've filled all my drawers – and these will be fresh out when we've sold some...'

'Yes, it's a pity we cannot display every pretty scarf,' Mrs Craven acknowledged. 'However, I do not think we should mix them with other stock – providing you have every scarf listed properly?'

'Yes, I have double-checked every item,' Beth said, 'and it is all in the stock book.'

'Very well. Clear up all these boxes if you please – and then call into the porter's room in the basement as you go for your lunch break. I shall allow ten minutes for you to ask Fred Burrows to come and take all this away.'

Beth thanked her and decided that she would visit the restaurant that day and see what it would cost her to have a cup of tea. Her staff discount allowed for twenty per cent off all food and drink, but it might still be too expensive for her small budget.

She found her way down to the basement and the porter's room, which was just off the stores for china, glassware and other goods. A man of perhaps fifty was piling boxes on to a trolley and looked slightly harassed.

'Hello, Mr Burrows. I'm Beth Grey from the first floor. Mrs Craven asks if you could fetch our empty boxes from the hat and scarves department please.'

'I've got one pair of hands, young woman,' the man replied and glared at her. 'I'm still delivering goods at the moment – why they thought one porter was enough, I don't know. I need a young lad to help me...'

'I'm sorry,' Beth said, because she could see that he still had many boxes to deliver. 'Perhaps I could give you a hand – I've got twenty minutes for my lunch break...?'

'You're sure you want to waste your time here?' he asked, looking at her properly for the first time.

'I'll only have a cup of tea anyway...'

'I'll give you one of those,' he said, calming down now he'd made his point. 'Could you pass those small boxes to me? Me name is Fred, miss – though you'd best call me Burrows if anyone's listening or they'll think we're courtin'.' The wicked gleam in his eyes made Beth smile as she handed him the parcels one by one, saving him from walking in and out of his stockroom. 'That's the last for upstairs,' he said when the trolley looked impossibly full. 'I've got the kettle on and there's milk – if you don't mind the condensed sort?'

'No, I don't mind at all,' Beth said and turned to watch as he poured water into a large brown pot. He swirled it around and left it while he put milk from a can into two mugs and then poured tea into them.

'There you go, miss. You tell your supervisor I'll be in to clear your boxes when I've delivered this lot to the gentleman's department upstairs.'

Beth nodded and drank her tea. Fred Burrows was a thin, wiry man with dark hair, grey eyes and thick eyebrows. He could never have been handsome but had a nice homely face and she felt comfortable with him now that he'd stopped being grumpy.

'I'd better get back,' she said when she'd finished her tea.

'Before you go...' Fred went over to his desk and picked up a box. 'This is for your department. I only found it after I'd delivered the others...'

'I'll take it for you,' Beth said, understanding that it was what he was asking. It would save him coming back for it – and he couldn't get another thing on his trolley.

She wished him luck and returned to the department. The box was labelled costume jewellery and so she took it to Sally's counter.

'What's this?' Sally asked, frowning.

'Mr Burrows found it behind his desk after he'd delivered the boxes for our department and he is a little busy, so I brought it for him...'

'The porter asked you to do his work for him?' Mrs Craven had heard and looked annoyed. Beth realised it was best to keep quiet about how she'd spent her lunch break.

'No, I volunteered,' Beth said. 'He is snowed under with work, Mrs Craven, but he said he will come for our boxes as soon as he's delivered his next load.'

'Very well,' Mrs Craven acknowledged. She looked at the label on the box and then on her inventory. 'This hasn't been listed here – really, it isn't good enough. Stock could go missing this way and then who would get the blame? It would be our department...' She added the box to her list and marked it as being delivered at a certain time.

Sally opened the box and started to take out the leather jewellery cases. When she opened them, Beth saw that each one contained an item of silver: bracelets, bangles, chains, brooches and lockets.

'How lovely – especially these with the greenish stones...' Maggie exclaimed. 'What are they?'

'Turquoise,' Beth, Sally and Mrs Craven replied in unison.

'My aunt has a brooch set with turquoise,' Beth said.

'I've seen them in Selfridges,' Sally agreed, nodding.

'I have a silver bracelet set with them at home,' Mrs Craven finished, looking sad.

Beth thought that perhaps her husband had given it to her but didn't ask, because clearly the thought of the bracelet hurt.

'I think they're American,' Sally added. 'I think a lot of the silver jewellery is from America – or perhaps from Mexico...'

'What makes you say that?' Maggie asked.

'Because they have a look – almost Aztec,' Sally explained and then laughed as Maggie's blank look deepened. 'I've seen a display of Aztec jewellery at the museum...'

'Do you often visit museums?'

'Yes...' Sally flushed. 'It's free and its warm and it's somewhere to go on my day off...'

'It's your turn to take a break, Maggie,' Mrs Craven said because an embarrassing silence had fallen. 'Go along now... and Sally, you can finish listing that last lot of jewellery and then go yourself. Beth and I can tidy up here after that wretched porter deigns to visit us...'

Beth thought Mrs Craven was being a little unfair to Fred Burrows, but she seemed a little on edge and it might have been because of the turquoises – or that Sally had let her mask slip a little, revealing the extent of her loneliness. Did their superior also feel alone now that her husband was dead? Beth would have liked to ask but knew she couldn't; things like that were personal and you didn't ask personal questions of your superior at work.

Beth and Mrs Craven spent the next few minutes checking all the boxes to make certain that nothing had been left inside and also checking the inventories to make sure that all the stock was listed in the appropriate books.

'Can you hold the fort while I have a break in my office?' Mrs Craven asked at last. 'I brought a flask of soup for today, because I didn't want to leave the department. I'll be close if you need me...'

Beth assured her that she was fine on her own. All the hard work was done and she had time to wander around the counters, looking at the various displays of beautiful bags, fine costume jewellery, gorgeous hats – and then her own counter, which she already knew almost by heart. She still thought the silk scarf she'd listed as swirls was one of the prettiest and was thinking of moving it to a more prominent place in her open shelves when the door swung back and Fred Burrows pushed his trolley through.

'All this lot ready to go then?' he asked.

'Yes, we've checked it all,' Beth said. 'Nothing has been left inside by mistake.'

'You're doin' better than most,' Fred said and grinned at her. 'I've rescued a silver-plated coffee pot from an abandoned tea chest and a pile of best china plates – and them lot upstairs ain't even got their counters straight yet...'

Beth helped him to pile the last of the empty boxes just as Mrs Craven returned to the department.

He leaned into Beth, whispering, 'Don't you go payin' restaurant prices for your tea, miss. Fred's always got a pot on the go and there'll be one for you whenever you like...'

Beth thanked him, her cheeks a little red as Mrs Craven glanced at her.

'Mr Burrows, I'd like a word with you...'

'Know what you're goin' to say...' he forestalled her. 'I've left the invoice on the counter so you can keep it for your files, Mrs Craven.'

'Very well – but it might have been serious. That jewellery was expensive.'

'That's why I put it safe,' Fred explained and winked at Beth. 'Tucked it behind my desk and forgot it when I brought the rest – but this young lady gave me a hand by bringing it up. All right?'

'Yes – but don't expect my staff to do your job in future, Mr Burrows.'

'No, ma'am, certainly not...' He grinned at Beth as he left and Beth saw a flicker of a smile in her superior's eyes.

'I didn't mind bringing it up,' she said.

'Best not to make a habit of it – supposing you'd lost it?'

Beth nodded, because she knew her superior was right. 'He had so much to do. I should think he'll still be delivering stock tomorrow...'

'Yes, well, just be sensible, Miss Grey...' Her superior sighed. 'I suppose you have noticed that he speaks better than most porters?'

'Well yes, he does,' Beth agreed.

'He was a schoolmaster but dismissed from his post for some misdemeanour – not that I've been told what it was. Mr Burrows was never arrested or charged with anything, but still... one must be careful...'

'Yes, I suppose so, but he seems honest and pleasant...'

'I agree and I shall give him the benefit of the doubt, but be aware, Miss Grey. That is all I am saying.'

Beth did not need to reply for the other girls had arrived back together, which meant that Maggie was a few minutes over her time. Mrs Craven looked at her watch and frowned but said nothing, though a few moments later she spoke to the junior privately. Beth saw the younger girl flush and apologise; she'd been enjoying her time with Sally and forgotten the rules about being back on time.

They were all admiring each other's counters and asking

various prices when Miss Hart walked in. Instinctively, they all went to stand behind their counters.

'I see you have everything done,' she said. 'No one else is as far on – I hope that stock has all been written up in the appropriate ledgers?'

'Yes, Miss Hart,' Mrs Craven assured her instantly. 'We are all making ourselves familiar with the stock so that if necessary we could stand in for each other during breaks or in the unfortunate circumstance that any member of staff is away ill.'

'That is one of the reasons I am here,' Miss Hart said. 'The junior in the ladies dress department has not turned up – and, since you are so far on, I want to borrow Miss Gibbs to help them out. Also, I need to remind you that there is a meeting at four thirty. Mr Stockbridge wants you all in the restaurant to give you a welcome talk – and we're hoping that Mr Harper may attend...'

'Miss Gibbs may help for a short time, but her place is here, Miss Hart. I would appreciate it if you remember that...' Mrs Craven suddenly realised what the floor supervisor had said. 'Mr Harper – the store's owner – is here in London?'

'He arrived in London yesterday and the window dresser has been to his hotel. When Mr Marco returned, he re-dressed two of the windows. Now Mr Harper wishes to address the staff in person. Please make sure that none of your girls is wearing make-up or perfume or jewellery, Mrs Craven.' Her narrow-set eyes went over all the girls, lingering longest on Beth. 'That is not your uniform, Miss Grey.'

'No, Miss Hart. I wanted it to be clean for tomorrow...'

Miss Hart nodded and frowned. 'It will do, I suppose – but you are all supposed to be dressed alike. Please make certain you wear the required uniform in future. A black dress is not good enough; it must be the same style and material – and it is better to order one from me than buy elsewhere.'

'Yes, Miss Hart,' Beth said meekly. She sighed inwardly for it meant she could not use the dress she was wearing for work and would have to purchase another uniform quickly or sponge the one she had every night.

'Very well,' the floor walker nodded primly. 'Miss Gibbs, come with me...'

Maggie threw a despairing glance at Beth but followed in the wake of the grim-faced floor walker. She looked as if she were being marched to her doom and Sally gave a little giggle as they left the department.

'Poor Maggie,' she said. 'But she's lucky. I wouldn't mind giving them a hand in the dress department.'

'I think Miss Gibbs is a little in awe of our floor walker,' Mrs Craven said. 'Miss Ross – please keep your pet names for after work. It might slip out in front of customers and that could result in a complaint.'

'Yes, Mrs Craven. I am sorry...' Sally looked suitably remorseful.

'I'm surprised Mr Harper is coming,' Mrs Craven said. 'I asked Mr Stockbridge about him, but they haven't actually met – only spoken on the telephone. Apparently, he was approached by a lawyer and given the task of setting up the store and hiring the staff. I think quite a bit of the merchandise has been sourced in America – and other countries – and been shipped in ready priced. Like your silver jewellery, Miss Ross. Some of it is quite stunning...'

'Miss Hart said Mr Harper only arrived in the country yesterday?'

'Yes, that was a little odd...' Mrs Craven replied and frowned. 'As I was saying, much of the stock must be American.'

'I think the jewellery will make a wonderful display,' Sally said thoughtfully. 'But unless the customers take to it, it may not sell...'

'Some of it is a little bold for my taste,' Beth agreed. She hadn't liked to offer an opinion previously. 'As you say, Miss Ross – it could be all the rage and we'll sell out quickly or it may just sit there.'

'I think we should have a display of it in the window,' Sally replied, 'but Mr Marco would never listen to me... or I don't think so...' Remembering his wink, she wondered if he might.

'You should not even suggest it,' Mrs Craven said. 'Mr Marco will tell you what he wants when he decides to feature merchandise from this department. I do not think he has requested anything yet...'

'Well, I think he's wasting an opportunity...'

'He may well have his own stock,' Mrs Craven said. 'Just at the start. It's what I'm looking forward to, seeing the blinds taken down so we can view the windows.'

'I've seen people trying to peer round the edges,' Beth said, 'but it isn't possible.'

'It's an idea they've copied from Selfridges,' Sally said. 'It should bring in a little crowd in the morning to see the displays revealed – and hopefully they will all come inside and buy something.'

'Oh, we shall be busy for the first week or so for the novelty,' Mrs Craven said. 'I am confident that once the customers see the quality they will keep coming.'

Beth looked at her. 'All the big stores in Oxford Street seem to be busy. I've only been up a few times before I applied to work here – and I thought they were all successful.'

'The big stores have huge turnovers, but they need it – for the rents, expenses and wages. To make a profit at the end of the year they have to have a better than average rate of sales. Otherwise their balance sheets will soon be in the red...' She saw Beth's puzzled look and smiled. 'I ran a small haberdashers for a few months before I came here and I learned how slender the margins can be in the retail area. If we have too much spoiled merchandise or items that do not sell... we shall need to have a big sale after Christmas and that can be difficult for a business like this... However, I am certain that our owner is well aware what a business like this needs. I believe he has several stores in America.'

'I think people will love the stock. I do...'

Mrs Craven smiled. 'I like what I've seen so far – though I'm not sure we're the right end of Oxford Street for some of it. We must hope that the ladies who can afford real crocodile hand-bags don't mind walking to this end...'

* * *

Beth went to the restaurant for her tea break. She discovered that for staff it was only tuppence for a cup of tea and a biscuit and another tuppence for a currant bun. She could manage on a bun until her evening meal most days, though if she went out in her lunch break she could do better from Bessie's.

By four thirty that afternoon, all the girls were familiar with the stock in their department. Maggie returned just as they were all going up to hear what the manager had to say. Most people were curious whether the owner would actually turn up to welcome them. Beth heard a whisper that he was disfigured and Sally said someone had told her that he was very old, while Maggie had been told he was a recluse and refused to be seen in public because he was so ugly.

Mr Stockbridge began by thanking them all for their hard work and asking them all to be in early the next morning for the big opening.

'Mr Harper is giving a prize of five guineas to the first customer – and a surprise to customer number one hundred, but only the staff know that. Also, the assistant who makes the biggest single sale will be given a bonus in their wages this Saturday. Every...'

His next words were lost in the murmur of excitement and approval and several of the men began to look about them. 'When shall we see him?' one of the men from the glassware department asked.

'He should be here at any moment... Now, as I was saying, every customer who comes through the door tomorrow will be offered a glass of champagne. Some of the assistants will be acting as waiters for the day –you know who you are.' He looked at them expectantly. 'Any questions?'

A few of the men looked at each other and then one of them spoke out, 'What sort of a man is he – this Mr Harper? Is he an American?'

'Well, yes, he is,' Mr Stockbridge said. 'I've spoken to him on the telephone but I haven't actually met Mr Harper as yet...'

'Is he a recluse then?'

'No, gentlemen, I am not...' A hush fell as someone stepped out to join the manager out front and Beth heard Sally's sharply indrawn breath beside her. 'I'm sorry I was late, but there was a problem with something that I couldn't leave to others – but thanks to one of your London cabbies, I finally made it.'

Mr Stockbridge moved forward, offering his hand. 'I'm pleased to meet you, sir – but I understood Mr Harper was an older man...' He looked puzzled.

'That Mr Harper is – or was – my uncle,' the newcomer said. 'It was Mr Gerald Harper who bought the store with the idea that I should run it. I am Ben Harper. Unfortunately, Mr Gerald had a heart attack two months ago and died just two weeks later and that is what caused my delay in getting to England. I've had to settle a lot of business in America before I could leave and so I had to leave it to you, Mr Stockbridge, and to Mr Marco – who is a good friend and knew what was happening, though he kept quiet about knowing me because I asked him to.'

There was a buzz of surprise, because this was very direct and frank information.

Mr Stockbridge looked stunned and then said, 'Does that mean that the store – all we've done – might be at risk...'

'No, I am one of the main beneficiaries of my uncle's will,' Ben Harper paused, looking round at them all. 'I have decided we should go ahead with the opening as planned, and that's what we'll do. It does mean we are on our own without the back-up of our American branches, but I do not intend that it should hold us back. I have big plans for this store and, if all goes well, others...'

'What happens to us if things don't go as you hope?' a man asked and there was a murmur of voices raised in assent. 'I gave up a good position to come here...'

'So did I...' came from several voices.

'I don't give up easily,' Ben Harper said and grinned, suddenly looking young, dynamic and very attractive. Every woman in the room smiled back. 'My uncle promised me this store to run – and I expected to be a partner and to take it over one day. Now I own most of it and I intend to fight for its survival... and I want all of you to help me by selling as much as you can on opening day to give us a cash flow...'

'You'll do it, sir...' Sally called out and several women said "yes" and clapped. They hadn't liked to speak out at first because women were still expected to know their place, in the home and at work.

Beth looked at her. 'Be careful,' she warned. 'Miss Hart is watching you.'

'I don't care,' Sally said and smiled. 'I've met him – and I'd back him all the way against a dozen Miss Harts...'

9

'What do you mean – you've met him?' demanded Maggie excitedly.

'Yes, I think you'd better explain,' Mrs Craven said as they drew away from their nearest neighbours into a huddle. Some of the men were firing questions at Mr Harper and he was answering them all with good humour and without rancour. Miss Hart had asked whether his policy was to give more women important jobs and he had answered her in the affirmative.

'I certainly do, whenever I find a woman who wishes for promotion and deserves it.'

'He was looking at Selfridges' windows and so was I,' Sally said in a whisper and grinned. 'We both thought one of the displays lacked something and we talked about it, that's all...'

Mrs Craven nodded. 'Best that you keep it to yourself,' she said and turned her head, listening. 'All the supervisors have been asked to stop and speak to Mr Harper. I suggest you three return to the department. Miss Gibbs, you can cover the hats. I shall join you there shortly and we'll speak more of this...'

She made her way towards the front while the shop workers began to file out. There was a lot of complaining going on as men grumbled about having left perfectly good jobs to come here.

'I reckon if this place shuts down, we'll all be out of work...' one of the men grumbled.

'Shouldn't worry about it if I were you,' Sally said cheerfully. 'You heard what Mr Harper said, he intends to make a success of it.'

'He's an American – why should he care what happens to us. He's like all the other rich men... as soon as the store is making money he'll sell and run back to America.'

'If he's rich, he'll use his fortune to keep the store. It sounded as if he wanted to,' Maggie said and then blushed as the man glared at her.

'Good for you, Maggie!' Sally whispered.

'Come along, Miss Gibbs,' Beth said. 'You too, Miss Ross. It isn't our business to discuss what our employer may or may not do – and we have our work to do...'

When they got back to the department, it was to discover that two more boxes had been delivered. Sally looked at them and then nodded.

'One is handbags and the other is hats. I think we should unpack them and get them written up before it's time to go home.'

I'll write up for you, Miss Gibbs,' Beth offered since she had nothing more to unpack. 'I should check the box and write up what is inside but leave them in the box in the stockroom. There isn't room to display any more – and it is always nice to keep a few things back to make a fresh display...'

'I've got room for my bags,' Sally said. She opened her box and took out six leather bags. 'These are only two and three guineas each. I think we'll sell more of these than those very expensive bags.' She wrote down the details in her stock book and then took the empty box through to the back room.

Beth had just finished helping Maggie to check the hats and list them when Mrs Craven arrived. She looked relaxed and more cheerful than she had after Mr Harper announced his reason for being late.

'Have I missed something?' she asked.

'We had another six hats and Miss Ross had six leather bags – cheaper ones this time...' Beth said.

'We'll leave the hats in the stockroom for now,' Mrs Craven nodded her approval. 'Well, I must say I approve of our new owner...'

'Did he have any more to tell you?' Sally asked eagerly.

'Not really...' Mrs Craven smiled at them. 'He is a forceful young man and I am certain he will make a go of this place. He told me that he and his sister bought some of the stock but his uncle had already purchased half of it before he was asked to take over.'

'The question is – did he buy the expensive stock or otherwise?'

'I think his sister was responsible for buying the earlier stock.' Mrs Craven looked at Sally. 'It makes sense of the distinction between the two sets of merchandise. Apparently, his uncle had two successful stores in New York. Our Mr Harper expected to join the staff there, but then his uncle suddenly told him about his London venture and asked him to take over...'

'Does his uncle have any children?'

'There is a daughter as well as his wife and two other nephews, but no sons,' Mrs Craven said, frowning. 'Mr Gerald has a sister, who is a widow, and a brother who is not interested in the stores...'

'Who told you all that?' Sally laughed.

'Mr Harper told us all. He was explaining that there was likely to be at least five or six beneficiaries in his uncle's will, but he has most of the London store, though nothing more.'

'It would be awful for him as well as us if it closed too soon...'

'Well, Mr Harper intends to do all he can to keep us going,' Mrs Craven said. 'Now, if you all tidy up and put everything away, I think we can leave. I suggest we might all go to a café and share a pot of tea – talk about things for a while. We shall not often be able to leave early...'

'Yes, I'd like that,' Sally said eagerly and Beth nodded.

Maggie hesitated and then agreed. 'I can't stop long,' she said. 'My mother needs help with my father – but I'll come for ten minutes or so...'

'It would be nice to have a little informal time together,' Mrs Craven said. 'I think we all need a little treat and I'll pay. We've all worked hard to set the department up...'

* * *

Beth decided not to mention Mr Harper's revelations to her aunt. It would only give Aunt Helen something to grumble about if she thought there was any chance the store might not succeed without its American backing, and she'd been a little easier to live with since Beth had found work. So she made their tea and ate the lamb chops, mashed potatoes and cabbage with mint sauce that her aunt had cooked, and talked about the lovely things they had in stock.

'I'll be surprised if that shop survives a year,' Aunt Helen observed as she dished up the suet pudding and treacle for afters. 'Who has the money to buy the scarves you spoke of – and those expensive bags...?' She shook her head over the folly of an American who clearly didn't understand that the ordinary British woman simply could not afford such highly priced merchandise. 'In a year or less, you'll be looking for another job, Beth...'

Beth didn't answer. She would have made a spirited defence of their chances, but after Mr Harper's upsetting announcement she thought her aunt might be right.

After she'd done the dishes, Beth made some fairy cakes and a batch of jam tarts. She would take one of each and a sandwich with her in the morning and eat them in the staffroom rather than visiting the restaurant or Bessie's café. If she was likely to be out of work again soon, she ought to save as much as she could.

Beth was thoughtful when she went to bed that evening. She'd wondered if Mark would be at her bus stop earlier, but there had been no sign of him and her feelings had been a mixture of relief and regret. She knew there was no point in hoping he would go out of his way to meet her when he was already married, besides, he'd been angry with her. No, he had forgotten his feelings for her and she must forget her hopes of marriage and happiness, accept that her dreams belonged to the past.

At least she had work for the moment and she was grateful that she would be paid on Friday night. It would be the first money she'd earned and very welcome now that the few pounds her mother had left had nearly gone.

'I shall go in early in the morning,' she told her aunt as she bid her goodnight. 'I want to be there when the window blinds come down for the first time so that we can see the displays – and all sorts of things are happening. All the customers are to be offered a glass of champagne. You should come, Aunt Helen, you might win one of the prizes...'

'I do not hold with champagne,' her aunt said, wrinkling her nose. 'A waste of money and a bad habit to encourage drinking during the day – and I've no time to waste queuing. I have work to do!'

'Yes, of course,' Beth said. 'Goodnight. I'll try not to wake you in the morning...'

She smothered a sigh as she entered her own bedroom. It was foolish to think that her aunt might take an interest in her place of work. Beth had hoped that she could earn promotion at Harpers and perhaps be able to have a place of her own – or one that she could share with friends, but now she feared she might be stuck here forever...

* * *

Sally frowned as she saw Mick watching her when she entered the hostel. He was standing in the doorway of the public house opposite, just staring across at her, his hands on his hips, a smirk on his handsome face. She felt tempted to wipe the smile off for him, but he would only laugh if she said something rude; it was best just to ignore him. He didn't call out or wave, though his gaze followed her inside, making her feel hot all over. Sally did her best to ignore him, but she was conscious of him all the same.

However, when she reached her room, for once she took little notice of the cheerless atmosphere. She'd been shocked and surprised to see the man she'd spoken to outside Selfridges the previous evening and a little smile had curved her lips until his announcement banished it. Sally hadn't been as upset as some others, because she'd never found it difficult to get work, but she liked the department where she already felt she fitted in with her immediate supervisor and the other girls. Mrs Craven expected loyalty and good work from those in her department and Sally liked her. She liked Maggie and Beth too and would be disappointed if she had to find a new job too soon. She'd stuck up for Mr Harper, but it wasn't truly up to him, because if his uncle's will didn't name him as a major shareholder in the store he might be voted out – and that would be a shame for all of them, including Mr Ben Harper.

Sally had hung up her coat when someone knocked at her door.

'Yes, who is it?'

'May I come in, Sally?'

'Yes, all right...' She opened the door to Sylvia reluctantly but then saw the other girl had been crying. Her hair looked messy and she had a bruised face, her mouth cut and bleeding. 'You'd better come in... what happened?' Sally asked as she shut the door behind her.

'I had an argument with someone...' Sylvia said and sank down on the edge of the bed looking miserable. 'I don't know what to do...'

Sally saw the desperation in her face and something clicked. 'Are you in trouble – with the law... or is it even worse?'

Sylvia half smiled. 'Even worse,' she whispered. 'I've been seeing someone – and I'm having his baby. I told him and asked him what he intended to do about it. He told me to clear off and then he hit me...'

'Rotten devil!' Sally said, firing up. 'You should go to the police...'

'You don't know him,' Sylvia said bitterly. 'If I did that I should end up in a back alley with my throat cut...'

'Oh, Sylvia!' Sally said, shocked by the flash of fear in the other girl's eyes. 'Why did you get involved with a man like that?'

'I didn't know what he was until it was too late,' she replied, brushing a hand over her eyes. 'He's rich and drives about in an expensive motor car. He gave me a lift when it was raining and he started sending me presents. I was dazzled by his lifestyle and I thought he loved me – and he spoke of setting me up in a flat of my own...' Sylvia's voice cracked. 'I nearly agreed and then someone told me that is the way Kingston works. Once he's got you where he wants you... he makes you work for him...' She lifted eyes filled with despair to meet Sally's. 'He brings other men to the flat and tells you to sleep with them to oblige him, and if you don't...' She gave a little sob of despair.

'Oh, my goodness!' Sally shuddered at the idea. 'That's terrible. You didn't get caught like that?'

'No, I refused and he told me we were finished – and I thought I was free and clear, but then...' Sylvia took a deep breath. 'I'm carrying his baby and he won't do a thing to help me.'

Sally looked at her with sympathy. 'So he roughed you up when you told him he was responsible?'

'No, he sent some of his men to the pub where I worked and

they wrecked the place. I tried to stop them and they gave me a good hiding – and then my boss told me I was bad news and sacked me.'

'He can't do that...' Sally protested but instantly realised that of course he could. Not only could her boss sack her, but if she was refused a reference, she would find it difficult to get another job. Pregnant and unmarried, her reputation would be destroyed. 'I'm really sorry, Sylvia.' There was nothing Sally could do to help her find a new job, but she could offer immediate help. 'Let me bathe your face for you, it might ease the bruising.'

'Thanks...' Sylvia sat patiently as Sally bathed her face with cold water. She winced a bit but bore it without comment until Sally had finished. 'I'm sorry to be a nuisance, but I didn't know who to talk to...'

'Have you any family?'

'No, I'm on my own,' Sylvia said. 'I had a brother, but he went off years ago and my mother died last year. I know you can't help me, Sally, but I just felt I had to tell someone...'

'If you like, I could write a character reference for you,' Sally said tentatively. She didn't really know Sylvia well enough, but she had to offer.

'I'll find a job somewhere – but they will throw me out once I start to show,' Sylvia said and took a deep breath. 'I've been a damned fool, but I really thought he cared for me.'

'You could go to the Salvation Army,' Sally said thoughtfully. 'They have places you can go to give birth – and I've heard they will have the child adopted.'

'Unless I get rid of it...' Sylvia's eyes flashed with sudden defiance. 'I don't want to give birth to that devil's brat!'

'Don't even think of getting rid of it,' Sally said and took hold of her arm urgently. 'Please, Sylvia, promise me that you won't do anything stupid. When I was in the orphanage, one of the girls tried to get rid of a baby with a knitting needle. She ruptured herself and they took her to hospital and she died.

Beryl was just thirteen and it was one of the wardens that got her pregnant. She told me, but no one else would believe her – at least, they made out they didn't.'

'Thirteen...' Sylvia's face was pale and frightened. 'Someone said if you sit in a hot bath and drink gin it brings on a miscarriage...'

'That's an old wives' tale,' Sally warned her. 'I think all those old remedies are useless. I know you can go to women who do it but I think it's dangerous...'

Sylvia looked at her eagerly. 'Do you know where I can find one? I'm nervous of doing it myself – but I can't let him ruin my life.'

Sally thought she'd already done that but kept a still tongue. There were women in back streets that got rid of unwanted babies for girls like Sylvia, but she didn't know of any in particular.

'I don't know of anyone – If you really want to do it, why don't you ask down Soho Square?' she said. 'The women who walk the streets must know about things like that – because some of them must get pregnant...'

'I daren't go back there in case Kingston sees me...'

Sally saw the expectant look in her eyes. 'I'll see if I can find the time,' she promised reluctantly. She didn't really want to speak to the prostitutes that worked the area, and risk being seen by someone that knew her, but Sylvia was in trouble. 'I'm making no promises, but I'll try...'

'Thanks, you're a real brick,' Sylvia said. 'I'm sorry to have dumped my problems on you, Sally.'

'We all need help sometimes,' Sally said and let her out.

She locked the door after her and sat on her bed, unsure why she'd promised to do something she didn't want to do for a girl she hardly knew – and yet but for the grace of God, there went she. Sally was often lonely and knew that if someone had offered her a new life, she might have snatched at it. She wouldn't be in any danger. The women of Soho might threaten her if they thought she was trying to move in on their patch, but she would make it clear it was the last thing she wanted. If they gave her a name that would be the end of it and Sylvia could make up her own mind what to do about her unwanted pregnancy...

10

'Good morning, Poppa,' Maggie said as she found her father sitting up in bed that morning, reading the previous day's paper. 'How are you?'

'I'm not too bad, my love,' he replied and pointed to something he'd been reading in the paper. 'It's about time those poor devils got a proper wage...'

Maggie saw that he'd been reading an article that said Mr Asquith was to introduce a bill establishing the principle of a minimum wage in the House of Commons, although he'd so far refused to agree to the Union's demand for five shillings a day for the men and two for the boys.

'Let's hope it means an end to the strike then,' she said and her father agreed, because the miner's strike was crippling industry. 'Is there anything you need before I leave?' she asked. 'I need to get to work early because it will be a busy day.'

'You get off, love,' he said and smiled at her. 'Your mother gave me a drop of my medicine just now so I shall rest for a while.'

Maggie bent and kissed his cheek. His skin felt dry and papery and a little overwarm. She saw the exhaustion in his eyes as he rested back on his pillows and her heart caught with pain because she knew he was suffering.

She left him lying with his eyes closed and went down to the kitchen. Her mother sniffed as she looked at her.

'Off to that job of yours, I suppose – and how I'm supposed to manage on my own, I don't know...'

'I thought you wanted me to work?' Maggie said and saw a flash of temper in her mother's eyes.

'None of that cheek from you, my girl,' Mrs Gibbs snapped. 'It's lucky Mrs Jenkins from next door comes in to give me a hand to wash him and get him on the pot.'

'I'm sorry, Muma. I have to go...'

Maggie escaped from her mother's stinging tongue into a bright fresh morning. She ran to catch her bus, tears burning behind her eyes, tears she refused to let fall. It hurt her to see her father lying in his bed dependent on others for everything and her mother's scolding made her feel wretched, because she enjoyed her work. They didn't pay her very much at Harpers, but she loved being there with the other girls and she would hate to give it up.

She caught her bus and smiled at the friendly conductor, who nodded as she paid for her ticket. The ring of his machine was bright and cheery like him and she began to feel better and to look forward to her day at work. It was opening day and she was excited by the thought of all the customers crowding in for their glass of champagne and the chance of winning a prize.

In Oxford Street, she disembarked from her bus and joined the little crowd of staff hurrying in through the side door. Across the street, a few customers had begun to gather, jostling for the best place to watch the unveiling of the windows. The salesgirls were chattering and laughing as they poured into the store, which seemed to be bubbling with excitement for the grand opening, and Maggie's excitement grew as she reached the first floor and went into her department. Sally was just taking off her coat and Beth came in behind her. Mrs Craven was already taking the covers off the hats on display stands. She gave an armful to Maggie, who took them to the stockroom and put them away tidily.

'They are going to take the blinds down now,' a voice from the doorway said and Maggie saw Miss Hart looking at them. For once she actually looked excited; the contagious feeling had spread throughout the store and Maggie couldn't resist a giggle as she saw Sally's expression.

'We are summoned,' Sally said. 'Best look sharp, Maggie love...'

Maggie nodded. She liked it when Sally called her Maggie, though she knew it was against the rules, but it sounded affectionate coming from her new friend and made her feel valued.

Down on the ground floor, the displays of glassware and china were exquisite; beautiful large vases and crystal glass that reflected the light touching on delicate table lamps and small onyx-topped tables, also pretty boxes of all descriptions and many small items that ladies might like to purchase. At the back of the ground floor was a cabinet displaying umbrellas and parasols as well as a selection of walking canes with silver tops. Maggie could smell the toilet soaps, perfumes and talcum powders that were displayed in glass counters and thought the delicious smell would make the customers want to stay longer and explore.

Mr Stockbridge was lined up with Mr Marco and the store owner. Mr Harper smiled at his staff, waiting until everyone was present and then told the window-dressing assistants to take down the blinds that had hidden the window displays. There was a chorus of surprise as the windows were revealed to show a series of tableaux that showed off most things the shop sold: models dressed in women's clothes, others in men's tailored suits. There was a penny farthing bicycle and a selection of sporting goods in one window, a table set with a white lace cloth and beautiful china and glass in another. An assortment of ladies' handbags was shown, as well as gloves, scarves and a small display of silver jewellery. Another window was made up with an array of gorgeous hats on stands of varying heights, and parasols with silver or ivory handles were suspended above them, the colours like those in a rainbow, the whole scene set against a backdrop representing a Parisian market. A ripple of applause spread through the assembled men and women.

'Very well, ladies and gentlemen – to your places,' Mr Stockbridge said and clapped his hands. 'Mr Marco, now you may reveal the windows to the world...'

As the outer blinds went up, they could hear faintly the cheers from outside the store and see the lights as cameras were flashed – and then, suddenly, a brass band began to play an American tune just as Mr Harper, who had been outside to admire the windows, now walked back in through the main door with a beautiful blonde woman on his arm.

'She looks like a film star,' Sally whispered to Maggie. 'Either that or she's American...'

'She's lovely and so smart...'

Maggie felt almost reluctant to leave the ground floor, which was where the champagne was about to be poured. She'd glimpsed a crowd of customers outside and would have liked to see them come in through the big plate glass doors but knew she must be upstairs ready to do as Mrs Craven requested once they arrived there.

'I liked the display of parasols hanging up,' Sally remarked as they emerged from the lift into their own department. 'The stalls looked like a picture I once saw of Paris...'

'Yes, I'm sure that's what it was meant to represent,' Mrs Craven said. 'It was a bit like a Renoir painting, I thought.'

'I've never seen one...' Maggie whispered. 'Have you?'

'Yes, quite a few,' Sally replied. 'I often visit the art galleries and museums. I like the Impressionists and that was what they were trying to achieve with that window...' She looked thoughtful as she walked to take her place behind her counter.

'I like them too,' Beth said softly to Maggie. 'One Sunday we might all go to a gallery – some of them open on Sunday mornings, I think...'

'I wish I could...' Maggie was wistful. 'I have so much to do on a Sunday...'

'Me too,' Beth smiled, sending her a sympathetic smile.

'Well, that was rather splendid,' Mrs Craven said. 'Now, girls, let us try to look busy. Have your account books out and Maggie you can help me rearrange that display of hats...'

Maggie hurried to do as she was asked, tingling with excitement at the thought that she might soon be serving her very first customers.

Sally stood in front of the glass cabinet containing her most expensive bags. She didn't think she could make them look any better than they did already and she felt quite calm, but that might have been because her mind was more on what Sylvia had told her than on worrying about the customers. Maggie was clearly nervous and Mrs Craven was giving her something to do to occupy her mind. Beth stood patiently waiting. Like Sally, she had everything arranged to its best and did not try to rearrange a thing but watched Mrs Craven change the position of three hats.

The first customer through the door was a very fashionable young woman wearing a smart grey wool suit with a red felt cloche hat and red leather shoes and gloves. Her bag was black and looked a little shabby compared to the rest of her outfit. She made straight for Sally's counter.

'I should like to see a leather bag,' she announced. 'I want black because it will go with everything...'

'Yes, madam, of course,' Sally took two from the counter and placed them on top. One was matt black leather and the other was shiny patent leather. 'These are the latest styles and priced at two guineas each...'

'Oh, is that all you have?' The customer looked disappointed.

'I wanted something more exclusive – like those in the window...'

Mr Marco had been given items from all departments direct from the American shipment, thus keeping the displays a secret to the last moment.

'We have the crocodile bags and a skin bag, but they are not black,' Sally said. She replaced the rejected items in the counter and reached round to the cabinet on the wall at the back, unlocking it and taking out first a dark grey lizard skin bag with a shiny clasp. 'This one is five guineas...' The price sounded shocking to Sally's ears when men were fighting for the right to earn five shillings a day, but some people could afford lovely things.

'Yes, that is beautiful,' the young woman replied and stroked it with her gloved hand. 'What about that one... the crocodile bag?'

Sally took the bag from the cabinet and placed it next to the skin bag. 'This is ten guineas, madam...'

'Expensive but beautiful,' the woman said, clearly awed. She opened it and looked at the silk lining inside. 'Yes, I think this is the one I want. Please wrap it well for me...' she handed over three crisp white five pound notes.

'Yes, madam.'

Sally wrote out the sales ticket in her book and accepted the customer's money, sending it off with her ticket to the office. She placed the skin bag back in its position in the cabinet and then began to wrap the expensive crocodile bag in layers of tissue. Once it was protected, she slipped it into a black bag with 'Harpers' emblazoned in gold on it and then the little ping behind her told her that the change had been returned. She counted the change into her customer's hand and gave her the receipt.

'Thank you for your custom, madam. I hope you enjoy your bag.'

'Oh, it isn't for me,' the young woman replied and laughed.

'My employer asked me to buy a present for his wife's birthday. I couldn't afford this lovely thing. Good morning.'

'Good morning, madam.'

Sally watched as the young woman left the department. She saw that Beth was serving two customers at her counter and Maggie was assisting her. Mrs Craven was showing another customer a hat and Sally hid her smile. The customer was a large lady and the hat she'd chosen to try on was far too fussy and young for her and Mrs Craven was diplomatically trying to steer her towards something a little less flamboyant.

Just then, two young women came in together and they made a beeline for Sally's jewellery counter. They looked a little out of place in their cheap clothing and shoes that had seen better times. Sally went to stand behind the counter and one of the young women pointed at a silver bracelet on the top shelf of the cabinet; it was quite chunky and had turquoise stones set round it and the price was a guinea. Sally wasn't sure the girls could afford the purchase price, but, when they asked, she brought it out and placed it on a tray lined with blue velvet.

'How much is it?' one of the girls asked.

'It says on the ticket, Mave,' the other girl told her. 'Look, it's a guinea...' She grinned at her friend. 'Big Tony give yer that much last night, didn't he?'

Sally realised that the girls were spending the money they'd earned in a less than respectable manner. She was a little surprised they'd ventured into the store and wondered if they'd sampled the free champagne – and yet Harpers was open to everyone.

Mave nodded, her cheeks flushed. Sally's opinion of the two was confirmed when the girl said, 'Yeah, but I've got me rent ter find for Sammy and yer know what he is if yer can't pay...'

'There is a cheaper one – at ten shillings and sixpence,' Sally said and took out a similar but lighter bracelet.

'I like this one best,' Mave said. 'Can yer lend me five bob, Shirl? I'll have enough fer this and me rent then...'

Sally replaced the rejected bracelet and waited while the two girls admired the bracelet on Mave's wrist.

'Yeah, all right,' Shirl agreed. 'But I want it back, right?'

'Yeah, o'course.' Mave grinned at her. 'Big Tony will be back ternight. He can't stay away from me...'

Sally's nerve endings tingled. These two were clearly street girls out for a spree on their ill-gotten gains and she wished she dare ask them what Sylvia needed to know but could not risk it. Someone might hear – and then Sally's job would be snatched away from her, her reputation in ruins.

She accepted their money and watched as they walked off, clutching the distinctive bag containing the little velvet-lined jewellery box. They were giggling and looking about them, enjoying themselves. Sally saw one or two of the other ladies look at them askance because their bleached hair and clothes shouted out their likely profession, but a customer was a customer and Sally had served them exactly as she would any other.

Beth had made her first sale and was looking pleased with herself and Mrs Craven had given two hats to Maggie to pack into their special boxes and was attending to the money. Belatedly, Sally remembered her supervisor's advice on having her tickets checked, but they'd all been serving at the same time and she'd checked it all herself. Both her customers had been quite happy and since the department was busy for the whole of the morning, she continued to check her own figures and change herself.

She had no trouble in selling to the majority of customers who came to her counter, though one woman complained about the price of everything she asked to look at and then went away without making a purchase. Everyone else bought something, though the ten guineas for the crocodile bag was the most expensive sale Sally made.

At twelve thirty, Mrs Craven sent Maggie and Beth off for

their break. The rush seemed to have cooled off and she came to stand next to Sally, looking pleased.

'I think you've made more sales than either Beth or I,' she said. 'How many pieces of the silver jewellery have you sold?'

'Five,' Sally told her. 'A guinea was the most expensive, but the pendants have gone well at eighteen and eleven – and two brooches went to one lady at fifteen shillings each. She wanted separate boxes, because they were presents for her two sisters. She thought everything was lovely and said she would be buying something for herself next week...'

'That's what I like to hear.'

'We've all been very busy and so have the other departments. Miss Hart came in while you were serving the lady who bought three hats – and she said there had been a constant stream of customers all morning.'

Mrs Craven nodded. 'I made one multiple sale that came to nine pounds – what was your best?'

'A bag for ten guineas,' Sally said. 'I didn't think my customer could afford so much, but she was buying it for her employer's wife and wanted the best...'

'It just shows you never know, I thought we'd have that bag forever.' Mrs Craven smiled. 'Oh, we have more customers...'

She went off to serve a customer with some gloves, as Beth was already serving someone, and Sally had another customer for her jewellery. The Mexican silver had proved a huge hit, perhaps because it was so distinctive and unusual, and even though quite expensive, some pieces were still reasonable enough to be bought by ordinary girls looking to treat them-selves. They might have to borrow to pay their rent, but a little excitement now and then brought a smile to everyone's lips.

Sally's thoughts returned to the young women who had bought one of the more expensive pieces. She wondered if Mave worked the streets in Soho or had a room where the men were taken by her pimp. She decided that she would take a walk round the square after work, find a café to have a cup of tea or a sandwich and perhaps bump into Mave or another girl who might give her the information she needed.

* * *

After Sally returned from her lunch break, Mrs Craven left her in charge. Several customers came in and Sally sold a cloche hat and a red leather handbag. Beth was the busiest now as people asked to see scarves and gloves. Gloves were something every woman wore when she went out, winter and summer, if she wanted to look properly dressed. Yet a few of Beth's customers walked away without purchasing anything.

When the department was temporarily empty, Sally asked her what reason the three women had made for refusing the scarves she'd shown them.

'One of them said she wanted a paler shade of blue, another said they were all too expensive and the third asked me if I could put one by for her – she said she would come back on Saturday.'

'What did you say?'

'I said yes and I've wrapped it in tissue and put it in my top drawer with a note of her name and how much there is to pay.'

'I'm not sure that is permitted,' Sally said. 'You should ask Mrs Craven, Beth. I don't think the management would approve.'

'Did I do wrong?' Beth looked anxious. 'She seemed sincere. She gets paid on Friday night and the colour is just what she has been looking for but she didn't have enough money to buy it until she gets her wages.'

'Well, I wasn't allowed to do it at Selfridges,' Sally said, 'but you need to ask Mrs Craven. Oh, that gentleman is at my counter...'

She walked towards the counter, where a well-dressed man waited for attention. 'May I help you, sir?'

'Yes, I think perhaps you can,' he said and smiled at her as he tipped his trilby hat. 'My secretary bought a beautiful bag from you this morning, for my wife's birthday – she told me about some special silver jewellery.' He looked down at the counter. 'Would you show me that bangle and some earrings please?'

'Yes, of course, sir.' Sally took out the best of the bangles, priced at three guineas, and a box with earrings that matched.

The man handled the bangle, nodded and said that he would purchase it but refused the earrings and pointed to a different style.

'I'd like to see those please...'

Sally took out the large loops. She had thought them too flashy for a gentleman's taste, but he smiled. 'Yes, I will take those too – for my friend...'

Obviously, the jewellery was not meant for his wife. Sally wondered about the person who would receive the earrings and bangle, but then put the thought from her mind as she double-checked the cost and asked for four pounds exactly.

She sent the money off and gave him his receipt with his packages.

'I'll be seeing you again, I dare say,' he said and flashed her a brilliant smile before walking away.

Mrs Craven had returned from her break and was talking to Beth. She frowned and Beth flushed and looked uncomfortable. Sally thought her friend looked close to tears, but she was lucky that they had Mrs Craven as their supervisor and not Miss Hart.

Mrs Craven approached the counter. 'Thank you for telling Beth she should not reserve goods. We were not advised on policy and therefore it wasn't her fault but I think it unwise to put stock away – it leads to mistakes.'

'Yes, I know,' Sally agreed. 'Some smaller shops will do it but most of the larger ones won't. People reserve stuff and then don't come back for weeks or forget it.'

'Hush – not another word...' Mrs Craven said as the floor walker entered the department, followed by Mr Stockbridge and Mr Harper. 'She doesn't need to know...'

Sally grinned and turned away to move some of the

jewellery about on the shelves. Their boss was certainly a good-looking man and she liked the fact that he was making a personal tour of the departments, taking an interest in everything. She'd sold far more in one day than she'd expected and, if the trend continued, would need more stock soon.

'Well done all of you,' Miss Hart said. 'You've made more sales than any other department – and, Miss Ross, you made the most expensive sale of the morning in this department. Congratulations. You will receive the sum of five shillings as a bonus in your wage this week.'

'I want to encourage my staff to work hard and achieve,' Mr Harper said and his eyes seemed to dwell on Sally for a moment, bringing a little flush to her cheeks.

'Have we been busy throughout the store?' Mrs Craven asked him.

'I believe sales are satisfactory on most floors,' he said, turning to her.

'Yes, but not as many sales in the men's department as on this floor,' Miss Hart put in importantly. 'The ground floor have made more sales overall, but there are more counters there – and nothing above six guineas was sold this morning. I dare say your sale may be the largest of the day, Miss Ross...' Her mouth drew back in a grimace, as if disappointed that it should have been Sally. 'Though a porcelain dinner service was inquired about earlier. If the customer returns that will of course be a bigger purchase...'

'We need both large and small,' Mr Harper said, looking enthusiastic. 'Come along, Stockbridge, we have other departments to visit...'

Another customer entered the department as they left and Sally returned to her counter. She was asked about handbags and sold a leather bag for two guineas and a silver pendant for ten shillings. Miss Hart watched her and then hurried off in her employer's wake.

'I think she was not pleased that you had made the best sale of the morning, Miss Ross,' Mrs Craven said. 'I cannot for the life of me think why...'

Sally grimaced. 'I don't think Miss Hart quite approves of me.'

'Maybe not – but I certainly do,' Mrs Craven said. 'I have a customer now – please excuse me...'

Sally returned to her post behind the counter, where she continued to sell steadily all afternoon; all the sales were from the silver jewellery now and she realised that it must be the display in the window that was bringing everyone in.

Smiling, she waited for the next customer. So far, everything was going really well. She would just have to hope that her excursion into Soho would go just as well that evening...

11

Beth felt really tired when she left work that afternoon. One of the last to leave, she saw Mr Marco and Mr Harper discussing one of the displays. The window dresser nodded to her and she summoned a smile, even though she felt weary. She hadn't realised that working as a sales assistant would be quite as hard and her back ached as she walked to catch her bus. She saw there was a sizeable queue and sighed, because if the bus was already half full she might not get a seat for ages. When the car drew up behind her, she didn't bother to turn her head until someone touched her on the shoulder.

'Will you allow me to run you home in the motor?'

Turning, Beth saw Mark looking at her intently and her heart turned over. His eyes were dark with passion and she felt the strength of his emotion touch her. Perhaps it was the look of appeal in his eyes that swayed her and she was agreeing before she thought of the consequences. Parked by the kerb, his motor car was a very smart vehicle with shiny wheels and green paintwork. Beth had no idea what kind of vehicle it was, for she had taken no notice of such things, but caught sight of the words De Dion on the back and thought it sounded French. The people standing in the queue were looking at her and she blushed, feeling embarrassed as Mark opened the passenger door for her.

Sitting in the front passenger seat, Beth looked at the man she had once loved so desperately. She felt exposed and nervous. 'I'm not sure this is a good idea... your wife...'

'Wouldn't mind,' Mark finished. 'I shan't drive you to a dark alley and ravish you, if that is your fear?' She saw a flash of annoyance in his eyes and felt embarrassed.

'Of course it isn't!' Beth flushed hotly. 'I'm living with Aunt Helen – I think you know where that is. Please stop before we get there, because I don't want the neighbours to gossip.'

Motor cars were still a rarity in her aunt's neighbourhood and she would have been noticed getting out of it from behind a dozen lace curtains, and that would be enough to set the gossips talking for a week.

'Poor Beth – always having to do the right thing. Don't you get tired of being a saint?'

'That's unfair,' she retorted. 'You don't understand – you have no idea how it was...'

'No, that's why I think we should talk,' he said and released the handbrake, heading into the traffic. He didn't look at her as he asked the question she'd refused to answer years earlier. 'Why, Beth – why did you choose your mother over me?'

'I didn't,' Beth said as tears stung her eyes. She felt the wind tug at her hat and put up a hand to hold it on, because although it was a pleasant evening the rush of wind as they drove faster was enough to blow it away. 'I begged her to let me marry you and to come and live with us, but she refused. She accused me of being selfish and not caring for her and said my father would be shocked and hurt that I could think of deserting her. She threatened to die in the infirmary rather than live as your dependent...'

'What had I done that she should dislike me so strongly?' he asked resentfully.

'I don't know – except that she wanted to keep me on her string. I think you might have stood up to her better than I did...'

Mark nodded but said nothing for a while. 'Yet you still chose to stay with her. She couldn't have forced you.'

'I wasn't old enough to marry without her consent, but more than that it broke my heart when she said that she would rather die than leave our home. I felt selfish and unkind – and I tried to explain, to tell you, but you were angry and you left me in a temper that night. You never gave me a second chance.'

'I believed you wanted someone else – and then I was told that you were easily led and not ready to settle down...'

'Who told you such things?' Beth asked, angry now.

'I called at your home the next morning but you were out. Your mother told me you had better prospects and asked me not to call again...'

'Mother said that?' Beth looked at him and saw the pulse flicking at his temple. She closed her eyes briefly as the pain struck. 'How could she? She never told me you'd been – I thought you'd deserted me and I wrote to you, but then I didn't post the letter. Mother said if you'd wanted me you would have kept coming back...'

'It seems that your mother was determined to keep us apart...'

'Yes, she was,' Beth agreed. She saw it clearly now. 'I kept hoping you might write to me or call, but you never did...'

Mark was silent. He drew up two streets away from her aunt's home, turned the ignition off and looked at her. 'Don't get out for a moment, Beth, please.'

'I should go...' She hesitated, feeling drawn to him by the look of longing in his eyes and yet she knew that it was useless. 'It is too late, Mark. I was barely twenty and my mother used emotional blackmail – and I lost you. I wish I could have explained better, asked you to wait...' She brushed away the tears from her cheeks. 'I am truly sorry that I hurt you. I loved you, but you're married now and...' Beth shook her head.

'Please, don't try to stop me leaving – and don't come to meet me again. It's no good...'

'I was a damned fool,' Mark said and she saw pain in his eyes. 'I should have known your mother was lying. I should have found you and made you tell me the truth...'

'You didn't and I was too hurt and proud to beg you to come back,' Beth said. She was trembling and her voice shook as she whispered, 'Goodbye, Mark, my dear. You know this has to end here...'

He leaned towards her and before Beth guessed what he intended, his lips were on hers; it was the merest touch, but she jerked back instantly.

'No! You cannot – you must not...' she cried, wrenched the door open and almost fell out in her haste. 'Goodbye, Mark.'

Beth did not look back as she walked hurriedly away. Tears were trickling down her cheeks as she turned the corner of the street. She brushed them away with her gloved hand and took a deep breath, trying to control her emotions before entering the house. Aunt Helen must not see her like this! She would lash Beth with words of scorn and that was the last thing she needed. No one needed to tell Beth that she had no chance of happiness with Mark. He was married and she would neither become his lover, nor would she destroy his marriage. It would be shocking if he were to divorce his wife for her – and the alternative was shame.

Beth had no choice but to forget him. The pain inside her chest was sharp, but she would hide it from her aunt and the world; she had no other course but to pretend that this had never happened. Even if Mark regretted his marriage and wanted her, it was impossible.

* * *

Sally found a café and sat down, ordering a cup of coffee and a ham sandwich. She felt she could afford to treat herself, because of the five shilling bonus she'd earned that day. She looked out on the square, watching as the dusk gathered. Soon, the young women who sold themselves to men for money would begin to walk up and down the pavements. Normally, Sally would not have ventured here at this hour and she was determined to leave as soon as she had managed to ask the question she needed to have answered.

Idly looking through the window, Sally suddenly saw the young woman named Mave. She jumped to her feet, threw the money for her bill on the counter and rushed out into the square. She ran after Mave and caught her arm, turning her to face her. Only then, did she realise it wasn't Mave but someone she'd never seen before in her life.

'Oh, I'm sorry,' she said. 'I thought you were someone else.'

'What the bleedin' hell do yer want?' the woman demanded angrily. 'If Sammy sent yer, yer can clear orf. I'm on me own now and I don't bleedin' care what he thinks...'

'I don't know Sammy,' Sally said desperately. 'I was lookin' for Mave...'

'What yer want wiv her then?' the woman demanded.

Sally hesitated, and then decided on a little lie. 'She was going to tell me where I could get rid of a kid...'

'Get rid...' the woman stared at her hard. 'Up the spout, are yer?'

'It's not me, it's my friend,' Sally said. 'I need to know – for her sake...'

The woman was silent for a moment, and then nodded. 'Happen I do know of someone,' she said. She took a pencil and a scrap of paper from her bag and scribbled a name and an address. 'Tell Dot that Vera sent yer... and she'll want payin', ten quid if it's yer first time. But I never told yer and if yer shop me to the law, I'll make yer wish you'd never been born...'

'I promise I won't. My friend is desperate...'

'I'll bet she is...' The woman leered at her, clearly thinking

Sally needed the name for herself. 'Ain't no shame in it, love. It's the bloody men what's to blame.'

Sally decided there was no point in denying the abortion was for herself because Vera wouldn't believe her. 'Thank you. I'll tell Sylvia how much it will cost her…'

'Be sure yer want it done,' Vera advised seriously. 'It might mean yer can't 'ave kids in future – and if yer leave it too late it can be dangerous…'

'Thank you, I'll tell her,' Sally tucked the paper into her jacket pocket and walked away. She had not gone more than a few steps before a man stepped out on to the pavement in front of her.

'How much?'

'I'm not interested,' Sally said, but he grabbed her arm.

'I'll pay yer ten quid for the lot…'

'No! Leave me alone…' Sally pushed at him, but his grip tightened and he muttered something about 'bloody prostitutes gettin' above themselves,' as he tried to drag her off. She struggled and he thrust her hard against the wall. Sally gave a little scream and then she saw the man who accosted her jerked back and sent flying onto the pavement.

Someone stood over him and there was a bit of shouting before the man in the gutter got to his feet and ran off. Sally was shaking as her rescuer turned back to her.

'Are you all right?' Irish Mick asked and she gasped in shock, but he looked just as shocked as he realised it was her. 'What the hell are you doin' up here?'

'I had an errand to run,' Sally said and her face was on fire. 'Thank you – I have to go…'

'I'll see you on the right bus,' Mick said and glared at her. 'Are you out of your mind comin' up here at night, Sally Ross?'

Sally hadn't realised he knew her name. She'd hardly spoken to him, though he'd looked at her many times and called out a greeting. 'I told you, I had something important to do…'

Mick had hold of her arm and was bundling her along the

street. 'Nice girls don't walk this square at night, especially alone,' he said. 'It's a wonder the girls didn't think you were a rival and set on you – and there's some here as would use you in a way you wouldn't like...'

'I'm not a fool,' Sally muttered angrily. His fingers were digging into her arm and hurting her. 'I had to do something for a friend...'

His eyes narrowed and she knew he was furious, but what was it to him that she was here?

'If I hadn't come along you might have been found in the river by mornin'.'

Sally bit her lip. She knew what she'd done was dangerous, but she'd promised Sylvia.

They reached the bus stop just as an omnibus pulled up.

'Get on,' he grunted. 'Don't come here again...'

'I don't know what business it is of yours...' Sally said, but he'd walked away and the conductor told her to move along. She did so, rubbing at her arm. There was sure to be a bruise in the morning. It was just as well her uniform had long sleeves or Mrs Craven would be curious!

Sally paid her fare and stared out of the windows at the lights of the town. It was a different London that came to life at night and she'd never been afraid to be alone before, but she'd had a fright that evening and it would be a long time before she ventured into the square again...

* * *

Sylvia took the address eagerly but frowned as Sally told her how much the procedure would be.

'He should be payin' for it,' Sylvia muttered, 'but he wouldn't give me a penny.'

'I haven't got much saved – but I'll lend you four pounds if you're short...'

'Thanks, Sally,' her friend said. 'I'll pay you back as soon as I can. You've done enough for me and I will repay you.'

'Vera said be careful you don't leave it too long, because if you're too far advanced it can be dangerous...'

Sylvia looked anxious. 'I'm not sure how far on I am.' She shrugged. 'I can't have it anyway so I've got no choice.'

'I wish I could do more...' Sally said, feeling anxious for her. 'Do you want me to come with you?'

'No, it's all right, I'm not frightened,' Sylvia said. 'When it's over, we'll go out somewhere together on me – the theatre. I like a bit of music hall...'

'Yes, so do I,' Sally agreed with a smile, 'but it's no fun alone, you need someone to go with...'

'Yeah – so we'll go together,' Sylvia promised. 'I'm off bloody men for good...'

Sally smiled and left to return to her own room. She'd delivered the address Vera had given her and now it was up to Sylvia. It was only as she sat down on the bed in her own room that she realised she would have to acknowledge Irish Mick in future. He'd saved her from a beating at the very least, and perhaps worse. Sally hadn't thanked him properly, but she would when she next saw him, though she wouldn't tell him why she'd been in Soho – it wasn't his business. Momentarily, she wondered what he was doing there, but then forgot it, because it wasn't her concern.

Sally was more than tired as she crawled into bed. It had been a busy day and she could have done without the trip into Soho, but she had wanted to help Sylvia and she had. Now she could forget it and think about the future.

* * *

Sally saw Mick the next morning when she left for work. He was waiting for her in the pub doorway and crossed over to speak to her. She couldn't ignore him after what he'd done to help her, so she stopped and looked at him warily.

'I'm sorry, can't stop – I have a bus to catch...'

'I know. You've plenty of time,' he said and his Irish accent was more obvious than the previous evening when he'd been angry. He was smiling and easy, more like his normal self. 'I was just wantin' to ask how you feel this lovely mornin', Sally Ross.'

Sally was nervous, unsure she wanted to be talking to him like this. 'Who told you my name?'

'Oh, I have my ways,' he said and grinned. 'As long as you're no worse for your nasty experience?'

'Of course I'm all right,' Sally snapped. 'You stopped that brute in time and I'm grateful. I am truly. It was foolish of me to go there, but I had to – I needed some information for a friend...'

'Well now, couldn't you have been after askin' meself?' he said. 'Anything you need to know, I'm your man... don't you be forgettin' that in future.' His eyes lit with a teasing smile that made her cheeks flame.

'That is kind of you,' Sally said, 'but I've no intention of going there again...'

'Sensible girl – more so if you hadn't gone in the first place.' His gaze narrowed intently. 'If it's yourself in trouble...'

'No, it isn't,' she said quickly. 'Now, please excuse me – I must catch that tram...'

Mick stood aside to let her pass and Sally hurried to the end of the lane and walked the few steps to the tram. She was only there a few seconds when it came round the corner, its bell clanging. Jumping on board, she breathed a sigh of relief and then laughed at herself. Sally knew she had no reason to fear Mick; he might be more familiar than she liked, but he would never harm her. She'd seen warmth in his gaze and understood that he liked her, but Sally wasn't interested in a man who worked as a barman. She wanted more out of life...

12

Beth noticed that Maggie looked pale and upset when she arrived for work on that Thursday morning. She had customers almost at once and it was not until they were told to take their break for lunch that she had time to ask her if anything was wrong. Maggie's eyes filled with tears, but she brushed them away and gulped as Beth handed her a handkerchief.

'It's my father,' she gasped. 'Oh, Beth, it was so terrible. He was in so much pain that he was crying with it and we had to fetch the doctor to him in the middle of the night...'

'I am so very sorry,' Beth said sympathetically. 'I could see that you were very upset, but it is understandable when your father is so ill...' She took a deep breath. 'I lost mine when I was still a child. I looked after my mother until she died some months ago. It is a very sad and painful time when someone you love is suffering...'

'I feel so helpless,' Maggie confessed. 'The doctor said that all he could do was to give my father more of the drug that eases him... but if we give him too much he might die.'

'That is an awful situation for you and your mother,' Beth replied sadly. 'And is there nothing more anyone can do for him?'

'He hurt his spine in an accident and his firm are supposed to pay him compensation because it was their fault – but that doesn't make up for the pain, does it? Besides, I don't think they've paid anything yet.'

'It doesn't help your father in the least,' Beth said. 'Money might help your mother to pay the bills, but it is your father who suffers – and both of you with him.'

Maggie nodded but said nothing. She wiped her face. 'I know crying won't help, but your sympathy brought the tears, Beth. My mother just doesn't seem to care about anyone but herself...' She drew a sharp breath. 'Oh, that is so awful of me and it isn't true. I'm sure it's the worry that makes her so harsh all the time.'

'Yes, people do become harsh when they're worried,' Beth said. 'I'm really sorry, Maggie. Would you like me to ask Mrs Craven if you can go home early?'

'No, please don't,' Maggie said. 'I was lucky to get this job and I don't want to lose it, even though Muma doesn't think the wage is very much – and I'm happier here than at home. I love my father, but he's either in pain or asleep... and my mother is always grumbling at me.'

'Yes, I do understand, more than you might think,' Beth said. 'My mother was often unwell and spent most of her time sleeping.' And the rest complaining!

'I do love Muma in my way... but just not as much as my father...' Maggie sniffed and handed Beth her handkerchief. 'Should I wash it for you and bring it back?'

'I'll wash it at home,' Beth said with a smile. 'I know there isn't much I can do to help, but I can listen if you want...'

'Thank you,' Maggie said and glanced at the big silver-dialled clock on the restaurant wall. 'We'd better go back or we might be late. I don't want to be fined on my very first week.'

'No, nor do I,' Beth agreed. 'I shall only just make my wage last out as it is...' Maggie looked at her and she pulled a wry face. 'My aunt takes half of my wage for my board and lodgings...'

'Oh, that's rather a lot, isn't it?'

'I suppose I've been living there for a few months and not paid for more than some shopping...' Beth smothered a sigh. 'It was hard enough when my mother was alive, but when she died, I was left with very little and that has all gone so I can't make a change even if I wanted to...'

'My mother spoke of taking a lodger in, but she was only going to charge five shillings for bed and breakfast.'

'I have my evening meal too,' Beth reminded her. 'My aunt's request isn't excessive. I know I couldn't afford to live anywhere else.'

'Sally wants a flat of her own and she suggested that I might move in with her,' Maggie said, 'but my mother would never let me...'

'I think it would be expensive, unless there were at least four sharing – and one would have to be a widow, so that it was respectable.'

'Sally said it didn't matter,' Maggie said and a little frown creased her forehead. 'Why does it make it more respectable if a woman is a widow?'

'It just does, that's all,' Beth said and laughed. 'Your mother would be shocked if you said the three of us wanted to live in a flat on our own, wouldn't she?'

'Yes, I know, but can you see why?' Maggie asked. 'If we are all respectable girls, where can the harm be?'

'In other women's minds I'm afraid. We should be thought fast,' Beth suggested with a smile. 'Come on, we'd better hurry or we shall be late...'

* * *

Sally was serving a middle-aged lady with a leather handbag when she saw the woman enter the department and her heart sank. She couldn't be mistaken; it was the street walker she'd met in Soho a couple of evenings previously. She'd tried to erase the memory and begun to forget the unpleasant experience she'd had there, but now it came back as she saw Vera make a beeline for her counter.

'Ah, miss,' Vera said. 'I was wondering if you could show me a silver bangle like my friend bought on the day you opened please.'

Sally remembered exactly which bangle Mave had bought, but there wasn't another just the same. 'These are all individual pieces,' she said, 'but I think this might be the nearest to the one you're seeking...'

Vera's gaze came up and registered both shock and recognition, but she recovered instantly as Sally brought out the bangle. 'Yes, miss,' she said. 'That is almost the same but just a little different – the stones are smaller. What are they called please?'

'Turquoises,' Sally said and prayed that Vera would not mention their previous meeting. 'This bangle is cheaper than the one your friend bought – it is seventeen shillings and sixpence.' And that was still more than many working girls could afford to pay.

'I like it better,' Vera said. 'Can I have it in a fancy box please? It isn't for me, it's for my sister. She lives in the country and she won't have seen anything like this before.' Vera winked at Sally. 'She'll think it's posh and that her big sister is rich.'

'I doubt many people in this country have seen this type of jewellery,' Sally said. 'The line is exclusive to Harpers and was recently imported into the country. I hope your sister likes it.'

'She will,' the other woman said and grinned as she offered the exact payment. 'Thanks very much, love – and don't worry, Vera ain't no snitch...'

Sally kept a straight face as she handed her the little bag with the distinctive logo. 'Thank you,' she said. 'We are grateful for your custom.'

'Bye, then,' Vera said, 'take care of yerself...' She winked again and walked off, almost walking straight into Miss Hart. The superior floor walker looked down her nose at her as if she were something the cat had fetched in. 'Watch out, missus, yer face'll crack if yer smile...'

Sally caught her breath as she saw the outrage in Miss Hart's eyes. The floor walker came straight up to her, her expression sour. 'Was that a friend of yours, Miss Ross?'

'No, Miss Hart, just a customer. She bought a silver bangle...'

'I'm not sure we wish to encourage women like that into the store...' Miss Hart sniffed disapprovingly.

'I was told to serve everyone in the same manner when I worked at Selfridges, but if you are ordering me not to serve a common woman...?' Sally left the question hanging and looked as innocent as she could.

Miss Hart glared at her. 'Nothing of the kind! We are here to serve and I suppose her money is as good as the next person's – but you should be careful not to allow familiarity, Miss Ross. It would be unwise to be seen to fraternise with a woman of that sort...'

'Is something wrong?' Mrs Craven asked as she approached. 'I was just about to ask you to take over the department while I have my break, Miss Ross.' Her eyes met Miss Hart's glare. 'I feel happy to leave the department to Miss Ross – unless you wish to remain while I take my break, Miss Hart?'

'No, I have other things to do. Excuse me, Mrs Craven – Miss Ross, I shall be watching...'

'What happened?' Mrs Craven asked after she'd gone.

'She thought one of the customers was too friendly, that's all,' Sally answered but blushed.

'She is right, Miss Ross – even if I do not like the way she speaks to you and Maggie, I must agree that you should be careful. However, I do not think you encouraged that young woman to be familiar, though she appeared to know you.'

'It was merely that I had served her friend with a bangle and she wanted one similar.' Sally didn't enjoy lying to Mrs Craven, but she couldn't tell her the truth. What Sylvia was planning to do was illegal and Sally had broken the law by giving her the address of the back-street abortionist. Her supervisor would think she had been very foolish and perhaps she had, because if Mick hadn't happened to be there when she was attacked... It was odd that he was, Sally's thoughts switched as Mrs Craven went off to take her break. What had Mick been doing in that part of London?

She dismissed the question as a smart young woman entered the department and walked towards her. 'I should like to buy a handbag – I want a good one. I've seen something I like in the window... Ah yes, that red one there...'

Sally took the bag from the cabinet. It was one of the less expensive bags and the customer took a long time to make up her mind. Beth had two customers, which left Maggie to serve a middle-aged lady with a hat. Sally couldn't see what was going on properly because she was busy showing her customer various bags, but when she finally settled on the first red one, Sally saw that the woman had at least ten hats on the counter and was pointing at another in the cabinet, clearly asking to try it on. Since Sally was free, she walked over to join Maggie, who looked pink and flustered.

'Can we help you to decide, madam?' she asked and smiled at Maggie. 'Please put these away, Miss Gibbs, while I attend to this customer – you wanted a black hat, I think?'

Maggie hurried to tidy away the rejected offerings, clearly relieved that Sally had taken over.

'Well, yes, or a grey one,' the customer said. 'Nothing frivolous, because it's for a funeral, but I want to be able to wear it for work. I can't afford these fancy prices...' she frowned at a ticket of two guineas.

Sally glanced around the cabinets and stands and spotted a black cloche with a plain ribbon band. She knew it was priced at twelve shillings and swooped on it.

'Now this would suit you well, madam –it is a perfect shape for your face.'

Sally offered the hat and the customer took it, glanced at the price and then tried it on. It suited her well, but she frowned and drew her mouth in and then looked at the ticket again.

'Yes, well, I think this might do,' she acknowledged. 'Twelve shillings – far more sensible than that the other girl showed me, though still expensive. I normally pay seven and sixpence at the most! I thought this shop would be more reasonable than Self-ridges, but some of your prices are ridiculous.'

'Yes, a little expensive for this end of town,' Sally agreed with her. 'I think Mr Harper wanted to give our customers a wider choice – and we do have all prices in stock of most things.'

'You seem a sensible young woman,' the customer said and shot a look of malice at poor Maggie. 'I think it very foolish to leave an untrained girl in charge of a counter like this...'

'Miss Gibbs is a junior and learning,' Sally said smoothly. She whisked the customer's money away in the cash dispenser and packed the hat into a smart box. 'I do hope you will be pleased with your purchase, madam.'

The customer was admiring the box, which was striking and looked mollified. 'It's a good thing you're in charge here,' she said as Sally counted her change out. 'The hat is lovely quality, even though it's too much money. I dare say I shall shop here again and tell my friends.'

'Please do,' Sally said and smiled.

'Thank you,' Maggie said, coming up to her as the customer disappeared through the glass doors and they swung to after her. 'She terrified me. I just didn't know what to do...'

'All bark and no bite,' Sally said and laughed. She picked up one of the hats that Maggie had not tidied away yet just as Mrs Craven walked in through the opposite door. Her back to her supervisor, she laughed at Maggie as she put the hat on and pretended to admire her reflection in the mirror. 'I'm not sure it is my colour – have you something else in a paler shade and not too expensive. Oh, and more veiling, I need more veiling...'

'Miss Ross!' the sharp tones of the floor walker made Sally freeze. She took off the hat as she turned to meet the cold gaze fixed on her. 'What do you imagine you're doing? These hats are not to be played with – and if you've damaged it, you will be fined...' Miss Hart snatched up the expensive hat and looked at it. 'As I thought, the silk is torn just here – you will be fined two shillings a week until you have paid its price...'

'Just a moment,' Mrs Craven spoke from behind the floor walker. 'I believe you are mistaken, Miss Hart. I asked Miss Ross to try on that particular hat as I am thinking of buying it for a friend. May I see the tear?'

Miss Hart glared at her and handed her the hat. One little fold of tulle had frayed out slightly and Mrs Craven tucked it back in place; there was no actual damage.

'There, nothing is harmed,' Mrs Craven said. 'I shall be purchasing this hat – so there is no need to penalise Miss Ross for this slight mishap.'

'Well!' Miss Hart looked as if she might explode and walked off angrily.

Mrs Craven waited until she'd gone and then raised her brows at Sally. 'What was that all about?'

'It was my fault,' Maggie said hastily. 'Sally helped me with a difficult customer. I told her I was terrified and she was just teasing me, pretending to be a fussy customer...' Her cheeks went bright red. 'I'm sorry...' She looked to be on the verge of tears.

'Miss Hart is rather particular,' Mrs Craven said in a flat tone. 'However, I have to agree that the assistants are not supposed to try on the merchandise for fun. It was not wise, Miss Ross. Luckily, no damage was done this time and I did always intend to purchase the hat, but...'

'It was the customer who did the damage,' Maggie said. 'She was pulling at it and I didn't dare to say anything...'

'Well, we shall say no more about it,' Mrs Craven said, 'but be careful, Miss Ross. Miss Hart has clearly taken your name down and further black marks might lead to an official reprimand – and even dismissal...'

'Thank you, Mrs Craven,' Sally said meekly. Inside, she was raging with anger. The floor walker had taken a dislike to her and Sally knew that in future she would have to be very careful when Miss Hart was near or she would have her out on her ear!

* * *

Sally was still brooding on her wrongs when she reached her room that evening. She was home earlier than usual, because she'd decided to spend some time washing and drying her hair. Although she wore it collar length, it was thick, dark with a hint of red, and had a mind of its own and she needed to towel dry it thoroughly and then finger wave it and clip it, letting the waves dry in place. The ends would just flick up themselves. If she let it grow longer, it would wave and curl naturally about her shoulders, but she needed it to be neat for work.

She boiled a kettle on the little gas ring and made a pot of tea and was just about to start washing her hair when someone pounded on her door. Frowning, Sally went to open it and saw Sylvia standing there looking pale and swaying on her feet.

'You look dreadful...' Sally said, realising instantly that the older girl had been to the abortionist's. 'She did it then?'

Sylvia stumbled into the room and Sally caught her as she almost fell. She led her to the bed and Sylvia collapsed on to it. 'I'm bleeding again,' she said. 'She had a job to stop it, but then she said it was all right and told me to go home and stay in bed for a day or so... but I've bled all over the sheets. I don't know what to do...'

Sally didn't know what to do either. When she'd told Sylvia of the woman called Dot, she'd warned her that there might be unpleasant consequences, but she didn't like the sound of the bleeding.

'Did she say what to do if it started again?'

'She said I couldn't go to a doctor, because they would put both of us in prison – and I had to promise I wouldn't before she did it. I was warned that if I opened my mouth, I would be sorry. She has two great sons and I dread to think what they'd do to me if I went to the law...'

'That's awful,' Sally felt anxious and wished she'd never told Sylvia about the woman. 'I'm sorry. I thought she knew what she was doin' or I wouldn't have given you the address.'

'What should I do?' Sylvia asked, clearly on the verge of tears.

'Are you still bleeding?'

Sylvia didn't answer and when Sally looked at her, she saw that her eyes were closed. She appeared to have lost consciousness and Sally could see a small pool of blood spreading on her bed. A feeling of panic went through her as she realised Sylvia could be seriously ill. What was she going to do?

She couldn't just let Sylvia bleed to death. Sally knew she had to fetch a doctor or the girl she'd tried to help would die – and it would be her fault for telling her about the back-street butcher that had ended the life of the child inside her and nearly killed Sylvia into the bargain.

'I'll get help,' she said, but Sylvia couldn't hear her. Leaving her lying on the bed, Sally ran downstairs and out into the street. She wasn't even sure where the nearest doctor was, because she'd never needed one. Then, as she saw Mick emerge from the pub opposite, she remembered that he'd told her to come to him next time she needed help. Without considering the consequences, she waved frantically at him and he came running.

'What is it, Sally? I can see it's trouble...'

'My friend Sylvia had an abortion and now she's passed out in my room and the blood won't stop. I need to fetch a doctor...'

'That's somethin' you can't do, Sally,' Mick told her. 'You'll all be in trouble. Leave it to me. I know someone who will help her. Go back to your room and wait. I'll send my friend to you and she'll do what she can. If she can stop the bleedin', it's best if we take your friend somewhere else – this has to be kept quiet or she'll be in trouble with the law, and you for helping her.'

Sally nodded, feeling frightened and distressed. She should never have gone looking for help in Soho, she'd only made things worse.

Hurrying back to Sylvia, she found that the girl was conscious again.

'Someone is coming to help you – not a doctor, no one who will turn you in to the police. Let me help you to sit up and I'll make you a drink while we wait...' Doctors were bound to report bungled attempts at abortion, which could be punishable by the law.

'Thank you,' Sylvia's words were almost inaudible. 'I've made a mess over your candlewick cover... I'm sorry.'

'I can take it to the laundry and no one will know.' Sally made cocoa and gave a cup to the other girl. Sylvia's hand shook as she sipped it, but she'd managed to get most of it down by the time someone knocked at the door. Sally opened it and admitted the woman who stood there. She was in her forties and her hair was a frizzy bleached blonde, but her eyes were kind and under-standing as she took in the situation. She deposited the bag she was carrying on the floor near to the bed.

'Mick sent me. I'm Bridget,' the woman said, looking from one to the other. 'Who have we here then?'

'I'm Sally and this is my friend Sylvia.'

Bridget nodded. 'Will you lie back on the mattress, lovey, and let me take a look?' she said to Sylvia, her manner calm and unflustered.

Sylvia looked at Sally, who nodded and smiled, and then did as she was told.

'Sure and it's a wicked mess that butcher made for you. She's torn you, so she has – but Bridget will stop the bleeding and put a stitch in to repair the bit I can see – as for the inside, well, only the Good Lord knows the truth of it.' She gave Sylvia a small bottle of Irish whisky. 'Drink a little of that and it will dull the pain a wee bit...'

Sylvia took it and drank several mouthfuls and then handed it back.

Bridget removed a small brown bottle from the bag she carried and poured some liquid on her hands, washing them all over with the iodine. She poured more on to a piece of white linen and bent to look at Sylvia's torn and bruised feminine parts.

'This will sting, lovey,' she said, 'but it's necessary or we'll have you dyin' of the infection, so we will – now grip young Sally's hands and hold tight and I'll soon have you right.'

Sally took her friend's hand while Bridget dabbed her with the iodine and then stitched her flesh. She whimpered and cried out a few times in pain, but Sally gripped her hands tightly and soothed her the best she could, watching as the silent tears trickled down Sylvia's cheeks. Bridget stood back as she finished her work and nodded.

'You'll do now, lovey. It's a pity you didn't come to me at the start, for I'd have made a better job than the butcher you paid, but you'll live – I can't promise that you'll be able to have children ever, but pray to the Good Lord and mayhap he'll hear you.'

'Thank you...' Sylvia accepted the small bottle of whisky once more and drank some more. 'I can't pay you...'

'Mick asked me to come, I'll take no money from friends of Mick,' Bridget said. 'Now, he said you were to come with me, if you can manage it – he'll take you somewhere safe and I'll watch over you until you heal...' She looked at Sally. 'Can you help me get her outside? Mick will have a cab waiting to take her off...'

'You're very kind,' Sally said. 'I could manage a few bob if...'

Bridget gave a cackle of laughter. 'Mick would have the skin off me back, so he would. Keep your money, me darlin'. You're his Sally and he thinks the world of you, so he does...'

'He hardly knows me and I don't know him,' Sally said, blushing a fiery red.

'Mebbe you don't know him yet,' Bridget said with a knowing look, 'but Mick knows you, lovey – and, as far as he's concerned, you're under his protection. Next time a friend of yours is in trouble, go to Mick...'

Sally nodded but said nothing, uncertain of how much she wanted to rely on Mick, even though he'd helped them this time. After all, she hardly knew him. She looked out of her door. No one was about. Turning, she beckoned the others forward, and, slipping an arm about Sylvia's waist, helped Bridget to support her down the stairs. The door was left half open, but Sally couldn't bother about that, her concern only for getting her friend away before they were discovered.

Mick was waiting outside. Sally could see him in the shadows, avoiding the glare of the street lamp. His dark eyes flicked to Sally and then the girl she was helping Bridget to support.

'I'll take care of this now,' he said and swept Sylvia up in his strong arms. 'Thanks, Bridget darlin'. I'll be seein' you – and, Sally, get back and clear up. We need this kept as quiet as possible.'

Sally nodded. She turned and ran back up the stairs and along the landing to her room. As she went inside, she saw Jean looking at the bloodstains on the bed and the scrap of linen with iodine and blood all over it. When she turned, there was a look of glee mixed with triumph on her face.

'They say the quiet ones are always the worst...'

'What are you talkin' about?' Sally said, knowing she had to deny everything unless she wanted this spiteful cat to blackmail both her and Sylvia for the rest of their lives.

'It's obvious, ain't it?' Jean said gleefully. 'Someone had an abortion and it happened here...'

'Absolute rubbish,' Sally said. 'I brought a young lad who fell from his bike and cut his knee badly up here. He bled all over my candlewick cover, so I fetched a nurse to him. She sewed him up and she's taken him to the hospital for further treatment.'

Jean's gaze narrowed with spite. 'I'm not fallin' for that one...'

'I don't mind what you think,' Sally said, facing her down. She was angry now and no longer afraid. 'You can think what you like, but you have no proof – it's your word against mine and everyone knows what you are.'

'Sylvia isn't in her room...' Jean challenged, leering at her in triumph.

'No, she came to tell me half an hour ago – she has gone to stay with her cousin for a few days.'

'She had an abortion and you helped her,' Jean said spite-fully. 'I know it. Just watch out, yer snooty bitch, I shall prove it and then I'll have the law on yer both...'

'You may do your worst,' Sally told her and opened her door. 'Now, please get out of my room – and if you come in here again when I'm out, I'll report that you stole money from me. I had five pounds on the side of my bed in coins and notes and they've gone. You'll lose your job and probably go to prison...'

'You bloody liar!' Jean screeched. 'I never touched any money.'

'Prove it...' Sally said, her eyes narrowed dangerously. 'Now get out or I'll start yelling and calling you a thief...'

Jean glared at her and then left. Sally locked the door after her. She leaned against it feeling sick and shaken, because Jean knew the truth even though she couldn't prove it. Sally would have to warn Sylvia to say she'd been staying with her cousin and she'd make sure that she kept her door locked in future.

Jean would try to blackmail them both, but the only way to deal with her was to be bold and stand up to her. She was a bully and Sally had met her sort in the orphanage. There was always one who tried to rule the other children and make their lives a misery. Sally had had to face her nemesis down and fight her before she'd stopped the constant mockery and hair pulling. She knew how to deal with Jean, providing that she could never prove what had gone on here this night.

Stripping the candlewick cover from the bed, Sally was relieved that the blood had not gone through to the blanket below. She would take the bedspread to the laundry on her way to work the next day and stick to her story of a boy falling from his bike. She would also need to slip into Sylvia's room and clean that before anyone else poked their nose in...

Undressing later that evening, Sally finally had time to lie back on her pillows and think. Mick had made things right tonight and she owed him a debt of gratitude – but she hoped he wasn't expecting too much in repayment. Bridget said he thought the world of her, but surely that couldn't be true?

Sally thought about Mick for a moment. He was good-looking, cheerful and friendly – and he'd done her a good turn, but she didn't really know him...

13

It was halfway through their second week of trading and the first rush of customers at Harpers had tailed off. The newspapers had made a big splash, giving the new store the thumbs up, but now they had fresh stories. Harpers still had lots of shoppers coming and going, but the sales were more infrequent. In the first few days it had seemed that almost every customer bought something, now some left without making a purchase. Sally was still making the most sales, but the customers at Beth's counter seemed more difficult to please. Several times she'd shown them the expensive silk scarves, only to be told that the customer could buy better at Selfridges or one of the other department stores. Beth didn't think it was necessarily true but reported the trend to Mrs Craven.

'Well, I think that is just annoyance speaking,' her supervisor said. 'One thing I cannot fault is the quality of our stock. I shall pop into some of the other shops in Oxford Street on my half day and have a look at the scarves. If I agree that ours are too expensive, I'll put in a report to the management.'

'It's not something I'm doing wrong?'

'I don't think so for a moment,' Mrs Craven said as the floor supervisor entered the department. 'Return to your counter. I suggest you do a stock-take on your scarves. I should like to know what has sold so far...'

Beth returned to the counter. Miss Hart walked up to Mrs Craven and began to explain something to her.

Sally was busy at her counter. She made a sale of a leather bag and then a piece of silver jewellery. After her customers and the floor walker left, the department was empty apart from the assistants. Mrs Craven beckoned to Beth, Maggie and Sally.

'There is to be a meeting this evening in the restaurant,' she told them. 'Mr Harper is going to make an announcement, so I would advise you all to be there.'

'Let's hope everything is going well,' Sally said. 'Otherwise, we could all be lookin' for a new job soon...'

'Don't jest,' Maggie shivered. 'I like my job here.'

'We all like our jobs,' Mrs Craven said. 'Maggie, you and Sally may go to your lunch break. Beth and I will keep the flag flying...' She suddenly realised she'd broken her own rule as Sally laughed. 'That is enough of that, Miss Ross. Off you go – Miss Gibbs too.'

'Yes, Mrs Craven,' Sally said, but her eyes were dancing with mischief.

Beth smiled but shook her head. It showed that their supervisor was getting to know and like the girls that worked in her department and she'd made a simple mistake. Beth thought it showed she was human and she liked her all the more for it.

Three customers entered the department the moment that the others had departed and two of them made a beeline for Beth's counter. The first was one of the customers who had refused to buy the previous day, claiming that the silk scarves were cheaper elsewhere.

'I think I'll buy that pretty green scarf with the wavy lines,' she said to Beth. 'It is expensive, but my husband says he will buy it for my birthday and I haven't seen one I like as much anywhere else...'

Beth felt vindicated and smiled inwardly. She took the scarf out and displayed it over her hand. 'Is this the one, madam?'

'Yes, and it is as lovely as I remembered.' The customer nodded and looked pleased. 'I thought I'd seen something better for less money, but it wasn't as nice as this when I went back...'

Beth took her money, sent it off in the pulley system to the cashier's office and then wrapped the scarf carefully in tissue and placed it in one of the distinctive black and gold bags. She returned the change to her customer, checking it carefully, bid her goodbye and turned to the next.

'I am sorry to keep you waiting, madam. How may I help you?'

'I want a good-quality scarf,' the woman said. 'I can just see something in that drawer – I think the colour is magenta...'

'Oh yes, that is one of our very best,' Beth told her with a smile. She took the scarf out and displayed it and her customer asked if she could try it on, preening in front of the small mirror on the counter.

'Lovely, just what I wanted – and the price is reasonable too,' the customer said. 'I'm so glad Harpers has opened. I used to have to go to Knightsbridge for what I wanted, but I shall shop here in future.'

Beth thanked her and she went away with her purchase, smiling. Beth made a note in her stock book with a feeling of satisfaction. She'd thought that particular scarf would lie in the drawer for ages, but, as she was fast discovering, there was a customer for everything. You just had to be patient and wait.

* * *

'What would you do if the store did close?' Maggie asked Sally as they sat over their pot of tea and sandwiches. The two of them shared a snack at Bessie's when they got the chance, because it was cheaper than eating in the shop restaurant and taking sandwiches from home to the nearest park would eat into the time they were allowed for lunch.

'I'd find another job in retail somewhere,' Sally said, looking thoughtful. 'I hope it doesn't happen, because I need decent references and a steady job or future employers will think I never stop anywhere.'

'I doubt I'll get a job I like as much,' Maggie said. 'Muma will make me stay at home and help her. She says she could earn more if she went out to work and I stayed home to look after my dad.'

'Perhaps she could,' Sally agreed. 'That would be a shame, Maggie love. You need to get out and make friends. If you could get away on a Sunday, we could go for a walk together – listen to a concert in the park and have tea.'

'I wish I could.' Maggie sighed. 'Muma expects me to be there – she pops out to see her friend on Sunday afternoon. She says it's the only chance she has to have some time to herself...'

'It's a pity,' Sally said. 'I like you, Maggie, and I'd like to share a flat with you – Beth too, if she would...'

'Beth's aunt expects her to help out at home,' Maggie said. 'I think she gets nagged if she's late back.'

'I don't have anyone to care what time I get in,' Sally said. 'I always thought it would be lovely to have a family – but I sometimes wonder if I'm better off being free to do as I please.'

'I'd rather live at home than in a hostel,' Maggie told her. 'You've told me it's not very nice. At least Muma keeps everywhere spotless. She never used to nag as much before Poppa had his accident, but she's changed a lot since then.'

'I suppose it's worry,' Sally said and Maggie's eyes stung with sudden tears.

'I don't mind so much for me – but I hate it when she hurts my dad's feelings. I've seen it in his eyes and I want to shout at her to stop, but he shakes his head at me and I know arguing would make things worse.'

'Nothing is straightforward, is it?' Sally's eyes flicked across the café as she saw two girls come in. 'Don't look over there, Maggie. I don't want her to notice us...'

Maggie wasn't sure what she meant, but then the two girls came up to their table. 'So this is where yer get to,' one of the girls said with a nasty little sneer. Maggie instinctively disliked her. 'You don't mind if we share yer table – all the others are full...'

Sally got to her feet at once. 'As a matter of fact, I do,' she said. 'Come on, Miss Gibbs, we're leaving. I'm not sure why, but there's a bit of a stink in here now...'

Maggie felt herself flushing hotly. She saw a look of hatred in the other girl's eyes and allowed Sally to lead her up to the counter to pay.

'Who was that?' she asked as they went outside. The sky was clouding over and it felt as if there might be some rain before long. 'I didn't bring a coat. I hope it doesn't rain before we get back...'

'Her name is Jean – I don't know her friend – but she is a nasty piece of work. If she approaches you when you're on your own just ignore her, Maggie.'

'I wouldn't want to know her,' Maggie assured her. 'We should find somewhere else to have our sandwiches for a while.'

'I'm not going to let her scare me off,' Sally said. 'If she causes trouble I'll ask Bessie's husband to get her to leave next time.'

Maggie nodded. Her mother had always warned her to stay clear of that kind of girl at school.

'Common girls! They use bad language and they can be violent,' Mrs Gibbs had told her daughter. 'We're a decent family and we keep ourselves to ourselves – so mind what I say and have nothing to do with that sort.'

Maggie would certainly stay away from Jean and her friend. If Sally hadn't been with her, she would have been too embarrassed to just get up and walk away. If she had to take her lunch break alone, she thought she might try somewhere else, even if she could only afford a cup of tea.

* * *

Sally frowned as she tidied her hair in the cloakroom. Jean had deliberately chosen their table just to make things awkward for her. She was spiteful and a bad enemy and Sally wondered if she ought to think of moving away from the hostel where she was staying. Yet it was close enough to Oxford Street to be a cheap bus ride in the morning and she could walk home at night, providing it wasn't pouring with rain. If she moved she might have to go much further afield to find anything as cheap.

If Beth and Maggie were able to share a small flat with her, she would leave the hostel in a heartbeat, but they were both tied to their homes. She wouldn't mind sharing with Mrs Craven, although perhaps that wouldn't do because her supervisor might feel it was inappropriate. Sighing, she thrust Jean's spiteful leer out of her mind and focused on the meeting with Mr Harper that night. What would he have to say?

14

The three girls and Mrs Craven stood together close to the back of the room. They'd stopped to clear everything up before they came and only just avoided being late because customers had seemed to crowd in just before closing time.

'I hope everyone is here,' Mr Stockbridge said as they joined at the back. 'Please everyone, be quiet now, because Mr Harper wants to talk to you all...'

The attractive young man moved forward and took a moment to look round at all the expectant faces. 'I'm pleased to tell you that I have some good news for you, ladies and gentlemen. The opening week went well, better than even I hoped.' His eyes moved round the room. 'Our situation is this – my uncle bequeathed me a forty-nine per cent holding in Harpers of Oxford Street, and my sister has thirty-one percent. My aunt holds the balance and they have agreed they are happy for me to continue to manage the store.'

There was a sound as of an indrawn breath as everyone felt relief at the news.

'And are you planning to continue to run the store – or will you sell as soon as you can make a profit?' one of the bolder men asked.

'I don't foresee that happening,' Ben Harper said. 'As long as I can make it grow, I prefer to run the business rather than take my capital and run.' He smiled in Sally's direction, or so she thought. 'The sales thus far have been encouraging – particularly in the millinery and ladies' goods department. Fashion is just behind and the ground floor is holding its own – it seems the English gentlemen are reluctant to take the lift to the upper floor and the sales there are lagging a little.'

'Lazy devils, men,' a woman's voice said and someone sniggered next to her.

'Perhaps we ought to rearrange the departments,' Ben Harper said, 'but we'll give things time to settle. Mr Stockbridge will be announcing a bonus system in the next few days and I hope that may encourage the gentlemen upstairs to be more energetic in their efforts.'

'Most of 'em round here think as we're too expensive,' one of the men said. 'Some of the suits belong in Knightsbridge rather than the wrong end of Oxford Street. We can't sell them because they're too dear.'

'I shall be asking the heads of departments to give me a report on sales at the end of the first month,' Ben Harper pounced on his comment. 'Any opinions on stock, prices or the window displays will be listened to carefully. I may be re-organising the display team and I shall put out a suggestion box so that anyone can post their ideas.' His gaze moved over them once more and seemed to linger where Sally, Beth and the others were grouped. 'Are there any questions?'

'What do we do if certain items sell out?' Sally spoke out then and his gaze rested firmly on her. 'The silver jewellery has sold well, even though it's a bit expensive, and we need fresh stock if we want to keep selling at the same rate.'

'Your name is?' he questioned, his gaze intent now.

'Miss Ross,' Sally said. 'Certain items have sold out and we need to replace them – but not necessarily with the exact same thing. Can you source the silver bangles easily?'

'Yes, I believe so,' Ben Harper replied and smiled. 'My sister, Miss Jenni Harper, chose the silver jewellery and the bags – and I could arrange for her to visit the department and speak to you about it.'

'I think we need to replenish the stock soon,' Sally said and then blushed as everyone looked at her. 'But some of the departments aren't as busy and that might be down to the stock...'

'That is what I wanted to hear.' Ben Harper's eyes seemed to smile as they dwelled on Sally. 'I've worked in my uncle's stores in New York for three years, but London is a different market and I need to learn what sells here. Jenni is in charge of the buying for all the stores – but she's over here in England at the moment, sourcing British goods for the store in New York.'

'Why can't we have more British goods here?' one of the men asked.

Ben Harper turned to discuss the possibility with the speaker and Maggie looked at Sally. 'I wouldn't have dared to speak up like that,' she said admiringly. 'You're so brave, Sally.'

'It needed to be said,' Sally murmured softly. 'Besides, some of the stock just isn't suitable for our customers and I think a lot of it is in the men's department. British men want the same thing they always buy and some of the things, well, they're a bit too natty for our men's more conservative taste...' Most men Sally saw in the streets looked less than smart in their crumpled trousers and jackets and they would consider the American stuff too flashy with its wide lapels and fancy binding. Only a few had their trousers crisply pressed, because that needed to be done every day and cheap material quickly went shiny and baggy at the knees.

Maggie giggled and then flushed as Miss Hart glanced at her severely.

'Careful, Maggie love,' Sally hissed. 'You don't want her getting her claws into you too.'

The meeting had broken up and everyone began to file out.

Miss Hart made a beeline for Sally, her expression one of outrage.

'How dare you speak out like that, Miss Ross?' she demanded. 'Mr Harper wanted to hear from senior staff – not the likes of you...'

Sally stared at her but made no reply. She was about to walk on when someone caught her arm. Turning, she saw Mr Harper smiling at her.

'If you're not in too much of a hurry, Miss Ross? I should like you to give me ten minutes of your time... in my office please.' His voice carried a hint of command and everyone wondered if Sally was in trouble.

She went with him obediently and Miss Hart turned her baleful gaze on Maggie. 'She won't last here,' she said spitefully. 'She'll be out on her ear before six months is up – or end up where girls like her usually do, in the gutter... and you'd be well advised not to follow her lead!'

Maggie gasped at the floor walker's spite but said nothing. She was grateful when Mrs Craven touched her arm, shaking her head.

'Why does she dislike Sally so much?' Maggie asked Mrs Craven.

'Take no notice of her, Miss Gibbs. I think our floor supervisor has just had her nose put out a little and she is letting off steam...' Or perhaps it was just the jealousy of an older single woman for a young and very pretty one.

Maggie nodded gratefully. She hurried to put her coat on and leave, because she wanted to catch the next bus. Her mother would already be looking for her, but she did hope Sally wasn't in trouble...

* * *

'Please sit down, Miss Ross,' Ben Harper said, indicating the chair opposite the large mahogany desk. 'Don't look so nervous. You're not in trouble.'

'Thank you,' Sally said and sat down. He remained standing and looked down at her for a moment, his expression thoughtful. 'I hope you didn't mind my speaking out, sir?'

'It was what I'd hoped for,' he said.

'I felt you needed to be told about the stock. Some of it isn't right for this area of London...'

He nodded and frowned. 'In the New York store we have more departments on one floor. These premises are small by comparison. Do you like your job, Miss Ross?'

'Yes, sir.'

'Good. I like staff to be happy. I'm not certain...' He paused then, 'My sister Jenni will be returning to New York in a couple of weeks. She also has shares in one of the stores there. I've decided to stay on here, at least for the foreseeable future. We have to make this place pay and quickly. Stores like this can sink or swim in the blink of an eye. My uncle wanted to open a store here, because he loved London and England – he said the English had more class. I don't want to let him down, Miss Ross.'

'I'm sure you can make it work, sir,' Sally said, meeting his look honestly. 'Some of the stock is probably more suited to Knightsbridge – especially in the men's department. Only a few men can afford to pay the prices you're charging, most working men wouldn't dream of paying so much.' The suits were a bit flashy for English taste and didn't have that quiet look of elegance that British men preferred.

'I didn't want the store to be a bargain basement...' he said, 'but perhaps the suits are a bit too pricey...'

'There is a middle ground...' Sally suggested.

'I suppose there must be,' he said but looked doubtful. 'We've always stuck to the best and that's how my uncle made his fortune. However, neither of us knew London as well as we thought...' He was silent again and Sally wondered what more he wanted to say. Then he nodded to himself and brought his gaze back to her. 'I need to speak with Jenni and then I may want to talk to you again, Miss Ross. My sister has worked in the stores longer than I have and I need to consult her...' He smiled at her and Sally's heart missed a beat. 'Thank you for listening and for your advice – but you must be anxious to get off...'

Sally could have told him she had nowhere she wanted to go but kept the information to herself. She went back down to fetch her coat and found Mrs Craven about to leave for the night.

'I waited for you,' she said. 'You're not in trouble?'

'No – he wanted to talk that's all. I think he's realised that some mistakes were made with the stock. His sister does the buying and she's used to stocking the best for their exclusive stores in New York. He's going to talk to her and then we may see changes...'

'As long as you haven't been unfairly dismissed,' Mrs Craven said. 'I'll get off then. I'm meeting friends for some supper this evening. They are two spinster ladies that lodge with me at the boarding house, Minnie and Mildred; it's Minnie's birthday – and they made me a beautiful tablecloth for mine...'

'How lovely,' Sally said and envied her. 'Have a good evening. I'll see you tomorrow...'

They parted outside the shop. Sally decided to catch the bus home. She would see if Mick was around and ask him for news of Sylvia...

15

Rachel had arranged the meal out in a quiet restaurant as a treat for Minnie and Mildred, of whom she felt protective. Minnie was a particularly sweet lady with a lovely gentle nature and it was for her that Rachel had purchased the hat Miss Hart had accused Sally Ross of damaging. It was Minnie's forty-eighth birthday and she had never been taken out for a meal to a restaurant in her life.

The dining room was lit by shaded lamps that shed a soft light over the pretty tables. Each of them had red cloths and a tiny arrangement of a carnation and a sprig of fern. The cutlery was spotlessly clean and the glasses polished so that they sparkled in the light. When Rachel's beloved husband had been well, it had been their favourite place to come for celebrations.

Minnie was actually trembling with excitement as the head waiter led them to a secluded table in a corner by the window. It was one of the nicest and Rachel had asked for it specially. The waiter beamed at Rachel.

'Madam, how wonderful to see you again,' he said, and for a moment sympathy was in his eyes, though he was tactful enough not to mention her bereavement. 'I was hoping that we had not lost you for good...'

'I brought my friends, Miss Minnie and Miss Mildred – it is Miss Minnie's birthday, Mr Henry.'

'Twenty-one years young,' he responded gallantly and bowed over her hand, making her giggle and blush like a young girl. 'How delightful – a birthday dinner. I shall ask chef to make sure everything is perfect for my three favourite ladies.'

'Minnie, he was flirting with you,' Mildred said and frowned in disapproval, but Rachel smiled.

'Mr Henry is always charming,' she said. 'My husband brought me here often and the food was always good.'

'It must be expensive,' Minnie said, in awe of her surroundings. 'You already gave me that beautiful hat, Rachel dear...'

'I like coming here too,' Rachel assured her. 'I am earning a good wage now, more than they're refusing to give those poor miners, and I wanted to celebrate with my friends.'

'You should have a nice gentleman friend to take you out,' Minnie said, looking at her with warmth and kindness. 'You're far too attractive to spend the rest of your life alone.'

'Minnie – you should not make personal remarks...' her sister reprimanded, but Rachel just laughed and shook her head.

'If I fell in love again I might marry, because I knew what it was to be truly happy, but I haven't met anyone I feel remotely that way about,' she said. 'I don't see why I shouldn't go out sometimes and have a little pleasure – and I'm looking forward to sharing my evening with both of you.'

Mr Henry had returned with a bottle of wine on ice, which he placed at their table with a flourish. 'Compliments of the management,' he said and beamed at them. 'We are so happy to have Mrs Craven and her friends with us this evening.'

The menus were produced and everyone chose from the extensive list. Minnie had roast chicken, Mildred chose plaice done in a white wine sauce and Rachel asked for a steak, medium rare, accompanied by French fries, mushrooms and a salad. For starters, the sisters had fruit juice and Rachel had smoked salmon mousse, which had always been her favourite.

She had wondered if it might make her feel sad to come here without her husband, but she found that the serenity and warmth of the place, combined with Mr Henry's charm and the sisters' chatter, made her happy. It seemed that at last she'd found a way to put the hell of the last months of that terrible illness to a far corner of her mind, where it was no longer as powerful.

Minnie tasted her wine and giggled as the bubbles went up her nose. It wasn't champagne, but a pleasant sparkling rosé that she discovered she liked.

'Whatever Papa would say, I don't know,' Mildred said, tasting hers suspiciously. However, as the meal progressed, she finished one glass and allowed Mr Henry to pour her a little more. Minnie had two glasses and was perhaps a little tipsy when she finished her coffee cream gateau at the end. Mr Henry then produced a pot of coffee and the meal finished with little mint creams covered in chocolate.

'That was the nicest meal I've ever had,' Minnie said when they had done. 'I don't know how to thank you enough, Rachel dear.'

'It was my pleasure,' Rachel said. She stood up and Mr Henry came hurrying over to help them on with their coats. She smiled and thanked him. His special attention had made them all feel welcome and the food had been excellent.

'Do not stay away so long next time, madam,' Mr Henry said and she felt warmed by the smile he gave her. 'And you must bring your ladies again...'

Rachel assured him she would and they all left. The evening air was cool after the warmth of the restaurant, but they soon caught a bus that took them back to Mrs Malone's lodging house.

'That was the best night of my life,' Minnie whispered as she kissed Rachel's cheek. 'You're a lovely lady and I'm glad you're my friend...'

'It was very kind of you, Rachel,' Mildred said. 'I too, enjoyed the evening.'

Rachel's eyes were a little moist as she kissed Minnie's cheek and then her sister's and wished them goodnight. She went into her room, feeling more relaxed than she had for some time. For a long while after her husband's death, she'd felt as if her life was over, but the new job at Harpers and the friends she'd made here had brought her back to life.

She was thinking about what Minnie had said as she prepared for bed. Rachel was still young enough to marry again but knew she would have to really love a man before she could marry him. She wasn't ready to consider it yet, because she was still grieving. She'd been lucky when she was given the job at Harpers because it meant she could live comfortably with the occasional luxury like that evening's meal.

Rachel had neglected her friends after Paul's death, refusing invitations to dine at their homes, her grief making her solitary, but she was ready now to resume the life she'd known. Mr Henry had been sympathetic but tactful enough not to mention Paul's death, which made Rachel feel better. One of the worst things about losing someone you loved was all the well-meaning people who kept saying how sorry they were. She would write a little note to two of her closest friends, asking if she might call on a Sunday. Now that she'd made a start, she could invite other friends to the restaurant she liked so much...

* * *

Sally paused outside the public house where Mick worked as the manager. She didn't want to go in, because she knew that a young woman alone in a pub drew comments that ranged from impertinent to rude. Sally was about to turn away when Mick came out to her.

'Was it me you were lookin' for?' he asked with a warm smile.

'Yes...' Sally glanced over her shoulder. 'I wanted to ask about Sylvia – is she all right?'

'Your foolish friend is recovering well,' Mick told her with a slight frown. 'The divil's own work I've had to make her stay in bed, but she's on the mend now. I dare say she'll be back in a day or so...'

'Oh, thank goodness!' Sally was relieved. 'I've been worrying about her.'

'I'd have told you if there was anythin' to worry you,' he said, and his eyes seemed to caress her. 'I could take you to see her, but I'm on nights all this week and you're working every day.

'I get Monday afternoon off,' Sally said, 'but she may be back by then. Tell her to be careful of Jean – she thinks she knows everythin' but she's only guessing.'

Mick nodded, his eyes narrowed. 'I doubt your friend will stay long at the hostel. She told me she was going back home for a while – she comes from Cambridgeshire, so she says.'

'Sylvia isn't London born.' Sally took a deep breath. 'I haven't thanked you properly for what you did for us...'

'I did it for you,' he said and his grin took her breath away. 'Sure, you don't know it yet, Sally lass, but you're special to me...'

'I'm not that grateful,' Sally snapped and he laughed, seeming delighted with her spurt of temper. 'You've been a good friend, but I'm not going out with you.'

'Now did I say you were? When I'm after askin', you'll know.'

His mockery made her glare at him. She turned on her heel and stormed off. She glanced back and saw he was still watching her, laughing at her outrage. Sally was tempted to make a rude face at him, but it would only make him laugh more, so she raised her head and went into the hostel without giving him the satisfaction. He was a devil and didn't deserve she should speak to him – and yet he'd saved Sylvia and her from endless trouble, because the law was very strict about abortions.

Going up to her lonely room, Sally calmed down. Mick had

only been teasing her and she shouldn't let him make her so angry, because she knew it amused him. She was smiling when she locked the door behind her. For a while she'd been worried that Sylvia might die, but Bridget had sorted her out and Mick had taken care of the rest. He was a good friend – perhaps the only person in the world she could rely on...

* * *

Beth told her aunt the good news when she got home. 'The store did well the first week or so,' she said. 'Mr Harper was pleased and he's giving us a bonus system...'

'Well, that's a blessing, I suppose,' her aunt said. 'I've copied the pattern for your work dress and bought some material from the market. I don't think that floor supervisor will know the difference, but it cost half the price they wanted to charge you for a second uniform.'

'Oh, thank you, that is very kind of you,' Beth said, because it meant she could afford a second work dress now rather than waiting. 'Is there anything I can do to help you?'

'Just do your normal chores,' her aunt said, nodding. 'I wasn't sure it would work out when I first took you in, Beth – but you've settled in nicely, found work for yourself and the money you bring in pays the coal and electric. We're lucky to have the electric. A lot of houses in London are still on the gas. I prefer electric for working at night.'

A little smile touched her mouth and Beth nodded. Sometimes her aunt seemed to be thawing towards her, beginning to appreciate her and be pleased with her company.

'Do you need to work every night?' Beth asked doubtfully. 'I thought perhaps we might go to a concert together one night... or to a play, if you'd rather...'

'A concert?' Her aunt stared at her oddly. 'I used to like music. I played the piano as a girl. My teacher said I might be good enough to go on the stage, but then Mother died and

Father sold the piano. He couldn't bear to hear me play, because it reminded him of her – and I started to sew clothes for others…'

Beth hadn't known of her aunt's lost dreams. It made her realise how sterile and empty her aunt's life must have been for years. It wasn't any wonder she'd resented her prettier sister. Beth wanted to show sympathy but guessed it would not be appreciated; Aunt Helen had put the past firmly behind her.

'So you enjoy music then?' Beth asked.

'I do – I'd like to go to a concert with you, Beth. If you book our seats, I'll pay my half.'

'Yes, we'll go on your birthday – and I'll pay for the tickets.'

Aunt Helen looked at her sharply. 'You can't afford that out of your wage, girl.'

'I'm getting five shillings' bonus this week,' Beth said. 'My sales have been really good these past two days and I've earned the weekly bonus.'

Aunt Helen hesitated and Beth knew she was considering whether to ask for her half of the extra, but she decided against it.

'Very well, you may spend the money on a birthday treat we shall both enjoy.'

Beth thanked her and tried not to feel slightly resentful that her aunt seemed to think that any increase in wages was half hers.

Going into the kitchen, Beth set about cleaning the cooker and the sink before washing the floor. When it was all neat as a new pin, she went up to her room and prepared her clothes for the morning. The dress she wore for work each day had to be sponged and pressed to keep it looking fresh and clean. When she had a second dress, she could wash this one, but for now sponging and pressing would have to do.

Beth sighed but knew she was lucky. Aunt Helen wanted her own way in most things, but Beth was still able to afford the things she needed every day. She would have preferred to spend what little she had over on a pretty dress, but she did need a second for work and Aunt Helen had saved her at least ten shillings. She knew Miss Hart would not be able to tell the difference once she put on the lace collar that all the girls wore with their neat black dresses.

As she slipped into bed at last, Beth was feeling tired but content. It had been a long, busy day. Sally had spoken out for all of them, because their departments all needed more stock. After two weeks of busy trading, much of the best had gone. Beth was happy with the scarves that had been chosen for her counter, but she knew that some of the men were grumbling because she'd spoken to Fred Burrows as she was leaving that evening and he'd told her there was discontent on the men's floor.

'Too bleedin' dear, them fancy suits are,' he'd said. 'Especially, them smart frock coats with the astrakhan collars. Pardon me language, miss, but I've 'ad it in me ear all week. They get the customers, but the stuff ain't movin', and it ain't likely to if yer ask me, and they don't reckon that's fair to them, 'cos they never get a bonus.'

'Oh dear, that is a shame – and it's too soon for a sale,' Beth had said.

'Ah, well, they'll have to do somethin', you mark my words.'

Beth had smiled and bid him goodnight. She hadn't wanted to be late and had hurried to catch her bus. Each night, she looked round, half hoping that she would see Mark but knowing it would be wrong if he came looking for her. Mark hadn't loved Beth enough to wait for her. He'd married someone else and that meant that she could never find happiness in his arms.

Sighing, she turned out her light. Aunt Helen only had the electric downstairs. Up here, they still used oil lamps. Still, most houses in the area had no electric at all. Aunt Helen kept a store of shillings for the meter and they had a good coal fire when the weather was cold.

Beth turned over in bed and closed her eyes. She fell asleep almost at once and dreamed of an ocean and a sunlit beach, though she'd only ever been to the sea a few times and it was nothing like the miles of golden sand she saw in her dreams.

As she slept, the dream changed and where the silence of the beach had been broken only by birds screeching, there was suddenly the sound of guns booming and she saw men lying everywhere, men with broken bodies and sightless eyes, their clothing stained with blood.

Waking with a shiver, she wondered where such an awful dream had come from and then remembered Fred had talked of some old soldiers he knew who had fought in foreign parts. One of them had lost a leg and another his sight, fighting in the second Boer War, which had ended eleven years earlier. She shivered, feeling cold all over. Aunt Helen had made them cheese on toast for supper so perhaps it was the cheese that had brought on the nightmare. It was something that happened to her now and then, especially if something was playing on her mind.

Beth decided to go down and make herself a pot of tea. It was almost six in the morning and she didn't think she could get back to sleep after a horrible dream like that...

16

Sally was serving a customer who was after a silver bangle the next morning. There were only a couple left and the young woman looked disappointed to be shown only two examples.

'I wanted something a little wider,' she complained. 'I'm sure you had lots more when I looked the first time.'

'We've had a run on them,' Sally said. 'I've been told that we shall have more stock soon – however, these two are much cheaper than the wider ones and they look very smart worn together. Why don't you try them on like that?'

The customer hesitated and then slipped both over her hand and held her wrist up to admire the thin bands of silver, one of which had the turquoise stones and one that was just plain.

'Yes, that is nice – and different,' she said, studying them carefully. 'The bangle was a gift for my sister...'

'She could start a little collection,' Sally said, 'and you could purchase the two for the same price as one wider bangle.'

'Yes, you are right.' The customer beamed at her. 'I shall take both. I think Amie will like them.'

Sally placed the bangles in a box and wrapped it in tissue. She sent the money off to the cashier's office and placed the box in the distinctive black and gold bag.

'These are so smart,' her customer said as she took it. 'It looks as if it might have come from a Bond Street jeweller. I think my sister will be thrilled.'

'I do hope so,' Sally replied. 'We should have new stock in quite soon – perhaps you might think of buying your sister something to match the bangles at Christmas?'

'Yes, I might,' the woman said. 'I have my eye on a couple of pieces I should like for myself too, but I'll come in again next month and see what is new...' She smiled at Sally. 'I love the way your windows here reflect things that are going on, like spring, Easter and that one with all the parcels and the birthday cake was wonderful.'

'Yes, Mr Marco is so clever,' Beth said. 'I loved that one too...'

The sound of a ping told Sally that her change was back and she removed it from the container and counted it into her customer's hand. The woman nodded, smiled, bid her good morning and left. It was only then that Sally became aware of the very smart young woman watching her, her dark-eyed gaze narrowed and thoughtful.

'I'm sorry to keep you waiting, madam.'

'No, not at all,' she replied and smiled. 'I'm not a customer and I enjoyed watching you serve, Sally. It is Sally Ross, isn't it?'

'Yes...' Sally hesitated and then, 'You're Miss Harper. Mr Harper's sister...'

'Yes, I am.' Jenni Harper advanced, her hand held out. Sally took it and they shook hands. 'I've very pleased to meet you and now that I've seen you in action, I think my brother was right.'

Sally wrinkled her brow, uncertain what Miss Harper meant. 'I'm sorry. I'm not sure what you mean...'

Jenni Harper laughed. 'No, I'm sure you're not, Miss Ross, for I know my brother and he would not have said much before consulting me. He is five years younger than me and I have more experience with the stock – but I understand from Ben that you and some of the staff have strong opinions on my choices?'

'I hope I haven't offended you, Miss Harper,' Sally said and glanced at her supervisor, who was serving a customer with hats. 'It was just that we need more of certain pieces of stock – and the men's department find the expensive suits unsuitable for conservative British pockets.'

'You mean they don't want to pay for a good suit,' Jenni said, nodding. 'Yes, I do see that, Miss Ross. I hadn't been to this end of Oxford Street when I helped my uncle buy that stock. I've sourced some good-quality merchandise here in England for our New York stores and I thought it would sell here. Back home, we sell to men who want the best and they are willing to pay our prices for good styling and quality cloth. I've spoken to the supervisor of the men's department and I've sourced a lower-priced range for them. I've decided I'll have the very expensive suits shipped back to New York and we'll feature them in our winter sale.'

'That is a good option,' Sally said, smiling easily now. Apart from a slight accent, there was nothing to show that Miss Harper was American, but she was clearly friendly and outgoing. 'We have the chance to sell the less-expensive stock here and the bulk of the sales are sure to be a middle range. Good sporting jackets and slacks could be a strong seller for the summer, I think.'

'Do you speak from experience?' the older woman seemed really interested and Sally blushed.

'I worked in Selfridges for a few months. I knew one of the staff from the men's department and he told me that was their strongest seller. British men tend to buy a suit that lasts them for years and more often wear a jacket and slacks – unless they have to have a suit for work. That's why the lower-priced range is best, because who wants to spend the earth on a suit for office work?'

'Clear thinking,' Jenni said. 'A good suit is a sign of affluence at home and men like to look as if they've got to the top.'

'Yes, I'm sure those that can afford it do here, too,' Sally agreed. 'But they visit Knightsbridge or one of the specialist tailors to have them made to measure – and they go for something quieter, more subtle.'

Jenni nodded as if she agreed, then, 'My uncle should have done his homework before he bought, shouldn't he? What other mistakes have we made between us?' She really wanted to know and wasn't angry or indignant because she'd been told of possible errors.

'I thought some of the skin bags would never sell,' Sally told her. 'However, I have managed to sell two for special gifts – but I think the lower-priced bags go more quickly, so we will need larger numbers of those. We still have sufficient in stock, but I think we'll need more in a month or so.'

'Good, that is exactly the information I need,' Jenni said. 'My brother has some ideas he wants to put to you, Miss Ross. Will you come to supper with us this evening? It will be a quiet meal in a quaint little pub by the river, so you need not dress for the occasion.'

Sally's nerve endings tingled with excitement. She'd thought Mr Harper would forget all about her after their brief interview, but it seemed he had consulted his sister about her. Now she couldn't wait to discover what the brother and sister meant to suggest...

'Is everything all right, Miss Ross?'

Mrs Craven had served her customer and now she approached, looking a little uncertain.

'Mrs Craven?' Jenni Harper offered her hand. 'I am Mr Harper's sister and the buyer for this store – for the present anyway. My uncle helped and it is too big a job for one, so we'll be delegating in future. I've been consulting Miss Ross and what she has to say is interesting. I should like to hear what you have to say about the rest of the stock...'

'I am pleased to meet you, Miss Harper,' Mrs Craven said and smiled. 'I was concerned – Miss Ross isn't in trouble?'

'Far from it,' Jenni said and smiled at Sally. 'I think you'll find she is to be offered a promotion. Now, tell me, how do you feel about the millinery and the scarves?'

Mrs Craven walked off with their visitor and Sally turned to a new customer, feeling a tingle of excitement but not quite believing she'd heard right. Did Miss Harper really mean they were thinking of giving her a better job?

Pulling her thoughts together, she concentrated on her customer, a young woman wanting a leather bag. Sally showed her several and she finished up buying a tan leather bag with a flap and a plain brass clasp. She then asked to see some silver earrings and bought those too, which meant by the time she'd been served and gone, Jenni Harper had left the department and Sally realised she hadn't given her an answer about having supper with them that evening.

However, Mrs Craven came up to her a few minutes later and told her that Miss Harper would call for her at closing time. 'You're to go up to the office and she will be waiting for you and she says she won't be changing for the evening, so you're not to bother.'

Sally would have liked to go home and change, but perhaps it didn't matter. She was after all just an employee and it was a business meeting rather than an invitation to dine.

'It seems that you may be leaving us soon,' Mrs Craven said. 'I shall be sorry about that, Miss Ross – but if it means a better job for you, then I am, of course, pleased for you.'

'What kind of a job?' Sally asked, not sure whether to be nervous or excited. 'Did she say anything?'

'Miss Harper did not explain, but she said that she must spend most of her time in New York. It is therefore her intention to stay here a little longer and train you to do whatever it is they need you to do... All very mysterious.'

'Miss Harper buys for the New York stores. She asked me my opinion of the stock and I told her honestly – but I have no idea where to source what the shop needs. I'm just a sales assistant.'

'Well, she didn't say she wished you to do the buying,' Mrs

Craven said. 'If you feel the work offered is beyond you, you can always turn it down.'

Sally nodded. Her stomach was fluttering with nerves and she felt on edge. Perhaps she ought to have kept her opinions to herself. She'd always been outspoken and now she'd got herself in too deep!

* * *

Sally bought a new lace collar so that it was clean. She washed her hands and face in the staff cloakroom and used a tiny drop of lavender water behind her ears. It was forbidden for work, but surely in the evening she was allowed to wear perfume if she chose?

Miss Harper opened the office door immediately Sally knocked. She had her smart coat on and carried a large leather bag and a sheaf of files, smiling as she saw Sally. Now that she was less nervous, Sally had time to notice the difference in her style. English women tended to go for prettier, softer styles that were feminine as well as stylish. Miss Harper's clothes had a sharp crispness about them that gave her a style all her own.

'Good, you are prompt and I have a car waiting. My brother will join us after his meeting finishes, but it will give me a chance to go through certain things before he arrives.'

'Are you returning to America soon, Miss Harper?' Sally asked as they walked down the stairs together.

'I had planned to travel on the Titanic on its maiden voyage,' Jenni said and sighed. 'It would have been an exciting trip, but I've managed to sell my ticket to someone who desperately wanted a stateroom and I'll stay another few weeks. If you're to take over my job, you'll need help for a start…'

'Take over your job as a buyer for the store?' Sally gasped and felt her spine tingle. They had reached the front of the store and she saw an expensive car waiting at the kerbside. Its paintwork was yellow and black and it gleamed, the chauffeur dressed in sober grey sitting up front. 'Are we going in this?' She laughed. 'I've never even seen a car like it, let alone ridden in one.'

'Well, there is always a first time.' Jenni smiled. 'Don't imagine we've always been rich, Sally – I may call you Sally, I hope, and you must call me Jenni. We're going to work closely together and be friends...'

'You're taking my breath away...'

'Am I?' Jenni's eyes sparkled with mischief. 'That was rather the idea, because I know a good thing when I see it and I don't want you to refuse Ben's offer.'

'I have no experience of buying,' Sally told her truthfully. 'I spoke out, but it was just my instincts – I know nothing of sourcing merchandise...'

'You will when my brother and I have finished training you,' Jenni said. 'My uncle threw me in the deep end when I was sixteen, Sally. I was told to buy the stock for his latest store and to make sure it was good stuff and then left to get on with it – but don't worry, I shan't do that to you.'

Sally slid into the back seat of the stylish vehicle, inhaling the distinctive smell of leather and an expensive perfume.

'Oh, that is lovely perfume,' Sally exclaimed. 'So delicate and yet... intriguing...'

'Got it in one,' Jenni said. 'It was given to me by someone called Elizabeth Arden. She brought it back from Paris, where she went to learn more about cosmetics for women. She is someone you will learn to know as her products become famous. I've already bought some of her face creams for the American stores. We do not have it here yet, but I shall rely on you to let me know when the time is right. As she develops the treatments available to everyone rather than just those who use her salon, we shall be able to stock them...'

'Elizabeth Arden... is she an American?'

'No, Canadian, but she is going to open her business in

America and I'm certain it will be a huge success once she has enough products in her range.'

'It must be exciting,' Sally said and her nerves tingled, but with pleasure this time rather than apprehension. 'To discover new products and introduce them – especially beautiful perfumes and clothes...'

'Ah, so you like clothes.' Jenni nodded and smiled. 'I love fashion, but a buyer for a store like Harpers has to keep up with all kinds of products. I want to introduce more departments as we go along – cosmetics and a children's department as well as others. We'll need more staff, but we're feeling our way just now. It is hard work to buy for a store this size, Sally, and we sometimes make mistakes and then we get the blame if sales are poor. However, you have a good eye and if you learn to listen to those who have to sell the merchandise you will soon learn.'

'I'd like to try,' Sally said, even though her stomach was tying itself in knots. It would be fun to research things – and to travel. 'I suppose it means travelling to various parts of the country to see things before you order?'

'Yes – you would need to travel by train for the time being. I'll ask my brother to teach you to drive and then we'll get you a car or perhaps a van; it's always nice to bring some new stock back if you can...'

The car had driven them smoothly through the dusk towards the river. Sally looked out at the old-fashioned inn and was immediately enchanted. A gas lamp hissed in the yard out front and she could hear horses in the stables at the back.

Inside, the ceilings were low with smoke-blackened beams and the tables were from another century and polished oak. Harding's was an old, well-established firm, the building going back to the seventeenth century. Small oil lamps on the tables gave it an intimate feel and there was a wonderful display of flowers in an inglenook fireplace.

'I adore places like this,' Jenni said as the waiter came to show them to their seats and handed them menus and a wine list. 'It's Ben's favourite in London.' She looked up at the waiter. 'My brother will be joining us later, Edwin – we'll have a bottle of your finest medium white wine, chilled please.'

'Very well, Miss Harper. I know you like the best...' He smiled at her and went away.

'It's chilly this evening,' Jenni said and shivered. 'It's April and I thought it might be a bit warmer by now. New York can be bitter in the winter, but when it's warm there, it's warm.'

Sally laughed. 'Our spring and summers get all mixed up. Even in June you will still get cool evenings sometimes.'

'Give me Florida or California,' Jenni said. 'I usually head for the sun once I've got the stock sorted for the winter. I don't think I'd want to live over here – but Ben says he likes it and if the store goes well, I think he may make London his home.' Sally caught a twang in her voice then and she sounded more American, but it wasn't there all the time.

'It's a shame that you had to miss your chance to travel on the Titanic,' Sally said. 'I was reading all about it – they say it's wonderful and has all the luxuries you could think of aboard ship...'

'Well, there will be another time.' Jenni laughed. 'I couldn't just throw you to the sharks, Sally. Ben seemed to think you could manage, but I've promised to stay until sometime in May. I'll help you meet your first suppliers and tell you how to get a better price out of them. They always start at least twenty per cent above their bottom line.'

Sally looked up as the waiter approached. He poured them a glass of wine each and she took a sip. It was crisp and clean and she liked the taste, which she thought a little fruity. 'Thank you, very nice.'

'Do you appreciate wine?' Jenni asked her.

'I rarely drink it,' Sally admitted. 'If I have a drink, which is only for special occasions, I normally have a sherry or a port and lemon.'

'Yes, I've heard that a lot over here,' Jenni said. 'My aunt always drinks champagne, but she was brought up with money. My uncle made his by working his guts out – and my parents had a small hardware store in a one-horse town. They both died of a fever. Aunt Ella asked me to stay with her after our parents died and my uncle sent Ben to college. I started work in the store. I had three weeks working on the counters and then he told me I was the buyer and to get on with it. All I had was a list of names and a store to fill.'

Sally looked at her in awe. 'That must have been frightening?'

'I was scared to death at first – but I bluffed my way through and I was lucky enough to find a new dress designer at the launch of his business. His collection sold out in weeks and that gave me confidence. I've gone for new designers, new suppliers, as often as I can, and several of them have been winners. I had one total failure, but that was because he cut the quality on his range after I'd bought it – I didn't take his next collection and no one else did either.'

Sally understood then that buyers could be influential to the prosperity of small businesses and felt the responsibility of making those kinds of decisions.

'For a start, either my brother or I will be at your shoulder and you'll need our approval before you place the order,' Jenni told her. 'You won't be dealing with the men's department or anything on the lower floor. Mr Stockbridge and Ben will see to most of that... so it's jewellery, bags, scarves, gloves and fashion. I think you should be able to manage that easily. You have common sense and a good eye, I don't think it will take you long to pick it up, Sally. I have every confidence in you.'

Sally didn't say anything, because this all seemed too good to be true. Why should Jenni and her brother trust her to buy for the store? She had no experience whatsoever and her casual advice had been meant only as a guide in response to his asking questions. Surely this was a dream and any minute she would wake up!

'What are you thinking?' Jenni asked.

'Only that it is a big responsibility.'

'I told you, I had no one to help me. You will have us...' Jenni's bright eyes seemed to challenge her, setting her on her mettle.

'Well, if you think I can do it...' Sally was doubtful, but just then Mr Harper entered the room and her eyes were drawn to him. He was dressed in a very smart suit that she thought must be bespoke and Savile Row, and looked clean-cut and hand-some. For a moment, her heart raced as she saw his smile and then he was at their table.

'Miss Ross,' he said and offered his hand as she stood. 'Jenni – I'm sorry to keep you waiting. Have you ordered?'

'No, we waited for you,' Jenni said. 'I should like the salmon and asparagus in aspic followed by Dover sole and sautéed pota-toes with peas...'

'Miss Ross?' he asked with a lift of a fine brow.

'Could I have the same please?'

'Of course – and I think I'll have a steak and chips with mushrooms...'

The waiter was summoned to take his order and a glass was brought for him to share the wine.

'So, Miss Ross,' Ben Harper asked, his eyes bright with antic-ipation. 'Jenni has told you of our idea for you to take over the buying for the London store – jewellery, bags, fashion; all the things you women adore?'

'Yes – but I don't know why you thought I was suitable,' Sally said honestly. 'I gave you my opinions based on what I'd seen, but I know nothing about buying.'

'Jenni knew less when my uncle gave her the job,' he said cheerfully. 'Besides, she will show you the ropes before she leaves London – and I'll still be around. Mr Stockbridge and Marco are good at what they do and they will buy for the other departments until we find the right men for the job – though your opinions will be valued if you feel they're going wrong...'

He grinned at her and her heart took an odd leap. 'Whenever you want to try a new supplier, you convince me or Jenni first. That way, I carry the can if things go wrong.'

'I should like to try,' Sally said. 'I know I have a lot to learn – but it should be exciting.'

'It's hard work too,' Jenni said. 'I'll be in touch when I can, but don't expect another visit for at least four to six months after I leave...'

'Jenni has two stores to stock in New York,' Ben Harper said, looking at her fondly. 'She is the best sister in the world, Miss Ross – and I know she gave up the voyage of a lifetime to do this for me.'

'Yes, you owe me,' Jenni said and threw him a look that spoke volumes. 'I'll think of a way for you to make it up to me, little brother.'

Sally laughed at the banter between them. They were both vibrant, dynamic people and she'd never met anyone quite like them. Both were attractive and made their clothes, rather than the other way round. Sally had never been part of a family and the warm teasing that went on between them made her feel good. They were warm people, she sensed that both were shrewd when it came to business – but Jenni was firmly on her brother's side. She wanted Harpers of London to be a success and so she was willing to give up a maiden voyage on the wonderful new White Star liner.

'Well,' Ben said as their salmon was brought. 'So you've accepted the position, Miss Ross, and was the salary acceptable to you?'

'I don't think it was mentioned,' Jenni said. 'We thought twenty pounds a month to begin – and if the store flourishes we will double that in six months' time...'

'Twenty pounds a month...' Sally swallowed hard. She wasn't sure she'd heard correctly, because it was far more than she'd ever earned in her life. 'That is quite a lot...'

'Not for a buyer,' Jenni told her. 'I make a hundred and fifty dollars a month now and I'm thinking of pushing for a raise. It's a huge responsibility and you will earn your money, Sally. You will be responsible for sourcing new goods, getting stock to the store, pricing and making sure that the newest lines get prominent positions in the windows. It means longer hours, Sally. The extra wage will be earned, I promise you...'

'Yes, I'll want your opinion on the window displays too,' Ben Harper told her seriously. 'I think some of the windows we've had could do with improvement. Jenni rearranged one herself the minute she got here... Marco has flair, but he needs new ideas, as we all do.'

Sally came back down to earth. She would have to put in lots of extra hours to get on top of a job like that – but it was just what she needed. She'd spent hours just wandering at night, not wanting to go back to the dump she lived in, but now she would be able to stay in her office until later... and she could look for somewhere better to live.

'I might look for a room nearer the store,' she said. 'I don't mind working after hours. I've nothing to go home for...'

'Don't you have a family – or a boyfriend?' Jenni looked sympathetic.

'No, I was brought up in an orphanage,' Sally said. They could have got that from her records if they'd looked it up; they probably knew it already but wanted to hear her story. 'I have no one of my own.'

'Well, you do now,' Jenni said. 'I want us to be like family, Sally. If you feel passionately about the store, you will do your best and that's all any of us can do...'

Sally nodded. She was enjoying her meal, she'd never tasted anything quite like the salmon before this night and the Dover sole just seemed to melt in her mouth. The rest of the evening rushed by and before she knew it, Ben Harper had driven her back to the hostel and was bidding her goodnight.

'I'm glad you're with us, Sally – really on my side.' He got out and opened the door for her, giving her his hand to help her out.

His eyes went disparagingly over the hostel. 'No wonder you want to move – I'll see what I can find closer to the store. You can afford something decent now.'

Sally thanked him. It was only when she was inside her own room that she realised Mr Harper had called her Sally and held her hand a second more than he needed to.

A little frown touched her brow because she'd learned to be cautious where men were concerned and she knew it wouldn't do to admire her employer too much. Jenni was straightforward and meant it when she said she wanted them to be friends – but was it ever possible for a woman to be friends with a man? Sally knew it would be easy to lose her head over someone like Mr Harper.

Something drew her to her window and she looked down into the lane. Mr Harper's car had gone but Mick was standing outside the pub, looking up at her window. With the light behind her, he could see her and she drew back, letting the net curtain fall back into place and drawing the heavy cotton ones behind it. Mick had obviously seen her arrive. Was he thinking she'd been out with her fancy man?

Sally waved and decided that she would tell him about her new job the next time she saw him. She didn't want Mick to get the wrong idea. Sally might like being given a special meal out and offered a job with a much better wage, but she wasn't daft enough to lose her head over a man the way Sylvia had, even out of gratitude...

17

'How did things go?' Mrs Craven asked Sally when she entered the department the next morning. 'Did you take the new position? I really hope so, because I think it will suit you, though I should not wish for the responsibility. At my age, I couldn't stand the extra hours...'

Sally smiled. Mrs Craven was making a joke to let Sally know she didn't resent her getting the promotion.

'Yes. I've just come in to sign off my stock book and then I'm going upstairs to Miss Harper's office.'

'She's not going straight back then?'

'Miss Harper considers it more important that I should learn from her,' Sally said. 'She has done it as a favour to her brother – but it was because I spoke out the way I did about the jewellery and things. I just hope I don't let them both down.'

'You won't do that, Miss Ross.' Mrs Craven smiled. 'I shall miss you. I don't know if they will replace you in the department...'

'Jenni said she would speak to you about that,' Sally hesitated, then, 'I think Maggie could take over Beth's counter and you could take over my counter...'

'And leave the hats to Miss Grey?' Mrs Craven nodded

thoughtfully. 'Yes, that is what I have been thinking, Miss Ross – your counter is the one that needs the most experience and Miss Gibbs is more confident now.'

'We don't really need a junior if we keep our own counters tidy, except perhaps on Saturday...' Sally stopped and blushed. 'I'm sorry. I'm not trying to tell you how to run the department, Mrs Craven. It sounds as if I'm getting too big for my boots, but really I'm not.'

'Not at all, Miss Ross,' she said. 'I have thought there could be more efficiency in the whole store and I shall tell Mr Harper of our ideas. After all, it isn't just sales that make a store a success; if money is wasted it will fail anyway.'

Sally nodded. 'I am going to find somewhere better to live – perhaps a small apartment. I'd like to share but...' She left the words unsaid because it seemed like cheek to ask her supervisor if she would like to share with her.

'You are wondering if we might share a flat?' Mrs Craven hesitated and then nodded. 'I think it might work now that you have been promoted. I have considered it for myself, but an apartment for just one is expensive... we might visit a few together and see how we feel...'

Sally felt a rush of pleasure. 'I'd love that,' she said eagerly. 'Thank you for considering it, Mrs Craven.'

'At work it must continue to be Mrs Craven and Miss Ross, but in private you could call me Rachel if you wish.'

'Thank you, yes, I shall,' Sally told her, glowing. 'I can't believe I've been so lucky...'

'No, I think you have the potential,' Rachel said seriously. 'I knew from the first that you were different. You will do well – and I wish you all the luck in the world.'

'I shall visit the departments regularly,' Sally said. 'It's why Jenni gave me the job, because she can't be here all the time and she says a buyer needs to know all the merchandise, what is selling and what is not...'

'Yes, she is right; I believe it's the only way,' Rachel said.

'You'd best get off then and I'll tell Miss Grey and Miss Gibbs of their new positions...'

Sally left the department and went to the lift to take her to the office on the top floor, but just as she approached, it opened and Mr Harper walked out with a beautiful red-haired woman on his arm. He was smiling at her, and she was gazing into his eyes – neither of them noticed Sally.

'You're a wonderful guy, Ben Harper,' the woman gushed. 'You've made my trip to London so great, I can't tell you...'

'It was my privilege, Selina,' he murmured. 'I have enjoyed being with you...'

He'd had a blonde on his arm on opening day and now a redhead! Mr Harper obviously liked to play the field.

Sally laughed inwardly. She'd been thinking he might be interested in her, but now she knew it was highly unlikely. The woman with him looked rich, was obviously American and laughed a lot in a loud way.

It was strange that she looked so out of place in the store where Mr Harper and his sister seemed to blend in. Yes, they had slight accents and some of the words they used were pronounced differently, but they were neither brash nor arrogant and the gulf between them and this woman struck Sally immediately. She smiled at herself as she went on into the lift. That would teach her not to get ideas above her station!

* * *

'I think it's wonderful that you've been given the job,' Beth said and smiled warmly at Sally as she went to wish her well during her tea break. 'We shall all miss you and hope to see you sometimes.'

'I'll be around,' Sally said. 'You three are still my friends and I want to keep in touch. At least I shan't have to worry about Miss Hart picking on me after this promotion. I'm actually above her in the scale now. Just be careful she doesn't pick on you and Maggie instead.'

'She won't like you being above her,' Beth warned. 'I'd still be careful of her, if I were you, Sally.'

'She doesn't worry me,' Sally said. 'Maybe we'll have a little get-together one day. I'm going to find a small flat and you could visit on a Sunday for tea.'

'Oh yes, I'd love that, if I could manage to get away,' Beth said. 'I wish you lots of luck and I'll miss you.' Leaving Sally to her new job, Beth returned to the department.

Beth felt a little strange to see Maggie at her counter, but like Sally she believed that the younger girl was capable of managing it alone. She herself was happy to have the hats, because some of them were so beautiful it was a joy to handle them.

She served her first customer at a little after nine and sold two sensible felt hats – a brown with a feather and a grey with a smart bow at the back. The customer had asked her to model the grey one so that she could see the back and had been pleased with the effect.

'You can't really see it on yourself, even with the mirrors,' she'd told Beth. 'I'm starting a new job and I want to look smart but not fussy – and those hats are just right.'

After she'd left, Beth saw that Maggie was selling a scarf and Mrs Craven was wrapping a leather bag. She decided to update her stock book and then went to the little room at the back and brought out two new felt hats, neither of which had been on display before, adding them to the list.

It was an hour before she had another customer, although both Maggie and Mrs Craven were busy. Beth rearranged some hats in the counter and sighed, wondering how Sally was getting on in her new job. She'd made it sound both nerve-wracking and exciting and Beth envied her a little. It must be exciting to take on such a challenging job, though, on reflection, Beth didn't really wish to be in Sally's shoes.

At eleven o'clock, she had three customers on the trot and then Mrs Craven told her to take an early lunch. 'Two of us need to be in the department all the time, which means that Miss Gibbs will take her time off next and me last. I'm sorry I cannot let you go together, but one isn't enough to run this department.'

'No, that would be awkward, customers might be waiting for a while,' Beth agreed. She'd thought four of them excessive for a department of this size, but less staff might make things difficult during holiday times or when someone was ill.

'I shall have to talk to Mr Stockbridge about relief staff,' Mrs Craven said. 'We don't always need a junior, but if you were ill or I perhaps, it could make things difficult.'

Beth agreed and left to have her lunch. She'd brought a cheese sandwich and some rock buns and thought she would go down to the basement and have a word with Fred. He would make a pot of tea and share it with her and she would give him a couple of her rock buns. Beth found it pleasant to sit and talk to Fred about his life and his family rather than go out to a busy café where she hardly got time to eat before she had to get back to the store.

His face lit up with a big smile when he saw her and he immediately put the kettle on. Fred had his own sandwiches, but he didn't say no when she offered him the rock buns and she noticed that he ate one immediately with his first mug of tea.

'How are things with you today, Fred?'

'I've been rushed off me feet,' he said. 'I had a load of new stock for the men's department. I've been up there three times – and I've brought some of those fancy suits back down.'

'What will happen to them?' Beth asked, curious now.

'I think Miss Harper is shipping them back to the States, leastwise that's what she told me. She's leaving the rest, but these are special and she says they will sell like hot cakes where she comes from.'

'They must be richer in New York than we are.'

'Right, I reckon some of 'em are drownin' in it,' Fred said and cackled with laughter. 'That's why my eldest boy is off to the States shortly...' He looked at her proudly. 'He's been offered a job on that fancy ship – the Titanic. Have yer heard of it, miss?'

'Yes, I have,' Beth said and smiled at his obvious pride. 'What does your eldest boy do, Fred?'

'Jack is a steward with the White Star Line,' Fred said proudly. 'That's a good job. When I was his age, I was running messages until I worked my way through teaching college – I just hope we don't get any wars to mess things up.'

'Your son wouldn't leave a good job to volunteer, would he?'

'Not Jack, no, he's got a head on his shoulders. I was thinking of young Timmy – he's just seventeen and all he can think of is that he wants to be a soldier.'

'Well, that's a good job too, and we're not at war anywhere at the moment, are we?'

'No, not that I know of,' Fred admitted. 'But I've friends who fought in the Boer War and there's always a chance of a flare-up abroad somewhere – in India or one of the colonies. Tim will be off to sign for King and country as soon as he's eighteen and then I'll be on me own again...'

Beth nodded sympathetically, and for a moment she remembered having an odd dream about war, probably brought on by Fred's tales about his service. She knew that his wife had died some years back and he was often lonely because his sons had busy lives of their own. She also knew that the reason he'd been dismissed as a schoolmaster was because he'd disagreed with the governors over caning boys. Fred wouldn't have it in his school and so he'd quarrelled with an influential man and been asked to leave.

'I'll come and see you sometimes,' Beth promised. She made a mental note to ask Aunt Helen if she could have him for tea on a Sunday. Her aunt might refuse, so she wouldn't mention it yet. 'I miss my father, Fred. Did I tell you he was a doctor?'

'That you did, miss,' Fred said and smiled at her. 'You'll make some lucky man a fine wife one day – good cook you are.'

'I don't think I'll ever get married...'

'If you don't, it will be from choice – a lovely girl like you should have dozens of offers...'

Beth smiled sadly and then found herself telling him about Mark.

He shook his head over it, then muttered. 'Damned fool – begging your pardon for my language, miss, but it makes me spit. He should have looked after you instead of thinking of himself...'

Beth laughed. 'No wonder I like visiting you,' she said. 'You make me feel so much better. I have to get back to my work now. I envy your son his job on the Titanic. It must be wonderful to travel and see the world...' Beth asked him if she could see his newspaper, which was the *Evening Standard*, and turned to the page advertising concerts. 'I'm looking for a concert to take my aunt to,' she confided and he nodded. 'I think Harry Lauder should be a safe choice, don't you?'

'Depends whether your aunt prefers more classical music, or the popular songs. You could always take her to the ballet if you're not sure – most ladies like that...' Fred sighed. 'My wife would have loved to see Anna Pavlova, God bless her soul.'

'Yes, so would I,' Beth told him and smiled. 'I don't think we could afford the ballet – but a nice show with lots of singing and jokes should be all right.'

'My missus liked that as well...' He smiled at her. 'You'd best get back, miss, or we'll both be in trouble.'

Beth left him to finish his lunch and went back to her department feeling more cheerful. She would miss Sally now that she'd moved up in the world, but Fred would always be there for her.

'I'll leave you in charge of the department now,' Mrs Craven said when she went to lunch a little later that day. 'It seems so strange without Miss Ross here...'

'I wonder how she is getting on,' Beth said and sighed. She knew she was lucky to have this job, but somehow the spark seemed to have gone out of things since Sally left the department. Beth's life seemed a bit empty when she thought about going back to her aunt's house. She would do some cooking and cleaning and then go to bed ready for work the next day. Her thoughts went briefly to Fred's son, who would be sailing on the Titanic and how exciting it must be to travel in such a luxurious way...

Shaking her head, she smiled. There was no way she could afford the sort of prices those passengers must have paid...

18

Jenni handed Sally a long list of suppliers. It extended to more than two pages of neatly typed names and addresses.

'These are manufacturers and suppliers here in Britain,' she told Sally. 'I have not included the American suppliers I used. I will still do the ordering back home, but I shall rely on you to let me know what is needed and whatever mistakes I make. Don't be shy, because unless you tell me, I can't know. I feel we should source as much as we can from British suppliers...'

'The Mexican silver has gone really well,' Sally reminded her.

She felt as if she was walking through fog. Jenni had been bombarding her with information for the past hour and she was trying to keep up with everything she'd been told. One thing she had gathered was that she had the use of this office, which Jenni was sharing with her brother.

'Ben won't be here most of the time,' Jenni told her. 'Those filing drawers are for the orders and Ben often dives in to look at things, so don't expect them to be where you left them. My brother has his own system, which is to put the files down anywhere.' She smiled with a kind of fond exasperation. 'I think you may do much better with sourcing new lines over here in future, Sally. We'll visit as many of those firms I mentioned as we can before I leave for New York – but if you really need to ask me something, send me a telegram. I'll cable you by return. Mostly, you and my brother can settle things here...' She looked at Sally and grinned. 'I know I'm a pushy bitch, Sally. I'm expecting too much too soon, but I need to get home...'

'I'll catch up,' Sally said and laughed at her employer's colourful language. It certainly made her feel at ease, because Jenni treated her like an equal rather than an employee. 'I can make contact with the salespeople, either by visiting or the telephone...' She eyed the instrument dubiously. Sally had never needed to use a telephone, though Jenni had explained how to and it sounded simple enough.

'Sit down at the desk,' Jenni invited and, when Sally did so, pushed the instrument towards her. 'Now, pick up the earpiece and hold it to your ear as I showed you. The girl on the exchange will take the number and put you through.'

'Who shall I ring first?' Sally's nerves jangled for a moment.

'Why not try that jewellery manufacturer in Hatton Garden? Make an appointment for this afternoon and we'll go together, see if we can source a new line in silver jewellery.'

'Yes, I will.' Sally picked up the telephone. She spoke into the mouthpiece and gave the number she wanted. 'Good morning,' she said in a firm but polite voice as it was answered, 'I am the jewellery buyer for Harpers of London and I wish to speak to your head of sales...'

Jenni nodded encouragingly as Sally spoke. She made an appointment for two that afternoon and thanked the person on the other end, replacing the earpiece on its hook.

'Good start,' Jenni made a sign of approval. 'Now, look at number three on the list. They have representatives. Ring them and ask someone to call tomorrow.'

Sally did as she asked and then did the same with half a dozen other suppliers, who stated they had representatives who would call.

'That will do for now,' Jenni told her. 'I think we'll have sandwiches and some coffee and then get off to Hatton Garden. I'll let Miss Summers know.'

She went to the office door, called the secretary, and ordered sandwiches and coffee and her car for one o'clock.

'We could have got the underground to Hatton Garden,' Sally told her when she came back and drew up a chair at the desk.

'You will make your own arrangements next time,' Jenni said, 'but I hate the subway at home. It smells and it's dark. Give me a comfortable car with a chauffeur any time.'

Sally laughed. 'I never had that luxury until I met you, Jenni. It was a treat to go on the underground for us kids from the orphanage.'

'It's sad that you never had a family,' Jenni said, looking sympathetic. She hesitated, then, 'Do you think you will like this new job? My brother was carried away with the idea, but we did rather dump it on you.'

'It was a shock, but I'm getting used to the idea. I'll tell you more in a few days,' Sally said. 'I'm still trying to get it all straight in my head at the moment...'

'I know it's a lot to ask,' Jenni agreed. 'It took me a while to find my feet back home. I don't mind telling you that I've made a few mistakes here, Sally. I didn't buy enough of that jewellery you've been selling and I bought too many expensive suits. I thought British men looked smart and would be sure to buy at least a couple of suits a year, but I've since discovered that only the wealthy ones have more than one suit...'

'Someone once told me that even the aristocratic men buy just a few good clothes from their tailors and keep them forever,' Sally said with a smile. 'It's men in business that buy the suits, but they don't want the kind you stocked; it's normally pinstripe or good wool tweed for them, something that lasts. Your idea of buying a good suit off the peg is new here, Jenni. The thirty-shilling tailors are usually busy. Some of our stock is priced at five pounds and above, and for most ordinary men that is a fortune. Only the gangsters can afford our prices.'

'That's why I'm taking some of the more expensive suits back to New York with me when I leave,' Jenni said and glanced at her wristwatch. 'I should have been on board the ship by now.'

'Do you regret staying on for a while to help Mr Harper?'

'Yes and no.' Jenni made a wry face. 'I regret I don't get to travel in that glorious stateroom, but my brother needs my help, so the answer is no, I'm glad to help him. Maybe I'll get to travel on the Titanic another time – coming this way perhaps. It won't be quite the same as the maiden voyage, but it's still a wonderful ship.'

'Fabulous,' Sally agreed. 'I've only read about it in the paper, but I'd love to be on it.'

'I'd like to take you to New York one day,' Jenni said and laughed as she saw Sally's reaction. 'However, it's these suppliers here that we need to get sorted... Come in...' She answered the knock at the door and the secretary brought in a tray of sandwiches and a pot of coffee.

'I know you like yours black, Miss Harper, but I wasn't sure about Miss Ross – so I brought milk and sugar...'

'Thank you. I do take milk and sugar, Miss Summers.'

'Cucumber and cress and smoked salmon with cucumber,' Jenni remarked, examining the sandwiches after the secretary left. 'Eat what you wish, Sally. You'll need something inside you. We may have a battle on our hands. The first lesson in dealing with a new supplier is to refuse their first price, even if it sounds cheap. We want at least ten per cent off whatever they say...'

Sally ate some of the sandwiches and drank two cups of coffee. Jenni did the same. She was slim, but she didn't hold back when it came to eating and Sally assumed she used up a lot of nervous energy because she was never still for five minutes. Jenni didn't sit so much as perch and she was up and down all the time, throwing out her arms to express her ideas, full of energy and the joy of living. It was the first time her American birth had really showed up the differences between them, because most English women were far more reserved.

They left before one o'clock so that they would arrive on time for their appointment. It wasn't the first time Sally had been to Hatton Garden. Since leaving the orphanage, she'd used the public transport, trams, underground and buses to see as much as she could of London, but it was the first time during working hours. Passing some bullion dealers, she looked at the heavy iron bars on the window. You had to ring a bell for admittance at most of the workshops and wholesalers here.

Sally was wearing her best jacket over a smart grey skirt with a white blouse that had a lace collar. She'd wanted to make a good impression and knew she would need to spend some of her wages to buy herself better clothes. As the buyer for Harpers, she needed to look the part and wasn't restricted to a uniform like the salesgirls.

They were greeted by a man in a suit: grey pinstripe, the trousers a little shiny, his black shoes polished so hard, Sally thought he must be able to see his face in them.

'Mr Heinrick?' Jenni asked. 'I'm Miss Harper and this is our buyer, Miss Ross. She is the one who will be dealing with you in future – should we wish to stock any of your lines.'

'Miss Ross, we spoke on the telephone.' He offered his hand. 'It was good of you to phone. So many others come without an appointment and it is not always possible for me to speak to them personally.'

'We are looking for a range of good-quality silver we can sell at a reasonable price,' Sally said. 'What can you show us please?'

Jenni gave a little nod of approval but said nothing, leaving it to Sally to lead the way. Mr Heinrick took them through to the workrooms, where four men were working on handmade silver items. It was fascinating to watch the silver being worked and for a moment Sally was mesmerised, but then she saw a man engraving a bangle and approached his bench, watching as he finished his work and then began to polish the silver. He held it up for her to admire. She saw at once that it was the equal of the silver she'd been selling but more reserved in taste; some of the Mexican silver had been rather flamboyant but perhaps that was why it had sold so well.

'Lovely,' she said. 'How many of these do you make in a day?'

'Depends on the order,' he said evasively and looked at his boss.

'We could manufacture about a hundred a day if every piece was same, but we work on orders. We are a bespoke firm, Miss Ross – that is why our prices are higher than some of the other jewellers in the Garden.'

'What would the price be to us on a bangle like this?'

'Again, it depends. Individually, I should charge fifteen shillings for a bangle of this quality, but if you ordered twelve, the price could come down to eleven shillings per bangle.'

Sally examined it. She knew she needed to sell it for nine-teen shillings and sixpence if she wanted to entice the customers. 'I need ten shillings a piece if I order a dozen,' she said. 'Now, show me something with stones set in the silver please.'

Mr Heinrick wrote something on his pad and someone brought a velvet lined tray with bangles displaying various stones set into the silver. Sally noticed at once that the quality was better than the Mexican silver and nodded.

'How much for these individually, and if I took a dozen?'

'It depends...' he began and then, as Sally frowned. 'Very well, Miss Ross – to you the price for a dozen assorted semi-precious stones, including amethysts, garnets and peridot as well as turquoise, will be fifteen shillings each. If you should require sapphires or ruby with diamonds, the price rises to between thirty shillings and two pounds and that is the best offer you will get in the Garden.'

'Good.' Sally smiled. 'We shall need twelve of the plain and twelve of the bangles set with semi-precious stones in our first order...' She glanced at Jenni and saw her nod of approval. 'I'd like to see some silver brooches – with a strong design, Art Nouveau would be good. I like enamelling if you have anything to show us...'

It took nearly two hours to go through all the stock and to sort out the prices. By the time they'd finished, Mr Heinrick had an order worth nearly two hundred pounds and they had a parcel of lovely jewellery.

'You amazed me,' Jenni said when they were sitting in the car on their way back to the store. 'I would have thought you'd been buying for a store for years if I didn't know better – how did you know what to price the goods at?'

'Because I knew what they needed to be if we were to double up on the profit,' Sally told her. 'Unless we can double and still sell at the same price as the Mexican silver, we might be stuck with some of it for ages.'

'I'll have some more of that Mexican silver sent out as soon as I can,' Jenni said. 'But I'll also be placing an order with Mr Heinrick to take back with me to America – I thought the quality was better than anything I bought...'

'The Mexican silver was something different,' Sally said, beginning to feel confident, 'that's why it sold so well for a start, but we'll need variety to keep customers returning for more. I'll find a few more suppliers, but we'll see how this stock goes first...'

'Had I known you could manage so well I might have sailed with the Titanic...' Jenni looked wistful as she glanced at her wristwatch – it was platinum and diamond with a diamond-set strap and obviously expensive.

'I fear it's too late, it must have sailed by now,' Sally said. 'Anyway, I don't know anywhere near as much about women's clothing – and we have three suppliers to meet tomorrow. They all agreed to send representatives in to see us. I think it will need both of us to make the decisions over the restocking...'

'Yes,' Jenni agreed. 'That is one we need two heads on – and Ben too, if he can spare the time – although my brother has a friend visiting at the moment. Dolores is an actress, Sally, and beautiful – though my uncle would have thought her vulgar. Some folk make the mistake of thinking that all Americans are vulgar, but some of us know how to behave...'

Sally laughed as she was meant to. For a moment, she felt like pinching herself. It wasn't five minutes since she'd been serving behind the counters with Maggie and Beth, and now she was on first-name terms with her employer and being taken all over London in her expensive hired car. Her thoughts went to her friends, because she liked Beth, Maggie and Mrs Craven, and hoped she wouldn't lose touch because of her promotion...

19

Listening to her aunt laugh, Beth felt that she'd chosen the concert well. The music had been lovely, but she'd laughed at the comedian Little Tich and enjoyed the well-known singer, Vesta Tilley, though it was a melody sung by Eugene Stratton that had brought tears to her eyes.

'Well, that was a proper birthday treat,' Aunt Helen said when they left the theatre and caught a tram home. 'I don't know when I've enjoyed myself so much, Beth. Thank you.'

'I enjoyed it too,' Beth assured her. She'd been anxious to pick a show her aunt would approve and felt relieved that it had all gone so well.

'My father never approved of the music hall or the theatre in any form,' Aunt Helen said. 'When your mother first started courting, I had to go with her, because our parents insisted – and your father took us to the theatre twice. I liked it then too but I'd forgotten how much...'

She looked thoughtful as she led the way into the kitchen and put the kettle on the gas hob. Beth cut them both a piece of seed cake and they ate their supper almost in silence. Her aunt seemed lost in thought and when Beth bid her goodnight, she merely nodded and sat dreaming over the teapot, clearly lost in her memories.

Had her aunt once had dreams of love and a family? Beth would never have guessed it, but now she wondered. Her grandfather had by all accounts been very strict. Beth's mother had been allowed to marry, but Aunt Helen had stayed at home to care for her father until he died, making her living by sewing for other women. Was she ever envious when she made beautiful evening gowns for others, knowing that she would never have a chance to wear such things.

It had taken all of Beth's bonus to pay for their treat. She couldn't afford to do it again for ages, but she would save what she could and perhaps they could visit the theatre again nearer Christmas, which was ages away yet.

Turning over in bed, Beth heard her aunt come upstairs at last. She was glad that she'd had the idea of taking Aunt Helen to the theatre as a birthday gift and hoped that perhaps it would lead to a better understanding between them.

It would help if she earned a little extra every week, but she couldn't expect to get a bonus all the time and she wasn't due for a pay rise yet. Maggie had got hers early, because she'd moved up from junior to sales staff, but Beth would have to wait a little longer. Still she liked her job and after seeing how long Sally's hours were now, Beth didn't think she'd want her job. Promotion sounded wonderful and it was, but it also brought a lot of work and responsibility.

* * *

It was Tuesday morning and Sally was at her desk, busily working her way through the list of firms she wanted to visit when the door of the office opened and Ben Harper walked in. He looked at her and his face was as white as a sheet. Sally's heart missed a beat because there was clearly something very wrong.

'Have you seen Jenni this morning?' he asked.

'No, she hasn't come in yet.'

'She must have heard the news,' he said and sat down heavily in a chair. 'It sank – can you believe it? They said it couldn't sink and it went down so fast, hundreds of them died. If Jenni had been on board...' He gasped and ran his fingers through his hair before turning to her. 'It's all due to you, Sally Ross! If you hadn't spoken out, Jenni would have been on that ship... she's alive because I asked her to stay on and teach you her job...'

Sally gasped. 'You don't mean... the Titanic has gone down? They said it was so strong... how could it happen? Did someone attack it? Was it an explosion?' She shook her head in disbelief. Everyone had said it was the safest ship ever to sail and it had sunk on its maiden voyage.

'The news is filtering in bit by bit,' Ben said, sounding shocked. 'I've heard they hit an iceberg and went down before any rescue ships could get there... The worst thing is they're saying in the paper that the ship didn't have enough lifeboats. A lot of the passengers must have died...'

'Thank goodness Jenni didn't take that ship!' Sally said, deeply moved. The shock and horror of it made her feel sick for a moment.

'Amen to that,' Ben agreed, 'but one of her friends may have – and Marie had her young son with her. Jenni will feel terrible if they didn't get off in time...'

'Yes, of course she will,' Sally agreed, realising how it would make her employer feel. 'It is absolutely terrible – and I know there were hundreds of people travelling steerage. They were looking for a new life in America, and now...' Tears were trickling down her cheeks, because it was just so sad. All those people dying in a freezing sea when they'd expected to have a wonderful voyage. Her first relief that Jenni Harper wasn't on board had given way to distress for the people who had perished.

'I must go to the hotel and speak to my sister,' Mr Harper told her, seeming to summon his strength. 'If she hasn't come in, it's because she is too upset. I know Jenni; she will be blaming herself for her friend being on that ship.'

'Yes, of course,' Sally agreed.

After he'd gone, Sally continued to feel sombre. She was in need of company and decided to leave her work for a while and seek out her friends in her old department. It might be a good idea to see how the new stock was doing compared to the Mexican silver they'd been selling.

Mrs Craven smiled at her as she entered the department. Beth was serving a customer with hats and Maggie had just sold a silk scarf, which she was carefully wrapping in tissue.

'I thought you might visit us,' Mrs Craven said. 'I've put some of the new stock out this morning, and I've already sold two of the bangles with semi-precious stones.'

'That is one of the things I wanted to discuss,' Sally said. 'Did you think it compared well with what we had previously?'

'The bangles are better quality and they sell for the same price. I don't think you need to buy much more of the Mexican silver, Miss Ross. The customers seem to think the new stock is better value.'

'Yes, it is,' Sally agreed.

They spoke for a few moments of the other stock and she made notes in her book, because Maggie needed more gloves in the small size and scarves in muted shades rather than the bright colours that sold less often.

'Have you heard the news?' she asked when Mrs Craven had finished outlining their recent sales. 'Mr Harper told me a few minutes ago. It is so shocking – the Titanic hit an iceberg, last night I think. The news is uncertain at the moment, but they're reporting that not enough lifeboats were supplied and that means hundreds of people died in the sea...'

'Oh no! I hadn't heard. Fred's son was on that ship as a steward,' Beth said and gasped with horror.

Sally and Mrs Craven turned to look at her. She'd finished serving her customer and had come over to speak with them when she heard the terrible news.

'He was so proud of him getting that job and now...' A tear trickled down Beth's cheek. 'It will break his heart...'

'I'm so sorry,' Mrs Craven said. 'Would you like to take your break now and go down and speak to him?'

'Yes please,' Beth said, hesitated, then, 'I wanted to tell you, Miss Ross – we have sold all but one of our black hats...'

'Thank you. I ordered a new range and there are several smart ones in black. The company director promised me they would come in today or tomorrow.'

Beth nodded, turned away at once and left the department.

'It makes it personal when you know people who were travelling on the ship,' Sally said. 'Miss Harper would have been on it had she not stayed behind to teach me her job... but she sold her ticket to a friend who had a small son with her...'

'That is terrible for her,' Mrs Craven agreed. 'She will feel guilty about the people who died, because she is safe.'

'Yes. Mr Harper told me the news and then went over to his sister's hotel to see if he could comfort her...'

'A tragedy like that casts a shadow over everything,' Mrs Craven said, looking pale and concerned. 'It's all the more dreadful because everyone thought that ship was so sturdy.'

'I can hardly believe it...' Sally shook her head. 'I just feel like crying, but I have work to do. I wondered if you would like to have some travelling dressing cases here. Some of your customers for bags might like to buy them....'

'I think they would do better to stay with luggage on the ground floor,' Mrs Craven said. 'The silver jewellery and the bags keep me busy. I see I have a customer now, please excuse me...'

Sally nodded. Maggie was serving two customers with gloves, so when a lady walked in to look at hats, Sally stopped to

serve her and ended up making a good sale of three expensive
creations.

'I think you have the magic touch,' Maggie said when the
customers had all been served and gone. 'Beth showed that lady
some hats yesterday, but she bought nothing then.'

Sally nodded. 'I think they look at our stock, think they're
too expensive and then try elsewhere and come back when they
can't find anything as nice for the price. However, I've found a
new range and I think they will sell at slightly lower prices,
which means we may do even better.'

'Beth thinks we haven't been selling enough hats,' Maggie
told her. 'She will be pleased if your new range sells well.'

Sally nodded and left them to get on with their work. Beth
had been too upset to speak about her work much, but Sally
would make a point of talking to her later, when she'd had a
chance to get over her first shock.

As she entered the lift, Miss Hart was coming out. She
looked upset and stared at Sally for a moment as if she wanted
to speak, but then shook her head and walked off. Clearly she'd
heard the news and wanted to discuss it but not with a girl she
disliked for some unknown reason...

* * *

Beth could see that Fred had heard the news. He was sitting on
his chair, his face ashen and his eyes dark with grief. She saw
that a mug of tea stood cold on the bench beside him and he was
staring vacantly into space.

'Oh, Fred, I'm so very sorry,' Beth said and went to sit on a
stool by his side. She reached for his big, work-worn hands and
held tightly to one of them, feeling his fingers curl about hers.
'It's terrible news, but you mustn't give up hope. Some people
will survive...'

'He's just a steward – it's women and children first, that's the
law of the sea, as it should be. My boy wouldn't try to take a

place that a woman or child could occupy. Them boats must have been loaded afore they cast off...' He shook his head sorrowfully, looking at her with misted eyes. 'My boy told me there wasn't enough lifeboats, but they never thought it would happen in a million years – it was supposed to be the one that was safe...' A little sob escaped him.

'They would've needed crew to row the boats,' Beth said, trying to cheer him. She could almost see the panic amongst the people on board and hear the screams as they fought to get into the lifeboats and discovered there were not enough. It must have been terrible and she could not imagine how it felt to know you would die in icy cold water in the dark...

Fred felt the shiver run through her. 'My boy knew what could happen. He had no fear of the sea. He would try to swim for it – maybe he managed to hang on to a boat until rescue came.'

'Did a ship come to the rescue?'

'The paper says it was the Carpathia,' Fred said in a low voice that was choked with emotion. 'Arrived a couple of hours after it sank, but there were only a few hundred survivors in the boats – that means fifteen hundred or more died. The paper says they don't know for sure how many were in steerage, but that may be just a tale...'

Tears trickled down Beth's cheeks and she put her arms about Fred's shoulders and hugged him. She felt him let go and sob and she wept with him. After a minute or two, he snorted and pulled back, taking out a rather grubby handkerchief to wipe his face.

'This won't do, miss. My boy wouldn't like it. If he went down with that ship, he was doin' his duty by the passengers and that's how he lived.' Fred wiped his eyes and looked at her. 'I know my Jack's gone. He would never take a place that a lady or a child could take. I'm proud of him, miss.'

'Yes, you should be,' Beth said and wiped her own cheeks. She felt a warm caring sensation towards this man who had taken the loss of his eldest boy so bravely. Fred was like the father she'd loved and lost too soon and she made up her mind that she would secretly adopt him. Fred wouldn't know, but if there was anything she could do, Beth would do it. Little things like bringing in cakes and buying him some cigarettes and a card on his birthday. 'You're not the only one worrying, Fred. I think the nation will worry and wait with you...'

Fred nodded, but his smile didn't reach his eyes. 'You get back now, miss,' he said. 'Thank you for thinkin' to come down to me; it helped and I shan't forget. Go on now, I'll be all right. I'll see my boy in Heaven one day.'

'Yes, of course you will,' Beth said and kissed his brow before she left him. Her heart ached for him and for all the others who had lost friends and relatives on that ill-fated ship. She knew that there was only one God and yet at times like this it was hard to reconcile that with such a terrible tragedy. Why would the god who had died for them demand such a sacrifice of lives?

20

Sally was on the telephone when the office door opened and Miss Summers brought in a tray of coffee and sandwiches.

'You didn't ring, miss,' she said as Sally replaced the receiver. 'But I thought you must be hungry... you didn't go out for a break, did you?'

'I didn't feel like eating and I wanted to check some of the departments,' Sally told her. 'It is such dreadful news, Miss Summers. All those people drowned like that...' She shuddered as the horror of it hit her again. There had been so much optimism and hope when the ship was launched and it all seemed like a nightmare.

'It doesn't bear thinking of,' the secretary said and gave a little shiver. 'I was envious of those rich folk who could afford to travel on that ship, but now I feel lucky.'

Sally agreed wholeheartedly. 'Yes, me too. I've written a couple of letters – can you type them up properly for me please, rephrase them perhaps? I'm not much good at writing letters...'

Miss Summers picked up the papers Sally indicated and smiled. 'I'll correct the spelling, Miss Ross, and rephrase a couple of sentences, but they'll say the same thing.'

'They are just re-orders really,' Sally said, 'but I tried telephoning and neither of the firms was answering...'

'Perhaps it's because of this trouble,' the secretary said. 'This tragedy will have touched many people, not just those rich enough to travel first-class...'

'Yes, you're right,' Sally said.

She ate a couple of the sandwiches after the girl left and drank a cup of coffee, but she wasn't very hungry and was about to start telephoning again when the door opened and Mr Harper entered.

Sally hung up immediately, her nerves tingling. 'Is Miss Harper very upset?'

'Devastated,' he said and sat down opposite her. He looked as if all the wind had been taken from his sails. His normal confidence was gone and he seemed vulnerable to Sally. 'She's been trying to get news from New York and various news agencies, but so far she hasn't been able to get confirmation of whether or not her friends survived.'

'I'm so sorry...' Sally hesitated, then, 'A member of our staff had a son on board. He was working as a steward, I understand...'

'Good grief! That makes things worse,' he said and took a sandwich, eating it and then started on another. 'Sorry – was this your lunch?'

'I've had all I wanted. You're welcome to finish them...'

'Thanks, I didn't bother with breakfast once I heard the news.' He picked up the spare cup Miss Summers always brought and poured his coffee black, adding sugar. 'Can you tell me where I'll find the man who has probably lost his son?'

'It's Fred – he works as a porter. He'll be in the basement unless he's delivering.'

Mr Harper drank his coffee and made for the door, then stopped and looked back, 'Would you have supper with Jenni and I this evening? She needs cheering up and she thinks a lot of you, Sally.'

'Yes, of course, thank you.'

He went out and Sally got on with making her calls. She wanted to establish who had new lines, which firms had representatives to send and which she would need to call on herself. Yet for the moment it was difficult to put the terrible news from her mind...

* * *

Jenni had obviously been crying. She'd bathed her face and applied some face powder and a little lip rouge but still looked pale, her eyes a little puffy.

'No news yet?' Sally asked and Jenni shook her head.

'There is a possibility that Marie may be on the Carpathia,' she said huskily, 'but it hasn't been confirmed.'

'Don't give up hope,' Sally said and squeezed her hand.

'No, I shan't,' Jenni said. 'I'm sorry I didn't get in today – did you need me?'

'I changed my appointments to meet reps to another day,' Sally said, deciding it was best to change the subject. 'I also spent a lot of time checking stock throughout the store, including the departments that I'm not responsible for – and you'll be glad to know that there is a slight improvement in the sales in men's clothing.'

'So you were right,' Jenni approved. 'Good. Now, Ben and I have a bit of news for you – we've found you an apartment only a couple of streets away. It is over a tobacconist's shop and it has three bedrooms – I thought you might want to share with friends...'

'Yes, I should prefer that,' Sally agreed. 'Mrs Craven – she's the supervisor in my old department – she says she may be ready to move into a flat with me...'

'Well, that is perfect.' Jenni smiled a little sadly. 'It's good to have a friend and now that you're the buyer she can share with you without it being awkward on either side...'

'Yes, that's what we thought,' Sally said. 'How much is the

rent a week?'

'It's twelve shillings and sixpence,' Jenni told her. 'I know that is quite a lot, but if you share...'

Most rents were between five and seven shillings and sixpence, but Sally had expected that a flat within walking distance of the store might well be more expensive. On her own she might have thought it too much, even though she would be earning more now, because there were lots of other expenses when you lived in your own flat, but together they could certainly manage it.

'I'd like to see it and to take Rachel to see it,' Sally said. 'If she likes it, we shall probably be able to afford it between us...'

'Ben was thinking he might make you a rent allowance...'

'No,' Sally said, perhaps too quickly because it made him look at her. 'You've already given me a huge rise. I won't let you give me an allowance, but thank you for the thought.'

Mr Harper was silent, but Sally thought she saw reproach in his eyes.

Jenni prattled on about helping her to get the lease settled. 'You may need to put a deposit down. If you do, I'll help and you can pay me back,' she said in a practical tone that needed no reply. 'The flat is unfurnished, but I'm sure you can buy furniture second-hand and carpets and curtains are already in place...'

'That is good,' Sally said. 'I've bought quite a few things of my own since I've lived at the hostel, but I'll need a bed and something to sit on...'

'Well, as I said, most things you can buy in a second-hand shop and if you choose carefully they can look really nice. Ben has bought some beautiful things cheaply for his place...'

Her brother was still silent. He ate his meal without making a remark as his sister chattered, but afterwards asked if Sally would like him to drive her back to the hostel. She hesitated, but then, realising she might have offended him, said that she would like it, if it didn't take him out of his way.

'I should not have offered if it bothered me,' he said sharply.

They parted from Jenni soon after. Her hire car was waiting to take her back to her hotel and she kissed Sally's cheek before she left. 'I shall be in as usual tomorrow,' she promised. 'We have a lot of work to do and I've realised that brooding won't do me the least good...'

Sally kissed her cheek and Jenni was driven off to her hotel suite. Mr Harper held the passenger door of his car for Sally and she slid into the seat, the smell of the leather greeting her like an old friend.

'Thank you for cheering Jenni up,' he said as they drove off into the darkness which became lighter as they left the old-fashioned inn and nosed into the busier streets. Here, the street lights were brighter and the shop windows were a feast for the eyes as they passed the large stores, inhabited now only by their nightwatchmen.

Mr Harper didn't say a lot until they were almost at Sally's hostel, then he glanced at her briefly.

'It wasn't my intention to offend you, Sally. I know you have no family to help you out and I thought an accommodation allowance might be useful. My uncle gave Jenni her own small apartment when she was twenty-one and until then she lived in one of his properties rent-free.'

'Miss Harper is your sister,' Sally said. 'People would think the worst if you paid my rent...'

Mr Harper had stopped the car engine. He turned to face her. 'What would you think, Sally? I'd hoped you might trust me...'

'I'm sorry...' Her cheeks were flaming but she knew this was the time to be honest. 'I left my job at Selfridges because the floor supervisor wouldn't keep his hands to himself; when he threatened to get me sacked if I didn't do what he wanted, I'd had enough...'

'The bastard. Give me his name and I'll make him wish he'd

never been born.' His eyes bored into hers. 'Do you really think I'd do something like that, Sally Ross?'

Sally shook her head. 'No, and it was stupid of me to think it,' she said. 'I know you have far more glamorous girlfriends... and I was flattering myself you'd be interested. I'm an idiot. Will you forgive me?'

'You are an attractive young woman and you've had an unpleasant experience,' he said softly. Then he leaned towards her, his lips brushing her cheek lightly so that she hardly knew it except that her heart lurched. 'I never want to hurt you, Sally. I like you very much, but we don't know each other yet...'

'No, of course not...' Sally was embarrassed. He must think she was a conceited fool, imagining that every man who looked at her wanted to jump into her bed. For a moment, she wished the ground would open up and let her through. Not knowing what to say, she got out of the car, looked at him and then ran into the hostel.

Alone in her room, Sally's racing heart slowed and she was able to think clearly. Shocked, she realised that it was probably her own feelings that had made her imagine Mr Harper might have more than work on his mind. She found him very attractive and the touch of his lips on her cheek had set her heart racing.

She was such a fool. She hardly knew him, even though sometimes all it took was one look. Sally knew that the very first time they'd spoken outside Selfridges and compared notes on the windows, she'd felt a strong pull of both liking and sensuality. Had Mr Harper taken her in his arms and kissed her thoroughly, she might have stayed there... and that would be madness. He was her boss and perhaps a friend. Anything more could only end badly. Besides, he wasn't thinking that way about her. He could take his choice of many lovely women and she could never be more than one of the crowd...

Once again, her cheeks burned and she decided that from now on she would be very correct and proper in all her dealings with the handsome and too likeable Mr Harper.

Beth rested with her eyes shut, but she wasn't sleeping. She'd discussed the tragedy of the Titanic with her aunt when she got home that evening and, to her surprise, Aunt Helen had cried. She seemed to be showing her softer side more often of late.

Beth's tears had been shed for her friend earlier and it was still him she was thinking of as she lay staring into the darkness. Fred wouldn't sleep this night, she knew that for sure, and wished she'd been able to do more for him. All Beth could do was to take him an apple pie she'd baked that evening. She would give it to him and hope he understood.

Beth was aware of feeling lonely. She thought that her awareness of Fred's loneliness had made her realise her own need of someone special more than ever before. Mark hadn't tried to contact her since she'd told him not to and she knew that was right and proper. He was married and there could never be anything between them. Beth had thought she would dedicate herself to her work, but of late she'd begun to see that she needed more.

She acknowledged that she was lucky her aunt had taken her in, because otherwise she would have been worse off, but if there was nothing more for her to look forward to... Beth shook her head and told herself not to feel sorry for herself. It was Fred she ought to be thinking of. She'd mentioned to Aunt Helen that she would like to bring him home for tea, but her aunt had not answered. Perhaps she might try to save a few shillings so that she could take him out instead.

As the weather got warmer, Beth could suggest an outing to the park or the Serpentine and they could take a picnic she would prepare. She smiled and nodded as she realised that a picnic hamper would be the answer. Fred might not want to make small talk with her aunt, but a visit to the park would be pleasant and he could even bring his younger son along if he wished. Beth's father had bought a wicker hamper they'd taken to the park years ago and she still had it in her room.

Feeling better, Beth allowed herself to relax. Fred was being brave and she was lucky to have a comfortable home when so many others didn't, so she shouldn't let the lack of romantic love in her life get her down. Many young women had to settle for a similar life, looking after parents and working for a living. It was silly to hope for something she knew could never happen.

Her thoughts drifted to Maggie, who had a much harder time at home. Maggie's father was getting worse, his pain almost unbearable now, and her mother seemed to put more and more of his care on to her daughter.

'She wasn't there when I got home last night,' Maggie had confided in a rare moment when they had time to talk. 'Poppa was awake and asking for a drink, the range had burned low in the kitchen and the dinner wasn't even started...'

'Perhaps your mother got caught in the rain,' Beth had suggested because it had poured down for a while. This summer, although warm some days, was wetter than usual.

'No, I don't think so,' Maggie had replied, looking thoughtful. 'She was dry when she came in – and she didn't want anything to eat. She said she'd been to visit a friend and that she was enti-tled to a little bit of peace for herself...'

Beth's eyes closed as she thought about her friend's problem, but there wasn't very much she could do for her other than listen when Maggie wanted to talk.

She drifted into a heavy sleep but woke with the screams of drowning men in her ears. For a while the image had been so vivid and Beth knew she'd been reliving the tragedy of the Titanic in her dream.

She shivered because it had been so real that she'd actually felt that she was in the water struggling to stay afloat and then a man had swum up to her and grabbed her. He'd kept her head above water and someone had hauled her into a boat, but when she looked for the man who had saved her, he'd disappeared.

'Where are you?' she whispered and she knew without understanding why that the man who had saved her was Fred's son.

It had been so real, but it was only a dream, like the one she'd had after Fred talked about his old comrades in the war. Beth shook her head as she got up and pulled her dressing gown on. She needed to clear those vivid pictures from her mind and a cup of tea would help.

* * *

Fred seemed quiet but determined to keep a brave face when she visited him during her break the next morning. He was wearing a black armband over his shirtsleeves but so were several of the staff as a mark of respect for those that had died in the terrible disaster. A kind of hush hung over the shop that morning as everyone came to terms with what had happened.

'I made this for you,' Beth said and gave Fred the apple pie she'd baked for him. It seemed woefully inadequate, but she didn't know what else to say or do.

'You're a kind lass,' Fred said and there was a hint of tears in his eyes, but he didn't break down. 'I'll repay you one of these days...'

'Perhaps you would come on a picnic to the park with me

one Sunday afternoon?' Beth suggested. 'My aunt never usually wants to stir from the house when it's warm and I should enjoy it.'

'A lovely lass like you needs better company than an old codger like me...'

Beth smiled and shook her head. 'Perhaps I could ask Maggie to come with us – and you could bring someone... make a little party of it.'

Beth knew that all he had was his youngest son, but she didn't say more, just let him turn it round in his mind.

'They have concerts in the park and I like music,' he said at last.

'Yes. I love listening to brass band concerts,' Beth said. 'My father always used to take me to listen to the Sally Army – and some of the bands who played in the working men's clubs used to have a competition in the park. My father used to love listening to them.'

Fred looked at her and she could see the glisten of tears in his eyes. 'Ah, you're a lovely lass, miss – and I'd be honoured to take you for a picnic in the park when it's a bit warmer.' He hesitated, then, 'You can come to tea at my place this Sunday if you like, meet my son and his young lady...'

'Thank you, I'd like that very much,' Beth accepted, even though she wondered at the invitation so close to the news of the tragedy. She finished the mug of tea he'd given her. 'I'd best get back, Fred. I don't want to be late, because there are only three of us now since Miss Ross was promoted to buyer...'

'Now, she's a pleasant young lady,' he said, nodding. 'She's been down to see me a few times, telling me what to expect in the way of new stock.'

'We don't see as much of her now,' Beth told him. 'Miss Gibbs was only saying how much she misses her earlier this morning.'

Beth missed Sally's cheerful manner and knew that they all felt a little bereft with her gone from her counter, even though she popped in every few days to see how things were going.

Beth was thoughtful as she walked back to the department. Passing Mr Stockbridge, and then Mr Harper, who was talking to a young, dark haired woman, very smartly dressed, she nodded in reply to his brief good-morning. It was good to see their employer about the store – and he always seemed to have a young woman with him.

Mrs Craven was serving a pretty woman with one of the new silver bangles when Beth took up her position at her counter. Two women were admiring various hats and she was soon drawn into a conversation about the merits of a velvet cloche against a wide-brimmed straw.

* * *

Maggie watched as both Beth and her supervisor served a succession of customers. She'd sold two silk scarves that morning and a pair of grey leather gloves, also two pairs of white cotton ones, but felt restless and wished that Mrs Craven would tell her to go to lunch.

'Miss Gibbs, you may go,' her supervisor said at last. 'I should have told you to go as soon as you could after Miss Grey returned.'

'Yes, Mrs Craven...' Maggie went to fetch her coat and then left hurriedly. She wanted to do some shopping in her break that day and would buy a sticky bun somewhere and eat it in the restroom when she had her afternoon break.

It was her mother's birthday the following day and Maggie had already purchased a pretty scarf from stock, using her staff discount. However, she wanted to find a nice card and perhaps buy either some chocolates or a small bunch of flowers.

She was hurrying along the busy pavements of Oxford Street when she bumped into someone and dropped her purse. The coins fell out and rolled away from her until someone stopped

them with his foot. He bent to recover them and handed Maggie
the two shillings and sixpence, which was all the purse had
contained.

'Here you are, miss,' the young man said, handing them
to her.

'Oh, thank you,' she stammered and blushed. 'I'm so
clumsy...'

'I'm sure you're not,' he said and smiled at her. 'Where are
you off to in such a hurry?'

'To buy my mother a birthday card...' Maggie's cheeks were
on fire as she saw the smile in his eyes. 'I have to get back to
work – and I haven't done my shopping yet...'

'Then I mustn't stop you,' he said. 'I'm sure you have a lot
to do...'

Maggie blushed yet again and accepted the money from his
hand before entering the shop selling stationery, newspapers,
books and an array of fountain pens. She looked at the pens
wistfully, because she'd bought one for her father for his
birthday the previous year – before the accident that had
brought him so much pain. He'd been so thrilled with the gift
and talked of being able to write his crossword out with it. His
pain was now so bad that he no longer did the crosswords in his
newspaper.

Blinking back her tears, Maggie made her way to the counter
selling birthday cards and asked to see a selection. She found
one with drawings of violets and a sentimental verse inside and
chose it for her mother. After she'd paid for it, she wrote the
greeting, addressed it and placed the stamp on the envelope,
posting it in a box on her way back to the shop.

Beth and Mrs Craven both had customers when she entered
the department and as soon as she'd taken off her coat, Maggie
was back at her counter. She served three customers in quick
succession and then turned to serve the next.

'May I see some leather gloves please...? I know it is the
wrong season, but leather gloves are so acceptable as a present,

aren't they?' It was true, because most women wore gloves whenever they went out, leather for cooler days and cotton or lace for summer.

Maggie looked up at the man standing before her counter and found herself blushing once more as she realised it was the gentleman who had rescued her coins in the street.

'Oh...' she exclaimed, then, 'what colour would you like to see, sir?'

'Navy blue,' he said, 'or French blue as my sister calls that colour...' He pointed to a pair of gloves on the second shelf up.

'We have them in a size small or medium,' Maggie said, avoiding his blue gaze.

'What size do you take?' he asked. 'My sister is a similar size and build to your own...'

'I take the smaller size,' Maggie said and slipped one of the pair on to show him how it looked.

'Yes, that looks neat,' he said and took her hand. 'Lovely soft leather – I think Vera would like wearing those. How much are they please?'

'Twelve and eleven pence,' Maggie told him. 'I know they are expensive, sir, but they are good quality.'

'My sister would skin me alive if they weren't,' he said and laughed, his face alight with mischief. 'Sisters are like that, aren't they?'

'I don't know. I'm an only child...'

'Oh, poor you,' he said instantly. 'Vera is sometimes difficult to please, but I wouldn't be without her. Yes, I'll take the gloves – and do you have a scarf to go with them?'

Maggie sold him the gloves and a pretty navy and white spotted scarf. He took two pound notes from his wallet and paid her and she packed the items into one of Harpers distinctive bags. He thanked her and left.

Maggie saw Mrs Craven speak to Beth and then leave the department for her own break. After that, the floor was quiet as for once they had no customers.

Beth came over to her and smiled. 'Did you get what you wanted?'

'Yes – a pretty card and I bought some scented notepaper. I saw it and thought my mother might enjoy using it...'

'I'm sure she would,' Beth said. 'I might get some for my aunt.' She hesitated, then, 'Would you like to come to tea with us on Sunday?'

'That's so kind of you,' Maggie said and sighed. 'I shall have to ask my mother. She might have plans of her own. It is wearing for her all day on her own looking after my father...'

'Yes, I know it must be,' Beth was sympathetic, because every day she asked Maggie if her father was better. 'But you should have some time to yourself too...'

'I know...' Maggie couldn't meet her gaze. 'I can't leave her on her own on Sundays at the moment...' Tears stung her eyes, but she blinked them away. 'It isn't that I don't want to come, Beth...'

'Perhaps another week,' Beth suggested and moved away as two customers entered.

Beth was immediately busy showing hats to two older women and then Maggie found herself showing a young woman some of the silver bangles. She took out each of the bangles in turn, making sure to put away those that were rejected. The customer looked at every bangle in stock and then shook her head over one with three turquoises inset.

'I don't like any of them – I preferred the ones you had when the other girl was serving,' she said. 'Perhaps I'll have a look at some bags instead...'

Maggie replaced the rejected bangle in the counter and turned to take out three bags from the cabinet behind her. When she placed them on the counter, the woman frowned and shook her head.

'No, I shan't bother. I'll look elsewhere...'

Maggie bit her lip as the young woman walked off. She had just replaced the bags when Mrs Craven returned and Maggie went back to her own counter. She sold three scarves and it was nearly an hour later when Mrs Craven came up to her looking worried.

'Miss Gibbs, did you sell a silver bangle with amethysts set in it – three in a row...'

'No, I haven't sold any jewellery, I did show some bangles to a customer, but she didn't buy anything,' Maggie said and felt a shiver down her spine. 'Why – is something wrong?'

'I know that bangle was there when I went to lunch,' Mrs Craven said. 'I was showing it to a customer earlier this morning and now it isn't there...'

Maggie stared at her in dismay. 'I did show a woman some silver bangles, but I put them away each time she asked to see another...'

Her supervisor looked at her hard. 'Are you certain, Miss Gibbs, because it is definitely missing and it isn't entered as sold...?'

'I know I didn't leave anything out when I turned away to get those bags,' Maggie said, but she was feeling sick inside. Had she allowed a piece of expensive jewellery to be stolen from beneath her very nose? 'I know I showed my customer three bangles – the one with garnets, one with pearls and one with amber...'

'You are certain you did not leave the counter open while you turned your back?'

'Quite certain,' Maggie said. 'I didn't see the bangle with amethysts in the cabinet when I served the customer...'

'I know it was there earlier.' Mrs Craven frowned as she looked at her counter.

Maggie was sick with apprehension, because if the bangle had somehow been stolen then she would probably be blamed and she couldn't afford to pay for the loss. Remembering what Miss Hart had said to Sally about the slight damage to the tulle on a hat, Maggie feared that she would either be made to pay or be given the sack.

Beth was glancing across at them both. She was still serving a customer, but when the sale was complete, she came over to join them.

'Is something the matter?' she asked.

'There is a silver and amethyst bangle missing,' Mrs Craven told her. 'I know it was there earlier and now it isn't... You didn't serve at my counter, Miss Grey?'

'No, not this morning,' Beth said. 'I was busy when Miss Gibbs was serving that customer with bangles, so I didn't see anything untoward...'

'This is a serious loss,' Mrs Craven said. 'I shall have to report it to Miss Hart or Mr Stockbridge...'

Maggie drew a sharp breath. They would blame her and she would be dismissed. Her mother would be angry and she would never find another job!

'I know I put everything away,' she said. 'I didn't see the bangle there when I took over the counter...' She broke off, because Miss Hart walked in at that moment.

'Back to your counters,' Mrs Craven said. 'I shall report the loss, Miss Gibbs, but I'm not blaming you – anyone might be responsible...'

Maggie nodded but felt guilty. She averted her gaze when she knew Miss Hart was looking at her but felt hot and uncomfortable.

'Miss Gibbs, come here please,' Mrs Craven called to her a few moments later and Maggie went with her heart in her shoes. 'Miss Gibbs, I owe you an apology...' Mrs Craven was saying and held up the bracelet with three amethysts. 'It was in my top drawer beneath my receipts book. I remember now, I put it there in a hurry earlier...'

'Oh, thank goodness you found it,' Maggie said and burst into relieved tears. 'I'm so sorry...'

'No, I am the one who should be sorry,' Mrs Craven said. 'I thought you must have been careless and instead I am the one at fault.'

'Well, I think it very fortunate that the item was found,' Miss

Hart said disapprovingly. She glared at Mrs Craven. 'This is not the standard I expect from your department, Mrs Craven. You came to us with glowing references...'

She sniffed, walked around the department looking for something else she could criticise, but finding nothing out of place, gave a little toss of her head and stalked off.

'I am truly sorry for suspecting you of being careless, Miss Gibbs,' Mrs Craven said and looked upset. 'I didn't mean to make you cry.'

'It isn't the bangle,' Maggie sniffed. 'I think I'm just tired. I was up all last night with my father and I'm so worried about him.'

'We need privacy,' her supervisor told her. 'Beth, let me know if I'm needed.'

She led Maggie into the little office and sat her down in the only chair, perching on the desk next to her.

'Do you want to talk about it, Maggie? I didn't realise your father was so ill...'

Maggie caught back a sob and then told her all about her father's pain and his deepening reliance on the laudanum the doctor had prescribed. 'He had some kind of a fit in the night,' she said, breathing deeply to steady herself. 'For a while he was shouting and his eyes were wild. He accused my mother of trying to kill him and then he ended by sobbing in my arms...' Maggie looked into the sympathetic face of her supervisor. 'It was awful to see him so broken. I've always been close to him and I know she doesn't look after him as I do...' She wiped her eyes with the handkerchief Mrs Craven gave her. 'But she wouldn't really try to kill him... would she?'

'I'm sure she would not,' Mrs Craven said. 'It is the effect of the drug. I suspect he has been taking too much, but I know it does help to dull the pain, if only by sending the patient to sleep – but some people have terrible side effects and it sounds as if your father is suffering from them if he is hallucinating. If possible, you should cut back on the amount he takes.'

'He is in so much pain, but I shall try,' she said and drew a shaky breath. 'Thank you for talking to me. I feel a little better.'

'Do you feel able to resume your duties or do you need a little time?'

'I'm all right now,' Maggie said and smiled. 'I was worried I would lose my job and when you said it was your fault, I just broke down.'

'Understandable with all your personal worries,' Mrs Craven said and smiled. 'We must both return to our duty, Miss Gibbs – but if you have worries in future, please come to me.'

Maggie nodded and thanked her. She went back to her counter feeling a little less anxious. Her job wasn't well paid but it meant a great deal to her and if she'd been sacked she knew it would have been almost impossible to find another she would like as much.

22

Maggie left work at the usual time that evening and caught her bus home. She walked to the end of the road and turned into the narrow street where her father's terraced house was situated. The front step looked neglected and had obviously not been cleaned for a few days. Making a mental note to scrub it the next morning before leaving for work, Maggie went round to the back and entered through the kitchen door. Immediately, she knew that her mother was not here. The range had been left to die down and it was almost out.

Maggie fetched in coke from the shed in the back yard and made up the range. She filled a kettle and put it on the hob. It would take a while to boil because the fire would need time to get going.

Where had her mother gone? Looking around, Maggie thought she must have been out most of the day, because nothing had been cleaned and the ironing was still piled high in the basket. She thought her mother must have left soon after she did, because even her father's breakfast dish and cup were still in the sink.

'Muma... where are you?' she called, but she knew her mother was not in the house. 'Poppa – are you all right?'

A chill settled over her as she ran up the stairs. How could her mother just go out and leave him all this time? The house wasn't cold, because it was spring, but he needed more warmth just lying in bed all day and the heat from the range normally kept his room warm.

As she burst into his bedroom, Maggie saw her father sprawled on the side of the bed, his legs dangling over and his head back at an unnatural angle. She could smell the acrid odour of human waste and knew that he had soiled himself; it was probably the reason he'd tried to get up.

'Poppa… it's all right, I'll soon have you clean again…' Maggie said and went to him, but the moment she touched his hand, she was shocked by the coldness of his flesh. 'Poppa… no, please no!' Her cry of anguish turned to noisy tears as she looked at his face and saw the colour of his skin. 'Oh no, Poppa, my dearest one…'

Maggie knew that she was too late. Her father had died, alone and in pain. He must have been trying to reach the toilet and had slumped over the bed. She saw the empty laudanum bottle lying on the ground near his body and groaned. It had been full when she left him that morning…

Tears cascaded down Maggie's cheeks. For a few moments all she could do was cry bitter tears and call to her father to wake up, but she knew he wasn't going to.

She had to fetch help. It was too late for him, she knew, but a doctor must be called, and the undertaker. Drying her eyes on the sleeve of her dress, Maggie went back downstairs and round to her next-door neighbour.

Mr Jones opened the door, took one look at her face and said, 'I'll come right away, lass. Your dad, is it?'

'I think he's dead,' Maggie said and drew a shaky breath. 'I need to let the doctor know and…' Her voice failed her, but she lifted her head. 'I think the police ought to come too…'

Her neighbour looked grim. 'Aye, lass, I reckon as you're

right. Your mother not there again? She's been out quite a bit lately...'

Maggie nodded, swallowing hard. 'The range was out...' she said and saw him frown. 'Father has soiled himself trying to get out of bed by himself...'

'You go into the kitchen with my Mabel,' Mr Jones said kindly. 'I'll take a look for myself and then fetch the doctor. He will decide what you need to do next, Maggie lass.'

'I'll go back in and wait,' Maggie said in a whisper. 'Tell Mabel I'll pop round later – I don't want to leave him alone...'

'If that's what you want,' her neighbour agreed and smiled sadly. 'It's not your fault, lass. I saw Rob last week and he told me what a good girl you were to him. I'm only sorry I wasn't here today, but I've been working extra hours this week.'

'Thank you,' Maggie said.

She turned and went back to her home. The kettle was beginning to boil, so she moved it off the heat and went back up to her father's room, opening the window a little to freshen the air. For a moment she wondered whether to clean him before anyone came but decided that it was best to leave everything as it was, including the empty bottle.

Maggie tried to shut out the awful suspicions crowding into her mind. No, she mustn't let herself think such terrible things. Mrs Craven was right when she said the drug had given her father hallucinations. Her mother would never have deliberately given him an overdose and then gone out, leaving him to die alone – would she?

Knowing she must fight such suspicions, Maggie sat on a chair next to her father and stroked his head. 'I'm so sorry, dearest one,' she whispered as the tears trickled down her cheeks. 'I did love you and I'm sorry I left you alone all day. I should have stopped here with you...'

Maggie wasn't sure how long she sat there alone with her father, but it wasn't long enough. Suddenly, the doctor and her neighbour were there and then the doctor had sent Mr Jones to summon the police. They arrived and took notes, asking Maggie endless questions about what time she'd got home and where her mother was now.

'I don't know where she is,' Maggie answered honestly. 'I caught my usual bus home at ten minutes to six and it must have been nearly half past when I got in. The range was out, so I made it up and put the kettle on – and then went up to my father...' Her voice broke on a sob.

'I think you should take Miss Gibbs next door,' the police constable said to her neighbour. 'Get her some hot sweet tea and feed her. We'll finish up here and bring the key round...'

Maggie protested but she was overruled and taken to sit in the warm kitchen next door, where Mabel Jones gave her a doorstep of bread and dripping and a mug of hot tea with about three sugars in it. She could hardly force the dripping down, but the hot tea was welcome and she gratefully accepted another one.

'It's the shock, that's what it is, love,' Mabel said and looked distressed. 'A lovely man, your dad, Maggie. Every day he went to work he had a smile and a wave for us – and if there was ever anything he could help with, he was there.'

'Yes, I know,' Maggie dabbed at her wet cheeks. 'He was lovely and I loved him.'

'Aye, you would,' her neighbour said. 'I told yer ma I'd look out for him if she let me know she was goin' somewhere, but she's too proud, that mother of yours.'

'I don't know how she could leave him,' Maggie sobbed. 'It's my fault. I should have stayed home and cared for him...'

'No, of course it ain't, love...'

'Muma was tired from looking after him on her own...'

'The money the firm awarded him could have paid for a nurse,' Mabel told her and shook her head. 'A thousand pounds is a lot of money, Maggie. Your ma didn't need to do everythin' herself and so I told her – she told me to mind me own business...'

Maggie stared at her in shock. 'They paid my mother a thousand pounds? I didn't know any compensation had been paid...' Her mother hadn't mentioned a word and nor had her father and that must mean he didn't know!

'Yer dad paid into a fund at work and the firm had to pay the same – insurance it was and your ma got the money a month ago...'

Maggie felt the anger stir inside. Her father need never have been left alone. Any of the women in the lane would have sat with him and helped to keep him clean and comfortable for a few shillings a week or even better, Maggie could have stayed home to help – and her mother had kept the news of the compensation to herself... Why had she done that when she could have made life easier for all of them? And why had she chosen to go off and leave him all day?

23

'I've asked Miss Hart if we can have the junior from the dress department for a few days,' Mrs Craven told Beth the next morning. 'Miss Gibbs sent word that her father died yesterday and she needs to be at home for couple of days...'

'Oh, poor Maggie,' Beth said, feeling her eyes sting with tears of sympathy. 'I know she thought the world of him and she must be so upset.'

'Yes, I am sure she was,' Mrs Craven said and looked sad. 'This is where we miss Sally. We don't actually need four of us all the time, but there's no doubting it was easier if someone was off sick or gone to lunch.'

Beth nodded, but her thoughts were with the young girl who must be grieving for her father. She decided that she would go round to see Maggie after work, to show they were thinking of her.

June Brown was duly sent round from the dress department and Mrs Craven showed her the counter Maggie served from. It was the easiest of the three and so she settled into it soon enough and Beth noticed that she made several sales during the morning, though one young man entered the department, took a look at the scarf counter and left again without asking to see anything.

Fred came up with a box of new hats during the morning. He winked at Beth and whispered to her, 'I've got some news for you,' he said. 'Pop down for a minute on yer break and I'll tell you.'

Beth smiled and nodded, wondering what it could be. She had to be patient and wait because June had asked for the first lunch break and Mrs Craven went next, leaving Beth in charge. Fortunately, no one wanted to see jewellery or bags while Mrs Craven was gone and Beth had only two customers for the hats. June sold another scarf, but Beth noticed she didn't write it down afterwards and went to her.

'Did you forget to cross that scarf off the stock at the back of your book?'

'I didn't know I had to,' June said and looked sulky. 'I haven't crossed anything off. We don't do it that way in my usual department...'

'Let's have a look in the receipt book...' Beth checked and saw that she hadn't written anything but the word 'scarf' and the price. 'How shall we know which items you've sold?'

Maggie would not know what had gone when she returned to work, which made nonsense of all the hard work they'd done setting up the stocklist. Feeling annoyed on behalf of her friend, Beth checked the price of the scarves sold against the prices. She had to go through several drawers before she discovered that a green silk and a blue plaid scarf had been sold. She drew a line through each and showed June what she'd done.

'Please make sure to do it in future,' she said and went over to the jewellery counter as two customers entered.

After serving them with both bangles and two brooches, Beth returned to her own counter, where a lady was waiting, looking impatient.

'I'm sorry to keep you waiting,' Beth said, 'but we're short-handed just at the moment...'

'That girl hasn't had a customer all the time you've been serving. She deliberately ignored me...'

'Perhaps she was worried about making a mistake,' Beth said, but knew that June was still sulking. She served her customer and debated whether to say anything, but Mrs Craven returned then and so she decided to leave it to her supervisor. However, June had a customer almost immediately and Beth noticed that she wrote the sale in the back of the stock book afterwards.

'You may go to lunch now, Miss Grey,' Mrs Craven said.

Beth hesitated but went without speaking to her supervisor. After all, it wasn't her place to discipline the young girl and she'd already put her back up by telling her what to do. Since June might be asked to serve in their department again in the future, Beth didn't want to make an enemy of her.

Fred had the kettle boiling when she arrived. His attitude was such that she knew something had happened and when he beamed at her, she felt a little thrill of pleasure.

'You've had some good news,' she said, sensing what it must be.

'Aye, miss, I have,' he said. 'My boy is alive. Jack is on the list of survivors on board the Carpathia...'

'Oh, that's wonderful news, Fred,' Beth exclaimed. 'I am so glad!'

Fred had been certain that his son would have died, as so many others had on the Titanic. She wondered what Jack Burrows' story was, how he had survived when more than half the passengers and crew had drowned but didn't ask. Fred would tell her when he knew the whole story, for the moment she would just celebrate the news with him.

'I thank God for it, miss.'

'Do you know when he will be home?'

'They say the survivors will be taken to America. No doubt they'll want his testimony, to know how he escaped from a bitter grave. Jack will find another ship and work his passage home, as soon as they say it's all right for him to leave. If I'm lucky, he'll send me a telegram. I ain't heard from him yet, but I saw his name in the list of survivors.'

'I'm so happy for you,' Beth said and recalled her dream of being rescued from icy waters by a man she'd hadn't seen clearly but had known was Fred's son. She didn't tell him of her dream because he might think she was making it up, but she'd known somehow that Jack was alive.

'The paper I read says one of the stewards from the Titanic saved several passengers' lives,' Fred went on as he passed her a mug of hot sweet tea. 'Half the boats only had a few people in them when they were launched and this steward dived into the water and pulled some women and a little boy to safety. They said the steward's name was Jack – I think it might have been my boy...' Fred's eyes glistened with tears. 'He's a champion swimmer, always has been – and he did a course in lifesaving...'

'Oh, Fred...' Beth swallowed her tears. It was so close to her dream that she was overcome. 'You must be so proud...'

Fred nodded and sipped his tea. 'I thought he would go down with the ship if there wasn't enough room for everyone, but he'd go in after a child or a woman – that's my boy all over...' He smiled at her proudly. 'Both of them are like little fishes in the water, my boys.'

'It was such a terrible disaster, but if some are saved we have to thank God for it.'

'Aye, that we do, miss,' he said and smiled. 'There's the hand of God in it, sure enough.'

Beth sipped her tea. She didn't tell him about Maggie's father dying. Fred had seen Maggie with her, but they weren't friends and it would only dim his happiness. She would tell him another day perhaps.

After she'd drunk her tea and eaten the rock cakes she'd brought to share with him, Beth returned to the department. June was serving at her own counter and it wasn't until later that she noticed a red hat was missing from the glass cabinet behind her. She checked her stock book and saw that it had not been crossed off, though it was there in her sales book, just a hat priced thirty shillings. Crossing it off her stocklist, she waited until June was free and went to tell her about it.

'You forgot to cross that hat out in my stock book, Miss Brown.'

'So what?' June said. 'You knew it had gone, so what does it matter?'

'Because if I hadn't noticed, I might have thought it had been taken...'

'No one can tuck a hat like that in their pocket,' June said rudely. 'Anyway, that's your job. I didn't want to work here. I like where I work...'

'As a junior, you can be asked to work anywhere,' Beth said and frowned at her. 'Just because you don't cross stock off like this in your department, doesn't mean it isn't a good idea.'

'You're a fusspot,' June muttered sourly.

Beth would have said more but had to return to her own department because two customers were ready to be served. They both wanted hats for a wedding and took almost half an hour to choose them. Beth was tidying up afterwards when Mrs Craven came up to her.

'Miss Brown complained that you've got it in for her, Miss Grey – will you tell me what you were saying to her earlier please?'

Beth hesitated because she didn't like going behind June's back, but she had to answer her supervisor. 'I asked her to cross something off when she sold it, that's all...'

Mrs Craven nodded. 'I've reminded her to do that for her own counter twice this morning. I think Miss Brown has an easier time where she normally works. In future, report any lapses to me and I will deal with it.'

'Yes, Mrs Craven. I thought she would listen and learn from it – as we all did...'

'I shall speak to her myself,' Mrs Craven promised and went back to her own counter.

Beth got on with her own work. She fetched two fresh hats from the stockroom and made the necessary adjustments to her records. She didn't much like the new junior and hoped that Maggie would be back sooner rather than later.

* * *

There was no one in Maggie's house when Beth arrived that evening, so she went next door to try to find out where the girl was staying. A middle-aged woman with a plump, smiling face opened the door to her and nodded when she asked for her friend.

'Come in, miss,' she said and stood back to allow Beth to enter. 'Our Maggie is the kitchen with my husband and son. The men have been working on the docks all day so you'll have to excuse the way they look...'

'I didn't want to disturb you,' Beth said. 'I just came to make sure Maggie was all right and offer to help if I could...'

'Beth!' Maggie cried and jumped up as she saw her. 'Thank you for coming round. I'm staying with Mabel for a couple of days – my mother has... I don't know where she is...' her voice caught on a sob. 'She'd been gone most of the day yesterday and she hasn't come back...'

'I'm so sorry...' Beth put her arms about her and gave her a hug, feeling her tremble. Maggie was clearly very distressed and she was glad she'd come. 'I'm sure she is safe somewhere... but you don't know where?'

'It's my belief she took your father's compensation money and went off with her fancy man...' Mabel said and then gasped as Maggie looked at her in shock. 'Sorry, love, I didn't mean to say that... but she did have another man...'

'Why didn't you tell me before?' Maggie said, clearly devastated by the blunt statement.

''Cos my Sam told me not to,' Mabel said and looked guiltily at her husband. 'Me and my big mouth, Maggie. Sam told me not to tell yer...'

Maggie raised her head proudly as she looked at Beth. 'I don't know if it's true, Beth, but Muma didn't tell me she'd got the compensation payment and I don't think my father knew either...'

'He must 'ave signed it for her to get the money,' Mabel said and stood with her hands on her hips. 'I saw her with a new coat and hat the day afore she went off. She made him sign it if you ask me – and that's not all she did, I'm thinkin'...'

Beth saw the pain and distress in Maggie's face. 'Are you all right here, Maggie? You could come and stay with me for a while...'

Maggie's face lit up, but then she shook her head. 'Your aunt would never agree...'

'I'll take that risk,' Beth said. 'We can share my room and you can pay for your food...'

'Perhaps in a few days...' Maggie glanced towards her neighbour. 'I ought to wait to see if my mother comes back...'

Mabel sniffed but said nothing. Maggie looked so pale that Beth wished she could persuade her to come away with her then. It must be uncomfortable stopping with someone who talked about her mother like that.

'Well, the offer is there,' Beth said. 'I shall be glad when you're back to work, Maggie. We've had the junior from the dress department and she's made mistakes. When I tell her, she sulks. I miss you.'

Maggie smiled and gave her a quick hug. 'I'll come when I hear from my father's brother. I've sent him a telegram and I hope he will come so that we can have the funeral. I'm not old enough to sign the forms and, with my mother missing, I can't pay for...' She gave a little sob of despair. 'I don't know what to do...'

'You should get your things and come to us,' Beth said,

knowing she risked her aunt's displeasure but willing to suffer it for Maggie's sake. 'You can't go back there on your own after what happened.'

Maggie shuddered. 'I don't want to...' she said and lowered her voice. 'Can I really come to you?'

'Yes – now if you want...'

'I'll come in a few days if I can,' Maggie said. 'Mabel and Sam have been good to me, but Mabel can't keep me forever, she's got enough to do with her family...'

'I'd 'ave yer, love,' Mabel said, 'but you'll be better with yer friend...'

Beth kissed her cheek. 'I'll share my room with you,' she whispered. 'I've got a good double bed. It's better than staying here and you mustn't try to live by yourself.'

'Thank you, I shall come,' Maggie said and hugged her. 'As long as your aunt doesn't mind...'

* * *

Aunt Helen pulled a sour face when Beth told her where she'd been and what she'd told her friend.

'You might have asked me first,' she said in a complaining voice. 'I hope you're willing to pay extra for her food and the extra expense of a third person in the house?'

'Maggie will pay for her food and anything she uses,' Beth said. 'If you don't like her, she will find somewhere else to stay, but she is a lovely, polite girl, Aunt Helen. I think you will like her if you give her a chance.'

'Well, I suppose... as long as she pays her way,' Aunt Helen sniffed. 'I suppose we can't refuse the girl a place to stay for a while – especially if her mother has gone missing...'

'Yes, things may change if Mrs Gibbs turns up. Maggie is anxious in case she has had an accident...' Maggie hadn't actually said anything of the kind, but Beth wouldn't tell her aunt what Mabel Jones had implied. If the gossipy neighbour was to be believed, Mrs Gibbs had gone off with her husband's compensation money and her lover. It sounded awful when said in that casual way, but Beth knew that it could be true. Maggie had told her that a thousand pounds had disappeared and no one had seen anything of her mother since she'd left the previous day.

'My mother didn't tell me she had the compensation money,' Maggie had said. 'She grumbled for ages that the firm hadn't paid up, but when it came, she didn't tell me – and I think she'd been drinking when I got home once or twice...'

'You told me she was tired and worried,' Beth had comforted. 'Perhaps the money is in the bank and your mother might have gone to stay with relatives or something.'

'She doesn't have any,' Maggie had replied. 'Poppa told me she was brought up in an orphanage and had a terrible time... I just wish she'd left me a note so I knew she was all right.'

'She will come back,' Beth had told her, though she didn't quite believe it herself. Why had Mrs Gibbs gone off like that without a word to anyone? She'd kept the compensation a secret from her daughter and there was some mystery about how Mr Gibbs had died. 'Keep your chin up, love, and come round to me if you're miserable where you are.'

Maggie had promised she would. Beth knew her friend wasn't happy staying with her neighbours but needed to wait for her uncle to turn up and arrange the funeral. She was her father's nearest relative if her mother was missing, but her uncle would sort all the details out for her – not least who would pay for the funeral. Maggie had no money and she thought there wasn't much of value in the house. If the compensation money could not be found, Maggie's uncle would have to pay, at least until his sister-in-law had been found and made to repay him.

Beth could not understand how Mrs Gibbs could steal her husband's compensation and run off with another man, if that was what she had in fact done. Surely, she owed a duty of care to both her husband and her daughter to use that money for their benefit.

What kind of a woman would leave her husband to die in a cold house while she ran off with a thousand pounds of his money? The answer wasn't pleasant and made Beth feel sorry for her friend's hurt, because Maggie must have reached a similar conclusion.

Lying sleepless in her bed, listening to the wind in the eaves and the rattle of some loose boarding somewhere, Beth puzzled over the problem. Maggie had no one to help her other than her father's brother. Perhaps he would ask her to live with him and his family. Maggie hadn't seemed to think it was likely and perhaps she didn't want that anyway. It was no use; Beth couldn't solve her friend's problems. She'd offered a bed here and that was all she could do...

24

It was another two days before Maggie returned to her job in the department. She was looking tired and her eyes had shadows beneath them, but she gave Beth a wan smile when she walked in and hung up her jacket.

'The police won't let us have the funeral yet,' she told Beth when they had a few minutes to talk. 'My uncle has taken charge of it all and he said I could stay with him if I wanted... he lives out in the suburbs and it would be expensive travelling in every day.' She hesitated and looked at Beth shyly. 'May I stay at yours for a while, please? I'm not sure what I want to do, but I don't much like my aunt or my cousins and my uncle was calling my mother bad names.'

'Of course you can stay with us,' Beth told her. 'Aunt Helen is expecting you – she fusses sometimes, but we get on reasonably well. I think you'll be happy enough once you settle down.'

'Thank you so much,' Maggie said. 'I've packed my things into two bags I found in the cupboard under the stairs. Uncle Morris will let me know when we can have the funeral. He says Poppa had an insurance that will pay for it – but he says my mother owes me half of the compensation money because Poppa left half of what he owned to me...'

'Your father must have made a will. Do you think your mother knew about it?'

'I don't know,' Maggie replied with a shrug. 'I don't care about that money – it won't bring him back, or her: it's blood money!'

'Have the police been able to trace her at all?'

'No, they say there is no sign of her,' Maggie said, 'but we know that she cashed the cheque a week ago and walked away with all that money tucked into her handbag...'

'Why didn't she put it into a post office account?' Beth said. 'I have one. I only have a pound saved so far, but it's safer than keeping it in your bag or under the bed.'

'I think she was planning to leave,' Beth said. 'I asked Mr Jones and he told me it was true that my mother had a fancy man... He worked down the docks, same as my father. Mr Jones thinks she went off with Bill Rumble and that he planned the whole thing to get the money.'

'Did he know how much your father was owed?'

'He was in charge of the payout, because he was one of the men concerned with workers' rights. He must have known exactly what Poppa had paid in and how much he would get for such crippling injuries.'

'He couldn't have planned the injury surely?'

'Mr Jones says he could have engineered the accident, and Bill Rumble has disappeared – he didn't go to work the day my mother went off...'

Beth looked at her in dismay. 'That would mean he had planned your father's death... and to run off with your mother...'

Maggie nodded, her face pale. 'Mabel says it's murder and if the police catch them they will both hang...'

'No!' Beth cried and her hand went to her throat. 'That can't be true, surely?'

Maggie's eyes brimmed with tears she struggled to blink away. 'I knew she didn't love him and she didn't want to look after him – but I can't believe they planned it all right down to the accident.' She caught back a sob. 'It's so awful, Beth. I can't bear to think about it.'

'Poor you,' Beth said, feeling dreadful for her friend. 'Let's hope your mother has a good explanation for what she's done...'

'I wouldn't press charges for my share of the money,' Maggie said. 'I've never wanted the money and I'd rather have my father back and without the pain – but if they planned to hurt him, they deserve to be punished. My uncle says they've conspired to diddle the insurance and Poppa's firm, as well as him and me...'

'That's so upsetting for you...'

'I couldn't wait to be back with you and Mrs Craven...'

'Well, I'm glad you're back,' she said and squeezed her hand.

'I don't know what I'd do without my friends here...'

Beth nodded, but there was no time to say more because customers had entered the department, and for the rest of the day they were busy serving. At the end of the afternoon, they left together.

Maggie looked pale and anxious, clearly nervous of her reception, as they boarded the tram to go home, but, to Beth's surprise, Aunt Helen had tea almost ready and she'd put some flowers out of the garden into Beth's room just in case Beth brought her friend home.

'Come in, Maggie,' she said when the girl hovered in the kitchen doorway. 'Any friend of Beth's is welcome – and I want you to stay for as long as you like.'

'Thank you so much; it's very kind of you to have me,' Maggie said, then, 'I'm not sure what to call you?'

'Just call me Aunt Helen as Beth does,' she smiled. 'You look pale and cold – go closer to the fire and warm yourself through.'

Beth gave her a grateful look. Aunt Helen nodded her head but didn't say anything more, leaving Beth to see about supper while she poured from the large brown pot of tea brewing on the table.

'I shall leave you two girls to eat and clear up,' she said after she'd drunk a cup of tea with them. 'I'm off to see a customer this evening and I'll expect you two to be in bed by the time I get back...'

'Will you be late, Aunt? Shall I leave the door on the latch?' Beth asked.

'No, I'll take a front door key with me,' her aunt said. 'I know I can trust you to do all your chores, Beth.'

She nodded to Maggie and went off to change her clothes. A little later, they heard the front door shut after her.

'I have some baking to do,' Beth said when they'd finished eating. 'Can I leave washing up the supper things to you?'

'Yes, of course,' Maggie agreed. 'I'm glad to have something to do. You must tell me what else needs to be done...'

'There is a carpet sweeper under the stairs,' Beth said. 'You just push it and it picks up the bits of cotton in Aunt Helen's room – but watch out for her needles. They are expensive and she grumbles if I break them...'

'I'll make sure I pick up anything as I see it,' Maggie promised. She went to the cupboard in the hall and got the sweeper out and a few minutes later Beth heard her pushing the little machine back and forth.

Beth cooked the pie for the following day and made some jam tarts. She made more than usual to allow for a third person in the house and then washed the pans she'd used. By the time Maggie returned, they were both ready to go up to bed.

Maggie looked exhausted, but it was more mental than physical because neither of them had been overworked. Beth decided not to say anything to her friend. Maggie had to get used to her new life and nothing Beth did or said could ease the worries that lodged at the back of her mind; she would just have to live with them until her mother was found and the case was closed...

* * *

Beth and Maggie had both been up early to prepare for work the next Monday morning and they had washed their breakfast plates before Aunt Helen rose and came downstairs.

'The kettle is boiling,' Maggie told her. 'I've got time to make a pot of tea for you before we leave, if you wish?'

'Get off with you the pair of you,' Aunt Helen said but smiled at her. 'You don't want to be late – and, Maggie, if you're in charge of a counter now, they should pay you the same wage as Beth gets. You want to speak up for yourself.'

Beth looked at her as they left the house together and walked to the next street where they could catch a tram that would take them all the way to Oxford Street. It was quicker than the omnibus that Beth sometimes caught in the evenings so they would be in nice and early.

They were actually some of the first to arrive and Fred was just unlocking the staff entrance. He smiled at them and stopped to chat for a while, telling them he'd had a telegram from his son confirming that he was alive and well.

'Jack is going to stay in America for a few weeks,' he said happily, 'and then he'll work his passage home.'

'It's wonderful news,' Maggie said. 'I'm so pleased for you.'

The two girls left him to his work and went up to their department, arriving just as Sally came in.

She hesitated and then approached Maggie, kissing her cheek. 'I heard about your father, Maggie, I am so sorry. Is there anything I can do to help?'

'I'm staying with Beth's aunt for the moment,' Maggie said, 'and my uncle has taken charge of... everything...'

'Well, I'm here if you need me,' Sally smiled at them both. 'You two are early this morning,' she said. 'I'm glad you're here, Beth. You can tell me what you think of the new silver stock – is it as popular as the bangles Miss Harper bought?'

'It depends on the customer,' Beth replied honestly. 'I think the older, smarter women prefer the new stock, but some of the younger women like the Mexican silver best.'

'Yes, that makes sense to me – the Mexican bangles were

thicker and looked more for your money, but the new ones are finer and the stones are beautifully cut.' She nodded thoughtfully. 'I bought some different lines from a new supplier yesterday. Some of the bangles have pink or green enamelling and I'm trying a gate-link bracelet in gold. I've only bought half a dozen rose-gold bracelets, but they're rather lovely.'

'Do you think we shall sell gold here?' Beth asked, frowning. 'Might it not be a step too far for our customers?'

'Perhaps – that's why I've only bought a few to try. I got a good deal on the whole package, but I'm not going to sell them cheaply. People will think they're not real gold if I do that, so I'll put the full price on them and see what happens.'

She crossed over to the cabinet and checked the bags. Three of the most expensive skin bags were still there, though the department sold at least one good leather bag most days.

'I think we'll send the skin bags back to America next time Miss Harper visits,' Sally said. 'I don't think these three will ever sell...'

'I almost sold one the other day,' Beth said. 'The customer really wanted it but she couldn't afford it. She asked if she could leave a deposit and pay so much a week, but I told her we were not allowed to do that, so she said she would come back for it sometime.'

'Well, it's likely to be a while before Miss Harper returns, so she'll get her chance.' Sally smiled at them. 'They look wonderful on display, but I shall stick to medium-priced leather bags as the bulk of the stock.'

'We have a steady turnover of those,' Beth agreed and looked at her with interest. 'Do you enjoy your new job, Miss Ross?'

'You can still call me Sally when we're alone; I shan't charge you sixpence to know me,' Sally said with a cheeky grin. 'Yes, I do enjoy my job, Beth, the women's clothing and this department is special to me.'

Beth nodded. 'Have you found your new flat yet?'

'Unfortunately not...' Sally shook her head. 'Mrs Craven and

I are viewing one this evening. It has three bedrooms, a kitchen, a sitting room and a bathroom. The first one we saw was much bigger, but they let it to a family rather than two women alone – thought we might not be able to pay the rent.' She sighed. 'I have a meeting with Mr Marco in five minutes, so I'd better go...'

'I spoke to him yesterday,' Beth said. 'He came up to the department to look at our stock, asked us what we thought we would like to see in one of his windows and he asked for some of the new hats, which he thought were attractive...' She smiled. 'He said if we had anything we were stuck with, he could use it and then write it off as shop soiled to help us out... Maggie and I were laughing and even Mrs Craven smiled...'

'Yes, he can be quite a character,' Sally agreed. 'But he has a point there because I know some of the window display stock does get damaged. So far, anything like that has been marked up cheaply and offered to staff... which seems to please everyone.'

'Oh, I didn't know that; I'll look out for a bargain...' Beth quipped as Sally prepared to leave the department.

She went to her counter and began to lightly smooth a felt hat with a soft brush. Hats that were left out on stands didn't get dusty because she covered them with silk every evening, but customers often tried the hats on and they did sometimes leave fingermarks that needed to be smoothed out on the felts.

Sally spoke to Maggie for a few moments and then Mrs Craven arrived and she had a word with her before leaving.

'You two are in nice and early,' Mrs Craven said, smiling at them as she removed her hat and gloves. 'I spoke to Sally about another junior to be shared amongst the departments for when staff are off sick or on holiday. She offered to have a word with Mr Stockbridge for us. I should like a girl I could train myself – the girl Miss Hart sent us when Maggie was away was not suitable for our department.'

Miss Hart visited every department each day. As the floor supervisor, or floor walker as was the official term for her post, it was her business to see that every counter was staffed, stock in place and any problems reported to her. However, because of her attitude towards her staff, Mrs Craven preferred to ask Sally to have a word. As the buyer for the department, her opinion would be listened to.

'Aunt Helen thinks that Miss Gibbs should be paid more now that she is working as a counter assistant,' Beth said. 'I agree, but she will never speak up for herself...'

Mrs Craven nodded and smiled. 'And that is why I spoke to Sally about it. I do not think there is any point in asking Miss Hart about a wage rise for a member of staff...'

Beth nodded her agreement. She took some of the velvet trays out and brushed them, rearranging the silver items attractively before placing them back in the counter and then the first customer of the day walked in, making straight for Beth's counter.

25

Returning to her office after making a tour of the various departments and noting that the ground floor was exceptionally busy, Sally was about to ring for coffee when Mr Harper walked in. He was wearing an open-necked shirt, dark blue blazer and grey flannels that morning and looked so attractive that her breath caught in her throat. Normally he wore a suit when he came to the store, but she sensed this was only a flying visit.

'I just popped in to give you this...' he said and handed her what looked like a letter. As their hands brushed, Sally felt a flicker of something in her chest and knew that she had to avoid looking at him or she would give herself away. 'It's a letter from one of our suppliers praising you for your efficient manner in sorting out a recent difficulty.'

Sally looked at it and smiled. 'They had a strike of their Jewish workers in the clothing industry and I accepted the shortfall and got what I needed from an out-of-town supplier – but I told them I would re-order as soon as they were back to normal.'

'Well, they wrote to me to thank me for my patience – but it was you not me, Sally Ross.' He glanced at his watch. 'I have to go. I'm driving a friend of mine to an appointment...'

'Have a nice time, sir...'

He glanced back and grinned at her. 'It's just good business, Miss Ross. I have to keep the ladies happy...'

Sally watched him leave and frowned. What was that supposed to mean? He'd been seen with several different young and beautiful ladies and the gossips had him down as a playboy, but she knew he worked hard. Was it possible he was just working to keep everyone happy when he escorted his friends wherever they wanted to go?

Shrugging, Sally rang for her coffee. Mr Harper was a very charismatic and handsome man. She would be mad to let herself think of him as anything more than her charming boss...

* * *

Sally glanced up as Jenni walked into the office later that day. Jenni's face looked pale, her eyes dark shadowed. Sally could see at once that the news was not good and stood up, anxious to offer help or comfort.

'Your friends?' she asked.

Jenni looked strained as she said, 'My friend was drowned, but the boy was plucked out of the water by one of the stewards and helped into a boat.' A little sob escaped her. 'Tommy was playing somewhere, down with some of the Irish children, and Marie couldn't find him when the ship struck that iceberg. By the time she got him on deck, all the boats had been launched. One of the crew signalled to a boat to come back and he tried to help them climb down a ladder on the side of the ship, but it was listing badly. They both fell into the sea – and then this steward went in after them. He got the boy first and another woman, but Marie had disappeared. He looked for her for some time but couldn't find her – they say she must have been sucked under by the pull of the ship as it sank...'

'How dreadful,' Sally said and went to put an arm around Jenni's shoulders. She could see how devastated her employer was.

Jenni shook her head, moving away as if she found it unbearable to be touched. 'I'm all right – but it means I have to leave at once. I've booked a passage on the same ship as I travelled over on and I go tomorrow – so that means you're on your own, Sally.' Jenni looked at her oddly. 'I had thought to stay longer, but that boy needs a friend and his father is a busy man – a general in the army. He doesn't have much time for little Tommy and I think Henry may be too wrapped up in his own grief to see what his son needs.' Jenni blinked hard. 'It's my fault Marie was on that ship and I owe it to them to be there...'

'Yes, I see how you would feel that, but of course it isn't your fault,' Sally agreed. 'Don't worry, Jenni. I shall not let you down, I promise. Mr Harper is here and I can consult him if I'm not sure about anything...'

'I know that,' Jenni said and sighed. 'Ben is capable of running this place alone, but he can be too impetuous; I was meant to supply the rock he could cling to. I feel I'm throwing you in at the deep end, Sally, but I must leave immediately.'

'I understand,' Sally said. 'I'll ask your brother for his advice on anything new until I'm certain of my facts...'

'Be careful, Sally...' Jenni said suddenly and she was frowning. 'I love Ben to bits and I'd do anything for him – but I know he has had quite a few girl-friends. They never last long and he just moves on to the next one. You're not like the others and I would hate you to get hurt...'

Why would Jenni think she needed to warn her? Had Sally shown that she liked her boss a little too much?

Sally caught her breath. 'I like Mr Harper, but I shan't be foolish enough to give my heart away,' she said, though she was half sure she might already have done so. 'I know he wouldn't – couldn't – marry a girl like me...'

'I'd be happy to see him settled with someone like you,' Jenni contradicted, 'but he's always played the field and I don't want him to do you wrong – so be careful around him...' she sounded more American somehow in her concern.

'Thank you for the warning,' Sally said and forced herself to appear unconcerned. 'I'm sorry you're leaving and I hope you can sort things out for your friends...'

'I'll do my best,' Jenni said and smiled oddly again. 'Expect long cables from me. It will cost a fortune, but Ben can pay.' She swooped on Sally and kissed her cheek. 'Take care of yourself, my friend. I'll be back before you miss me and then we'll get to know one another properly...'

Sally sat looking at the door as it closed behind Jenni, feeling slightly bewildered. Sometimes, she thought she was walking in a dream, because everything had happened so quickly. One minute she was just a salesgirl and the next she was buying the stock for the whole of the first floor. If anyone had told her she would be given this job, she would have laughed in their face and she didn't really understand why she'd been chosen. The only reason she could think of was that she'd spoken out when her employer needed someone with a voice, someone to show him a beacon of light and believe in his ability.

He'd been quite clear he wasn't interested in her as a woman. Had he seen something in her manner that told him she felt more than an employee should for her boss? Perhaps her feelings had shown despite her attempts to hide them.

For a moment she cringed with embarrassment. She needed to be sensible and make a better job of hiding her feelings.

Sally wished Jenni Harper could be here to help her for another couple of months. She'd hoped for the other woman's support for a while longer, because it was a huge responsibility to buy for a store like this and she would have to ask Mr Harper for his advice more than she would wish. She admired Mr Harper, but she must distance herself from him, because it was the sensible thing to do.

Sighing, Sally applied herself to her list and crossed out two names. Neither were willing to send representatives and the voice on the telephone when she rang had been less than encouraging. She would consult Mr Harper on certain others, but now it was time she left for an appointment with another working jeweller in Hatton Garden. Silver jewellery had been one of the store's early successes, far more than Jenni Harper had foreseen when she decided to try a few lines, and it made sense to build on what was doing well.

26

Beth was busy most of the morning. Given her break, she went down to the basement to have a cup of tea with Fred and share the coconut tarts she'd made the previous evening. He was in a cheerful mood now that his son had confirmed he was alive and well and the time flew by. Several days had passed since the tragedy and Beth's plans to visit Fred at his home had been postponed, partly because of the tragedy and partly because Maggie had moved in. Now she wanted to put that right and show him she was a friend.

'We should have a picnic in the park this weekend, because it looks like being fine,' Beth said. 'I'll make the food and bring a basket with me and we can listen to the band as we eat.'

'What about that friend of yours?' Fred asked. 'She seems a nice young lady. I'll get my youngest son to come along and we'll bring some food too – make a celebration of it...'

'I'll ask if she would like to come,' Beth promised, bade him farewell and went back to the department.

Mrs Craven sent Maggie for her break next and they managed all three counters between them for the next half an hour. Mrs Craven took her break between half past one and two in the afternoon; it seemed to be the time when they were least busy, and although Maggie had a customer, Beth didn't. She noticed that Maggie's customer was a young man and that her friend seemed to be blushing a lot. After he'd gone, Beth went over to her.

'I think that particular gentleman has been in before?'

'Yes, he has,' Maggie confirmed. 'He bought a scarf and gloves for his sister and his mother liked them, so he has bought something similar for her...'

'I think he comes to see you,' Beth teased. 'I'm sure he came in the other day and left without asking for anything when he saw you weren't here.'

'Oh, don't,' Maggie said and her cheeks were pink again. 'I'm sure he doesn't come for my sake...'

'I can see he likes you,' Beth told her. 'It's nice that he admires you, Maggie. He looks to be a very pleasant young man...' And good-looking!

'But I can't... Muma would say I was far too young to encourage followers...'

Beth laughed at her look of embarrassment. 'One young man who likes you isn't encouraging followers, Maggie. If he asks you out to tea one day, you should say yes.'

'He won't!' Maggie said and shook her head. 'Besides, Muma would say that a nice young lady doesn't go out to tea alone with a gentleman she hardly knows.'

'We'll see,' Beth said with laughter in her voice. 'Would you like to have a picnic in the park, listen to a concert with me, Fred and his son on Sunday afternoon?'

'Oh yes, that would be lovely,' Maggie said and her face lit up. 'That is – if your aunt says it is all right...' Doubt flickered in her eyes and she looked both young and vulnerable.

'There are two of us to do the chores now,' Beth replied. 'We'll have the house sparkling clean, so she can't raise any objections. Besides, why should she? She could always come too if she wished...'

* * *

In the event, Aunt Helen was asked but refused because she was going out to visit a customer and have tea with her.

'I've known Martha Hale for years,' she confessed. 'I made clothes for her when her husband was alive and for both of her daughters. She was saying that she gets very lonely on a Sunday, the only day her cleaning woman doesn't come in, and both her daughters are so busy, she only sees them once a month...'

'That will make a nice change for you, Aunt,' Beth said, genuinely pleased. 'You would be welcome to join our picnic, but you'll enjoy tea with your friend.'

'Perhaps another time, Beth, my dear,' her aunt said and Beth sensed how much her aunt had softened in the past few weeks. She knew Aunt Helen really liked and approved of Maggie, who, she said, was a very thoughtful and well brought up young lady, and decided that must be the reason for the marked changed in her attitude.

Maggie had made cocoa for them all on the second night of her stay and she'd started taking a cup of tea up to Aunt Helen in bed. Although her aunt told her she shouldn't bother, Beth noticed that she drank it and seemed to linger a bit longer in the mornings, enjoying being spoiled.

The two girls caught a bus to the park after Sunday lunch and met Fred by the bandstand, as agreed. Beth's eye was caught by a poster on the railings advertising the newly set-up Royal Flying Corps, with a picture of a dashing young man in a smart uniform.

Fred's son, Timmy, was with him and also a sulky looking young woman whom Timmy introduced as Dot. Her hair was a suspicious shade of blonde and she was wearing more than a little rouge on her lips. Her shoes were high, shaped heels and her dress was pale green and had a big frill around her ankles that looked far too good to go boating on the water or sit on the grass.

The weather was mild but certainly couldn't be called hot. Both Beth and Maggie wore simple linen skirts to ankle length with white blouses and neat collars fastened with little ribbon bows. They had straw hats and little jackets that fitted into their waists, Beth's dark blue and Maggie's a jaunty red. The colour made Maggie look very pretty and Beth saw Fred's son look from Dot to Maggie more than once and frown as he compared the easy way one fitted in and enjoyed the company. Dot picked at the food she was offered and complained that it was too hot and boring sitting around in the park, whilst everyone else enjoyed the picnic.

Fred had brought a bag with a couple of cricket stumps, a ball and a bat, and they amused themselves for a while when the band went off for refreshments. Timmy was a brilliant bowler and he caught both Dot and Maggie out first ball. Maggie laughed and told him how clever he was and Dot sulked. Beth managed to send him running after the ball three times before she was caught.

Maggie was fielding when Timmy had his turn at the bat and she jumped up and just missed the ball he sent flying, but someone behind her shot his hand up and caught it.

'How's that?' he called and Maggie and Beth both turned to look.

Beth immediately recognised the young man who had come into Harpers a few days earlier to buy scarves and gloves and Maggie blushed scarlet as she saw the laughter in his eyes.

'Good catch, sir,' Timmy said sportingly. 'Would you like to have a go and see if I can return the favour?'

The young man came forward and offered his hand. 'Ralf Higgins,' he said and accepted the bat. 'Pleased to meet you all...'

Timmy did the honours all round and Ralf took the bat. He sent the girls flying after the ball half a dozen times, but then he was caught out by Beth, who just happened to be in the right place at the right moment.

'Well done, Miss Grey,' Ralf said. 'You're a better catcher than my sister Maisie – and she would love to be here to join us this afternoon. Whose turn is it now?'

The band had just begun to file back to their seats and so they all took their places. Ralf just naturally seemed to find a place next to Maggie and Beth noticed that he talked to her easily and naturally in a low voice and that she was no longer blushing but smiling happily.

'Did you see the poster advertising for men to join the new flying corps?' he asked. 'It looks good fun and rather tempting.'

'The clothes he was wearing in that post looked very dashing,' Maggie said teasingly and Ralf laughed good-naturedly and admitted it was half the draw, though he thought he would like to learn to fly.

At some time during the band's performance, Dot became thoroughly bored, so Timmy made an excuse and left them all to it. Beth saw Fred frowning at his son's retreating back but whispered to him that band music wasn't everyone's favourite.

'He's too young to be seriously courting,' Fred said and sighed. 'I dare say it won't last, but she's older than he is and I fear she's got her claws into him.'

'I think you may find that his eyes are opened sooner than you think,' Beth said and clapped as the concert finally ended. 'I did so enjoy my afternoon.'

'As did I, Miss Grey,' Ralf Higgins told her. 'I was wondering if you would allow me to take you all to the ice cream parlour before we leave for home.'

'I think I should be gettin' on,' Fred said. 'I've things to do. Thank you – both of you for that delightful picnic and your company this afternoon. I cannot recall ever having a happier time.'

He offered his hand, but Beth gave him a kiss on the cheek. She would have hugged him, but there were ladies and gentlemen strolling in the park and a public display of too much affection might have been frowned on, even though it was for a man who might have been her father.

As Fred walked off, Beth looked at Maggie. Her cheeks were glowing from the fresh air and she looked so pretty. Her eyes sparkled with anticipation and Beth understood that she did not want their afternoon to end yet.

'Very well, just for half an hour then,' she said and Ralf gallantly offered them an arm each, which they took sedately, and they walked slowly across the smooth expanse of lawn to the little parlour where there were tables.

Ice creams were ordered for all three of them, strawberry for Beth, vanilla for Maggie and chocolate for Ralf. There were little straw umbrellas decorating the ice cream dish and glacé cherries and angelica. From Maggie's face, Beth could see that she had never been taken out for such a treat before and she was glad to see her enjoy herself.

After half an hour, she reminded Maggie of the time, Ralf settled the bill and insisted on walking them to catch their bus. Beth noticed that he stood watching them until they turned the corner on the bus and that Maggie was looking very thoughtful.

'He seems a very nice young man,' she ventured and Maggie blushed.

'He was telling me about his sister and his mother,' she said. 'His mother is a widow and his sister is hoping to marry next year. Ralf is the breadwinner for his family, because his father left very little money, but his uncle gave him a good job in his office. He works at one of the large import firms down near the docks and lives in Southwark – though he would like to join the Royal Flying Corps, I think.'

'He has been telling you a lot,' Beth said. Ralf Higgins had seemed a properly dressed and well-behaved young man, and clearly had responsibilities to his mother and sister. That probably meant he would be steadier for it and Maggie should be safe to be gently courted by a young man like that, because she was very young and, by the sound of it, Ralf would not be ready to marry for some years.

'I like him,' Maggie said simply. 'I was embarrassed when he came to my counter and said flattering things, but now I know he just wanted to get to know me...'

'Has he asked to see you again?'

Maggie looked at her appealingly. 'He asked if we could all meet for tea next Sunday afternoon. He wants to take us both out, Beth. Do you think we might go?'

Beth nodded, because it was the only way Ralf Higgins could hope to court this innocent young girl. He could certainly not ask her out alone and Beth was the closest she had to a sister. It would mean playing raspberry for some time, Beth knew, but she was prepared to do it for her friend rather than have her sneaking away to a clandestine meeting that would only bring shame and disgrace on both her and Ralf.

'Yes, I see no reason why not,' Beth agreed and squeezed her hand. 'You must promise me that you won't do anything foolish or run off to meet him on your own at night. Your mother may come back and your uncle and aunt would certainly drag you off to live with them if you were in trouble...'

'No, they would disown me,' Maggie said, looking sombre. 'But I'm not ready for anything like that, Beth. I should be too frightened and I don't think Ralf would ask me to do anything not quite nice.'

'I should hope not,' Beth said. 'I was just thinking of the gossips, Maggie. It is so easy for a young woman to lose her reputation and once lost it can't be regained.'

'Yes, I know,' Maggie said seriously. 'I'm happier living with you and Aunt Helen than I've been for a long time. It was all right at home when my father was well and bringing in a decent wage, but since his accident...' her voice broke on tears. 'I shan't abuse your kindness and I know it's a lot to ask...'

'No, it isn't,' Beth said and placed a hand on her arm. 'I shall enjoy coming for walks in the park and to tea. I am your chaperone and it's the only way my aunt would let you meet a young man – or me...'

'I'll be your chaperone when you start courting,' Maggie said and giggled, but Beth shook her head.

'I haven't told anyone else – but I did love someone,' she said. 'My mother was ill and I couldn't leave her. He didn't understand and he went off in anger and then... he married someone else.'

'Oh, my poor Beth,' Maggie said and slipped an arm about her waist sympathetically. 'He wasn't worthy of you, Beth. He doesn't deserve you – and you will find someone much better, I know you will...'

Beth smiled and squeezed her hand. 'Thank you – and I'm happy to have you staying with us. Aunt Helen has taken to you and she's been nicer to me these past few days.'

'Good,' Maggie said. 'I like her and it's no trouble for me to make a little fuss of her.'

The girls got off the bus and walked back to the house in a companionable silence. Aunt Helen had just got in and was looking pleased with herself as she filled the kettle.

'No doubt you two could do with a little supper?' she asked. 'I shall just want a hot drink as I had a really big tea – well, you never did see the like! Salmon sandwiches, crumpets and honey and three kinds of cake. We talked and laughed for ages – if I hadn't thought of you girls, I dare say I might be there still.'

'I'm glad you had such a nice time, Aunt,' Beth said. Aunt Helen was glowing and looked a younger, happier person.

'Yes, I did – and Beryl has asked me to make it a regular thing, so I shall have to leave you girls to look after yourselves on a Sunday afternoon...' She nodded to herself. 'I hope you had a good time and behaved yourselves?'

'Yes, Aunt, of course we did. We had a lovely picnic and enjoyed the concert very much.'

'Good.' Aunt Helen looked complacent. 'I'm glad you've had the sense to make yourself a respectable friend, Beth. Maggie is a proper person for you to enjoy your leisure time with and you will be good for her. It has worked out very well... very well indeed.' She nodded to herself as if pleased over something more than the girls' friendship.

Beth and Maggie exchanged looks. It was all Beth could do to keep from laughing, but she did, because it looked as if her aunt had made the excursion on Sunday afternoon easier for them. It wasn't that they wanted to lie to her, because the meeting with Maggie's new friend was perfectly innocent, but Beth knew that had she been the one to meet a new friend there would have been endless questions asked.

'Yes, I think so,' Beth said. 'I think I shall go and wash my hair – if you will excuse me...'

Beth left her aunt and her friend talking. She needed to be alone for a few minutes. Talking about Mark had made her realise that she still felt a hole in her life where the thought of him had dwelled for so long. Yet she knew that she must forget the feelings she'd once had for the young doctor. Her chance for a life as his wife had gone and she was not sure she would ever find another man she could love or trust.

As she filled a jug from the kettle and added cold water, she looked at her shoulder length fair hair in the heavy old-fashioned dressing mirror and for the first time considered cutting her locks off to a more manageable style. She lifted her heavy hair off her shoulders and held it up – what would she look like if she had it shorter?

Hearing Maggie come upstairs, she let go of her hair and began to pour water over it, soaking it before rubbing in the lilac scented soap she used and working it through her thick tresses. It normally took three big jugs to rinse her hair thoroughly and a heavy bucket to carry down the stairs to empty in the yard in the morning.

Maggie came in as she was rinsing for the third time.

'Let me do that for you,' she said and darted forward. 'Close your eyes so that the soap doesn't sting them. You've got such lovely hair, Beth. It's a pity no one gets to see it properly.'

Beth was happy to let her friend rinse her hair and sat drying it on the towel after Maggie insisted on taking the bucket from the washstand downstairs and emptying it straight away.

'I could have done that in the morning,' Beth said when Maggie came back up, 'but it was lovely of you to save me the effort.'

'It wasn't any trouble,' Maggie said. 'Why don't you have your hair cut a bit shorter so that you don't have to pull it back in that knot?'

'I must admit I've thought about it,' Beth admitted. 'How short do you think I should wear it?'

Maggie took the comb and ran it through the thick pale hair admiringly. 'I think if we took about four inches off the length it would curl just above your collar and look really pretty.'

'I saw hairdressers in Oxford Street the other day,' Beth said. 'I could probably book an appointment in my lunch break...'

'Why go there and spend a lot of money?' Maggie went to her bag beside the bed and took out a pair of scissors. 'I used to cut my mother's hair and I cut my next-door neighbour's daughter's hair. Will you let me do it for you?'

Beth hesitated and then nodded. 'Why not? It's time I made a change and I'm fed up with all the trouble it takes to wash...'

She sat with her eyes closed while Maggie snipped round her head, lifting hair and cutting great chunks off the length, far more, it seemed to Beth, than she'd suggested. It was too late to quibble now and so she resolutely kept her eyes shut until the other girl told her to open them and then looked in the old-fashioned dressing mirror. A gasp escaped her as she looked at her reflection and saw a pair of sparkling green eyes and hair that curled round her face and over her ears with golden tips.

'You couldn't see the true colour of your hair before,' Maggie said and smiled. 'You look really beautiful, Beth – not so strait-laced, which you aren't at all.'

Beth knew what her friend was saying was true. Her mother had never wanted her to cut her hair and, looking after her, there just hadn't been time to think of her appearance.

'Yes, I think I look better,' Beth said and thanked her again. Aunt Helen might have something to say about it in the morning, but Beth didn't really care. Her new hairstyle had made her feel better about herself and nothing could spoil that...

27

Sally was checking some stock and ticking it off on her list when Mr Harper walked in that morning. It was midweek and Sally hadn't seen him for a few days, since Jenni had left for New York in fact. She supposed he'd been busy escorting one of his girl-friends about town.

'Have you heard from Miss Harper?' she asked, because passengers sometimes sent postcards when the ships called in at the port in Ireland, which was the last before several days at sea, though if it was important there was always a telegraph.

'No, I don't expect to,' he replied, looking distracted. 'I took her out for dinner the evening before she left and we spoke at length then.'

'Oh...' Sally attached a price tag. All the tags were written in a thin spidery hand with a special nib and indelible ink so that they were clearly legible. 'I thought she might have some message...'

'For you?' He stared at her hard. 'Do you need her advice? You seem to be managing well to me.'

'I don't want to make a mistake – and you haven't been in for a few days...' She avoided looking at him, because his intent looks made her heart thump.

'No, I suppose I haven't,' he agreed. 'I have some friends over from America and I've been busy with them...' He hesitated, then, 'If you've got time, I'd like you to cast an eye over some of the other departments... Just take a look and tell me what you think. Stockbridge was talking about stocking silver-plated teapots and sets. Back home they prefer silver...'

'I do too,' Sally replied. 'But a lot of customers can't afford them.'

He nodded. 'Marco told me to ask your opinion on various things. I know it isn't your job to buy for the whole store, but he has a high regard for your taste – and since he's a friend, I think you might help by looking in on the other departments when you get a chance...'

'Yes, of course.' Sally smiled. 'Mr Marco is generous and brilliant at designing the windows. I had a very good meeting with him the other day...'

Mr Harper's eyes seemed to bore into her, making Sally's spine tingle. 'He told me – in his opinion you could run the place...'

Sally wasn't sure if he was praising her or resenting her. His eyes were narrowed, so intent that she thought he was testing her – looking for something. If she hadn't known better, she would have thought he was interested in her, but she understood it was just business.

'I am quite sure I couldn't, sir...'

He frowned. 'It is possible that I might have to return to America soon...'

'A problem?' Sally asked and then flushed. 'Sorry – not my business...'

'It is personal,' he said, his voice harsh. 'Something I prefer not to speak about...'

'Yes, of course,' she said. He was making it clear that she was merely an employee. 'I shouldn't have asked.'

He nodded as though he agreed. 'Jenni wanted to stock real silver tea services, but I told her that I thought plate might be better. I didn't think we could sell a solid silver tea and coffee service complete with tray.'

'I very much doubt it,' Sally confirmed his opinion. 'However, you might sell one piece by piece. I think a young husband might buy the pot first and then the cream and sugar, and possibly the coffee pot as an anniversary present – or that might be something a doting father might buy his daughter...'

He looked interested. 'Do they often buy sets like that over here?'

'I think those that want real silver do,' Sally told him. 'You can often find second-hand sets on the market; they look the same but have different years in the hallmarks and that's how they've been built up. You'd need to be rich to buy the whole set, of course, and those customers usually go to Garrards or one of the Bond Street shops.'

'I'll talk to Stockbridge,' he said. 'I've never heard of it being done that way – but if you think...'

Sally stood up and brought a list to show him. She'd discovered the silversmith whilst looking for more jewellery manufacturers. 'Look, here they are – finely made tea ware in polished and beaten silver. You could telephone and ask for an appointment and then see what they say about selling the pieces singly.'

'Yes...' He sounded distracted and when she glanced up, he was looking at her oddly. 'What is that perfume you're wearing?'

'I'm not; it's just a rose perfumed soap.'

'It's very... nice...' he finished lamely. For a moment, something burned in his eyes. 'It's a pity Jenni had to leave. She has so much experience of these things – and she likes you...'

'I didn't get to know her long, but Jenni has been good to me and I like her,' Sally said a little shakily. 'Is there anything else, sir? Only I have several telephone calls to make this morning before my first appointment...'

'In that case we'd better get on with work, Miss Ross...'

'Yes, Mr Harper. Was there anything else you wanted to check with me, sir?'

'Give me your list of suppliers please.'

He took it from her without looking at her and walked away to stand by the window. She saw him take a gold-banded fountain pen from his top pocket and strike through the list a few times, and then he brought it back to her and laid it on the desk.

'I want a stock report on your department by the end of the week and whatever advice you have on any other department,' he said. 'Now, I have an appointment. Good afternoon, Miss Ross.'

Sally felt as if someone had stuck a long hatpin into her and let out all the air inside her. She'd been aware of tension in him. With most men, she would have thought the look in his eyes meant he was interested in her, but Mr Harper wasn't like any other man she'd ever known. The trouble was, she didn't know him and yet she felt something inside her pulling her towards him.

Sally shook her head. If she felt attraction, Mr Harper didn't and she was foolish to waste her time thinking of him. She'd seen him leaving the store with several different beautiful women and the whisper was that he'd been photographed leaving a nightclub in the early hours with an English lady with connections to the aristocracy. Sally hadn't seen the newspaper report herself, but several girls had and the rumours went round the store like wildfire. What chance had an East End girl against women like that?

She looked at the list. He had crossed out at least ten of the most promising items she'd sourced, but she wasn't sure whether he'd done it for good reason or just because he could. At least half of the items were things she was certain would sell well. She sat for a moment in thought and then shook her head; she was going to order those items she'd chosen so carefully and if he noticed, she would take the consequences, but she doubted he even knew what he'd struck out.

Smiling, she reached for the telephone, lifted the earpiece and asked for a number...

* * *

Sally was thoughtful as she got off her tram and walked the last few yards to her home in the young women's hostel. Because her mind was busy, she didn't see Mick until he stepped in her way, preventing her from moving on. She looked up in annoyance and then relaxed as she saw him.

'Oh, it's you,' she said. 'I was hoping I might see you, I wanted to ask about Sylvia.'

'She's on her feet again and she's found a job over in Southwark.' Mick's eyes never left her face. 'She asked if you could get her stuff from her room and bring it across to the pub. She says you've got her key and wants you to hand it in for her – but she says the rent is paid.'

'Why doesn't she do it herself?' Sally frowned, because Sylvia was asking a lot.

'What's the matter?' Mick drawled. 'Is it yourself gettin' too high and mighty to do a favour for a friend now that you're the buyer for your fancy man's shop then?'

'No, of course not!' Sally blushed furiously. 'That's a rotten thing to say – and he's not my fancy man!'

'Is that right?' His eyes met hers. 'Well, your friend is after being at my place for the next hour or so – if it's not too much to ask.'

'Damn you!' Sally said and twitched by him, furious at his goading.

She went into the hostel and marched straight up to Sylvia's room. The key was in her bag, where she'd kept it since that night, and she let herself in, picking up Sylvia's stuff and throwing it on the bed in a temper. There were two cases on the top of the wardrobe. She dragged them down and threw the first things in, then realised that unless she packed them properly, she wouldn't get everything in. So she took everything out, folded it neatly and packed the cases. Then she checked the room, under the bed and in the drawers and the wardrobe.

Satisfied that the room was empty of Sylvia's stuff, Sally went out into the hall and saw Jean watching her from the stairs. 'So you do know where she went,' Jean said spitefully. 'I know what happened that night and one day I'll prove it...'

'You're a nasty bit of work and I never listen to a word you say,' Sally said and ignored her.

Jean pushed at her as they passed on the stairs, but Sally resisted the instinctive urge to give her one back.

'You'll get yer comeuppance one of these days...' Jean called after her spitefully.

Sally would be glad when she could move out of this place for good and thought of the most recent flat she'd seen with Rachel Craven. It had been dirty and smelly and they'd turned it down immediately. Finding a place to live was proving far more difficult than Sally had ever imagined.

Crossing the small alley to the pub, she carried both the cases inside and stood looking round. It was nicer than she would have thought, the oak wood shining and decorated with horse brasses and buckets of bright geraniums at either end of the bar. Several oak tables were set at intervals in the large room, though most of the men sat or stood at the bar. Couples sat drinking at the tables and Sylvia was sitting at one in the corner talking to an older woman.

Sally walked towards her and Sylvia jumped up, waving as she saw her. She came rushing forward to take the bags from Sally and ushered her to a spare seat.

'I've got everything,' Sally said. 'Mick says you're all right – are you?'

'Yes, I'm fine now, honestly.' Sally turned as if to leave, but Sylvia caught her arm. 'Sit down, Sally – please, just for a moment. This is my friend Marlene – she owns a pub/restaurant over in Southwark and she's given me a job waiting tables and behind the bar.'

Marlene didn't get up. Her hair was blonde and she was wearing bright red lipstick. At first glance she might have been mistaken for a street walker, but when she smiled, something told Sally that there was no nonsense about this landlady.

'Pleased ter meet yer, Miss Ross,' she said and extended her hand across the glasses on the table. 'Sylvia told me what yer did fer her and I reckon yer must be a good friend. Sylvia will be all right wiv me – I'll take care of her and if ever yer in a spot of bother yerself, just come and see me...'

'Thank you, Miss... Sorry, I don't know what to call you...'

'I'm Marlene to me friends and a holy terror to them what ain't,' Marlene said and grinned at her. 'I can see yer a decent young lady, so I shan't ask yer to have a drink wiv us – but don't forget. Me pub is the Anvil and Hammer and we sell the best beer in London – and that includes Mick's, even if he is me best mate.'

'Thank you,' Sally said. 'I shan't have a drink, but I will sit with you for a moment.'

'I can't pay what you lent me yet,' Sylvia said awkwardly.

'Don't worry about it,' Sally said. 'I've been given a much better job and it's more money, so keep what I lent you, Sylvia. I'm glad you've found a decent job and that things are all right now.'

'Yes, they're fine...' Sylvia looked at Marlene and blushed. 'I know what a fool I was and I shan't be taken in like that again.'

'You aren't the only young woman to be led astray by a smooth tongued man,' Marlene said. 'You were just lucky you had good friends, otherwise it might have ended very differently.'

'I thought you'd decided to go back to the country?' Sally asked.

Sylvia shrugged. 'It was so boring. I couldn't put up with it, so I came back and asked Mick for a job – he sent me to Marlene, so I was lucky.' She looked at Sally oddly. 'Mick is a lovely bloke, Sally.'

'He was a good friend to us both,' Sally acknowledged. She was aware that Mick had been staring at her for a while and got to her feet. 'I'd better go now. Good luck, Sylvia – and thank you, Marlene. It was nice to meet you.'

'Don't you forget me,' Marlene told her and smiled. 'I've always got room for another pair of hands...'

Sally nodded but made no reply. She walked towards the door and then stopped and went up to the bar, looking straight at Mick.

'Thank you,' she said. 'I'm grateful for what you did for us.'

'It's what friends do,' he said. 'Don't forget I'm here when you need a friend, Sally.'

'I don't expect to be here very long,' she said. 'I'm looking at another flat with a friend of mine tomorrow evening and we hope to rent it together, if it's worth havin'...'

'Then I hope you'll be happy,' he said, but his eyes were hard.

'Mrs Craven is the supervisor for the department I worked at first,' Sally told him sharply. 'She is a widow and very respectable, Mr Whatever your name is...'

'It's O'Sullivan, if you're askin'.' The twinkle was back in his eyes. 'But my friends call me Mick – as you know well...'

'Thank you, Mr O'Sullivan,' she said and glared at him. She flounced off with his laughter in her ears, feeling annoyed.

* * *

'Yes, this is the best we've seen and at a rent we can afford,' Rachel agreed when Sally declared that she loved the small flat just off Kingsway they'd just been shown. 'I suggest we tell the agent that we want it immediately or it will be gone and we'll lose it again.'

It was the third possible flat they'd been shown by the same agent. The first had been bigger and they'd both liked it, but the owner had wanted a family because he wasn't sure two women would be able to pay the rent; the second had been damp and smelled unpleasant, but this was just right.

'It is perfect for us, Rachel,' Sally said. Two bedrooms of similar size, each with a double bed, wardrobe, chest of drawers and bedside chest. The sitting room had a sofa and two chairs, a bookcase and a little coffee table. It was a little bare, but they could buy a few bits and pieces to make it look more like a home; the bathroom looked quite new and was a real luxury because they would only have to share with each other, and the kitchen, though tiny, was adequate for their needs. 'We can walk into work from here.'

A strike had started in the London Docks and was turning nasty in recent days, the van drivers who had tried to break the stranglehold the Dockers had were attacked and threatened. The papers had hazarded a guess that the unrest might lead to a larger strike that affected transport all over the city, but if that happened it would still be easy to get to work from this flat.

'I have some small things I can bring with me. I've been storing them,' Rachel smiled her agreement. 'Yes, I like it very much, Sally, and I hope we can secure it this time.'

'We'll tell the agent now,' Sally said. 'I have my five pound deposit ready, do you?'

'Yes, of course,' Rachel said. 'I think three pounds and ten shillings a month is quite reasonable for a flat in this area, but they have asked for a steep deposit from us.'

'Mr Bramble told me the owner wanted security. He thinks if we can pay ten pounds' deposit to the agent, we shall pay our rent every month – and we were turned down last time because we had no male relative to vouch for us.'

'I know how you feel,' Rachel said and laughed softly at Sally's look of outrage. 'Not only do we not have the vote, we cannot even go into a public house alone without being thought fast or a woman of the streets. It is high time women were given the vote, don't you agree?'

'Oh yes, I do,' Sally replied and her eyes lit fervently. 'Jenni Harper mentioned something about being a member of a group for women's emancipation, but we had so much to cram into such a short time that we didn't explore it...'

'Yes, I must admit she did push you in at the deep end rather,' Rachel said as they went through to the hall, where the agent was waiting for them, looking rather impatiently at his silver pocket watch.

'We've decided to take it,' Sally said decisively. She opened her bag. 'We can pay you the deposit and the first month's rent now if you wish...'

'Could you come into the office in the morning tomorrow?' he asked, looking relieved. 'I'm glad you like it, Miss Ross – Mrs Craven. Your references are all in order, of course?'

'I have one from a former employer,' Rachel said.

Sally hesitated, then, 'Yes, Mr Harper will give me one, I'm sure.'

'I know that you are both perfectly respectable young women, but we do have to ask for these things...'

'I shall bring them in the morning,' Sally said, mentally grinding her teeth. Would the agent have been so fussy if they'd been men? She doubted it and it made her angry, but she held the irritation inside. It meant she would have to ask Mr Harper for a reference, but there was really no one else she could ask.

'Well,' Rachel said as they walked away. 'All we can hope is that we're lucky enough to get the tenancy this time...'

'Yes, fingers crossed,' Sally said. 'We have the money and we're respectable – but we almost have to grovel to be allowed to rent a property.'

Rachel nodded. 'That's one of the reasons I joined one of the women's movements recently. I've been to a few meetings. We listen to talks from men and women who believe in the cause and then have tea and sandwiches. You should come with me, Sally. I could just see you standing up on the platform hectoring the ladies on to civil disobedience if our demands are not met.'

Rachel was teasing of course, but Sally silently agreed. A growing resentment had been building deep inside her for a while. She'd seen the posters for women's suffrage and read about it in the newspapers, but until now she really hadn't thought about joining the Movement. When you were too busy trying to earn a living, it was hard to think of anything else, but these days Sally moved about the city on business and it had woken her up to the fact that women still did not get a fair deal when it came to wages and so many other things, although she herself was lucky. She'd been given a job that many employers would not think of trusting to a female. The Harpers had accepted that a woman could work as well as any man, but not many would agree with them. Old habits and thinking died hard. Changes had been made in parliament; the wages for women chain makers had been raised from the pittance it had once been and other small improvements had been made in conditions for female workers. Yet many people's attitudes did not change.

'Would you take me with you next time you go to one of your meetings?' Sally asked.

'Yes, of course I would,' Rachel said. 'I should like that very much. I do hope we shall get our flat, Sally. I am really looking forward to it...'

28

'Have you heard that Miss Ross and Mrs Craven are moving into their flat this evening?' Maggie asked when they had a moment to talk that morning in May. 'They were speaking about it just now when Miss Ross came down to check on that new silver jewellery. Some of it is so pretty – have you seen it yet?'

'I heard they had got the lease of a flat and would be moving in soon.' Beth smiled at the younger girl's eagerness. 'And yes, I have seen the enamelled jewellery – it is gorgeous. I would love to own just one piece of it, but I shall have to save for ages before I can buy anything.' She frowned. 'I think Miss Ross had difficulty with some of the dress stock, because there was a strike by Jewish workers in the rag trade that lasted around three weeks and that meant some of her suppliers couldn't deliver.'

'Yes, I read about that in the *Daily Herald*,' Maggie said. 'Ralf buys that paper and he gives me his copies sometimes...'

'Yes, I've seen it but I haven't bought it,' Beth said. 'Sally was clever. She went to a small country manufacturer and bought new stock from them – nothing seems to stop her finding something new and interesting.'

'That is why we're busy,' Maggie said. 'I love that Art Nouveau pendant with the pink enamelling and pearls. It costs three pounds and fifteen shillings and even with my ten shilling rise, I can't buy it yet.'

Beth made sympathetic noises, but that was something you had to accept working in a store like this; there were always lovely things in stock that were way beyond your own purse.

'At least we get to see and touch lovely things.' Maggie nodded and turned away as a customer entered the department and walked towards her counter.

Beth thought that Maggie looked prettier every day. She was brushing her hair a softer way now and her eyes were bright, her lips more often curved in a smile than not. It was now the end of May and they'd been out to tea with Ralf twice on a Sunday now, as well as several walks in the park and visits to the ice cream parlour, and Ralf's charming attention had made her friend blossom into a more confident and lovely young woman. Even though they sometimes had to dodge the rain, it never spoiled their afternoon.

Ralf had explained to Beth that he did not expect to marry until after his older sister was married. He had a wedding to pay for and must see his mother well settled before he could start to make plans for his own life, but he saw no reason why Maggie and he should not enjoy each other's company. As he'd explained to Maggie, although he wished to join the Royal flying Corps, he could not afford to give up the job his uncle had given him, which was better paid.

Beth enjoyed their weekly trips out and, as Aunt Helen now went out every Sunday, saw no reason why they should stay home. It was nice to see Maggie and her young man happy together and quite innocent.

A walk in the park or a little trip on the boating lake was pleasant for them all and Beth was not made to feel in the way; Maggie could not have gone without her. Besides, she was grateful to the younger girl for cutting her hair into the bouncy style she now enjoyed. Beth had attracted the attention of some young gentlemen as she walked through the park with the young couple but had studiously avoided the intimate stares some of them gave her.

A part of Beth envied Sally and Mrs Craven their move into a spacious flat of their own, though her life at home was much better these days. Beth wasn't sure how much of that was due to Maggie's presence; because there was no doubt that the young girl had charmed Aunt Helen. She smiled more and Beth sometimes heard them laughing together in the kitchen or the parlour. There were also the Sunday afternoon teas, which seemed to make Aunt Helen very happy. She had certainly mellowed recently and it seemed to be connected with her Sunday outings. Her manner was kind and concerned when she gave Maggie the news that the police had been round to say they were releasing Mr Gibbs' body for burial.

Having decided that he'd died of an overdose of laudanum, whether by accident or intent, the verdict of the inquest had been left hanging but the funeral was scheduled to go ahead. Maggie had had a day off work for it, refusing all offers to go with her, and had returned home in the evening looking pale and wan, but Aunt Helen had produced her favourite seed cake and made a fuss of her and she had soon begun smiling again.

Of Maggie's mother, there had been no sign. The police were still searching for her and the man who had gone missing on the same day she had disappeared. The money she'd taken was clearly lost to Maggie, but she'd told Beth that she didn't want a penny of it anyway.

'It's blood money,' she said fiercely. 'I wouldn't have it even if she gave it to me – and I never want to see her again.'

'She is still your mother,' Beth reminded, but Maggie shook her head.

'You and Aunt Helen and Ralf are my family now. I don't want anyone else.'

She wouldn't talk about the day of her father's funeral, but Beth gathered from odd comments she made that her uncle had wanted her to live with him and his family but she'd refused.

Her aunt hadn't really wanted her, so in the end he'd given Maggie her way, telling her she could come to him if she needed help.

'I would rather live in a hostel like Sally Ross did,' Maggie had told Beth. 'I'm so glad I live here with you and Aunt Helen.'

Beth was glad she did too, because it had made her life easier. They shared the chores between them, which meant they had more time to go out, and Aunt Helen allowed them to go to a church social one evening. There were various stalls, people playing cards, as well as a tombola, and lots of food, tea and orange squash. Beth wasn't in the least surprised when Ralf had turned up half an hour after it started and bought them both a gingerbread man and then won a little china fairing for Maggie on the hoopla stall.

He had walked home with them later and Maggie had asked him in to meet Aunt Helen. She had told her that he was a friend she'd known for a while and asked if she might ask him to lunch one Sunday.

Beth was shocked when her aunt had said she would be happy for Maggie's friend to come and have lunch with them. He'd sat and talked to her about his mother and sister for an hour before he left.

'Well, what a nice young man,' Aunt Helen had said after he had gone and nodded at Beth. 'It's a pity you don't have a pleasant young man like that to ask home, Beth. Really, my dear, it's time you looked for someone – unless you want to be an old maid like me...' She went into a trill of laughter as if it was a great joke.

Beth was astonished. She'd been nervous when Maggie had marched straight in with Ralf, but it seemed that she could do no wrong – only a short time earlier Beth would have been in trouble for being home late. The change in her was a mystery.

It was on her mind as she went down to the basement for her break at work later that morning. Fred had the kettle on and she asked him if he wanted to have tea in the park that Sunday. He looked pleased and they chatted for a while.

'My Jack will be home in two weeks,' he said. 'He's found a good job with the Hamburg-American line. They've made him up to senior steward as a reward for the lives he saved, and he's gettin' more money than he did with White Star. He reckons the owners have all learned their lesson and they'll none of them send another ship out without enough lifeboats for all. Jack had to give written evidence for the inquest, though he couldn't get back in time himself – but he'll be back by mid-June...'

'Oh, that's so exciting for you, Fred.' Beth was pleased for him. 'You'll have to bring him to one of our picnics when he gets home...'

'Yes, I'd like that.' He beamed at her. 'I still wake up and thank God every morning because my Jack was spared – and for you, too, miss, because you've made all the difference to my life...'

'I like talking to you, Fred,' Beth said. She'd missed her father for such a long time and she'd taken to the caretaker as a man she could rely on. 'I'm so happy you work here...'

Beth realised that her life had improved in these past three months since she'd begun working for Harpers. She had friends now, her job and a little money in her pocket. Because of her friendship with Sally, she knew that the store was doing well and that Mr Harper was pleased with the level of sales. Like other members of staff she'd wondered if the store would be sold off because it was no longer part of a much bigger chain, but now it looked as if everything was going well. She hoped so, because life was good and she wanted it to continue...

29

'I've been looking at the sales figures,' Ben Harper said one morning at the beginning of June as Sally entered the office and found him bent over the sheets, which had been sent up from each department. 'Several have shown a distinct improvement since the first month and your old department is surging ahead...'

'Good...' Sally's heart did a little happy dance as he smiled at her. 'Do you think it will be enough to keep your partners satisfied?'

'My aunt has decided not to sell her shares.' Ben looked thoughtful. 'She told me that she had confidence that I would make a success of the business, so I imagine she will be happy if you continue to show improvement, Miss Ross.'

'I only buy the stock for two departments,' she replied, turning aside from the look in his eyes which seemed to see into her heart. 'It is a joint effort, Mr Harper. Mr Stockbridge and Mr Marco do most of it between them... and you, of course.'

'I've merely agreed with suggestions from my manager and you, Sally Ross,' he said. 'I feel that those in day-to-day contact with the stock are better placed than I to make decisions...'

'Yet we all know you're watching, Mr Harper,' Sally said, a little defiantly.

'Still so formal' He raised his eyebrows. 'I thought I might have been forgiven by now...'

'I have nothing to forgive you for,' Sally said, her pulse racing. What did he mean? 'You've given me a chance to do something I enjoy – I am extremely grateful.'

'Not grateful enough to let me take you to dinner this evening?'

Sally drew a deep breath and then smiled. 'As your employee I should be delighted to have dinner with you, Mr Harper.'

'Good. I think of you as a friend, not just an employee – and we should celebrate our first three months,' Mr Harper said and grinned. 'Now, I want you to take a look at these lists I've drawn up – I think we should start thinking about our winter stock and Christmas too, indeed it is high time we did...' It was barely summer, but already it was time to think about Christmas stock, because the new lines were being shown now.

'Shall you have a special Christmas display throughout the store or just in the windows?' Sally asked, interested, as she accepted the catalogues and saw the photographs and drawings of festive stock. 'Oh, you've included a selection of Fair Isle jumpers for the men's department. I suggested them to Mr Marco because he asked me what I thought was a nice gift for a gentleman friend...'

Mr Harper nodded. 'It seems so odd to be thinking of winter and Christmas when it's a lovely summer day, doesn't it? But that is what retailing is all about. We have to decide what will sell next season well in advance, and that's why we sometimes make mistakes.'

'I think these will sell,' Sally said confidently. 'They're not too expensive and most men feel comfortable in these sleeveless pullovers at home... or at least I think they will...'

'We can none of us be certain, it's all about having the courage of our convictions,' Mr Harper said. 'My uncle had something similar and some of my friends wear them. I think they're a safe bet. Now, what do you think of these overcoats with astrakhan collars?'

After discussing various lines, they moved on to Sally's departments and he mentioned a couple of lines she'd chosen from the lists he'd crossed through, saying how well they'd sold and apparently forgetting what he'd done. Sally thought it best not to remind him.

They spent another hour discussing future orders for the shop and then Mr Harper departed to keep an appointment with his lawyer, promising to pick her up that evening, and Sally went on her usual tour of the store. She visited as many departments as she could each day, asking questions, checking rails and talking to all the salesmen and women, whether in her department or not. It helped her to have a good idea of what was selling and what was sticking. She'd made it her policy to keep the orders small and manageable, preferring to re-order more often rather than order too much and have it hanging there forever. It made more work for her that way, but she enjoyed being busy and expected others to work as hard.

Catching a look of resentment from one of the salesgirls in the dress department, Sally approached her and asked her if there was anything troubling her.

'I never seem to do anything but unpack new stuff,' the girl said. 'I've had to iron six wool skirts this morning, because they had creases in them.'

'You're June Brown, the junior on this floor?' Sally frowned as the girl nodded. 'Well, June, all I can say is that you should think yourself privileged to handle such lovely things. I should've loved to have your job when I was sixteen.'

June sniffed and looked even sulkier.

Sally stopped to have a word with the senior saleslady and asked about the latest costumes.

'They're selling really well, Miss Ross,' Mrs Simpson said with enthusiasm. 'The younger women love those skirts –

they're not easy to walk in because they're so narrow round the ankles, but they do look stylish.'

Sally felt pleased. She hadn't been sure whether or not to stock the hobble skirt. It had made its first appearance amidst a chorus of protest two years earlier, several cartoons and scathing articles about its impracticality covering pages of the popular papers. However, fashionable young ladies liked them and enjoyed the skirts, some of which were so narrow that it was actually only possible to take the tiniest of steps. The skirts Sally had found, however, were narrow about the calves and then frothed out in a little frill at the ankles, which gave the wearer slightly more freedom.

'Yes, I thought they might appeal,' Sally said. 'I'm thinking of buying one myself...'

'You'll need to be quick,' Mrs Simpson told her. 'We've sold five this morning. I was going to suggest that you re-order.'

'I'll inquire what else they have in a similar style,' Sally said. She didn't often re-order the exact garment, because what sold one day might not the next. Fashion was such a changeable thing.

Just as she was about to leave, Mr Marco entered and she stopped as he smiled at her. His hair was dark, wavy and a little too long for business, but he was an artist, born of an English mother and an Italian father, and his charm was in his smile and his teasing sense of humour, also his dark brown eyes that were warm and melting.

'Ah, Miss Ross,' he said. 'I wanted some of your wonderful new hobble skirts for my display – they are so delightful and the way the ladies walk in them makes them look like little birds twittering on the branches...'

'You are very naughty, Mr Marco,' Sally said and smiled. 'I'm glad you're going to feature them, because I have some rather smart new ones in stock. I was wondering if you might set a scene at a garden party for us. You could show off our hats and pretty dresses, but also some sporting goods as well...'

'I was thinking of doing a cricket window since we have all the wonderful matches going on at Lord's and on village greens everywhere, but I also need a rowing regatta... anything to celebrate summer...'

'We are thinking along the same lines,' Sally said, smiling.

'As always! Any ideas are welcome. Now run along, I shall not keep you,' he said and waved her away. 'You have so much to do, pretty Miss Ross...'

Sally laughed and moved on. The window dresser often said things like that but she knew that it was just his way. Some of the girls whispered that Mr Marco's lover was a man, but she ignored them. Whether it was true or not, it was his affair and made no difference to her – even though most of society did not see it that way.

Sally moved on to her favourite department. She was just in time to see Rachel packing a beautiful skin bag, one of the most expensive they had in stock. Stopping to speak with Maggie, she asked her if the scarves were selling as well as ever and the girl's smile shone out.

'I've sold five already this morning. We've been really busy, Miss Ross. Everyone says it's nice because we always have something new.'

'Good, that's what I like to hear,' Sally replied. 'I've spoken to Mr Stockbridge about you being promoted to the position of salesgirl as you are now in charge of your own counter – and he has promised to come back to me later today.'

'Oh, Sally, thank you!' Maggie cried and then blushed as Mrs Craven looked at her. 'Sorry. I should have said Miss Ross...'

'We'll overlook it this once,' Sally said and gave her a wink that no one else could see.

She moved on to Rachel's counter, addressing her as Mrs Craven because there were customers about and they'd agreed they would still use the formal address, even though they were now living in the same flat.

'I wanted to tell you I'm going out for supper this evening,'

Sally said. 'Mr Harper asked me and I agreed. I didn't want you to wait for me when you got home.'

They'd been sharing the flat for a while now and made a point of telling each other if they intended to be out for the evening.

'Oh... no, of course not,' Rachel said. 'I was thinking I might go along to that meeting of the Movement, so I shall probably just have a sandwich and a pot of tea.' She smiled. 'I've actually got Minnie and Mildred to come along to the meetings at last... and hopefully you, too?'

'I'll do my best...'

Sally nodded and moved away as another customer approached the counter. She stopped to speak to Beth, looking at the latest display of hats and making a mental note to buy some prettier styles. There were rather too many sensible felts and most of the fancier stock had gone. Beth had had a run on the straws because of the warmer weather, which was making women feel like dressing up in their finery.

Sally left the department but just as she approached the lift, Miss Hart came up to her. The look on her face told Sally that the floor supervisor was not happy.

'Miss Ross, I wanted a word with you!' The supervisor gave her a vitriolic look.

'Yes, Miss Hart – what may I do for you?'

'It is what you have done...' She took a deep breath. 'Why did you go over my head and ask for Miss Gibbs to be made up to full sales assistant? I do not take kindly to you interfering in my job...'

'Is it your job?' Sally asked, giving her a hard look. 'I understood that Mr Stockbridge was in charge of the staff wages, as well as many other things – however, if it was your job to bring it to his attention, why did you neglect to do so? Miss Gibbs should have been paid a full wage from the moment she was put in charge of a counter. Mr Stockbridge thanked me for bringing it to his attention...'

Miss Hart glared at her and for a moment Sally thought she wanted to hit her, but then she turned on her heel and strode off. Her job was to oversee the various floors, help in whatever way necessary, to point out any mistakes or faults and move staff between departments if there were absentees, but wages and promotion were not her prerogative. Mr Stockbridge was in charge of the staff – and had Miss Hart been doing her job thoroughly she would have spoken to Mrs Craven about it and then brought it to the attention of the manager.

It made Miss Hart hate Sally more than ever. Why she was so against her was a mystery, but Sally didn't let it bother her. She had a job to do and she did what she could to keep the store running smoothly, even if some of it wasn't her job. Mr Harper had made it clear he wanted her to speak up whenever she thought something needed doing so she had and if that annoyed Miss Hart it was too bad.

Returning to the office, she made some phone calls. The manufacturer had sold out of the popular skirts she'd bought recently, but there was a new version of the same style in a heavy silk and cotton weave and another in a material that they were describing as artificial silk.

'It is unofficially called rayon and it's a special process,' the salesman told Sally over the phone. 'We're describing it as artificial silk in our catalogue and I think it will be quite popular.'

'It makes the skirts cheaper,' Sally said, checking her pricelist. 'I'm not too sure about the artificial silk – but we will take two each in twenty-four to twenty-six and twenty-eight inch waists please. The younger ladies like to buy more often, but I feel our more mature customers prefer quality and will stick to the heavy silk.'

'I believe it is a material for the future,' the salesman said. 'The word artificial may put some off, but I think you will discover it is good value for money.'

'We can always buy more,' Sally said. 'I should like you to send me your autumn and winter catalogues please. I know it's hardly summer, but Mr Harper feels we should plan well ahead...'

Sally replaced the receiver. She had worked through the lunch hour and it would soon be time for her to be thinking about getting ready for the evening. A smile touched her lips as she decided that she would return to the dress department and purchase one of the new skirts for herself...

* * *

The lights were on in the flat when Ben Harper brought Sally home later that evening. She turned to look at him as he switched off the engine.

'Would you like to come up and have a cup of cocoa with us?' she asked.

'Your flat mate might object,' he said and looked at her strangely. 'I don't think I ought to barge in at this hour...'

Sally nodded and moved to open her door, but he put out a hand to stop her.

'Just a moment, please...'

'You wanted to say something?' They had talked of business for most of the evening, but also discussed music, plays on at West End theatres, the coming Olympics, and his hopes for the future of the store.

'Yes... I wanted to say that I like you very much, Sally Ross...'

He leaned towards her and she smelled the fresh tang of his cologne; it lingered on his skin, as if he'd just stepped from the bath and carried a hint of the outdoors. For a moment she thought he meant to kiss her and was mesmerised, gazing up into his eyes, but, with a great effort of will, pulled back.

'I have to go. Thank you for a lovely evening, Mr Harper...'

He nodded. 'I wanted to tell you before I go. I'm leaving for the States in the morning, Sally. I don't know how long I'll be gone, but I'm relying on you, Stockbridge and Marco to hold the fort while I'm gone...'

'No!' Sally was shocked. 'Why are you going? What happens to Harpers while you're away?' It seemed strange that he should leave when the store was still in its fledgling state.

'You will all carry on as if I was still here,' he said and there was something in his eyes that mocked her. 'I think you're quite capable of running this place all by yourself if I asked you to. Anyway, you're going to have to for at least a month and it may be longer. I don't have a choice.'

'But why?' Sally asked. 'Is it my fault?'

He laughed, his gaze mocking her. 'The whole world doesn't revolve around you, Sally Ross. I have important personal business and that's all I'm going to tell you.' He touched the end of her nose with his forefinger. 'Just take care of yourself and Harpers while I'm away.' He drew back, his look seeming to challenge her. 'Now go, before I say more than I should...'

The mockery in his look and his words stung her and she opened her door and sat half out, then looked back at him. 'Please come back safe...' And then she scrambled out of the car and ran towards the apartment building.

Sally didn't turn round when she got to the door, though she heard the car roar off through the night and knew he must be breaking all the speed limits. His news that he was leaving for America the next day had devastated her. Why had he suddenly made up his mind to go? Or had he been planning it for a while? Was he going back to see a woman he cared for...? Her instincts told her there was a woman involved and it was like a knife thrust in her heart.

Rachel was sitting on their sofa with a cup of cocoa and a magazine. She looked up and smiled as Sally entered. 'Did you have a good evening?' she asked.

'Oh, yes, pleasant,' Sally replied carelessly, though her heart was still racing. 'It was more of a business meeting really – Mr Harper is off to America tomorrow and I think he wanted to make sure that I was prepared to keep things steady until he returns.'

'Oh... that's a little strange, isn't it?' Rachel queried. 'After all, he made it clear that he needs Harpers to succeed.'

'Yes, and he still does,' Sally said, thoughtful now. There must be something more important to take him back to America. 'He is relying on all his senior people to keep the ship afloat while he's away.'

'How nautical.' Rachel smiled. 'Would you like some cocoa? I made extra and it only needs to be reheated.'

'Yes, I'll do that,' Sally said and went into their tiny kitchen.

She wondered what could be so important that it would force Mr Harper to undertake a long voyage when he must want to be here and oversee his fledgling business. Sally knew that Mr Harper wasn't a rich man. Most people thought he had to be just because he was American, but what he had was tied up in Harpers, so it must be urgent for him to leave at this stage – and he'd said it was important personal business. The belief that it was a woman grew and she felt a foolish ache in her heart. How ridiculous to fall in love with a man who didn't want her – but she had!

Why go now? She'd seen an odd look, almost of pain in his eyes when he spoke of his personal business and was certain he would rather be here in London. He'd been so enthusiastic when talking about the Christmas season to come.

Sally knew that her employer wanted Harpers to do Christmas in a big way. He'd talked of snow scenes in the windows and models of reindeer.

'I'd love to bring in live reindeer and a Father Christmas, but we don't have a toy department for the children,' he'd told Sally at dinner. 'I don't think it would have the same appeal for adults, do you?'

'No, not quite,' she'd affirmed. 'I think long wreaths of holly and glass balls everywhere will probably be enough – and some spectacular windows. We might have a Father Christmas in the window with his sack filled with presents...' Sally had laughed as an idea had occurred to her. 'Supposing we hired one of those mimic artistes? Have you seen them? They look as if they might be made of wax, because they have pale masks on their faces, and then they suddenly move and make people jump out of their skins.'

He had looked at her as if stunned and then a smile had spread over his face. 'We could have him in the window and when he moved, people would be shocked. It would cause a sensation...'

Sally's laughter had bubbled out at that. 'Yes, it might be fun. If he was dressed as Santa Claus and he sat on his sleigh and then got up and started to put presents into the sack...'

'We could have him move every fifteen minutes or something like that,' he had agreed. 'People would gather to see if it happened again...'

'He might ring a Christmas bell or something and invite people into the store – we could have a hot spiced drink to give away perhaps...'

'Has anyone ever told you that you're a genius, Sally Ross?' he had said and toasted her with his wine. 'Work on that idea – and talk to Marco about the other windows too. I think you can't start preparing for important events too soon... and don't forget the Stockholm Olympics in July. I know Marco has plans for that, but he would appreciate your input...'

Thinking back over the evening, Sally smiled. It had felt comfortable and right being with Ben Harper, and she knew she could be happy spending her life in his company... but she was just an employee. He couldn't have made that plainer when he mocked her, even though just for a moment she'd felt as if the air had tingled between them...

30

Beth noticed something different as soon as they entered the house that evening. There was a different smell – the distinct aroma of cigar smoke. She hadn't smelled that in her aunt's house ever.

'Has a gentleman been here?' she asked Aunt Helen.

To her surprise, Aunt Helen's cheeks tinged with pink. 'Yes, as a matter of fact – a friend of mine called to see me this afternoon,' she said. 'He bought me some flowers and stopped to tea. He liked your jam and buttercream sponge very much, Beth.'

'That was nice for you,' Beth said, doing her best to hide her shock as she hung up her coat and hat. 'Did you know he was coming?'

'Well, no,' Aunt Helen said. She hesitated, then, 'You know that I've been having tea with a friend on Sundays recently?' Beth nodded. 'Gerald Greene is Martha's cousin and he sometimes calls on her on a Sunday... We've become friends...'

'Oh, that is lovely for you,' Maggie said, genuinely pleased. 'It is nice to have friends – especially gentlemen, because they sometimes take you out...'

'Yes... as a matter of fact, Gerald is taking me to a theatre and supper afterwards...' Aunt Helen looked self-conscious.

'Tomorrow evening... so you girls will have to look after yourselves...'

'You mustn't worry about us,' Maggie said quickly. 'How lovely that will be for you. You must be so excited – what will you wear?'

'I think my pearl grey satin,' Aunt Helen said and blushed like a young girl. 'It is my best and I don't have time to make anything new.'

'It suits you well,' Beth assured her. 'What a lovely treat for you, Aunt Helen.'

'Yes.' Her aunt gave a little laugh. 'It was most unexpected, as were those delightful flowers. Please do go and smell them, girls, they are lovely.'

Beth was silent as she went through to the parlour to sniff the flowers, which were a mixture of roses and freesias and must have been expensive. She was shocked and surprised, for she had never expected her aunt to have a suitor.

Returning to the kitchen, she helped put their supper of macaroni cheese on the table. She felt pleased for Aunt Helen but wondered about the future if her only relative should decide to marry. Would Gerald come here or would Aunt Helen give up this house and move into his home?

'You're very thoughtful, Beth?' Aunt Helen said.

'We were busy at work. I think I shall go up when we've washed up – unless there is something I can do for you, Aunt?'

'Oh, no, I mean to have an early night myself,' her aunt said. 'Please don't worry, Beth, there will always be a home for you – though I am sure you will find a young man of your own one day soon.'

Beth shook her head. She would find it difficult to let herself love again and she would not marry simply for a home. If her aunt did marry, Beth would find herself a room in a lodging house somewhere, but it was a little unsettling to learn that Aunt Helen had an admirer...

'Gerald is taking me to the ballet,' Aunt Helen said excitedly.

'I've never been but he isn't a fan of Music Hall – though he says that at least three Music Hall artistes have been invited to perform at the Royal Command performance at the Palace Theatre for their Majesties in July...'

'Oh, how exciting,' Maggie said. 'I should love to attend the ballet. I read that Nijinsky's Faun was brilliant in Paris – though some people said it was a little... bestial...' she lowered her voice, hardly daring to say the word.

'Oh dear, that sounds unpleasant.' Doubt flickered in Aunt Helen's eyes, but then she shook her head. 'Well, Gerald is taking me to see *Swan Lake* so I hope there will not be anything bestial about that.'

'Oh no, I'm sure there won't,' Maggie said. 'The ballet I read of was in Paris – they wouldn't have anything like that here...'

Beth smiled at her approvingly and changed the subject.

After supper, the clean crockery was placed in the dresser and then the girls went upstairs to the room they shared.

'I didn't mean to upset your aunt,' Maggie said. 'I shouldn't have told her what the papers said about Nijinsky's Faun...'

'I doubt if her friend will take her to see anything remotely shocking,' Beth said. 'I'm not sure that Aunt Helen will truly enjoy the ballet – but she does seem to like this Gerald...'

'Oh yes, she does,' Maggie agreed. 'It will be so exciting if she marries him – perhaps they will let us have this house to ourselves then...'

Beth realised that Maggie didn't understand the seriousness of their situation, because it could leave them both homeless. Beth thought it more likely that the landlord would want to put a family in this house, but she wouldn't say anything yet. After all, Aunt Helen had only just told them about her friend...

* * *

Everyone knew that Mr Harper had returned to America, leaving Miss Ross, Mr Stockbridge and Mr Marco in control of the store. The supervisors and Miss Hart, the floor walker, all had their parts to play, but it was accepted by most that the orders came from the offices on the top floor. Miss Hart was the only one who spoke disparagingly of the arrangement, everyone else understood that Miss Ross was a good influence and that the store had improved under her aegis. Sales were increasing week on week now and even the menswear was selling steadily. As the summer progressed – one of the wettest on record – Mr Stockbridge was seen taking his stocklists into Miss Ross's office every week and the whisperers said she had the final say on most things. The dress department and the hats, bags and scarves were always busy and Mr Stockbridge had agreed with Rachel Craven that they needed an extra junior. He'd come to see her after speaking with Sally Ross.

'June is not well trained,' Rachel told him. 'We have valuable things here and I should prefer a young girl I can train myself.'

'Yes, I quite understand – and Miss Gibbs is now an excellent salesgirl, testament to your training.' He'd beamed at her. 'I've always thought Miss Gibbs an excellent young woman.'

'Perhaps you could choose someone like her for us again,' Rachel suggested. Mr Stockbridge had a daughter of around Miss Gibbs' age and she thought he might have a soft spot for her because of it.

'I'm glad he agreed that we could have a new junior,' Beth said after he'd gone and they were alone. 'June Brown just isn't up to our standards, Mrs Craven.'

'No, she is not,' Rachel agreed. 'Our department is still the busiest of all and we have an excellent turnover. I think you too should have a rise, Miss Grey, but I cannot ask for too much all at once.'

'Oh, I manage, just,' Beth assured her. 'I never have anything much left to save, but for the moment I'm settled at my aunt's – though if she gave up her house, I should not find it easy to pay my rent elsewhere.'

'Is it likely she will?'

'I'm not sure,' Beth replied honestly. 'My aunt has a gentleman friend – he has taken her to the ballet, which she enjoyed far more than she expected, and since then he has taken her out to dinner and the theatre twice. She has had him to tea several times and he is invited to lunch this coming Sunday...'

'It sounds as if he might be serious?' Rachel said and Beth nodded. 'Does that make you anxious?'

'Yes, a little. Maggie hasn't thought of it yet, but the landlord would never allow us to take over his house...'

Rachel nodded her understanding. 'Yes, I do see your concern. 'If we had a third bedroom, you might have shared it. However, I am sure you will find accommodation easily enough.'

'Yes – but it might not be quite the same. Some landladies are too fussy and others are not particular enough about their rooms.'

Rachel agreed. 'I had a good landlady, though she was inclined to be nosy. However, I'm sure your aunt will not leave you in the lurch. You will have time to look around...'

The conversation ended then because customers entered the department and all of them were busy serving throughout the morning. Beth sold five hats to one customer, who was getting married. The same customer bought gloves and scarves to match her hats from Maggie and went on to buy a new white leather handbag from Rachel.

'She spent a lot of money with us,' Maggie remarked when they were quiet for a few moments.

'Yes, for her wedding next month,' Beth confirmed. 'She said that she tried some of the other department stores but decided on Harpers because we are polite, friendly and our stock is bright and new all the time.'

'That is a real compliment,' Maggie said, smiling happily. 'I've just got my first proper wage – and I'm going to buy one of those new hobble skirts Miss Ross got recently. They are made of artificial silk and so smart – and nearly a third cheaper than the silk ones, which means I can afford it out of my savings now that I'm earning more.'

Beth had seen the skirts everyone was raving over but didn't feel she could afford to splash out on a fashion item. Her clothes had to last and yet when Maggie came back and showed her the deep blue skirt, she felt very tempted. Once, she might have asked Aunt Helen to make a skirt in the smart style for her, but now her aunt simply didn't have the time.

* * *

On Saturday evening, Beth sensed that her aunt had something important to say to her. She waited until Maggie had gone upstairs and then asked her to come into the parlour for a moment.

'Is something the matter, Aunt?'

'No, nothing – at least, I am a little concerned for you and your friend, Beth, my dear. I think you have realised that I have become fond of Gerald. He has asked me to be his wife...'

'Congratulations. I hope you will be very happy,' Beth said because it was all she could think of. 'When will the wedding be?'

'Quite soon, I believe,' Aunt Helen said and blushed. 'I hope you don't think I'm a foolish woman to rush into marriage with a man I hardly know?'

'Why should I think that, Aunt?' Beth asked and smiled, going forward to kiss her cheek. 'I really don't know him – but he seemed nice when he called for you.'

'I know it is quick,' Aunt Helen said. 'I am a little anxious for you and Maggie – if I give this house up, you will have nowhere to live.'

'When were you thinking of getting married?'

'In August...' Her aunt sighed. 'I know it seems rushed, but we're neither of us young and we do not want to waste the time we have. Gerald is taking me to Paris for a little holiday...'

'I see... Then Maggie and I had better look round for somewhere to stay...'

'I wish you had been a little older, perhaps then you might have taken over the house. It belongs to an elderly friend of my father, of course, but he had told me that he wished to sell with vacant possession and only his feeling of duty towards Papa had prevented him from turning us out before this, so he will be glad to have it back...'

'Yes, I understand...' Beth bit her lip. 'I shall tell Maggie when I go up and we'll find somewhere as quickly as we can...'

'No need to leave before the wedding. My landlord is bound to give you a week's notice...'

Beth kept silent with difficulty. Her aunt spoke as though it was an easy matter to find a new home just like that, but Beth knew differently. Sally and Mrs Craven had found it difficult enough. Beth and Maggie would find it impossible to rent a flat between them on their wages, and choosing a decent room to lodge in would take time. There was also the matter of things she owned that had belonged to her mother. Aunt Helen had allowed her to put things in her bedroom and the box room. She would either have to sell or to store her mementoes somewhere.

'Do you know where you will be living?'

'Gerald has a nice house out in Hampstead,' Aunt Helen said. 'I shall take some of my things, of course, but most will be sold. You could get a price for yours too, Beth.'

Beth nodded her assent. It seemed clear that she was not required in Aunt Helen's new life.

She left her aunt sorting out some of her remnants of material and went upstairs to the bedroom she shared with Maggie. It was going to be awkward telling her friend that they only had a few weeks to find a new home.

Maggie listened, seeming calmer than Beth had expected. 'I'm sure she is very excited,' she said and looked slightly uncomfortable. 'Ralf's mother told me that I could go and live with them... I can share with his sister until she gets married in

August and then have her room.' Her gaze dropped as Beth looked at her in surprise. 'I didn't tell you, because I wasn't sure – and I didn't want to let you down, Beth. I know your aunt has been better since I came…' her voice tailed off. 'Would you mind if I went to live with them?'

Beth took a moment to answer. 'I shall miss you, of course I shall,' she said at last. 'I've enjoyed sharing with you – it has been fun. And it's true; Aunt Helen likes you more than she likes me.'

'I didn't say that – just she's been easier for you to live with, Beth.'

'I think she was jealous of my mother and resented that she'd had chances she hadn't. I'm glad she has this opportunity to be happy and it makes things easier if I only have to find one room.'

'Yes, I suppose it might,' Maggie said. 'It's a pity you can't share with Sally and Mrs Craven…'

'If only there was a third bedroom,' Beth said. 'I would have moved in a like a shot – but they each have their own bed and I can't expect them to share with me.'

'I'm sorry, Beth.' Maggie put an arm about her waist. 'I shall miss you too. I wish you could come and stay with Ralf's family, because they're lovely – but there's only just room for me.'

Beth smiled at her. 'You know it means that his mother thinks you will marry one day?'

'Yes.' Maggie's face lit up. 'When he took me to tea, she made it clear that she liked me…'

'Then I am glad for you,' Beth said, though she was a little uncertain that she would wish to move into the home of the mother of the man she intended to marry.

'Mrs Higgins says that she has never known Ralf so happy. She thinks that he might have gone off and joined the Royal Flying Corps if it had not been for me…'

Beth nodded, wondering if that was the reason Ralf's mother had taken to his young lady so readily. Did she see Maggie as the lesser of two evils? Many people thought Maggie's sweet nature meant she was easy to influence, but Beth knew she had a mind of her own and hoped that it would not lead to conflict and unhappiness for the young girl one day.

'When shall you tell Ralf?' Beth asked.

'On Sunday when we all meet in the park,' Maggie replied, smiling. 'It will be lovely, all of us together – you and Fred and perhaps his son and girl-friend. She is a little sulky, but he's a nice young man.'

'Yes, very polite and helpful,' Beth said. 'I hope the sun shines. It spoils the picnic if it rains and we have to run for shelter...'

Beth lay wakeful for some time that night. She was glad for her aunt's sake that she was to marry, and relieved that Maggie had somewhere she could be happy, but she knew she would not enjoy the experience of lodging with a stranger. It was the reason she'd accepted her aunt's invitation to live with her, even though she'd known they didn't really get on.

31

Sunday was a lovely day. They all met in the park as arranged and settled down to listen to the concert, enjoying the feeling of being on holiday that the brass band gave. During the interval, Beth and Maggie set out the picnic on rugs they'd brought and everyone sat down to eat. After a while, Ralf and Maggie went for a stroll around the park and, a few moments later, Tim and his girl followed.

Beth saw Fred's worried look as he watched his younger son. 'Is something the matter?'

'He was talking about joining the forces before Christmas. He'll be old enough by then and it's all he wants to do…'

'I expect he thinks it will be fun,' Beth said. 'What does his young lady have to say about it?'

'Dot is encouraging him to join up. I think she imagines he will marry her then and they'll go somewhere more glamorous to live. She's heard about married quarters abroad and it sounds exciting.'

'Oh…' Beth placed a sympathetic hand on his arm, because he worried about his sons. Fred looked at her with warm affection; they were good friends and he treated her like a daughter at times.

A man was walking purposefully towards them and something made the back of her neck prickle. Fred turned his head to look at what had attracted her attention and then he was suddenly on his feet and gave a shout of pure joy before sprinting the last few yards to throw his arms about the young man. Beth rose more slowly to her feet, watching as the two men embraced and talked excitedly until Fred brought the stranger to meet her – and yet he wasn't a stranger because she knew him without any introduction.

'This is my Jack. I left a note at home to tell him where we'd be,' Fred said and looked as if he might burst with pride. 'The Americans gave him a medal for what he did when the Titanic went down – and he's been offered money and a fine job out there if he will go...'

'That is only deserved after what you did, sir,' Beth said and offered her hand. 'I believe you saved the life of a young boy – and I've been told he happens to be the son of a friend of my employer's sister...'

The man took Beth's hand, his strong fingers curling round hers for a moment. His dark eyes were curious as he looked at her, but he didn't smile. Beth allowed her arm to drop to her side as he let go. He seemed a little distant with her – and Beth didn't know why.

'I'm sorry,' Jack Burrows said. 'My father called you Beth – but I don't know who or what you are?'

'Jack,' Fred reprimanded, looking surprised. 'That's no way to speak to Miss Grey. She works for Harpers, same as me, and she has been a good friend to me...'

'Miss Grey...' Jack's dark eyes narrowed in thought, as if he imagined she was more than his father's friend. For some reason that made her laugh, because the very idea was just so ridiculous. 'Did I say something amusing?'

'No, of course not,' Beth said and forced herself to be serious. 'Your father and I are friends, Mr Burrows, that's all...'

Seeing Ralf and Maggie on their way back, Beth walked to meet them, giving father and son a chance to talk privately.

Maggie smiled at her happily. 'Ralf says I can move into his mother's house on my half day,' she-said and the delight was in her eyes. 'It means I shall be able to see him more often and we'll have more time to talk...'

Beth nodded and smiled at her pleasure. Yet she could see there was more causing Maggie's eyes to sparkle and then her friend shyly held out her left hand. On the third finger was a lovely cluster ring of garnets and pearls.

'Ralf asked me to be engaged and I said yes,' Maggie's voice was breathy with excitement. 'We still can't marry for a year or perhaps two, but at least we'll be engaged and we'll see each other every night and morning. We'll be able to travel in together on the trams.'

'Yes, that will be lovely for you both,' Beth said. As an engaged couple they would no longer need her as their chaperone and Beth knew she would miss the visits to the tea shops and the ice cream parlour. 'Congratulations, both of you. Ralf, you are a very lucky man.'

'I know I am,' he said, 'and I owe much of it to you. Had you not helped us, I should have had to keep buying gloves and scarves to see Maggie just for a few minutes.'

'Yes, we both wanted to thank you,' Maggie said. 'We're going to have a little party to celebrate and you must come as our special guest, Beth – do say you will.'

'Of course I shall,' Beth said and kissed her cheek. She offered her hand to Ralf, but instead he kissed her cheek. 'You're still my best friend, Maggie, and I expect to be a bridesmaid at your wedding.'

Maggie promised that she would be and the three of them walked back to join Fred and his elder son. Jack Burrows looked a little chastened and the glance he threw at Beth was slightly embarrassed.

Timmy Burrows and Dot returned just as the concert was

about to start again. Beth and Maggie had packed the remnants of their picnic into the basket and they retook their chairs. Jack Burrows was seated right on the end of the row and Beth studiously kept her gaze on the band and away from him.

Afterwards, Ralf suggested ice creams, but Dot said she wanted to go home and Timmy left with her, giving the others an apologetic shrug of his broad shoulders.

'I think I'll leave you younger ones to it,' Fred said. 'Jack – why don't you go? Miss Beth doesn't want to play gooseberry. If she has you to talk to, she doesn't have to...'

'Yes, of course,' he said. 'I'll see you at home later, Dad – and I'm sorry.'

'That's all right, son,' Fred said and smiled to Beth. 'I'm just glad to have you home – but you might owe an apology to someone else...'

Jack frowned but didn't say anything as he offered his arm to Beth. She hesitated and then took it, deciding it would be childish to refuse.

'We're having strange weather this summer, aren't we?' she offered as a truce and he grinned, suddenly looking rather handsome. 'Blazing sun one day and then torrents of rain...'

'Are your friends engaged?' Jack asked as they followed behind Maggie and Ralf, who were laughing and talking excitedly.

'Yes, just this afternoon. Maggie is going to be living with his mother from next week and I suppose Ralf thought he might as well make it official. I believe he is very much in love with her.'

'She is a pretty girl,' he acknowledged, still frowning. He cleared his throat. 'If I jumped to conclusions earlier, I apologise.'

Beth turned to look at him. 'Mr Burrows is a very kind and thoughtful man. I count him as a good friend – so when he believed you lost, I went out of my way to be of help.'

'He told me as much and far more bluntly, Miss Grey. I can only say I'm sorry. It was a stupid way to behave...'

'Not really.' Beth lifted her gaze to meet his brooding dark eyes. 'You thought I was some sort of harpy trying to take advantage of an older man and wanted to protect him...'

'I should've known you were not that sort of a girl...'

Beth laughed. 'I'm really not an ogress, Mr Burrows. If you're going to buy us all ice creams, then you should stop looking like a scalded cat. I shan't sink my claws into you.'

'I shall willingly buy the ice creams and tea if that will earn your forgiveness...'

'I think it might,' Beth said, giving him a naughty look. 'I think we should all have the knickerbocker glory today to celebrate Ralf and Maggie's engagement.'

Jack accepted her decree with good grace and went off to order the ice creams and drinks, refusing Ralf's offer to pay. He joined them at their table, a waitress carrying the loaded tray soon after.

'Was it very awful when the Titanic went down?' Maggie asked in a sympathetic tone. 'I know how brave you were...'

Beth noticed a nerve flicking at Jack's temple as he answered in a calm tone.

'I didn't stop to think about it,' he replied and Beth realised he'd been asked that question many times before. 'When the boy and his mother fell into that icy water, I just went in after them. I rescued as many as I could, though the mother seemed to have disappeared. I think she must have hit her head and gone down immediately.'

Beth shivered, remembering her dream when she'd seemed to be amongst those in the icy waters. It wasn't the first time she'd had odd dreams that seemed to come true, even if not in quite the way she dreamed them.

'It must have been terrifying for the passengers, especially when they realised there were not enough lifeboats for everyone.'

'The owners thought they would never be needed,' Jack said. 'It was designed to resist the worst of weathers, but when it hit that iceberg its construction worked against it somehow. There was a flaw in the design that no one had even thought of... and it resulted in far more loss of life than was necessary. Had we more boats, there might have been less panic in the launching...' His expression was grim. 'Some of the boats went off half empty. Many other lives could have been saved if they'd gone back to pick up the people in the water, but they were afraid of being sucked under when the ship went down...' His hand was shaking and his spoon clattered on to the table. He got up abruptly and left the table, going outside into the sunshine.

'I'm sorry,' Maggie apologised. 'I shouldn't have asked such a foolish question.'

'It wasn't your fault. He must still be upset,' Beth said. She got up and followed Jack outside.

He had only walked a few steps and was lighting a cigarette. He looked at her and blew out his match, returning the cigarette to his jacket pocket.

'Maggie didn't mean to upset you...'

'She didn't – everyone has questions.' Jack grimaced. 'Mostly the same questions. Sometimes I can talk about it – at others it all comes back and I remember just what it was like. The screaming and the crying – and the look on the faces of the men who knew they were going to die. Only strong swimmers like me were able to reach the boats. I begged them to go back for others, but they wouldn't...'

A shiver went down her spine as she pictured the terror and the chaos of that dark night. 'It must haunt you – but you did what you could...'

'For a child and a few women,' Jack said bitterly. 'The water was filled with desperate men. I would have just drifted away, because the boats couldn't take us all but someone hauled me into a boat and rowed away. Someone hit me on the back of the head because I was shouting, fighting to make them try to pick up more survivors, and I knew no more until I woke on the Carpathia...'

'I'm so sorry,' Beth said. 'It must have been terrifying for everyone.'

'You have no idea. Everyone says they're sorry, but they don't understand...' His eyes were dark with the horror of the memory.

'I know it hurts to lose those you care about. I can't know what it was like that night, but I do have some imagination...'

He stared at her as if he would deny her, but then the anger seemed to drain out of him. 'Of course you do. I'm sorry. I shouldn't take my anger out on you – it's the stupid fools who sent us to sea unprepared that are to blame.'

'Unfortunately, nothing the law can do will bring back those who lost their lives.'

'No, and I have to accept that I was lucky and not give way to guilt.' Jack smiled oddly. 'Shall we join your friends? I promise to behave...'

'I really don't feel like eating ice cream,' Beth said. 'I'll tell Maggie we're leaving and you can see me home – if you would like to?'

He looked at her seriously. 'Yes, Miss Beth Grey. I should like that very much. The only thing is – I have a motorcycle and side-car. Do you have the courage and will you trust me to drive you home in it?'

Beth stared at him for a long moment and then gave a little giggle, feeling reckless. 'Yes, why not?'

* * *

It seemed very formal to shake hands after what had seemed a death defying ride through the streets in Jack's sidecar. He'd given her a leather helmet and goggles to wear and she'd had to remove her Sunday hat. The wind had blown into her face, almost taking her breath away, and yet Beth found the experience both exciting and satisfying. She'd never done anything as daring in her life, but somehow after the talk about the Titanic it had seemed to be the right thing to do.

'That was fun,' she said and offered her hand. Jack took it but instead of shaking it, he bowed over it and then kissed the back. 'Thank you so much...'

'You're as lovely as Dad said you were,' Jack said and grinned at her.

Suddenly, Beth felt as if all the air had been sucked out of her. She smiled back a little tentatively.

'Would you allow me to take you out for tea next Sunday – I could call for you, and I promise not to bring the motorcycle...'

'Why not?' she said, finding it hard to speak. 'But I do hope you will take me for another ride one day?'

'Oh yes,' Jack said and his smile deepened. 'I think I can guarantee that, Miss Grey. I shall call for you at two next week – take care of yourself...'

Beth nodded, watching as he returned to the bike and went roaring off down the road. Several of the lace curtains opposite her aunt's house were twitching and a couple of neighbours had actually poked their heads out of their doors. Beth felt like shouting out loud that her escort was Mr Jack Burrows, a hero from the wreck of the Titanic, but instead she just smiled to herself and went into the house. After all, she wouldn't be living here much longer so what did it matter what the neighbours thought?

Aunt Helen had just come in herself and was putting the kettle on. She looked beyond Beth for Maggie.

'Maggie is still eating ice cream with Ralf,' Beth said. 'They became engaged today, Aunt, and she will be moving in with his mother on Monday afternoon...'

'We shall miss her smile and her chatter.' Aunt Helen sighed. 'Oh well, it was bound to come.' She looked speculatively at Beth. 'You will need some new clothes for my wedding, Beth. I would offer to make something for you – but if I gave you five pounds, you could buy something for yourself.'

'I can't expect you to pay for my clothes, Aunt. I'll wear my best blue dress and the hat that matches...'

'No – I insist,' Aunt Helen said and opened her bag. 'I always insisted you pay your way, Beth – and I didn't really need the money you gave me. Take this five pound note and make sure you buy something nice...'

Beth stared at the money, reluctant to accept it. She'd always thought her aunt needed her contribution.

Aunt Helen gave a sigh of exasperation and put the note on the kitchen table. 'It's yours. I expect you to buy something nice to wear at my wedding – perhaps a fine wool suit and a pretty hat in blue. Blue always looks nice on you, Beth. Perhaps it will help you to find a young man.'

Beth held her temper. She picked up the money and put it into her skirt pocket. 'Thank you, Aunt. That is very kind of you. I have seen a nice outfit at Harpers. I'll take a look in my lunch hour...'

32

Mondays were their official half day closing, though some of the staff stayed on after one to help with stocktaking if it was necessary. Sally visited the department and told Beth that she would be checking stock in her department that afternoon.

'Because you are by far the busiest department, I want to go through everything we've sold from the beginning and see what is left from the original stock – and what is turning over all the time. I'm going to need help. I wondered if you would stay behind for a few hours and help me.'

'Yes, of course I will,' Beth said, a little anxious. 'Do you think things have gone missing?'

'No, not at all,' Sally said and smiled at her. 'You're all so careful in this department. No, it's more a way of finding out just what is successful and what isn't, Mr Harper wrote me a letter and asked me to send all the information I could, because he is stuck in America for longer than he'd hoped.'

'Ah, I see.' Beth nodded her understanding. 'It's important that you send him full facts and figures.'

Sally frowned. 'I had thought he might return sooner.'

'I do hope he won't sell the store,' Beth said. 'It isn't easy to find somewhere to live even with a regular wage coming in. I've no idea what I'll do if I lose my job.'

'I thought you lived with your aunt?'

'Aunt Helen has suddenly decided to get married – in early August. I've got a few weeks to search for a room, but I can only look after work or on my afternoon off.'

'And I've asked you to work…' Sally looked thoughtful. 'I have two single beds in my room. I'm sure Mrs Craven won't mind if you stay with us – at least while you look for something else…'

'If you'd had a third bedroom, I would have asked.' Beth smiled. 'Thank you, Sally. At least I know I shan't be on the streets – and I really don't want to take just anything. Aunt Helen isn't the easiest person to live with, but her house is nicer than most of the others in our lane. If I could find somewhere closer to Oxford Street, it would save on the fares.'

'As I said, my room is big enough for two to share and I would be happy to give you a bed for a while,' Sally said. 'We share expenses and you can put five shillings in the pot to help cover them, as we both do each week.'

'I could pay seven and six – it's what I paid my aunt,' Beth said. 'Thank you so much, Sally – but you should ask Mrs Craven if she minds first…'

'Naturally I will, but I'm sure she won't mind,' Sally said. 'I've got work to do, but I'll come back at about a quarter to one armed with pads and pencils…'

* * *

Beth and Sally worked solidly for three hours that afternoon. By the end of that time, Sally had all the sheets of figures and stock-lists she needed and gathered them all into her folder with a satisfied nod of her head.

'I didn't mention overtime pay, but there will be five shillings extra in your wages on Friday,' she told Beth as they went downstairs.

Fred was still on duty. He'd been taking deliveries of new stock that afternoon and had waited to lock up after them, though Sally had her own key to the staff entrance.

'Been busy, ladies?' he said as he saw their smiling faces. 'I'm locking up now – have you finished for the day?'

'Yes, thank you, Fred,' Sally said and showed him her bulging folder. 'I've got work to do, but I shall do the rest at home this evening...'

'A lovely young woman like you should be out having a good time...' Fred looked at Beth and winked. 'I think you'll find someone is waiting for you, Miss Grey...'

'Well, she's free to go now, because we've finished,' Sally said. 'You get off, Beth, and I'll be down in a few minutes, Fred...'

'Righto, Miss Ross.'

'What do you mean?' Beth asked, but he just smiled mysteriously. Her curiosity was piqued, but when she emerged into the street, she saw that a man was leaning against a lamp post just outside. She caught her breath, looking at Jack Burrows in surprise. 'What are you doing here?'

'I thought it was your half day,' Jack said. 'Dad told me you were working extra hours – so I went somewhere for a couple of hours and came back. I thought I might see you home, Beth.'

Beth's heart did a little happy dance as she saw the smile in his eyes. 'Shouldn't you be at work or something?'

'I've got this week, including Sunday, to do as I like,' he said. 'Next Monday I report back to the ship and then we'll be off to New York. I shan't see you again until sometime in August, which is why I thought I'd meet you from work every day this week... make the most of the time we have before I'm on duty again.'

She looked up at him and then she smiled. 'I should like that,' she said. 'You can come back to the house with me – and stay for supper. It will probably be cheese or tomatoes on toast. Aunt Helen didn't cook a roast this Sunday.'

'Sounds wonderful to me.' Jack looked pleased. 'I didn't bring the bike tonight, but I could tomorrow...'

'Why not?' she said, feeling as though she was being swept up by a strong wind. 'It will give the neighbours something to talk about – but I shan't be living there much longer...'

'Oh, why?' Jack asked as they went to stand in the bus queue. 'Aren't you happy there?'

'I wasn't when I first moved in,' Beth admitted. 'My aunt is getting married and she will give up the house. It will be difficult to find anywhere as nice...'

Jack nodded but made no comment as they boarded the bus and moved down to the front. When the conductor came, he paid their fares, even though Beth offered her money.

Aunt Helen was in the parlour working at her sewing when Beth brought Jack in. She glanced up and then took her spectacles off to take a closer look.

'And who is this gentleman?' she asked.

'This is Fred Burrows' eldest son, Aunt Helen,' Beth said. 'I told you – he was commended for bravery. He works on ships as a steward and we're friends. Jack came to meet me from work and I've asked him to stay for supper...'

'Maggie hasn't come in yet,' Aunt Helen frowned. 'Well, Mr Burrows, perhaps you'd like to sit here and tell me a bit about yourself while Beth gets our supper ready. I made a cheese, onion and potato pie, Beth. You just need to pop it in the oven – and there are stewed raspberries and custard for afters.'

'You're in luck.' Beth smiled at Jack before abandoning him to her aunt's questioning. She expected that Aunt Helen would give him the third degree, but to her surprise her aunt's laughter reached her even before she'd put their supper into the oven to heat. She was setting the table when her aunt walked in followed by a grinning Jack. 'What was so funny?' Beth asked, looking at her aunt, but she merely shook her head.

'Mr Burrows has travelled a lot and he has a great many stories to tell,' she said mysteriously. 'I am sure he will tell you.' She disappeared into the pantry and brought out a bottle of pale ale and her favourite tipple, Jerez sherry. 'We can offer you a glass of beer, Mr Burrows, or a sherry?'

'Thank you, that is kind, but a glass of water is all I need,' Jack said. 'But don't let me stop you...'

'We seldom drink,' Aunt Helen said and put the bottles on the dresser. 'Do you not drink, Mr Burrows?'

'I find it best not to,' Jack said. 'In my job I see the effects of overindulgence all too often and so I hardly ever touch it...'

'Quite right,' Aunt Helen said and Beth could see her mentally ticking off another good conduct mark.

Jack said all the right things about her cooking as they ate and he told a funny story about an elderly passenger he'd served on board the ship that he'd sailed on from New York for his last voyage.

'He had a habit of popping his false teeth in a glass and leaving it in all sorts of odd places,' Jack told them. 'One of the young stewards saw them when he took the tray from the cabin but never thought a thing about them. They were thrown overboard with the rubbish and the poor passenger was forced to stick to soft foods for the rest of the voyage.'

'How awful for him,' Aunt Helen said. 'It isn't really funny – but you can't help laughing – but why didn't the steward realise what they were?'

'He told me that he thought the passenger wanted them cleaned – the way they put their shoes out, you know?' Jack grinned. 'It was his first job. He put the glass down with the used plates and turned away, meaning to come back, fetch the teeth and give them a clean – but when he looked, the Chinese cook's assistant had taken all the plates and thrown everything into the waste bin. Before he could be stopped, he'd disposed of the rubbish over the stern...'

'I didn't realise ships did that...' Aunt Helen said.

'We have to dispose of waste food,' Jack said. 'On passenger ships there can be quite a lot sometimes – besides, the gulls take most of it almost before it hits the water and if there's any left the fish will soon gobble it up.'

'Yes, well, I suppose it make sense,' she agreed. 'It just doesn't sound nice...'

'There are a lot worse things go into the sea than food waste,' Jack said, 'but we shan't talk about them at table...'

At that moment, Maggie entered the kitchen. She looked surprised to see Jack sitting at the table and then smiled. 'Please don't get up, Mr Burrows. I've just come to fetch the last of my things, Aunt Helen...'

'You're leaving us this evening?' Aunt Helen looked upset. 'I thought you might stay a few more nights...'

'I just have one more heavy case,' Maggie said. 'Ralf is in the hall with it. I thought I would just say goodbye...' She looked a little tearful, as if she'd only now realised that it wasn't so easy to say farewell to friends.

Beth stood up and went to her, kissing her cheek. 'You're not going to the ends of the earth,' she said. 'I shall see you at work tomorrow – and you will come to Aunt Helen's wedding still?'

'Oh yes, of course,' Maggie said.

'Well, take care of yourself, my dear.' Aunt Helen got up and took something from the dresser drawer. She put a small parcel into the girl's hands. 'A little present from me – I hope you'll keep in touch. Beth will give you my new address when I have it...'

Beth went out into the hall, where Ralf was waiting with a large suitcase. 'You should have come through,' she said. 'We were just about to make a pot of tea...'

'Thank you, but we shan't stop,' Ralf said. 'Mother didn't want us to be too late back...'

'Oh, of course...' Beth glanced at Maggie, smiled and then nodded. 'I'll see you in the morning...'

She watched as the two of them left. Maggie seemed a little

subdued and it made her wonder whether her friend would enjoy living under Mrs Higgins' roof as much as she'd thought she would...

Returning to the kitchen, Beth discovered that Aunt Helen and Jack were at the sink. Aunt Helen was washing the dishes and Jack was using the tea towel with authority.

'That's not the first time you've done that,' Beth said and Jack nodded.

'After my mother died, we had to look after ourselves. Dad brought us up to be independent – and my job has taught me to turn my hand to anything.'

'Yes, I suppose you have to do many things as a steward on board ship,' Aunt Helen said and he agreed.

'I keep the cabins clean and smelling fresh, change sheets, bring snacks and drinks to the staterooms, even a full three-course meal. When I'm not doing that, I serve at one of the bars – and, on occasion, I'm asked to dance with the ladies who don't have a partner. Then there are the gentlemen who need a hand getting to bed... and are occasionally unwell all over the floor...'

'You do have a busy time,' Aunt Helen observed as she poured the water away and wiped her hands. 'You will make someone a good husband, Mr Burrows...'

'Oh, I shall expect my wife to wait on me hand and foot when I'm at home,' Jack said and winked at Beth. Aunt Helen saw the wink and laughed.

'Well, I imagine you two might like a chance to talk over a pot of tea. I have some work to do. You may bring me a cup, Beth, and then sit and talk to your friend for a while – but don't forget you have a bus to catch in the morning...'

'Yes, Aunt Helen, thank you,' Beth said. 'I'll put the kettle on now...'

Jack sat down at the table as Beth put the kettle on the hob and her aunt disappeared into the parlour. 'Am I mistaken – or did your young friend look a bit upset?' he asked as she set a tray with cups and saucers, milk in a jug and the sugar bowl.

'I thought so too,' Beth said as she warmed the pot before adding three spoons of loose tea. 'Maggie was excited about going to live in Ralf's home, but she seemed nervous... a bit regretful...'

'Yes, I thought that,' Jack said. 'In a way, it's like living with her in-laws, and I'm not sure that ever really works.'

'Perhaps not,' Beth said. 'Miss Ross – she is the buyer I worked with on the stocktake this afternoon – has told me that I can share her room when my aunt lets the house go, just until I find somewhere else.'

Jack made a wry face. 'I know how hard it can be to find a decent room. We have shore time between jobs when we're overseas and on some of the runs it's almost impossible to find anything clean, unless you go to an expensive hotel.'

'Do you like working on the ships?' Beth asked. 'It seems to be hard work?'

'We earn every penny – but some of the passengers are generous and you make good tips. I save mine because I want a business of my own one day...'

'What kind of business?'

'I hadn't really thought of it, not seriously – just that one day I'd be my own boss...'

'It's something to think about,' she said, 'but I don't think you should rush into anything, Jack. You have a good job – you should enjoy that for a while...'

'Except that I'm not sure I shall enjoy being away from you for weeks at a time,' Jack told her. 'I'm fond of Dad and Tim – but there wasn't anything to stay put for until I went to bed last night and couldn't stop thinking about you and how I couldn't wait until Sunday to see you again...'

'Jack! You don't know me...' Beth gasped, her nape tingling at the look in his eyes.

Jack stood up and came towards her. 'I don't know you, Beth, and you don't know me – but what I do know for certain is that I want to be with you as much as I can...'

She smiled up at him. 'I'd like that very much, Jack Burrows – and I hope we shall get to know each other well, but...' Beth took a deep breath. 'It's too soon, Jack. I thought I loved someone once, but that didn't work out well, because I didn't know him – and I don't know you...'

'If I loved you, Beth, it would be forever,' Jack said, his expression so serious that something clutched at her heart. 'I'm not going to declare my undying devotion now – I know we need to take things slowly, but I'm hoping we can do just that...'

33

Beth felt as if she was walking on air when she got to work the next morning. She hung up her light jacket and tidied her counter, and then saw Maggie enter the department. One look at her pale face told her that something wasn't quite right.

'What's the problem, Maggie love?' she asked, putting the formality of their working titles to one side. 'Has someone upset you?'

'It's my mother...' Maggie spoke in hushed tones. 'The police came round yesterday evening and told us that she has been found...'

'They came to Ralf's home? How did they know you were there?'

'I gave my address to Mr Stockbridge as soon as I knew I was moving, and the police said they'd got it from the store.'

Beth moved towards her, putting an arm about her waist. 'What did the police say about your mother?'

Maggie's eyes filled with tears. 'She's very ill, Beth. They say she's dying in an infirmary. She doesn't have any money and they think... they say her accomplice took it all and then deserted her. She asked for me and they came round to Ralf's mother's house...' Maggie gulped. 'Mrs Higgins didn't know about the scandal and she was upset when the police came looking – Ralf said she didn't mean to be harsh, but she told me she would not have been as welcoming had she known what my mother was accused of...'

'Has your mother been accused of anything formally?'

Maggie shook her head. 'The police said she was too ill to question and they say that if I don't visit her by this evening, it may be too late.' Her eyes met Beth's. 'Ralf's mother says I should not go because it looks as if I'm condoning her behaviour. According to her, my mother is at the very least a thief and mostly likely a murderess...'

'Oh no!' Beth cried. 'She ought not to have said that to you...'

'Ralf said it would be better if I didn't go – but I have to, Beth. I know I said I didn't care, but she's dying...'

'Of course you must go,' Beth said sympathetically. 'Jack is going to meet me after work this evening, but we could both come with you...'

Maggie thanked her but had to take her place at her counter because they both had customers. During her break time, Maggie confided in Mrs Craven, and in the end it was she who insisted on accompanying her to the infirmary to visit her mother.

'It was kind of you to offer to go,' she said to Beth, 'but I feel this needs an older woman. Maggie quite rightly wants to see her mother, but she must not be compromised or bullied. I shall accompany her and then take her home and sort things out with Mrs Higgins.'

So it was arranged that Mrs Craven would look out for Maggie and Beth was able to go out for the evening with Jack, as they'd previously arranged. He took her to a small restaurant and they sat all evening talking and laughing over the excellent food.

'This is where I'm in my element,' Jack told her with a grin. 'I think I should have been a chef – or maybe just the manager of a place like this...'

'You like food,' Beth said and looked at him thoughtfully. 'And you've certainly learned how to look after people. Why don't you take a course in the things you don't know about managing a hotel?'

'I'd never given it a thought,' Jack said. 'I could study while I'm away – there must be places where I could take some sort of course to earn a diploma or a certificate...'

'It's something to think about for the future,' Beth said and smiled as he touched her hand. 'There's no hurry about any of it, Jack. I shall enjoy getting to know you when you're home – and I could write to you when you're away...'

'I probably wouldn't get them,' he said. 'We call in at various ports, but although I can send you cards, yours might miss me...' He looked at her seriously. 'While I'm away, will you get a photograph done for me, so I can take it with me in future...?'

Beth made a mental note to write him some letters, chatty, friendly missives telling him about her feelings and what she'd done at work. She would have a small batch ready for him to take with her photo on the following Monday and while he was away she would write about her life every day and give them to him for the next voyage.

She lay for a while that evening thinking about Maggie and wondering how she'd got on visiting her mother. It seemed unkind of Mrs Higgins to want to deny her, when she must know that Maggie was upset. Not for the first time, Beth wondered about her friend's snap decision to move in with Ralf's family. It had seemed a brilliant idea, but Maggie didn't really know any of them yet – even Ralf.

Beth knew it was easy to think yourself in love with someone. She'd loved Mark, but she'd been young then and she thought now that she would probably have realised that he was the sort of man who would sulk and get angry if he didn't get his own way, which meant that she might not have been happy with him.

For years, Beth had regretted having to give him up, but now she'd begun to see that perhaps Mark had never been right for her, and that meant her mother's refusal to let her go had been a blessing in disguise.

What Beth needed was a man who took things more in his stride – and she thought she might have met a man she could be happy with, but this time she wouldn't jump in too soon. Jack's job took him away and that was good because it gave them both time to think about what they really wanted...

Smiling to herself, Beth turned over and closed her eyes. She was feeling so much happier than she had for a long time and she thought it was partly due to her job and the friends she'd made at Harpers – but also because of a man's smiling eyes...

34

Maggie was in tears when the nurse told her that it was time for her to leave. Her mother was very weak, but she'd recognised her; she'd clung to Maggie's hand and begged her forgiveness.

'I never meant him to die...' she'd said. 'Forgive me... please...'

Maggie had mumbled something that sounded like yes, though she knew that inside she would never quite forgive what had happened to the father she loved so much, but it would be cruel to refuse a woman in such distress.

She would never know whether her mother had intended Poppa to take that medicine or whether it had just happened because he'd had enough of the pain, perhaps it was a bit of both. Maggie didn't even think of the money that had been stolen from him, it had never mattered to her. Nor did she feel pleased to see her mother lying there, the victim of a cruel battering that was slowly robbing her of life. She hoped the police would find and punish the man who had done it, but he was probably long gone on a ship and far away from justice.

They knew as they left the infirmary that Maggie's mother was unlikely to last the night, but Rachel persuaded her that it would be foolish to sit all night with a woman who had slipped into unconsciousness soon after begging for her daughter's forgiveness.

'She knows you came and you forgave her,' Rachel said as she took Maggie outside and led her to the nearest bus stop. 'None of this is your fault and you have nothing to reproach yourself for, my dear. Many a daughter would have ignored her plea for a visit.'

'Mrs Higgins thought I should. She will be angry that I ignored her advice.'

'Mrs Higgins is not your guardian or even your mother-in-law yet,' Rachel said. 'You moved into her house as her guest and if she feels she can no longer offer you a home – you can move out again...'

'Aunt Helen would take me back until she marries,' Maggie said. 'But then I'd have to find somewhere else – and I don't want to hurt or upset Ralf...'

'And he should not wish to see you upset either,' Rachel told her firmly. 'I know you love this young man, Maggie – but if he loves you, he will stand up for you to his mother...'

Maggie thanked her for her advice but continued to be nervous until they reached Mrs Higgins' home.

Ralf opened the door to her, looking anxious. 'We thought something must have happened to you – Mother was just about to send me to the police station...'

Maggie seemed to shrink into herself, answering defensively, 'We went to visit my mother. She is dying and in great distress. She wanted me to forgive her.'

Ralf shook his head as if dismissing her statement as unimportant, bringing tears to her eyes as she walked into the big, comfortable and spotlessly clean kitchen, followed by Rachel. Mrs Higgins turned reproachful eyes on her.

'You might have let us know where you were going, Maggie,' she said in a cold voice. 'Ralf has been worried to death. I told him you would have disobeyed us and gone to the infirmary, but he thought not...' she shook her head. 'After we took you into our family and treated you as a daughter...'

'I was worried, Maggie...' Ralf endorsed his mother's accusations.

Maggie's tears were not far away. She had been a fool to believe that Mrs Higgins really liked her. She'd taken her in so that she could control the girl Ralf wanted to marry...

'The police told me she was dying and in terrible distress – how could I not go?' Maggie was close to tears. 'Ralf, I'm sorry if you were worried – but I had to go...'

'No, Maggie, you did not,' his mother said. 'Really, if you are to live under my roof, you must observe some rules. It is quite shaming to know that you went to a woman who is guilty of theft and who knows what else...'

Maggie's bottom lip trembled, but she said nothing, struggling to hold back her tears.

'And what rule has Maggie broken by visiting a dying woman in distress?' Rachel cut in because she saw that Maggie was trembling and Ralf showed no sign of coming to her rescue. 'Any woman of feeling would understand that she must wish to see her mother at such a time?'

'And who are you?' Mrs Higgins stared at her furiously. She was not a large woman but her voice carried a piercing sharpness and her eyes were cold.

'I am Maggie's supervisor at work...'

'I do not recall asking you into my home – would you please leave at once?' the outraged woman demanded.

'Gladly,' Rachel said and sent her a look of utter disgust. 'I have no wish to stay – and if Maggie has any sense, nor will she.' She turned to look at the girl. 'There is a spare bed at the flat I share with Miss Ross. If you find it unbearable here, you are very welcome to stay with us...'

'That won't be necessary,' Ralf said, finding his tongue at last. 'Mother is just upset because we were worried – and I know Maggie wants to stay with us...'

Maggie looked at Rachel. 'Thank you for the offer, Mrs Craven. I shall not forget – but I do love Ralf...'

'Very well, I'll leave you here,' Rachel said. Her eyes met the angry stare of Ralf's mother. 'However, my door is always open to you, Maggie...'

Turning, she went out and resisted the temptation to slam the door behind her. Mrs Higgins reminded her of her own mother-in-law, but, if anything, she was far worse.

Rachel walked to the bus stop and waited for one to arrive, feeling frustrated. She would have liked to bring Maggie away with her. The girl's feelings were mixed up enough, regret and grief fighting with resentment at the way her mother had deserted her father. She needed kindness and comfort, not scolding for doing something entirely natural.

Boarding her bus, Rachel's thoughts dwelled on her own past as it drove off. She looked out at the lights of shop windows and found her thoughts drifting to the way her life had changed since she started working for Harpers. It was not only the job and the extra money or even the independence it offered her. Sharing with Sally had given her a settled comfortable life and she would not in the least have minded Maggie occupying the extra single bed in her room. She had a Chinese painted screen that could be erected to give them a little privacy, but it might be fun to share, all of them together, especially if Beth moved in too.

Yes, she rather thought she would enjoy that and she would monitor the situation with Maggie. She'd popped the idea on her suddenly, but if the girl was being made unhappy, she wouldn't stand by and let it happen... Maggie was almost like a daughter to Rachel – the daughter she'd never had.

For a moment she was overwhelmed by sadness as she remembered her husband's death, but then the grief faded. She wasn't that many years older than Sally, and Rachel was aware that she was not unattractive. If she wanted, there was still time to find happiness – to marry perhaps, someone she cared for...

As the bus slowed to a stop and she prepared to disembark, Rachel was smiling. She enjoyed her work at Harpers and she liked sharing the flat with Sally. She was in no hurry to make a change, but the shadows had moved away at last and she'd understood tonight that there was no way she wanted to be like Mrs Higgins – taking her own unhappiness out on others. Rachel had lost her husband, but she had a good job, a nice place to live and friends – in time there might be more.

* * *

Beth saw that Maggie looked pale the next morning, but she seemed to be fine once she started serving her customer and when Mrs Craven spoke to her later, she smiled and nodded. After they'd all been to lunch, there was an unusual lull between customers and Beth took the opportunity to ask her how she felt.

'I'm all right,' Maggie said. 'I shan't see my mother again, I know that – but I feel I've made my peace with her and I'm glad I went.'

'What of Mrs Higgins?' Beth saw her eyes darken. 'Was she very angry?'

'Yes, at first, but then she cried and said it was just that she'd been worried about me. I had to say it was all right, Beth – but it wasn't. She was horrid to me and rude to Mrs Craven. I think I made a mistake going to live there... she isn't nice at all, just selfish.'

'Oh, I'm so sorry,' Beth said and touched her hand in sympathy. 'You could come back until Aunt Helen marries...'

'Thank you, I know.' Maggie raised her head. 'I have to think carefully, Beth. I do love Ralf and he would be hurt if I said I couldn't live in his mother's house. It's difficult...'

'It must be,' Beth said, understanding her dilemma. 'It might be even worse if you were married – think what she might expect then. I do not think it is a good idea to live with your in-laws, unless you know them well and like them.'

'Yes, I shall think carefully,' Maggie said, 'but I don't want to rush into something else and find I've made a mistake again.'

'No, I see that,' Beth agreed. 'You take your time, Maggie love – but remember you have friends.'

'Yes, I know. Mrs Craven says I can stay in her room for a while...'

'Oh, I didn't know...' Beth's nape tingled. 'If I moved into Sally's room, we should all be together...'

'Just as Sally wanted,' Maggie said and the smile lit her eyes. 'It might be fun...'

'Yes, I think it would,' Beth said. 'I'm going to a Music Hall with Jack this evening. He wants to spend every evening with me until he leaves for New York next Monday.'

'You look happy,' Maggie said. 'I'm glad you've found some-one, Beth.'

'I thought you were happy too?'

'I was – I am...' Maggie looked at her and sighed. 'I was, but now I'm not sure...'

35

Beth loved every moment of the Music Hall. Being with Jack was enjoyable, even if they just walked through streets in the dusk of evening, holding hands. She was happier than she had been for a long time, the only shadow the knowledge that he would have to leave for his ship on Sunday afternoon. However, she spent as much time as possible with him that week and still managed to write three newsy letters in odd moments in her bedroom and on the bus to work.

'We'll say goodbye here,' Jack told her as he came round to take his leave of her on Sunday morning. 'I hate long goodbyes, Beth – and it won't be long before I'm home for another shore leave.'

Beth resisted the temptation to cross her fingers. She thought Jack was very brave to carry on working on board ship despite what had happened, but he didn't seem to fear the sea and she wouldn't let him see that she was anxious. Instead, she hugged him and gave him a sweet kiss on the lips and then thrust a little parcel wrapped in brown paper and string into his hands.

'What is this?' Jack asked, looking puzzled. 'You shouldn't buy me presents, Beth.'

'It isn't a present,' she said and smiled. 'Keep it and open it on board ship and you'll understand.'

He put the small package into his inside coat pocket and then picked up the bulging kitbag. 'I'll be back before you miss me,' he said and grinned.

'Of course you will.' Beth laughed. 'I'll be moving after the wedding – but Fred will know where I am...'

Beth went to watch as he roared off on his motorbike, her heart aching a little as she returned to the house.

Aunt Helen came downstairs dressed in her best navy blue costume with a red and navy hat and red gloves.

'Do I look all right?' she asked, a little nervously.

'You look very smart and attractive,' Beth said. 'Have a good time with your friends.'

Aunt Helen nodded, kissed her cheek and left. It felt strange to have the house all to herself. Rather than sit and brood, Beth decided to give it all a good clean and started by polishing the parlour. Her aunt had obviously been sorting through some papers and Beth tidied them into a pile so that she could polish the table top. Her eye was drawn to a life insurance document; the date was recent. It was odd that Aunt Helen should take out a new policy, although perhaps it was because of her marriage. She supposed people did that when they had someone else to consider.

Leaving the room tidy and clean and smelling of lavender, Beth went upstairs to turn out the bedrooms. Her aunt's personal business was her own and nothing to do with Beth...

* * *

Maggie stuck it out at Ralf's mother's house for nearly three weeks before she broke. She arrived at Harpers on a Thursday morning with two suitcases in her hands and another bag slung across her back. Beth had just got off the bus and she ran to catch her up and relieve her of one of the cases.

'What happened?' she asked as she saw Maggie's tear-streaked face.

'We had an awful row. Mrs Higgins couldn't find her grandmother's gold brooch. She said she'd been searching for it for days and practically accused me of stealing it, because she'd noticed me wearing a similar one – but Aunt Helen gave it to me the day I left her house.' Maggie sniffed hard. 'She has been unbearable ever since I went to my mother's funeral... I know she thinks I'm a thief... just like my mother, that's what she hinted.'

'Oh, Maggie love,' Beth said. 'What an awful woman she is – pretending to like you until you went there and making your life a misery ever since.'

'I wouldn't stay there after the things she said. I told Ralf that she'd practically accused me of stealing her brooch and she denied it. He told me I was too sensitive and I told him it was time he made up his mind whether he was a man with a will of his own or his mother's little lackey...' Maggie's eyes filled with tears. 'We had a terrible row and then I just packed my things and walked out. I didn't take her brooch, Beth. I think she lost it – it was quite old and the clasp was weak. She kept saying she would get it done, but she didn't and now she blames me.'

Beth sympathised. 'It is horrid to be accused of something you didn't do – and if people don't believe you there's nothing to be done...'

'I did the only thing I could. I opened my bags and told her to search before I left – and she said that obviously it wasn't in my things now or I wouldn't invite her to search, implying that I'd sold it.'

'What a nasty woman!' Beth said. 'Well, you're welcome to come to Aunt Helen's until Sunday morning. I'm moving out after the wedding and in with Sally at her flat. Sally and Mrs Craven insist that I stay with them while I continue to search for a room.'

'I'll speak to Mrs Craven later...'

The two girls left Maggie's cases with Fred. Beth didn't hear the conversation with Mrs Craven, but Maggie looked happy afterwards and told Beth that she was moving into the flat that evening.

'It makes more sense than coming to your aunt's for two nights – you'll have more than enough to do before the wedding without me in the way...'

'I'd like you to come round early on Saturday,' Beth said. 'Aunt Helen will be happy to see you and we can help her get her things ready...'

'I'd love to.' She smiled mistily. 'I feel so foolish, Beth. I thought I loved Ralf and I still do... but he's weak where his mother is concerned and I don't want to come second best all the time.'

'I know it hurts to lose the person you love,' Beth told her. 'Perhaps he will come to the shop and apologise once he's had time to think about it...'

'I'm not sure I want him to...'

Beth didn't try to argue with her. Maggie was feeling bruised and hurt and would need time to think about what she really wanted of life. For the moment that did not include Ralf.

As she turned round, she saw to her surprise that Aunt Helen had entered the department. She walked up to Beth's counter and smiled.

'What have you got that will suit me, Beth?' she asked. 'I've bought something in the dress department, but now I'd like a pretty hat, some gloves and perhaps a bag...'

36

Sally looked up from her work as Jenni entered the office that morning in late July, and then got up and went to greet her with a smile. She was surprised when the other woman put her arms about her and embraced her, kissing her cheek. Sally kissed her back.

'What a lovely surprise. I didn't expect you before Christmas...'

'I missed you – and you've done such a wonderful job here,' Jenni said. 'Marco told me that wonderful garden party window display was your idea. And the Olympic support window is fantastic, with its photographs of British and American athletes and our flags! Such a great idea for Harpers! I know it will come down soon, but quite a few people were admiring it when I arrived. Marco told me that was your idea too. You're a wonder, Sally, and I'm so pleased you came into our lives.'

'I've only done the job you gave me. Mr Marco and Mr Stockbridge have done their share.' Sally felt a warming glow at Jenni's praise. 'How are things for you – your friend? Does he blame you for the loss of his wife...?'

'Yes – and no,' Jenni said and grimaced. 'He knows it wasn't my fault, but he can't help feeling that if I hadn't given her my ticket she would still be alive…and that hurts…'

'I'm so sorry,' she said. 'It must be very hard for you?'

'Yes – however, Henry was glad of my help with finding a nanny for little Tom and he thanked me before I left – said that he hoped I wouldn't be away too long…' Jenni smiled. 'Thank goodness for the new steamships. Only a few years ago it would have meant weeks at sea to get here, now it's only a matter of days…'

Sally nodded, because the new fast ships had brought them much closer than could have been dreamed of only a few years ago. 'Is your brother with you?'

'No, Ben couldn't make it,' Jenni said and her smile disappeared. 'He has personal business, Sally. I don't know it all, but I know he's torn two ways. He needs to stay there for a while and yet his heart is here – he wants to make this store a success. In fact, he has to because we both invested everything we have in it…'

'So if it fails…' Sally was shocked. 'You could lose it all…'

'That is the size of it.' Jenni shrugged. 'It's the reason I came back before I'd intended. Ben is stuck back home and sends his regrets. I made time, Sally, even though I believed you could cope – but I know it was wrong to just throw you to the sharks and leave you…'

'It wasn't your fault,' Sally said. She wasn't sure what was keeping Ben Harper in America, but if it was a pretty woman he was taking a huge risk. 'I just hope I shan't let you down.'

'Ben believes in you and so do I,' Jenni said and she was smiling. 'I was wrong when I told you not to trust him, Sally – my brother really likes you a lot… and that threw me, I can tell you…' She laughed. 'Ben has always been a bit of a loner, but I think that might change… he seemed as concerned about you as the store…'

Sally drew a deep breath. 'Do you know when he intends to return?'

'No, he doesn't either...' For the first time, Jenni looked uncertain. 'I didn't know anything before – and it isn't my place to tell you – but Ben has his reasons...' She shook her head as Sally questioned with her eyes. 'No, I can't betray a secret, even though I trust you – you'll just have to wait until Ben gets here...'

'I shan't ask you to betray a confidence,' Sally said and stood back to gaze at her. 'You look wonderful, Jenni. I love that outfit...'

'Yes, I bought it in Paris last year...' Jenni said. 'It was my first time, but I'd like to go back – when I can. I've got to think about Henry and Tom for a while...'

'Yes, I suppose you must,' Sally said. 'I hope he appreciates you, Jenni.'

'Henry is still grieving for his wife,' Jenni said. 'I found a good nanny to look after Tom, as I told you, but he cried when I told him I was going to London for a couple of weeks...' She sighed and shook her head. 'I loved Marie and I love both Tom and Henry – I've always loved Henry, even before he married my friend. Marie was three years older than me and Henry saw me as a child...'

'You're a beautiful young woman, Jenni. He must be mad if he can't see that...'

'And you say the nicest things, Sally,' she said and laughed, banishing the shadows from her eyes. 'Why don't I take you to supper this evening and then you can fill me in on everything that has been happening over here...?'

'That would be lovely,' Sally agreed. 'I have a dress firm to see this afternoon and then I'm visiting a bag importer – I'd like your opinion if you felt like coming, Jenni. The bags come from Spain and are lizard or snakeskin and seem quite reasonably priced, but you could tell me what you think of the quality...'

* * *

Sally glanced in the mirror as she prepared to change for the evening. Jenni had liked the bags they'd viewed together and placed an order for the stores in America, praising Sally for finding the supplier.

'My uncle never gave me enough time to shop around,' she confided. 'I've sourced as many new lines as I can, but it's great having you on my team, Sally. We can help each other now... make all the stores more successful...'

Sally's smile faded as she thought about what Jenni had said concerning her brother. Ben Harper had personal business keeping him in America. It must be very important to make him stay away when his store was so new and needed his attention, but Jenni seemed to be on his side, whatever it was – and she'd come back, taking up weeks of her valuable time, because he couldn't...

Sally sighed. Jenni thought her brother liked his jewellery buyer a lot, but she didn't understand. Ben Harper might think she was good at her job, but he wasn't interested in her as a woman and that made her heart ache.

She shook her head. It was time to leave for the evening and feeling sorry for herself was a waste of time!

37

Aunt Helen was as nervous as a young girl on her wedding morning, but in the end she was dressed and ready, looking more attractive in a heavy cream silk dress and a fitted jacket than Beth had ever seen her. She had a soft pink hat with lots of tulle that she'd bought from Harpers and cream gloves and suede shoes.

'You do think I'm doing the right thing?' she asked Beth three times before the cab arrived to take the three of them to the church.

'Gerald is a nice man and, I think, fond of you,' Beth said. 'Just relax, this is your special day and you deserve to be happy.'

'You look lovely,' Maggie said and kissed her. She gave her a pretty handkerchief with blue embroidery as her little gift. Beth had given her some silk underwear, because it was pretty. 'He's bound to love you and you will be very happy.'

Beth and Maggie were both wearing pale blue with white hats, gloves and shoes. Their outfits were different but looked pretty together as Aunt Helen's attendants.

'I hope so,' Aunt Helen said. She picked up her handbag and took two small parcels out. 'These are for my maid of honour and my dear friend...'

Beth was standing with her aunt as a maid of honour and would also give her away. It would be a church wedding, and Aunt Helen's dress was ankle length, her hat almost as light and soft as a traditional veil. She'd thought the outfit more suitable for an older woman than a wedding gown and a long veil.

Inside the velvet lined boxes were little silver lockets on fine chains, both very similar in size and design. The girls thanked her and helped each other to put them on. Then the cab arrived and they went out into the street. The neighbours had turned out to watch and some of them waved, though others gossiped behind their hands, because everyone had been surprised when they heard that Aunt Helen was to marry.

The church was only two streets away and there were quite a few guests already seated. Vases of flowers made it smell lovely and lent their beauty to the solemn occasion as Beth walked down the aisle with her aunt holding on to her arm. She noticed that Aunt Helen's hand trembled slightly and she gave it a little squeeze.

Maggie had gone to sit with Jack, who had arrived home the previous evening. Beth had thought he wouldn't be back until after the wedding and was thrilled to see him. Mrs Craven was holding the fort in their department with staff drafted in from other areas. Sally had agreed that she would oversee things at the store so that Beth and Maggie could attend the wedding.

The ceremony was made pleasant because the sun shone through the windows the whole time and warmed the ancient building sending rays of colour over the worn flagstones. Soon it was over and everyone left the church behind the bride and groom to attend the wedding breakfast, which was held in a hotel nearby.

Beth knew no one other than the bride, Maggie and Jack. She'd met Gerald only a few times and even though he greeted her and Maggie politely, she felt that she was not part of his group of friends. She didn't know why but something about Gerald made her uneasy, as if he didn't want her around, and when Aunt Helen said she and her new husband were leaving an hour or so later for their honeymoon in Paris, Beth felt relieved that she could return to the house.

Most of her aunt's personal things had been taken to Gerald's home earlier that week. Only the beds, the kitchen furniture and a few pieces in the parlour remained. Someone would be coming to clear them the following week and Beth would leave on Sunday morning with her own belongings.

'It seems a bit empty,' Jack said when she asked him in for a cup of tea. Maggie had left them and gone back to the store, saying that she might as well see if she was needed before she went back to the flat. 'Will you mind sleeping here alone this evening?'

'I hadn't thought about it,' Beth said and looked about her. 'It does feel very empty – I suppose I could have gone straight to Sally's, but I thought I should clear up a bit. I'm going to leave the key with the next-door neighbour tomorrow and they will let the men in to remove the rest of the stuff on Monday. Aunt Helen doesn't want anything else; it's all been sold to a second-hand dealer...'

'What about your things? Will you have room for them all in the flat?'

Beth shook her head. 'I've got a few bits that are too bulky – your father said he could store them in his attic for me.'

Jack nodded and smiled. 'Why don't you show me?'

Beth led the way upstairs, indicating the two tea chests on the landing. 'I was going to ask the removal men to take them round on Monday...'

'What about the things you're taking to the flat?'

'I've two cases in the bedroom...'

'Right, I can get us a cab and he'll put all this lot on for you, Beth. We'll give him the address – and I can take you on the bike. We'll go to my father's place for the night and tomorrow I'll get your cases to the flat for you... It's Sunday, so I can make two or three trips if need be.'

'I don't want to put Fred to any trouble...'

'You can have my bed for one night,' Jack said. 'I'll sleep on the sofa in the parlour. I'm not leaving you here alone tonight, so no arguments – either I stay here with you, or we go to my father's house...'

Beth laughed and gave in, because he looked so determined and she didn't truly wish to stay here alone. The house seemed cold and lonely and she was glad that she'd accepted Sally's offer to stay with her. She didn't fancy living alone in one room in a boarding house; sharing with friends would be much more comfortable.

It took an hour to find a willing cabbie who loaded most of Beth's belongings into his cab, leaving her to follow in the sidecar of Jack's motorcycle with one small bag on her lap. Beth took a last look round, feeling a chill at the nape of her neck and the thought came to her that she hoped Aunt Helen would never regret what she'd done. Now why had she thought something daft like that?

Shaking her head, Beth pushed it from her mind. Aunt Helen must care about Gerald a lot or she wouldn't have married him... and yet the memory of that insurance policy niggled. Why had her aunt taken it out just before her wedding?

Beth decided it wasn't her business. She had her own life to think about now.

Fred welcomed them home and suggested they all have pie and mash from the shop on the corner for their supper, and Timmy was sent to fetch it while Beth was shown to her room.

It smelled of Jack's hair oil and shaving soap and she liked the way it was set out with lots of different objects that he'd brought back from his voyages overseas. She held a delicate shell against her ear and it seemed to sound like the sea. Smiling, she tidied her hair in the mirror as she heard Jack's voice calling her downstairs.

'The food is hot – come and eat,' he said and pulled out a chair for her next to Fred, sitting opposite her himself. Timmy sat at the far end of the table and grinned at her as he passed a dish of hot squashy peas.

'I bought these, my treat,' he told her. 'It's nice havin' you here, Miss Grey...'

'Oh, please, call me Beth...'

'Yeah, all right then,' Jack's brother said and grinned at his sibling across the table. 'When are you goin' to ask her and make it official?'

'When I'm good and ready and when Beth is ready too,' Jack said good-naturedly. 'You mind your tongue, Tim – or I'll clip your ear good and proper.'

'Tim is only joshing you,' his father said and smiled at Beth. 'Beth doesn't mind – do you?'

'No, I like being here with you all,' Beth said. 'I feel like one of the family when you tease each other...'

'You are,' Fred said and glanced at his eldest son. 'It isn't for me to embarrass either of you – but no one would be happier than I if you two got together permanently...'

'Give us a chance, Dad,' Jack said, but his eyes were laughing. 'I've only just got back. Beth and me – we had a week to get to know each other. I think she wants a bit longer than that to be sure I'm worth taking a chance on...'

Beth smiled, ate her delicious supper and said nothing. She didn't need to. This was a happy family and she knew she fitted in with them – and perhaps one day she would be more than an honoured guest, but Jack was right. They'd had just one week to get to know one another and Beth knew they needed longer. They needed time to think of the future and plan what they would do if and when Jack left the sea – and in the meantime she would carry on with her job and settle down to life at the flat with her friends...

* * *

Sally looked at the mahogany chest of drawers Beth had asked the furniture dealer to bring over for her. She'd hesitated to buy it, but Sally told her there was room to stand it in the alcove and so she'd purchased it to store her clothes and bits and pieces. It had gone in well, taking up hardly any space. In Sally's opinion it would look better painted white, but she didn't mind it as it was, because she was happy to share her room with Beth.

It had been lovely going out to supper with Jenni and they'd talked and talked for hours. Jenni was filled with enthusiasm for the store and they spoke of building it up even more and perhaps expanding one day.

'Ben would like to open more stores – perhaps another in London or other big cities over here,' Jenni had told her. 'It depends how well things go for him, of course. He couldn't think of it for a year or two, not until he pays off his debts...'

Sally hadn't known he'd got debts, but she knew nothing of his life. Ben Harper was a mystery to her and she was a fool to imagine herself in love with him.

Sally sighed as she undressed and got into bed. She could hear Maggie and Rachel talking in the next room and felt pleased; because this was the last night she would be on her own. It would be good to have Beth staying with her, at least for the time being. As for the future – well, Sally didn't know what to expect or what to hope for.

Jenni had hinted that her brother thought she, Sally, was special – that she meant something to him, but if that was the case why hadn't he made sure she knew it? Ben Harper was coming back to London as soon as his important business was finished. In the meantime, he'd told Jenni to talk to the staff and let them know that Harpers was safe despite his absence.

Sally knew that with all his money invested in it, Ben would have to fight for the survival of his business. It would take a lot of hard work to make the store successful and secure.

A little smile touched her mouth as she thought of the way Maggie had suddenly grown up after a quarrel with her boyfriend. Ralf might try to make it up with her, though he hadn't yet, but Maggie was getting on with her life and Sally had seen her laughing over a book Rachel had shown her earlier. Beth too had come through a storm and now seemed much happier. Sally's friend Sylvia was enjoying her present job and Rachel seemed less sad than she had when they first met. Her friends were all getting on with their lives and Sally knew that she would too.

For a moment a picture of Irish Mick came into her head, but she dismissed it. Sally was grateful to him for helping Sylvia, but, despite her knowing it was stupid, it was Ben Harper who made her heart sing.

Whatever was keeping him from returning to London, Sally could cope by simply getting on with her job. She had friends now and a life of her own and those days of wandering the streets because she didn't want to go back to her lonely room were over. Sally knew that she was looking forward to the future whatever it held...

MORE FROM ROSIE CLARKE

We hope you enjoyed reading *The Shop Girls of Harpers*. If you did, please leave a review.

If you'd like to gift a copy, this book is also available as a ebook, digital audio download and audiobook CD.

Sign up to Rosie Clarke's mailing list for news, competitions and updates on future books.

http://bit.ly/RosieClarkeNewsletter

ABOUT THE AUTHOR

Rosie Clarke is a #1 bestselling saga writer whose most recent books include *The Mulberry Lane* series. She has written over 100 novels under different pseudonyms and is a RNA Award winner. She lives in Cambridgeshire.

Visit Rosie Clarke's website: http://www.rosieclarke.co.uk

Follow Rosie on social media:

 twitter.com/AnneHerries

ABOUT BOLDWOOD BOOKS

Boldwood Books is a fiction publishing company seeking out the best stories from around the world.

Find out more at www.boldwoodbooks.com

Sign up to the Book and Tonic newsletter for news, offers and competitions from Boldwood Books!

http://www.bit.ly/bookandtonic

We'd love to hear from you, follow us on social media:

 facebook.com/BookandTonic

twitter.com/BoldwoodBooks

 instagram.com/BookandTonic

Lightning Source UK Ltd.
Milton Keynes UK
UKHW020813310120
357948UK00009B/268

9 781838 892036